The Queen of Killers

First sniper team's Bella Dwan broke formation and came to stand one pace to Athon's left. She showed her teeth to the Marines of second platoon in a grin. Her grin was no more friendly than that of a hungry shark.

"Lance Corporal Dwan," Athon said to second platoon, "will explain to you the operation and capabilities of the M14A5 sniper maser. She won't go into any great detail about how it functions; none of you have the advanced degrees in physics you'd need to understand them.

"Lance Corporal." He stepped aside.

Bella Dwan was petite and had what on another woman might be called an elfin face—as long as one didn't look into her eyes. They were cold and hard, and had made many a strong man excuse himself and depart for other environs. They called her the "Queen of Killers."

STARFIST: FORCE RECON

BOOK I

BACKSHOT

David Sherman & Dan Cragg

BALLANTINE BOOKS • NEW YORK

Backshot is a work of fiction. Names, characters, places, and incidents are the products of the authors' imagination or are used fictitiously. Any resemblance to actual events, locales, or persons, living or dead, is entirely coincidental.

A Del Rey Books Mass Market Original

Copyright © 2005 by David Sherman and Dan Cragg

Published in the United States by Del Rey Books, an imprint of The Random House Publishing Group, a division of Random House, Inc., New York.

Del Rey is a registered trademark and the Del Rey colophon is a trademark of Random House, Inc.

ISBN 0-345-46058-8

Printed in the United States of America

www.delreybooks.com

OPM   9   8   7   6   5   4   3   2   1

To:

Larry Smith
Corporal, USMC
1st & 2nd LAAM Bns
RVN, 1965–1968
Forever a Marine . . .
And a Good Friend

1946–2004

Semper Fi

BACKSHOT

PROLOGUE

"Look!" Jorge Liberec Lavager gestured heavenward at the meteor flashing across the sky. His daughter Candace was sitting on the bench beside him in the dark. "Some of the best things in life are free, Candie, and nature is one of them."

"I hope it doesn't hit anybody," Candace replied sarcastically.

"That's my girl!" Lavager responded cheerfully. He put his arm around her shoulders and drew her closer. "Most meteorites are harmless," he continued. "They burn up in the atmosphere before they reach the ground. They're nothing to be afraid of."

Candace sniffed. "I know that, Daddy." Although she was only sixteen, in the past three years since Annie Lavager, Lavager's wife and Candace's mother, had been killed in an assassination attempt aimed at him, Candace and her father had become extremely close. For his part, Lavager was impressed by his daughter's solid common-sense attitude toward world affairs. She was a realist and not afraid to speak her mind, and he appreciated that. Too many of the people around the former general—his aides, his cabinet ministers—only told him what they thought he wanted to hear.

She feigned a cough. "Daddy, must you smoke those foul cigars? You'll die of something if you don't quit. And besides, they're far from 'free.' "

"I am shocked!" Lavager said with mock outrage. "Shocked that anyone could refer to a prime cigar like this Davidoff Anniversario as 'foul'!" He chuckled. "And when you discount the things in life that are free, with what's left over you get only what you pay for. My first rule of economics, Candie. Besides, I'm going to die of something someday anyway, so while I'm alive I'm going to live." Lavager drew deeply on his Anniversario, a terribly expensive smoke imported all the way from the other side of Human Space. He savored the cigar's complex layers of rich flavors: a sweet earthiness tinged with a slight hint of leather and sweet spicy undertones, all blended into a smooth draw that burned perfectly. Slowly he let the flavors out through his nostrils.

"Father, don't talk that way!" Candace waved the smoke away with a hand. Ever since her mother's death, she had been very aware of her father's mortality, and the fact that some people on Atlas wanted him dead only added to her growing sense of uneasiness.

Atlas's major moon wasn't visible and the stars overhead shone with particular brilliance in the night sky. The lights from New Granum, the Union of Margelan's capital city, far below the mountaintop that was Lavager's getaway, glowed warmly down in the valley. Despite her best efforts to dispel the cigar smoke, a fine white cloud hung suspended in front of her father's face. The thought occurred to her that with the tip of his cigar aglow in the night her father might make a good target for someone hiding in the foliage below. She hoped the presidential security team watching over them from someplace out of sight was alert.

"I'm going to smoke this cigar right down to the band, Candie. Your mother liked the smell of them, and what was good enough for her is good enough for everyone else, including you, my dear." He drew again on the Anniversario.

Cigar smoke was a smell Candace had associated with her father for as long as she could remember, and she did really like the aroma of a good cigar. But their bantering about his smoking habit was a game father and daughter played, part of the ritual they followed when by themselves, which was not very often these days.

"Candie," Lavager said suddenly, "let's go to Ramuncho's! I'm hungry." Ramuncho's was his favorite restaurant in New Granum. He often dined there when his cabinet was sitting or when the planetary council, of which he was a member, was in session.

"Daddy, it's close to midnight! You have an important cabinet meeting in the morning."

"So what?" Like his daughter, Jorge Lavager often spoke just what was on his mind, inflaming his enemies and sometimes even his friends. "I'm hungry, I want some of Ramuncho's paella. Come on, let's go. You can drive."

"I can?" That offer almost made Candace start for the car. Then she caught herself. "What about your security detail? Daddy, you have to be more careful!"

Lavager made a dismissive gesture with one hand. "Let them sleep." Ever since the assassination attempt that had killed his wife, Lavager's aides had insisted on constant personal security for their head of state. Slipping off by himself, as he was proposing to do that evening, Lavager often gave his bodyguards fits. But giving in to the alarm in his daughter's voice, he relented. "All right," he sighed. "We'll order up a snack—but only after I've finished this cigar."

They sat quietly for a few moments. Candace hugged her father tightly. "Daddy, I don't want to lose you too," she whispered.

"Don't worry, you won't, Baby."

"But so many people in this world hate you."

"Yes, and some with good reason, Candie. I made a lot of enemies when I led our armies. I had to do things I'm not very proud of."

"But you're not a general anymore, Daddy. You're a statesman." She pronounced the word proudly.

"Yes, I surely am. But you know, once a general, always a general. You never really take that uniform off as far as some people are concerned. You're always on parade, as it were." He drew on his cigar and slowly exhaled the smoke.

Primarily an agricultural world, Atlas had early split into regional power centers that evolved into independent nation-states, rather than maintaining a centralized world government as had nearly all other human-settled worlds. Those nation-states, in the manner of nation-states throughout history on Earth, warred among themselves with the major center of power shifting from one nation-state to another over the years. The Union of Margelan, under a succession of astute leaders, most recently Jorge Lavager, had been highly successful for more than a century in defending its interests. Its military success had led it to impose certain demands upon the losers, mostly the cession of some territories and acceptance of Margelan's hegemony over others. The Union of Margelan's main adversaries had been the countries of North and South Solanum, Oleania, and Satevina. Margelan's main advantage, aside from excellent leadership, was the fact that unlike the other nation-states it had developed heavy industry that could produce the weapon systems needed to wage modern warfare—but over the years this had proved a tremendous strain on its economy.

Atlas was fortunate in one way, however. When the world was first settled three hundred years earlier, it had been on the fringes of Human Space, but by Lavager's time it sat astride one of the busiest spacelanes of the

Confederation of Human Worlds. That enabled the nation-states of Atlas, when they weren't at war with one another, to easily export their products to other worlds. Gradually it dawned on the politicians of Atlas that if they could attain a state of peace among themselves, no matter how uneasy, everyone would prosper. To that end it was agreed to form a League of Nations that would represent the interests of all the nation-states and, it was hoped, settle their differences amicably. The League had sat at New Granum since the end of the war that had established the Union of Margelan as the most potent military power on Atlas—Lavager's predecessor once removed had demanded that as a major concession for peace.

The League of Nations was a league in name only and its success at keeping the peace had been limited at best.

"Daddy, will there be another war?"

Lavager did not answer immediately. While he often entrusted secrets of state to his daughter, whom he secretly hoped might someday succeed him, there were things he would never tell her. "Probably," he admitted at last. "But," he added, "I have a plan."

"Daddy, the other day Beresford Tuchman stood up in the League and said that Margelan is not a state with an army but an army with a state. Everyone believes there's another war coming and that you will start it. The League is a joke."

Lavager laughed. "They've been saying that about us for years, Candie. Yes, the League has not been very effective, but it gives all the nation-states of Atlas a forum. That's important. But Candie, if I live long enough I am going to impose peace on this world. I'll do it by force if I have to but I'd prefer another method."

"Which is?"

"Ummm. I have something up my sleeve." Candace could not see her father's smile in the dark.

"Can you tell me?"

"Nope. It's something I'm working on." The silence between him and his daughter grew pregnant. "Damned fine cigar," he said at last.

"Daddy!"

"I'm developing something in our labs, and once it's ready I'm going to use it to impose order and tranquility on this world, and that is all I can tell you about it now, Candace." She cocked her head; her father used her proper name only when he was very serious. "This information must remain between me and a few others—and you never even heard what I just told you." What concerned Lavager most about his daughter's knowing too much was not that she would tell anyone—he knew from experience he could trust her with the most sensitive secrets—but the possibility of her being kidnapped and subjected to any one of many methods used to extract information from unwilling sources. A realist, he knew that if he couldn't prevent that from happening at least he could keep safe what he was doing in his research laboratories.

"A weapon," Candace snorted, a statement, not a question.

"Yes, of a sort." Lavager smiled. "Look, figure the politics. Our ambassador to the Confederation of Human Worlds recently filed a dozen dispatches reporting how a number of member worlds in the Confederation feel uneasy about our intentions in this sector of Human Space. We sit astride an economic lifeline here on Atlas. They're afraid that if someone succeeds in unifying Atlas he'll create a shipping bottleneck in these spacelanes and attempt to extract stiff tolls. As they see it, keeping us at each other's throats is in their best interests. So until I'm ready to show my hand, I've got to keep my plan under wraps."

"I understand," Candace conceded.

Lavager put his arm around his daughter again and

drew her close. "When the time is right—Well, I'd like a ham and cheese sandwich before bed. Care to join me?"

The pair stood and Lavager led the way back toward the house, followed silently by the presidential security team. In the sky overhead another meteor flashed brightly before disappearing over the horizon.

CHAPTER
ONE

Fourth Force Recon Company, Fourth Fleet Marines, Camp Howard, Marine Corps Base Camp Basilone, Halfway

" 'Toon, ten-hut!"

The Marines of second platoon, Fourth Force Recon Company snapped to attention at the command from their platoon sergeant Gunnery Sergeant Alf Lytle.

"Section leaders, report!"

"Squad leaders, report!" first section leader Staff Sergeant Suptra commanded in turn.

"First squad, all present and accounted for!" Sergeant Jak Daly shouted. His three Marines stood in a rank to his left.

"Second squad, all present and accounted for!" Sergeant Wil Bingh and his three men were directly to first squad's left.

The four Marines of third squad were also present. Fourth squad would have completed the front rank of second platoon, but it was on a deployment, running a reconnaissance mission for the army. Only the four Marines of fifth squad were present from second section; sixth, seventh, and eighth squads, along with their section leader, were on a mission in support of a peacekeeping operation somewhere else. All seven members of the platoon's sniper squad were present in the third rank, as reported by the squad leader, Staff Sergeant Athon.

Once the reports were complete, Gunny Lytle faced

about and Lieutenant Tevedes, the platoon commander, marched toward him. Lytle raised his hand in a sharp salute and announced, "Second platoon, all present and accounted for, sir!"

"Thank you, Platoon Sergeant," Tevedes said, returning the salute. "You may take your place."

"Aye aye, sir." Lytle executed an about-face and marched to his position two paces in front of Suptra.

Lieutenant Tevedes looked with pride at his Marines—*his* Marines. He'd previously served as a platoon sergeant and a platoon commander in a Fleet Initial Strike Team, a FIST. Before that he'd been first a recon-man, then a squad leader in Seventh Force Recon Company. This was his first command in Force Recon, and he looked forward to the day when his entire platoon would be sent out on a mission. Individual-squad and multi-squad deployments in support of Confederation army units or the armed forces of Confederation member worlds were the bread and butter of Force Recon, but platoon-size missions were nearest to the hearts of the platoon commanders; those missions were when they got to demonstrate that they could do more than train their Marines and provide them with mission planning and support, that they could successfully lead them in harm's way.

"I'm sure you will be happy to hear that sixth, seventh, and eighth squads have completed their phase of the peacekeeping mission with the army and will rejoin the platoon in a couple of weeks," Tevedes said.

The Recon Marines were too well disciplined to show a reaction, though they'd been looking forward to the return of the three squads—by tradition, when two or more squads returned from a deployment, the entire platoon was given a week's leave.

"That's what I thought," Tevedes deadpanned at their stone-faces. "Fourth squad is still bogged down trying to instruct the army on the difference between unconfirmed reports and the hard intel generated by Force Recon, so it'll be a while yet before they come home."

That brought out snickers from several of the Force Recon Marines and hoots from one or two. "Leave it to the doggies to not know the difference," someone murmured just loud enough for everyone to hear.

"Quiet in the ranks," Gunny Lytle said out of the side of his mouth.

"In other company news," Tevedes continued as though there hadn't been an interruption, "first platoon is deploying on a six-month training mission to Carhart's World, where they will establish a recon school and train the first generation of instructors for a new Carhart Armed Forces special forces reconnaissance unit. Add in travel time and whatever bureaucratic nonsense they'll have to deal with when they arrive on Carhart's World, and they'll probably be gone for seven months or longer. In the unlikely event that any of you don't understand the significance of first platoon's extended absence, it means there will probably be additional deployments for the rest of the company for the duration of that deployment."

There was little reaction to that news; as much as half of the company was on deployment at any given time anyway, and it wasn't all that unusual for a squad to have as little as two or three weeks, Standard, between deployments, though the normal rest and training period was at least two months Standard, and occasionally five or six months.

"The same squads from third and fourth platoons that were on deployments the last time I gave you an update are still on deployment, but I don't imagine we much care about when they're due back, not unless it interferes with our coming leave." Tevedes was right, his Marines were more interested in what they would be doing until sixth, seventh, and eighth squads returned.

He gave his platoon a bland look that could be interpreted as, "Don't ask me," then said out loud, "Everyone who's been in Force Recon long enough has run into a situation where you didn't expect to need a sniper, but suddenly you do. So we are going to spend the next two weeks on the range, where we will all fire sniper weapons for orientation and qualification."

This again was the kind of announcement that didn't provoke an overt reaction. They all knew that if a mission didn't require a sniper, the squad or squads that went on it didn't take sniper weapons either, so the training didn't make much sense. But it was an opportunity to fire—and qualify with—more weapons, and the Marines all enjoyed spending time on the range.

"Commander Obannion," Tevedes continued, "told me that came from very much higher-higher." Which probably meant Obannion, the company commander, got the orders from Lieutenant General Indrus, the commanding general of Fourth Fleet Marines. "So get ready to head for the range. You know what that means. We leave at oh-dark-thirty tomorrow morning. Transportation will be provided. Platoon Sergeant, dismiss the platoon."

"Aye aye, sir!" Lytle responded. He saluted Tevedes, who returned the salute, about-faced, and marched toward the company office.

Lytle waited until the lieutenant was halfway there, then faced the platoon and said, "You heard the man. Get your asses into the barracks and get ready to go play bang-bang with weapons most of us will never use."

Camp Hathcock Controlled Ranges, MCB Camp Basilone, Halfway

Camp Hathcock, like Camp Howard, was a small part of Confederation Marine Corps Base Camp Basilone. Camp Basilone itself sprawled over more than eighty thousand square kilometers, which was far more space than was required for the headquarters of a Fleet Marine Force and its attendant units. But Camp Basilone was also home to the Marine Corps Combat Development Center, where new tactics and most Marine-specific weapons and equipment were developed and tested—when six or seven FISTs assembled to run war games together, or in opposition to each other, they needed prodigious amounts of space to play in. Terrain and weather were also a consideration, and Camp Basilone provided a full range from semitropical swamp through desert, temperate forest, and savannah, all the way to alpine. The installation also included several built-up areas, ranging from rural villages to a mock-up of a major metropolis—every one of which could be used for live-fire training for the full panoply of Marine Corps weapons.

Camp Hathcock was the smallest of the "camps" that made up Camp Basilone, only five kilometers deep by ten wide, backed up against the Veridian Ocean, but its area of influence via firepower was far larger: Air and sea craft were banned for a distance five kilometers to its sides and twenty kilometers beyond the shore.

Warrant Officer Jaqua, Fourth Force Recon Company's training officer and range master, was ready for the platoon's recon squads when they reached the range. Masers slung over their shoulders, Staff Sergeant Athon and his sniper squad stood in a rank behind him.

The four squads of second platoon available for that training evolution formed up in front of the company training officer the same as they had for morning formation behind the barracks.

Jaqua stood, hands clasped behind his back, casually looking them over. "I know," he said before his inspection could make anybody uncomfortable, "that most of you have already done orientation firing of various sniper weapons. A couple of you have even fired all of them. But not one of you has fired any of them for qualification. We are going to spend the next two weeks correcting that deficiency."

Jaqua could say "deficency" without giving offense; in

addition to his Distinguished Blasterman and hand-blaster Expert badges, his chest bore the uncommon Expert Sniper badge with the scarlet pips that indicated he'd qualified at that level with all three of the sniper-specific weapons.

"We aren't going to overwhelm you with firing all of our weapons at once; we only have two weeks, and that's barely long enough to familiarize you with them. Instead, we will spend the first week concentrating on learning the maser. On Frigaday, you will fire the maser on the qualification range. Next week you will spend four days firing the mid-range projectile rifle and the long-range sabot. Next Frigaday, if you feel sufficiently comfortable with either of them, you will fire it for qualification."

He raised a hand to stop the groans of protest he expected and quickly added, "If you qualify with any of these weapons, that qualification will be entered in your Service Record Book and you will be authorized to wear the appropriate badge. If you fail to qualify with any weapon you fire for qualification, that failure will *not* be entered into your service record. There is no requirement in the Basic Reconman MOS for qualification with sniper weapons, so it wouldn't be fair to officially note any failure to do so. But qualifying with additional weapons will look good in your record."

He smiled. "Besides, some of you might decide you like firing sniper weapons and want to apply for sniper school. Force Recon can always use new snipers who have prior experience as reconmen.

"Now, I'll hand you over to Staff Sergeant Athon and his snipers for basic orientation." He made an about-face. "Staff Sergeant Athon, front and center!"

"Sir!" Athon sharply stepped in front of Suptra and saluted.

"Staff Sergeant, take command of the trainees," Jaqua said before he cut his salute.

"Aye aye, sir!" Athon held his salute until Jaqua cut his

and marched away, then stood with his feet at shoulder width and his hands on his hips, and ordered, "Lance Corporal Dwan, position!"

First sniper team's Lance Corporal Bella Dwan broke formation and came to stand one pace to Athon's left. She showed her teeth to the Marines of second platoon in a grin. Her grin was no more friendly than that of a hungry shark.

"Lance Corporal Dwan," Athon said to second platoon, "will explain to you the operation and capabilities of the M14A5 sniper maser. She won't go into any great detail about how it functions; none of you have the advanced degrees in physics you'd need to understand them.

"Lance Corporal." He stepped aside.

Bella Dwan was petite and had what on another woman might be called an elfin face—as long as one didn't look into her eyes. The other Marines of Fourth Force Recon Company were about equally divided as to whether, if she was seen off base in nice civilian clothes, she would look more like somebody's kid sister or like someone worth pursuing as a woman. But they all knew better—and no Marine who knew her ever saw her as a woman to pursue, much less as anybody's kid sister. Her eyes were cold and hard, and had made many a strong man excuse himself and depart for other environs. They called her the "Queen of Killers."

Dwan was a very unusual Marine. She was still under thirty and not yet through her first eight-year enlistment, which was the only excuse her chain of command had for not offering her a meritorious promotion to corporal. She was qualified as Expert with blaster, hand-blaster, and most sniper weapons. She wasn't qualified as Expert with the maser because she had surprised the competition-shooting community by earning the treasured Distinguished designation with the maser after only three years of part-time shooting in authorized competitions.

Dwan unslung her maser and held it across her body at

port arms. "This is the M14A5 sniper maser," she said, in a voice only slightly less elfin than her face. The weapon was little more than a meter long. Its rear half resembled the buttstock and firing group of the standard blaster carried by Marine infantrymen and Force Recon. Forward of that, the "barrel" group was a dull metal cylinder about three centimeters in diameter sitting in a short, knobby, wood forestock for almost its entire length. The barrel was slotted at regular intervals. Midway along the cradle, a handgrip dropped down. The "muzzle" tapered to a point, circled by a series of tightly spaced rings that diminished in diameter as they approached the point.

"The M14A5 sniper maser is an electrically operated, tightly focused, single-shot, shoulder fired, microwave weapon. It has a maximum immediate kill range of two hundred meters, and a maximum effective kill range of four hundred meters." Her grin broadened. "It can cause sunstroke at nearly a kilometer and severe sunburn at a klick and a half."

Then her smile tightened. "The M14A5 is a very quiet weapon. Someone with keen hearing can possibly detect it at a distance as great as five meters, but no farther. It fires a tightly focused pulse of high-intensity microwaves. A three-quarter-second pulse, at two hundred meters or less, striking a human target anywhere from the crown to mid-thigh, will kill before the full pulse has completed. To kill at four hundred meters, the entire three-quarter-second pulse must hit in the same point, somewhere between top of head and groin.

"The wave is so tightly focused—don't ask how, I don't understand the physics any better than you do—that it is virtually undetectable by any surveillance device not directly in its path. When the target is killed, it drops straight down and shows no external sign of being shot."

Her grin became wider than ever. "Gentlemen—that means you, Marines!—that means a sniper who is good enough at snooping and pooping can kill his—or," she cleared her throat, "*her* target without being discovered.

"Now, I know most of you badasses are Expert Blastermen, accustomed to firing plasma bolts at targets as much as a klick away and hitting them nine times out of ten, so you may be wondering what's so difficult about firing a weapon that can kill only up to four hundred meters.

"It's that three-quarter-second pulse. There isn't any recoil, or not much, but you have to maintain a solid lock on your aiming point for that entire three-quarters-second. You might be surprised at how many Marines can't."

Lance Corporal Wehrli from second squad raised his hand. When Dwan acknowledged him, he asked, "If that's so, why doesn't the maser have a stabilizing system?" He gritted his teeth when she gave him a you're-cute-when-you-ask-dumb-questions look.

"Weight and noise," she said. "Snipers have to be able to move slowly and silently. That means carry nothing you don't absolutely need. And every stabilizing device makes noise, no matter how slight. The maser gets heavier if it has enough shielding to silence the stabilizer. The more weight a sniper carries, the more chance he or she has of making noise. A silent sniper *makes* kills, a noisy sniper *gets* killed. It's that simple."

Dwan looked about, but nobody else raised a question, so she continued her lecture.

"Aiming is easy. You look through the optical sight, lock on target, and squeeze. The M14A5 is a line-of-sight weapon, and is unaffected by wind, weather, or gravitational effect within its effective kill-range. Which doesn't mean it isn't affected over ranges measured in thousands of kilometers, but that effect's from solar winds and Jovian-sized gravity wells. And by the time the waves travel that far, they're so dispersed it really doesn't matter.

"The basic elements of firing apply, BRASS: Breathe, Relax, Aim, Slack, Squeeze." She looked about for more questions, but when none immediately came, Staff Sergeant Athon stepped forward and took over.

"You all know the range routine for new weapons," he told second platoon. "I have all six of my snipers here, and there are twenty-three of you. Each of my people will take a squad, Sergeant Gossner will take the command element. They will give you dry-firing instruction, supervised by Gunner Jaqua and myself. We'll go right down the line. First squad, you go with Lance Corporal Dwan. Second squad—"

"Come on, big boy," Dwan said, stepping close enough to slap Daly on the shoulder. "Bring your kiddies with you." She marched toward a section of the firing line a hundred meters distant and didn't bother looking back to see if first squad followed—she knew they would.

Daly pursed his lips at the undue, almost insubordinate, familiarity of the "big boy" and shoulder slap—not to mention the insulting "kiddies"—but Bella Dwan was allowed to get away with minor infractions and insults, she was that good at what she did. Besides, like everybody else in the company, Daly was wary of her and didn't want to do anything that might provoke her anger; she wasn't known as "the Queen of Killers" just because of the look in her eyes. Everyone knew how she had earned the name.

With twenty-seven confirmed kills to her credit, she had more than any other woman sniper in the Confederation military—more than most male snipers, for that matter. But that wasn't why the men of Fourth Force Recon Company were wary of her.

A tall, strikingly handsome, and drunk—that's important, he was drunk—Marine who thought himself irresistible to women hadn't believed pixie-faced Bella Dwan when she repeatedly told him "no." Nor had he taken her seriously when she had told him he was about to lose the hand he put on an inappropriate portion of her anatomy. When he took further action with his inappropriately placed hand, so did she.

The navy doctors who operated on him successfully regenerated a new hand to replace the one Dwan had removed from the inappropriate part of her anatomy. But as a permanent reminder to him that when a woman repeatedly says "no," she really means it, they only regenerated one of his testicles.

The court martial board that tried him took his drunkenness into consideration and only gave him a General Discharge for Disciplinary Reasons instead of several years of hard time and a Bad Conduct Discharge for attempted rape. Of course then-PFC Bella Dwan had also taken his drunken state into consideration in refraining from killing him.

The court martial board that tried then-PFC Dwan found her not guilty of assault and battery, aggravated assault, assault with a deadly weapon (her hands and a knife she was carrying in a thigh-sheath), and several other charges, on the basis that she acted in self-defense and showed reasonable restraint.

And Bella Dwan *never* encouraged other Marines to make advances, or made advances herself. So the men she served with were always very careful with her.

Dry firing was an exercise all of the Marines had repeated many times since they first trained on the range in Boot Camp on Arsenault. Take a solid shooting position. Draw a solid sight picture on the target. Control breathing to steady the sights on the aiming point. Gently squeeze the trigger until the firing mechanism goes off and a plasma bolt, projectile, or beam moves downrange at the target. Keep the sights pinned on the aiming point all the while you're squeezing.

It's called "dry" firing because it's done with an empty weapon. Do the same thing with a loaded weapon and it's called "live" firing. During his dozen years in the Marine Corps, Sergeant Jak Daly had done countless hours of dry firing on all kinds of individual weapons. Dry firing wasn't any particular fun, but he knew it helped him get his first round on target when he finally got to live-fire the weapon—and getting that first shot on target, that *was* fun.

On the range master's command, Daly lowered himself into a solid prone firing position and swiveled the butt of the maser into his shoulder. Through the maser's sights he found the target, a simple 40-mm bull's-eye target fifteen meters distant, and aimed at the center of the smallest circle. A laser pointer that closely matched the weight and balance of a maser's power pac was used in the maser for dry firing. In the sights, the red dot jiggled around Daly's aiming point until he let out his breath, then it steadied down. The dot slowly spiraled until it settled where he wanted it, though it continued to move in a small circle, mostly inside the 5-cm bull's eye. He gave the trigger a steady squeeze until the red dot brightened, indicating the maser had fired. He kept the trigger back for a count of one-thousand, which he estimated was about three-quarters of a second, then let it go.

The circle described by the dot hadn't moved more than a millimeter or two during firing.

"Not bad, big boy," Dwan's voice said from too close to Daly's ear. "Your target's got some serious sick bay time ahead of him. If his doctors are good enough, they might even be able to figure out why he came down with a high fever."

Startled by her closeness, Daly rolled to the side away from her and jumped to his feet.

"What do you mean, 'sick'?" he demanded. "I was dead on for the whole time."

Dwan nodded. "Mighty fine shot—with a blaster, or any projectile weapon." She looked from the target and rose on her toes to lean close to his face, staring harshly into his eyes. "That much movement might cook an organ, but you need to hold steadier to cause severe enough trauma for a clean kill. Let me show you what I mean."

Dwan took the maser from his grasp and dropped into a modified sitting position, with her elbows locked on the insides of her knees instead of her knees tucked into her armpits, and aimed; Daly assumed the modification was because of her short stature. He studied the way she sat, he didn't think the flesh over any of the arteries in her arms was in contact with her knees; her pulse wouldn't affect her aim.

"Watch the target, not me," she ordered.

Daly jerked his eyes from her to the target. The red dot on the target didn't look like it was moving at all, not even when it briefly brightened.

"That's what we mean by 'steady,'" she said, hopping to her feet and shoving the maser at him. He grabbed it just as she let go of it. "Now try it again." She stepped back so he could resume his firing position.

Daly dropped into a sitting position, but Dwan nudged his shoulder with a knee. "Stick with prone for now," she told him. "It's easier."

Daly shot her a glance, but did as she said. He paid more attention this time to the almost imperceptible movements caused by the blood pulsing through his arteries, and shifted his position slightly so those points weren't in contact with anything. He chided himself mentally as he took aim; he'd learned on the range in Boot Camp how tiny pulses in the arms and legs could be transmitted to a weapon and throw off one's aim; he should have realized they'd have more effect on a weapon that needed to have a tighter lock on its impact point.

This time his aim was steadier. The dot didn't hold as tightly as Dwan's had, but the bobble was less than a millimeter.

"Is that good enough?" he asked, rolling to the side and looking up.

But Dwan was no longer there; she was five meters away, leaning over Lance Corporal Wazzen, giving the junior reconman instruction.

Daly shot a glare at her, but quickly wiped it off his face; he didn't want the Queen of Killers to see it. He resumed his firing position and tried again. After a few more shots, his dot held steady within its own diameter on every shot.

"If you can do just as well sitting and kneeling," Dwan suddenly said, "that's good enough to qualify as Marksman."

Daly rolled halfway to the side and looked over his shoulder. She was standing between his wide-spread feet, looking downrange.

"How long have you been there?" he asked.

"Long enough." She looked down at him. "Your Marines needed more attention than you did. You're pretty good, big boy. Try the sitting position now." She gracefully stepped from between his feet.

Daly swiveled up and around until he was sitting with his feet spread wide and his knees up. He pulled the maser into his shoulder and leaned forward until his armpits slid into position on top of his knees—the sitting position he'd been taught on the range in Boot Camp, the position he'd used in firing for qualification a dozen times since.

Suddenly, Dwan was on her knees next to him, forcing her fingertips between his armpit and knee, pads up. "Hold still," she snapped as she wiggled her fingers to where she wanted them. She held them there for a couple of seconds, then pulled her hand out.

"No good, you've got a pulse on bone, you won't be able to hold your aiming point. Remember how I sat? You should, you were eye-fucking me hard enough. Try it."

Daly remembered and turned red at her comment. "I wasn't eye-fucking you, Lance Corporal," he snarled, "I was studying your firing position."

She sniffed. "Call it what you will, I saw you."

Daly didn't confront Dwan further, but slid his feet forward a few centimeters and straightened his back until his elbows were inside his knees. The position felt odd.

"Now try it."

He steadied himself and aimed. The dot moved more than it had when he was prone, but not as much as the first time he tried prone.

"That's better, big boy," Dwan said, and clapped him on the shoulder. "Keep practicing." Then she moved on.

By the end of the day, Daly had spent two hours in each of the three firing positions used for qualifying with the maser. Dwan declared him good enough to qualify as Marksman, the lowest of the three noncompetition qualification rankings.

By the end of the week his proficiency had improved to the point where he was able to qualify as Sharpshooter with the M14A5 maser—he missed Expert by only two points out of two hundred.

The weapon Sergeant Jak Daly found most interesting the next week was the M111 sabot rifle with 10X optical sight. Unlike the M14A5 maser, the M111 had stabilizers in its forestock that the barrel rested on. The M111 was designed for long-range sniping: It fired a fin-stabilized 8-mm projectile, with a maximum effective range of one kilometer and a kill range several times that—even though a hit at three klicks would be due as much to luck as to skill, a hit in a vital spot would still kill at that distance.

"Never, *never* snipe with the M111 at less than five hundred meters!" Staff Sergeant Athon cautioned. "It makes a loud *boom* and has a fairly large muzzle-blast fireball. A sniper using the M111 needs that five hundred meters to have a chance of escaping whoever—or whatever—comes for him after he fires. A full klick is better: The rifle's report probably won't be heard at that distance, and the fireball won't be seen by anybody who isn't looking in the shooter's direction."

Daly qualified Expert with the M111. He chose not to fire the M2Z mid-range projectile rifle for qualification; two new qualifications were enough for now.

CHAPTER
TWO

Ramuncho's Restaurant, New Granum, Union of Margelan, Atlas

For Jorge Lavager, the Union of Margelan's leader and a representative to the Atlas League of Nations, dining at Ramuncho's in New Granum during work hours could be an ordeal, because everywhere he went the press was sure to follow. And in these times when the nations of Atlas seemed on the verge of a war that many commentators and politicians claimed would threaten the precious trade routes of the Confederation of Human Worlds in the Atlas Sector, reporters swarmed like bees about a honeycomb whenever Lavager appeared in public. So he dined during the off hours or late at night when business kept him in town, often in a back room reserved for his use, and always with friends.

To the great consternation of Franklin al-Rashid, his Chief of Security, Lavager had dismissed his bodyguards that night. "I can take care of myself," the old soldier told his security officer, patting the sidearm he always carried beneath his tunic.

"Sir, one of these times—" al-Rashid began. Lavager was a security chief's worst nightmare, always taking chances and never listening to sound advice.

"Not tonight, Franklin. Now go home, leave us to our dinner and cards."

After that night's dinner, cards consisted of some hands

at the ancient game of Hearts. Since they were lieutenants together, Lavager and his Army Chief of Staff, General Locksley "Locker" Ollwelen, had enjoyed a friendly competition seeing who could lay the queen of spades on the other. Just then, Lavager had the two of clubs in this hand, so it was his lead. On the deal he had not gotten the right suits to take all the points to "shoot the moon" and pile twenty-six points on the other players' scores, so he had deliberately shorted himself in clubs to break hearts first chance and maybe get away without taking any points at all. Henri Parrot, the Minister of Finance, had passed him the queen and the two of spades and the jack of hearts. He glanced sharply at the minister, who grinned behind his hand. The dreaded queen and two were the only spades in Lavager's hand!

Locksley shifted his cigar from one side of his mouth to the other, folded his cards into the palm of one hand and slowly rearranged them.

Lavager led the two of clubs. Locksley regarded his hand carefully before following suit, then took the first trick with the ace of clubs. He then led the ten of spades. Lavager played the two. He hoped someone besides Locksley would take the trick and then lead clubs, so he could drop the queen, but the old General took that hand as well. Lavager felt a sinking sensation in his stomach because he knew Locksley would lead a spade next, fishing for the queen and hoping he could make one of the others eat her and take the thirteen points that would add to their score.

Grinning evilly, Locksley next led the jack of spades. "Goddamn you, Locker!" Lavager shouted, slapping down the queen because he had no more spades and, according to the rules of the game, had to follow suit. Subsequently he took twenty of the twenty-six points that made the hand.

"Locker, how the hell did you know I was short on spades?" Lavager asked, shuffling for the next hand. He glanced at the score pad. He had eighty-seven points, Locksley none, Henri three, and Attorney General Fitz Cennedry, ten. Thirteen more points and Jorge Lavager would be out and Locksley would be the winner.

"I didn't. I've just been doing that for the past thirty years, just like you short yourself in a suit so you can unload points on me." Ollwelen grinned, puffing contentedly on his cigar. Often in their games neither Locksley nor Lavager won because their main concentration was on screwing each other, not winning the game, even though they played for money—a credit a point.

"Locker, I ought to put your ass back in the grass, remind you what's important in this life."

"Did you hear that?" Locksley turned to the attorney general. "Just another example of how power goes to the heads of politicians in this nation of ours—send a man off to war just so he can win at cards."

"War? Did I hear someone say 'war'? May I quote you on that?"

All heads snapped toward the door to the main dining room. There stood grinning none other than Gus Gustafferson, Galactic News Network's chief correspondent on Atlas.

"How the hell did you get in here?" Lavager asked. "Why aren't you in bed with some animal at this hour?"

Gustafferson made an airy gesture with one hand. "Ramuncho's gone home and I gave a note to a waiter." He waved a wad of credits in one hand and stepped unbidden into the room, making a show of waving the cigar smoke away from his face.

"Gutsy," Lavager said, "you could very easily get yourself shot busting in here like this." The reporter's nickname, one he hated but one Lavager delighted using, was "Gutsy Goofy," bestowed on him because he'd do anything to get a story and because his big ears and huge nose made him look stupid. He wasn't. What he was was an insistent, argumentative, opinionated interviewer who

never allowed the facts of an issue to override his precon-
ceived ideas.

"You can't shoot me, sir, members of the media are immune to assassination."

"Yeah, just like you're 'immune' to the truth," Attorney
General Cennedry commented sourly.

"How many billions of people have you misinformed
this week, Gutsy?" Locksley asked.

Gustafferson grimaced. "Touché, General. What's this I
hear about you going to war?" He made a show of activat-
ing his personal comp.

"Turn that damned thing off!" Cennedry snapped.

Gustafferson made a show of deactivating his comp and
putting it away. "I have a good enough memory," he murmured. "Statement?" he asked aloud, looking inquiringly
at each of the officials, holding out a fist as if it were a microphone, coming back to Lavager and smiling. "Anybody
care to talk about the imminent failure of your Five-Year
Plan?" He bowed toward the Minister of Finance, who
scowled. "What's going on out at that place near Spondu?"
The question was delivered like a cannonball, and it was
instantly clear why Gustafferson was there at that hour.

Despite himself, Lavager stiffened. The facility called
the "Cabbage Patch" was a high-security research center
in the mountains near the town of Spondu, about forty
kilometers northeast of New Granum. "That's a top secret
government facility, Gutsy. No comment. You know that."

"But Excellency," Gustafferson shifted now into his
falsely obsequious mode, "Everyone's talking about a
new superweapon you're developing out there. One
you're going to deploy to propel Atlas into the Confederation's economy."

"Only because you've been feeding everyone that crap
for the past six months, Gutsy," Perrot replied. "What we
have at Spondu is an agricultural research center."

"Uh huh. Sure it is. It just *used* to be a weapons research
facility."

"Things change, Gutsy," Lavager said as calmly as he could. "You know that. Hell, you change facts all the time in your stories."

Gustafferson ignored the jibe. "Come on, Jorge, an interview? Just fifteen minutes of your time?"

Lavager was not the kind of man who insisted on etiquette in his relationships with people, but the way Gustafferson used his first name was intended to insinuate a close personal relationship that didn't exist.

"See my Director of Public Affairs and take your place in line, Gutsy. When your number comes up, sure, fifteen minutes. Now get out of here. This is a private gathering and it's late."

"You don't have a private life, Excellency," Gustafferson said, grinning, but he turned to the door and left the room.

"Jorge, if you'd kept your security team on duty he'd never have gotten in here," the Attorney General said.

"Yeah, well," Lavager stared after Gustafferson, momentarily lost in thought, "those guys have a hard enough job as it is without me keeping them up all night to watch over our game. Gentlemen, we've got to find out who's leaking information about the Cabbage Patch. If that guy knows we're developing something up there, who else knows about it?"

Office of the Director, Central Intelligence Organization, Hunter, Earth

"So, Palmer, my dear fellow, tell us. What is going on in, what is it, the Cucumber Patch . . . ?"

"Cabbage Patch, not 'cucumber.'"

"Quaint name. Speaking of cucumbers, try some of these sautéed Vagarian cucumbers with a slice of this excellent Ciricussian bread. Delicious, I assure you." He twittered. "That's probably why I had cucumbers on my mind."

Palmer Quincy Lowell, Deputy Director for Intelligence, helped himself to the sliced cucumbers so generously offered by J. "Jay" Murchison Adams, Director of the Central Intelligence Organization and ignored the question of the Cabbage Patch while he enjoyed the cool taste of the succulent gourd.

"This wine is exquisite!" Somervell P. "Summy" Amesbury exclaimed. Amesbury functioned as Lowell's Chief of Staff. The three often lunched together in Lowell's office at CIO headquarters in the Fargo suburb of Hunter.

"That wine, my dear Somervell, is a specially imported vintage of Katzenwasser '48, which I received only last week. I was sure you'd appreciate it." Lowell smiled. He helped himself to a bread-and-cucumber sandwich, delicately wiping his fingers on the monogrammed napkins that were a staple feature on the table at the luncheon gatherings. "Gentlemen, do not overdo it," Lowell held up a well-manicured forefinger, "we have—I know you'll simply love this, Palmer!—creme d'collon soup with sherobie crotons as the main course!"

Palmer Quincy Lowell grunted with the pleasure of anticipation: Creme d'collon soup and especially sherobie crotons were a favorite of his and one of the reasons he weighed 170 kilos.

"And for dessert I have the most wonderful sherbet," J. Murchison Adams announced, taking another bite of his cucumber sandwich. He wiped his lips delicately and sighed. "But now, to business! I have a meeting with the Confederation Security Council tomorrow and I'm sure this business involving Atlas is going to come up. What is going on out there, Palmer? Who're your sources? And what in Human Space is this 'Cucumber Patch' place?"

"Ah, 'Cabbage Patch,' old boy. Our source is the chief of the trade delegation on Atlas, of course. He's a very experienced operative and has spread around quite a bit of money to develop his own stable of reliable informants.

You might recall, Jay, a line item in this fiscal year's budget, quite a sizeable sum—"

Adams waved the comment off impatiently. Budgetary matters, especially contingency funds for agent payments, were of little interest to him. His concept of what the Director of the CIO was to focus on was strategic intelligence, not the mundane day-to-day business of administering a government instrumentality. He left those details to his small army of accountants and clerks.

"Is Atlas and this impossible man, um—?" he turned to Amesbury.

"Jorge Liberec Lavager, Jay."

"—this Lavager fellow any real danger to our trade routes in the Atlas sector? That is what the President will wish to know tomorrow."

Someone buzzed. "Yes?"

"The soup course, sir," Adams's secretary announced.

"Aha! Send it in! Send it in!"

A functionary dressed in white from the CIO cafeteria wheeled in a cart with three steaming bowls of soup and deftly served them. The three officers sat silently until the man had departed. Then individually they sampled their soup, smacking their lips, wheezing in satisfaction, and grunting with pleasure; for a brief moment each was in his own little world of pure gustatory ecstasy.

"Lavager is an animal, Jay," Lowell replied at last, leaning back and patting his lips. "A military man, and you know the mindset of those little boys." They all chuckled. "He is developing some sort of superweapon." Lowell leaned forward as if to speak in total confidence. "We're not sure of its capabilities just yet, but we *are* certain he's going to use it to conquer Atlas and then start imposing demands on us based on his strategic position vis-à-vis our trade lanes with the outward worlds in that sector of Human Space. He is a dangerous man, Jay."

"One of your agents out there is that rather slick newsman Gustafferson, I believe? The GNN man?" Amesbury asked.

"He's developed some very reliable intelligence, Summy. He knows how to dig up a story. But he's one of several sources on the scene."

"And this 'Cucumber Patch' or whatever they call it is this Lavager's secret weapons lab?"

" 'Cabbage Patch.' Yes, it is, Jay. We haven't penetrated it yet but we will, we will."

"What do your analysts say about this info?"

"Oh, they evaluate this information as highly reliable." Lowell paused. "The desk officer, on the other hand, is not so sure," he said, carefully.

"Who's that?"

"Anya Smiler. She knows that area well," he added quickly, "she was there as an agent a few years back."

"God," Adams let out his breath, "it's been forty years since I was in the field, more power to the woman! But you know how these analysts are." He shrugged and raised a spoonful of soup to his lips.

"Yes, we've had our derrieres in the reeds, and the young are welcome to the field jobs," Amesbury laughed.

"Yes, yes," Lowell agreed quickly, "they sometimes do tend to go native on us, but I assure you Ms. Smiler is a very dedicated analyst. Hers is the minority opinion, I must add."

"And that is?"

"Jorge Lavager is a George Washington," Lowell answered, shrugging and tasting his own soup.

"Oh, come on! Are you joking? Palmer!"

"She thinks the man is no threat to the Confederation or to his neighbors on Atlas."

"Well," Amesbury turned to Adams, "we can discount that opinion! And the majority?"

"Lavager must be neutralized."

"Palmer, you'll come with me tomorrow. Bring copies of your full report for the other members of the Council. Now, gentlemen, we shall enjoy that sherbet and tomorrow—well, tomorrow, we shall propose picking somebody's cabbages."

CHAPTER
THREE

Apartment 1F, 4816 Hale Boulevard, Hunter, Earth

"Anya, are you listening to me?"

Anya Smiler looked slowly away from the window. A fierce storm was raging outside but that was not what she had been watching. "We'll have a meter of snow by midnight, if this keeps up," she said, just to say something. Her mind was on the meeting in the morning. "If it snows hard enough maybe they'll call it off and I can . . ." Her voice trailed off. She shook her head and turned away from the window.

"Anya, I was saying there's an opera Saturday night and I have tickets for us. It's Mozart's *Idomeneo* with Carmaggilo singing the lead role."

"That fat slob?"

"Anya!" Tim Omix snorted in exasperation. "What's gotten into you? You've been somewhere else all evening. If it wasn't snowing so heavily out there I'd go on home. It's something in that damn job of yours, isn't it? Don't you know it's not healthy to bring problems home from work?" He offered Anya a refill, and when she shook her head, he poured more wine into his own glass. He gulped it down and covered a satisfied burp with one hand. By Buddha's balls, he thought, I may as well get drunk, there won't be anything else here for me tonight.

Tim and Anya had been lovers for a long time, were in

fact on the verge of marriage, but Tim knew from past experience there'd be no romance between them that night, not with Anya so preoccupied. He also knew she wouldn't tell him what was on her mind because her work as an analyst at the Central Intelligence Organization was highly classified. He poured himself another glass of wine. "I guess I'll just get drunk and sleep on the couch, then," he groused.

Anya sat down beside Tim on the couch and took the wineglass he offered her. "I wish I could tell you about it, Tim."

"Well, tell me. Just put blanks in for the classified stuff." Anya laughed and kissed him. "Ah, you're all right, babe." He put his arm around her. "You haven't washed your hair today, have you? It smells good when it's dirty. In fact, I like you most when you're dirty and smelly and . . ." his right hand began to wander.

Anya pushed his hand away. "Go easy on that wine would you?"

Tim leaned back. "I'll get you later, lady. All right, go ahead, let it out."

"Tim, the positions we advocate at CIO are formed from the top down these days, especially with that bastard—" she hesitated to mention Adams by name, so ingrained was her sense of loyalty toward the agency "—in charge. It used to be, agents passed intelligence to us analysts, we, well, we analyzed it and passed it up to the bosses, and then they'd formulate a position. Now it's the other way around, we're given subtle indications by the bosses what the political atmosphere of the moment demands and then we find the intel to support it."

"So, if a certain analyst who shall remain anonymous develops an opinion that is contrary to that which is desired . . ."

"Yep. That's me—more and more these days. The former director put me at HQ because he knew I was very good at what I did. I was a good field officer, Tim. I know the craft. But with this new crew at the top . . ." She threw her hands up in frustration.

They were both silent for a while, sipping their wine. Anya and Tim were mid-level civil servants, professionals, the people who form the stratum of government that ensures its smooth functioning regardless of who was in charge. They were both at the height of their professional careers, both in their mid-forties, and very good at what they did, assured their assignments in Fargo at the seat of the Confederation government were gateways to further promotion. Tim's field was epidemiology. He worked at the Ministry of Health.

"Sooo?"

Anya sighed. "So there's this man somewhere. Some people think he's a threat to the Confederation. They want him neutralized. But, Tim, I know he's no threat to the Confederation."

"Hmmm. All right. I'll pretend to be a reporter from GNN. Now who is this guy?" Tim drained his glass, sat upright, thrust the empty glass out like a microphone, and stuck it in Anya's face. "Well, lessee, where was your last assignment, Ms. Smiler? Oh, out there, huh? Well, your man must be—"

"You'd make a good analyst, Tim."

"I am one, love. I analyze bugs, didn't I ever tell you? And I could tell you about a certain place that's 'quarantined' but really it's off-limits because on this world out there are these really strange . . ."

Anya put a finger to Tim's lips. "Don't say one more word, darling, because if you do I'll have to kill you."

Anya had been recruited into CIO right out of college. She had the right prerequisites, a degree with honors in economics and a minor in statistics. In her interviews she had impressed the recruiters with her high degree of intelligence and enthusiasm for the work the CIO did. She passed all the background checks with flying colors, and was willing to travel to some very remote and inhospitable places in her assignments.

At the time she was accepted into the organization, the leadership had been a lot different than it became in later years. When she was younger, the analysts at Fargo and the higher-ups in the organization had tried to base their decisions on sound analysis from experts in the field; the organization's top management was not so sensitive to politics then or as career oriented as it became under a succession of directors ending with Adams, the most careerist and politically astute of them all.

Adams and his associates had fallen prey to the oldest pitfalls of the intelligence business: Information is power, and if information is shared outside the community in its totality, the power it confers is diminished; only those with a "need to know" should share sensitive information and that "need" was confined almost exclusively to those who gathered it; and no one outside the intelligence community could be trusted to evaluate or protect really sensitive intelligence. So Adams released only the intelligence he felt it safe to impart to other officials, and when he did, he put his own spin on what it might mean.

Anya was not trained in clandestine, the so-called "black," operations. Her job as an analyst in the field was to fill a legitimate position in the economics section at a consulate or embassy and complete real work for the Confederation Diplomatic Service, but her pay and career track were controlled by CIO and, as she did her legitimate work for the embassy, she assiduously cultivated contacts among the local population, collected and analyzed all sorts of information on events in the world where she was assigned, and reported back to Fargo on a regular basis. As an adviser to the ambassador, Anya took advantage of every opportunity to meet the important people of the worlds where she was assigned, win their confidence, and pump them, ever so unobtrusively, for information of value to the Confederation. Many of those people knew full well what Anya's real function was, but they trusted her anyway because she had the kind of personality that made men want to put their arm around her shoulders and women invite her home for tea.

One of her early assignments was the Confederation embassy to the Union of Margelan on Atlas, and she had gotten to know the Lavagers, Jorge, his wife Annie, and their daughter Candace, who was only an obstreperously precocious five-year-old at the time. That was in the days before Lavager rose to the political leadership of the Union of Margelan, but Anya saw it coming and duly advised her superiors. Events proved her to have been right and identified her as a rising star among the CIO's analysts.

Anya came to like the Lavagers and was often a guest in their home for private as well as official functions. When Jorge seized power, Anya was personally very satisfied that having a man like Lavager in charge would be the best thing for the Union of Margelan and Atlas as a whole.

The prevailing attitude among the CIO leadership that Lavager was a threat to the Confederation really bothered Anya Smiler.

Tim had long ago passed out and now he snored happily on the couch in Anya's living room, snored so loudly he'd have kept her awake even if she'd been able to sleep, which she was not.

Anya tossed and turned, rearranged the bedclothes and pillows, but sleep would not come for her that night. Her mind ranged ahead to tomorrow—well, it was tomorrow already, as the clock by her bedside reminded her each time she turned in that direction. In a few hours Adams would meet with the President and inform her that Jorge Lavager posed a serious threat to the economic stability of the Confederation. If Madam Chang-Sturdevant accepted that analysis, the only course would be to remove him. The CIO had ways of doing that which were terminal and Adams had no compunction about using them. Would Madam Chang-Sturdevant agree, and authorize a clandestine operation to assassinate Jorge Lavager? Anya had never met the President, but from what she knew of the woman, she didn't think she was the type of politician who'd lightly order the murder of anyone, much less a head of state. Since she had been in office, yes, Chang-Sturdevant's government had intervened in the affairs of other worlds, but those interventions had been conventional military operations.

Anya smiled. Well, not all had been that "conventional." She thought of the Marines the Attorney General had arranged to have sent to Havanagas, and how they'd managed to upset everything there, and that Marine who'd been left behind on Kingdom. He'd actually managed to overthrow the government there. What was his name? Charles something. She'd seen the reports. Yes, and there was that business of the aliens nobody at Fargo was willing to admit existed. One benefit (or curse, depending on how you looked at it) about being an intel analyst at Fargo was you got to know a lot that other people wished you didn't—whether you were authorized to know those things or not, and there was a lot she knew that she shouldn't.

Anya sighed and rolled onto her back. She flexed her knees. Ah, that was better. Tim continued to snore. Were the concussions of that enormous snoring really shaking the bedclothes? If they were going to stay together, Tim would have to get that snoring fixed.

Back to Atlas. Anya reflected that dissident political elements on Atlas had already tried to kill Lavager, so she could see precisely how Adams would proceed to neutralize him. The CIO would use that as excellent cover to pull off a successful murder, blaming it on the Atlean factions that wanted Lavager dead. She could picture Adams smoothly assuring the President that no one would ever be able to trace the assassination back to Fargo.

Dammit, she thought, why can't I just let this go? What can I do about anything? What should I do? Events followed their own course, what effect could a slip of a thing like Anya Smiler have on them? Besides, the CIO paid her, paid her well enough to afford a great apartment and the lifestyle she enjoyed at Fargo and as long as they did, she owed them her silence. Silence? There was none of that in this apartment tonight.

Anya got up, went into the living room, and rolled Tim onto his stomach. That was better. She picked up a half-full bottle of wine, pulled a chair to the window, and looked out into the storm. It was really snowing out there; there'd be a meter of the stuff by dawn. Nice, she thought, how nature still ruled human events. That was one thing mankind had not yet made entirely superfluous. Oh, she thought, we can travel faster than light and kill just about anyone we wish, but still, many people won't make it to work on time today because of the snow. Maybe she'd be one of them. Well, she had enough leave saved up, she should take some of it, call in sick maybe. She took a long swig from the bottle. Good. She took another. Even better. She began to relax. Tim grunted from where he lay on the couch. That was nice, he'd stopped that infernal bellowing.

Okay, I'll just let it go. Why not? Bigger brains than mine will decide what to do about things on Atlas. I'll plan for retirement instead of worrying about things I can't control.

The snow swirled outside the window in mighty gusts. The last thing she thought before drifting off to sleep was that snowdrifts would be meters deep in the morning. The wine bottle fell from her hand and rolled under the chair. She slept at last and the curtains trembled with her snoring.

CHAPTER
FOUR

Major General Fitzter didn't bother looking at his primary staff when he said, "We need to find and fix their headquarters, ladies and gentlemen. I believe all of you understand the importance of finding and fixing it long enough for a reaction force to reach it."

The assembled officers all studiously avoided looking at the commanding general's eyes. The Silvasian Liberation Army's headquarters had been located many times in the seven months standard the 104th had been seeking it. But every time it was found, it moved before the division could mount an operation against it.

"It's evident that neither our own assets nor the navy's vaunted string-of-pearls is capable of locating the SLA HQ."

Lieutenant Colonel Kevelys, the division G2—intelligence—officer clenched his jaws and glared straight ahead; the assets that so far *had* located the enemy headquarters several times belonged to him. The problem wasn't *locating* the HQ, it was *maintaining* contact once the HQ was discovered. To date, every recon team he sent out either had to break and lose contact, or was killed in place. And of course, the navy couldn't locate the SLA headquarters, the rebels kept to deep forest where they were safe from orbital discovery and observation. If the navy had a warship in orbit, his recon teams could call down fire on the SLA HQ when they found it. But the navy didn't have a warship in orbit. And the rules of engagement wouldn't have allowed orbital fire on the HQ anyway.

"It's imperative that we find, fix, and fuck up the SLA HQ in order to bring this campaign to a close, so I've put in a request for assistance," Fitzter continued. This time he looked directly at Kevelys, who steadfastly glared at the same spot of wall at which he'd glared since the general began talking about the "intelligence failure."

"I've asked the Combined Chiefs for a Confederation Marine Corps Force Recon team," Fitzter said.

Kevelys opened his mouth to protest and began to stand, then thought better of it and remained sitting with his mouth clamped shut. He believed that for the army to call in the *Marines* was taking the admission of mission failure too far, but he wasn't about to argue with a two-nova officer, particularly one who happened to be his boss.

"Do you have something you want to say, Lieutenant Colonel Kevelys?" Fitzter asked coldly.

Kevelys was a good enough intelligence officer, and he'd been riding his reconnaissance company very hard to fix the enemy headquarters' location. He took it as a personal affront that the division's recon company hadn't yet been able to maintain contact long enough for a reaction force to hit it. But now General Fitzter asked for his opinion and he couldn't restrain himself.

"Sir," Kevelys said, lurching to his feet, "There is nothing the Marines can do that the army can't. Just give me a little more time and we'll find that HQ again and fix it this time."

"You haven't found it yet," Fitzter snapped.

"We have, several times, sir—as you well know," Kevelys rasped. "It's a mobile HQ, it moves every time we locate it, and we haven't been able to maintain contact when it moves—as the general also knows."

The commanding general and his intelligence officer glared at each other for a moment. Kevelys looked away first.

"I know that," Fitzter finally said. "And you're probably right that the Marines can't do a better job of locating the enemy HQ than our own assets can. But they can probably do *just* as good a job. A lot of good soldiers have died trying to fix the enemy's location—as *you* well know. Marines aren't very bright, and they don't like to break contact with the enemy once they've established it. If a Force Recon team manages to survive discovery, they'll most likely attempt to evade capture while maintaining contact. Maybe they'll manage to stay alive long enough to find out in what direction the enemy HQ heads so we can land a reaction force in its path."

Fitzter abruptly stepped away from the podium. "Let's let some Marines die for a change. Maybe that'll change our luck."

"Attention!" shouted the division chief of staff as Fitzter strode out of the briefing room.

Fourth Force Recon Company, Fourth Fleet Marines, Camp Howard, MCB Camp Basilone, Halfway

" 'Bout time you got here," growled Sergeant Major Periz. "Go right on in, they're waiting for you."

"Thanks, Sar'nt Major," Sergeant Daly said, ignoring Periz's remark; the company's senior enlisted man always accused squad leaders of being late, even when they were standing right there when the call for them to report went out. Daly stood at attention in the doorway of the company commander's office and rapped loudly on the frame.

"Come," Commander Walt Obannion immediately replied.

Daly took the two steps forward that placed him a pace in front of Obannion's desk and fixed his eyes on the wall directly above the company commander's head. He didn't even glance at the others in the office: Lieutenant Tevedes, Gunnery Sergeant Lytle, and Staff Sergeant Suptra.

"Sir, Sergeant Jak Daly reporting as ordered."

"At ease, Sergeant."

"Thank you, sir." Daly relaxed into a modified parade rest position, feet at shoulder width, hands clasped in the small of his back.

"Sergeant, we've got a recon mission for the army's 104th Mobile Infantry Division on Silvasia. It's pretty routine on the face of it, but there are extenuating factors that may require an extra measure of, ah, diplomacy." The corner of Obannion's mouth quirked in the beginning of a smile that he instantly repressed. "Everyone in the platoon's chain of command," he turned his hand to indicate the others in his office, "is in agreement that you're the most 'diplomatic' squad leader in the company. That's why I'm sending second platoon's first squad on a mission that even the most junior squad leader could successfully command. Do you understand?"

Daly managed to remain expressionless. "More or less, sir. I'd understand better if I knew what it was I need to be particularly diplomatic about."

"It's simple enough—for the right Marine. The 104th's G2, a Lieutenant Colonel Kevelys, believes that Force Recon has no capabilities his own reconnaissance people lack. And Major General Fitzter, the division commander, isn't convinced Force Recon can survive the mission. You will need to convince them, before you start tracking your target, that FR *does* have greater capabilities and that you *can* survive."

Daly lifted a hand and scratched the corner of his mouth. "Sounds pretty straightforward, sir. When do we leave?"

"Gunny Lytle has all your briefing materials. He'll probably send you off in three days. Any questions?"

"Nossir. At least not until I study the briefing materials."

"Then you are dismissed, Sergeant."

"Aye aye, sir." Daly came to attention, stepped back a pace, executed a parade-ground-sharp about-face, and marched from the office.

"Any words of wisdom for me, Sar'nt Major?" he asked as he paused next to the sergeant major's desk.

Periz rolled the Davidoff Anniversario he was chewing on from one side of his mouth to the other before looking up. "Daly," he drawled, "if you don't know how to handle a simple op like this by now without having your hand held, I need to start processing the electrons to transfer your ass back to a FIST."

Daly laughed. "Thanks, Sar'nt Major, I knew I could count on you." He whistled an aimless tune as he left the company office and headed for his squad's billeting area.

Commander Obannion waited until Daly was out of the company office and Sergeant Major Periz rose from his desk to join them, then said, "Daly's an outstanding squad leader. Or do any of you know something about him I don't?"

"I think he's about as good as I was before I accepted promotion to section leader," Periz said.

"Right now I think he could make an outstanding platoon commander in a FIST," Tevedes said.

Obannion nodded. "Outstanding in a FIST, I agree. But what about in Force Recon?"

Gunny Lytle looked bemused. "You know, sir, every time I try to teach him something, he already knows it. I don't know about platoon commander, but with a little seasoning, he could take on my job without missing a beat." He glanced at Suptra and added, "Sorry. I don't mean to imply that you couldn't do just as well."

"Anyone else?" Obannion asked, though Suptra was the only one who hadn't yet offered an opinion.

The section leader shrugged. "I wouldn't have any problem following him." He gave a wry smile. "Provided we had a tour between me being his boss and him being mine."

"Let's see how he handles his little bit of 'diplomacy,' then readdress the question," Obannion said. He turned to the waiting work on his desk and the others filed out.

Aboard Confederation Navy Starship *City of Dundee*

Three days later, second platoon's first squad boarded a navy Essay ferrying cargo to the landing ship, freight, CNSS *City of Dundee*. A petty officer third met them at the docking bay, clipped them onto a guideline, and towed them through the weightlessness of a navy starship in orbit to the cabin that would be their quarters for the duration of their voyage to Silvasia.

When they reached the cabin the third class slapped a diagram on the bulkhead just inside the hatch and said, "This schematic shows you where the galley, the gym, and the library are. You read it—"

"Thanks, petty officer," Daly interrupted him. "I've sailed on *Homdale* class ships before, I know how to find my way around. Is our use schedule posted there?" He nodded at a blank screen next to the schematic.

"Whatever you say, Sergeant," the third class said in a tone that made clear he meant anything but. "You know how to access it?"

Daly kicked into a gentle cross-cabin movement in the starship's orbital null-G and stopped himself with one hand next to the control panel alongside the screen. He touched the controls and the panel sprang to life, displaying the Force Recon squad's schedule for using the troop mess, crew's gym, and ship's library.

"If the jacks work, we won't need to visit the library unless we want the exercise of getting there and back," he said.

"I guess you know where the jacks are?"

"Wazzen, show the man."

Lance Corporal Wazzen, the squad's most junior man, grinned crookedly and reached over one of the wall-mounted bunks. He slid a small panel to the side, exposing the plug-in jacks for the ship's library.

"Anything else we need to know?" Daly asked.

The third class slowly shook his head. "Looks like you've got everything under control. Unless you need to know when we break orbit."

Daly tapped his wrist comp and looked at its display. "Scheduled for twelve hours, seventeen minutes standard from now," he said. "And the most junior of us has made more than a dozen jumps, so we all know that routine, too."

"Happy sailing, then," the third class said, backing out of the cabin. He closed the hatch, but not quickly enough to keep the Marines from seeing the disgusted expression that washed over his face—he'd been looking forward to making the Marines feel dumb by showing them things they didn't know about.

The Marines laughed at the closed hatch.

"Ah, sailors," chortled Sergeant Kindy, the assistant squad leader. "I guess they don't teach them anymore that one of the major functions of early Marines was keeping sailors in line aboard ship."

"That meant we had to know our way around their ships better than they did," added the senior reconman, Corporal Nomonon.

"They probably *do* remember," said Lance Corporal Wazzen, "and that's why they keep trying to make us look dumb."

The trip to Silvasia was uneventful. The four Marines spent several hours a day in the crew's gym, working out to maintain their physical edge. When they weren't otherwise occupied, they were plugged into the ship's library, refreshing their knowledge of the various Silvasian wars, learning everything they could about the current peacekeeping operation, the history of the 104th Mobile Infantry Division, and reading the bios and records of Major General Fitzter and Lieutenant Colonel Kevelys—Daly and his men wanted to hit the ground running, and they wanted to make an immediate and lasting impression on the army officers for whom they'd be working.

Receiving Barracks, Confederation Navy Base (Planetside), Silvasia

"So how are we going to convince that doggie light colonel?" Corporal Nomonon asked.

"*We* aren't, *I* am," Sergeant Daly replied. A wolfish smile flickered across his face as he looked at his men. "You know what a midnight requisition is. So does the army. But the army doesn't have a clue how we do it. I'm going to show him."

"Shit," Lance Corporal Wazzen muttered. "You do that once the army knows how we do it; how are we going to get any supplies we need that Mother Corps didn't have to give to us?"

Daly laughed. "Come on, he's a doggie, he's probably not smart enough to make the connection between what I show him and our midnight requisitions."

Sergeant Kindy shook his head. "One of these days, boss, you're going to say something like that where some doggie brass will overhear you. Then your sweet ass will be grass."

Corporal Nomonon poked him on the shoulder. "How do you know his ass is sweet, you two been doing something Mother Corps might object to?"

Kindy blushed and jabbed Nomonon back. "Shut your face. I'd go for Bella Dwan before I did that."

Nomonon shook his head. "Man, you must have one powerful death wish." He turned to Daly. "Boss, do we gotta take him on this op? He wants to go for Bella, he could blow the whole op and get us all killed."

Daly looked at the two as though he was considering whether or not to take Kindy along. Then he said, "Tell you what. Instead of me doing it by myself, we'll all show Lieutenant Colonel Kevelys that we have capabilities his troops don't."

"So what do we do?"

Headquarters, 104th Mobile Infantry Division, Confederation Army, Silvasian Peacekeeping Mission

The corner of Lieutenant Colonel Kevelys's mouth twitched in annoyance when an unexpected waft of air stirred a strand of hair that had dropped onto his forehead. He looked up, ready to snap at whoever opened his office door without knocking, but bit off what he'd been about to say when nobody was there and the door was closed.

He returned to the intel analysis he'd been studying. The enemy HQ had moved again, but not before killing the six-man recon team that had found it and reported its position.

In order to preserve his remaining reconmen, he was teaming them up, one reconman with five legs—regular infantry—for the search and locate missions. The success rate of the combined patrols in finding the enemy headquarters was nearly as good as the success rate of the pure recon patrols. Their failure rate in fixing the enemy's location until a reaction team could reach them was just as abysmal.

He looked up faster at another vagrant air movement. Again, nobody was there—but had he seen his door easing closed the last centimeter?

Moving only his eyes, he examined his office, looking into each shadow, at the sides of everything someone might conceivably be behind. He saw no one, nothing out of place.

He gave his head a sharp shake. This mission must be getting to him. He'd never before been on an operation where a division's reconnaissance battalion failed so consistently in its primary mission, or suffered so many casualties. *If only, if only—*

Maybe General Fitzter was right, maybe when those Force Recon Marines showed up and got killed it would change their luck. But where were the Marines? Their ship was in orbit, they should have reported in by now.

"What's going on here?" he demanded out loud as air brushed across his brow again. Had the door frame come loose, was there some loose paneling around it?

He got up from his desk, stomped to the door, and rattled it. It felt as solidly secure as ever. He opened the door and looked into the outer office. His analysts and communications people were all at their stations. He strode beyond them to the open outer door and stepped into the corridor. Nobody was in sight in either direction, so unless someone had cracked his door open and shut, then immediately jumped back to his station, nobody was playing a bad joke on him. He looked at the assistant G2, who seemed too preoccupied with what she was doing to notice if somebody had.

He shook his head. It was the operation, it had to be.

He stepped back into his office and eased the door closed, then jumped as a voice behind him, from near his desk, said, "Sir, Sergeant Daly, Fourth Force Reconnaissance Company, reporting as ordered."

Kevelys spun about and croaked out something incoherent. A disembodied head floated in the air in front of his desk. His eyes shot left and right. Another disembodied head floated in midair to his right, two more were suspended to his left.

Kevelys worked his mouth to make enough saliva to swallow, then shouted, "What the hell do you think you're doing?" Then added in a rising voice, "And how the hell did you get in here?"

"I believe you were expecting us, sir," Daly said blandly. "And if nobody on your staff told you our ship is in orbit, somebody needs some straightening out." His

head moved in a way that made Kevelys think he must
have shrugged. "Sir, my commander informed me you
have never worked with Force Recon before, so I decided
to give you a small demonstration of our capabilities. By
way of introduction, sir."

Kevelys had recovered his poise while Daly talked, and
now drew himself to his most commanding posture.
"Someone's head is going to roll!" he snapped. "I should
have been informed the moment you entered the base."

"Sorry, sir. Nobody knew we were here until I reported
to you."

Kevelys looked at him in utter disbelief. "Are you trying to insinuate that you simply waltzed into a secure
army installation and nobody saw or challenged you?"

"Nossir, I'm not insinuating that; I'm stating it as a fact.
Sir, Force Recon can go into—and safely return from—
places nobody else can enter."

Kevelys would have sagged into his chair if he'd been
standing behind his desk. But he wasn't, he was standing
midway between his desk and the door.

"Out of my way," he snarled, and staggered around his
desk to sit heavily. He looked hard at the Marines, but this
time he didn't look at their disembodied heads, he looked at
the apparently empty air below their heads. "I thought—"
he paused to swallow. "I thought Marine chameleons were
somehow visible. I mean if you look right at them and you
know a Marine is there you can see him."

"Yessir, that's true of the standard Marine chameleon
uniform. But Force Recon has greater need for invisibility, so our chameleons are more effective. We also know
how to move very, very quietly." His head vanished as he
donned his helmet.

"Take that helmet off!" Kevelys commanded. "I can't
see you."

"Aye aye, sir."

Kevelys spun to his left. Just a moment ago, Daly had

been to his right front. Now the Marine stood a pace away from his left shoulder.

"Nobody can move that far, that fast, without making noise!"

Daly's shrug went again unseen. "As I said, sir, we can move very quietly."

"This base has infrared sensors around the perimeter," Kevelys said, grasping at straws. "You couldn't have gotten past them without being spotted." He jumped as something unseen landed on his hands.

"That's my helmet, sir," Daly told him. "The infrared screen is in place. If the colonel would be so good as to put it on, he can see for himself."

Kevelys's hands shook as he wrapped his hands around the helmet. He looked at his hands and just barely made out a ghostly image between them, though it was so faint he wasn't sure the image wasn't really in his imagination. He turned the invisible helmet about and discovered it was only chameleon on the outside; he could see its insides, which were studded with a bewildering array of toggles and touch-spots. He turned the helmet so the screens faced front and placed it on his head.

In infrared, Daly's head showed so clearly Kevelys could make out details. Below his chin there was only the faintest smear of red, so slight it wouldn't be noticed by anyone not looking intently for it. Kevelys looked at the other Marines; they all showed the same.

"Buddha's blue balls," Kevelys whispered.

"Sir," Daly said after giving Kevelys a moment to digest what he was looking at, "if the colonel would like a further demonstration, he can sound an alert and see if base security can catch us as we leave the base."

"N-No. No, I don't think that will be necessary," the G2 said shakily. He leaned back in his chair, looking from one disembodied head to another. It seemed Marine Force

Recon did have at least *some* capabilities beyond those of an army division's reconnaissance battalion.

Kevelys looked at the very faint red smudges again. "How do you keep track of each other when you're on patrol?" he asked weakly.

"We've got real sharp vision, sir. That's a prerequisite for Force Recon."

CHAPTER
FIVE

Samlan Forest, Approximately 250 Kilometers from 104th Mobile Infantry Division Headquarters, Silvasia

A V-Hook, the army variant of the Marine hopper, a tactical troop carrier aircraft, inserted the Force Recon squad a day's walk from the area in which G2 thought the Silvasian Liberation Army's headquarters was hidden. The area was large enough that Lieutenant Colonel Kevelys would have sent in at least a half dozen patrols if he were using his own recon battalion. But Sergeant Daly had insisted the Marines go in alone, and Major General Fitzter had backed him up.

The four Marines followed a zigzag route to their area of operations, their designated patrol area. Even before they reached the AO they began finding signs of human movement among the numerous animal tracks. Once inside the AO they found more human tracks and encountered SLA patrols; one the first day, two the second, three during the third morning. The increasing frequency of patrols could be simple coincidence, they thought it more likely that they were getting close to the SLA headquarters.

They stayed on the move two-thirds of the day, nibbling recon rations, commonly called "ReRas," as they went. The ReRas didn't have much bulk, so their stomachs began feeling hollow after a day, but the ReRas provided all necessary nutrients for men moving slowly and on little sleep. The lack of bulk was important for a recon patrol that followed the injunction to "leave nothing, not even footprints." They wouldn't move their bowels until they returned from the patrol.

The going was surprisingly easy for a dense, trackless forest. The Samlan was multiple canopy; there was no place where the canopy had fewer than three levels of spreading branches, and some places had more than double that—the Samlan was one of the most heavily canopied forests in all of Human Space. The many canopies of the forest effectively blocked satellite communications and surveillance of the ground under them.

Sunlight reached the ground only where an upper canopy giant had died and fallen. Those scattered places were home to a profusion of new growth, saplings and ground cover of all sorts struggling for growth and life before taller-growing flora blotted out life-giving light and consigned them to premature death. Where the canopy remained intact, which was most of the forest, the tree trunks grew thick, with several meters of space between them. Little grew there, mostly analogs of moss and algae.

But animal life flourished on the ground. Herbivorous animals gnawed moss and algae from rocks and trunks, nibbled fallen branches and fresh leaves and fruits, crunched living bark from the trunks. Some animals made their living more simply, by preying on unwary herbivores. Insectoids scrabbled over the ground, devouring decomposing leaves and fruit missed by the browsers and scraps of flesh, blood, sinew, and bone left by the predators. And ate the waste of all the animals. Some insectoids fluttered about to land on the animals and scour their hides of flaking bits of dermis, or sink proboscides into their flesh to suck their fluids.

It wouldn't be accurate to say the Marines moved wraithlike; compared to their movement, the wraiths of Earth legend were noisy trompers.

Along the way, without disturbing dinner or diner,

they'd passed within touching range of a carnivore about to spring on a prey beast. They'd stepped over a venomous nyoka that lay in wait for something to come along and brush its trip-tail so it could whip its fanged head around in a killing strike. They'd stopped to let a foraging army of meat-eating hive insectoids pass less than a meter distant; the meat-eaters, which could sense warm-blooded animals tens of meters distant, ignored their presence. And they'd passed closely by many more animals and insectoids without being noticed.

With one exception: A browsing dreer bolted when Lance Corporal Wazzen couldn't resist petting the antelopelike animal.

Sergeant Daly was on Wazzen before the dreer completed its second bound, his helmet against his junior man's helmet, his voice carried by conduction through the helmets.

"Don't ever do that," Daly snarled. "If anybody's nearby he's going to wonder what startled that thing. Do you want a battalion of bad guys to start searching for us?"

"B-But it was so *cute*," Wazzen stammered.

"*Cute* can make you dead, Marine!"

"I won't do it again, Sergeant. I promise."

"See that you don't." Daly checked his sensors for any sign of human presence. There hadn't been any before Wazzen startled the dreer, there still wasn't. No sight, no movement, no scent. If there had been before, he would have initiated an immediate action instead of jumping on his junior man.

"Let's catch up."

Sergeant Kindy and Corporal Nomonon knew what had happened and that there were no enemy nearby; they had continued moving through the forest. The faint smudges they showed in infrared were almost as invisible as the two Marines were in visual light, but that didn't matter. What Daly had told Lieutenant Colonel Kevelys about how Force Recon Marines kept in touch wasn't totally true. They did have sharp vision, but their uniform shirts also had small ultra-violet lights on the shoulders. When Daly handed his helmet to Kevelys, he'd already turned off his UV tracker—and the Marines had their shoulder tracking lights turned off anyway.

Daly and Wazzen hustled to rejoin Kindy and Nomonon.

Daly was angry about Wazzen's dumb stunt, but he calmed down quickly. It was only the junior man's third mission. He had performed well on the first two and, until he gave in to the dreer's "cute," had done well so far on the current one. Official Force Recon policy was, one dumb mistake and you're out. But Daly believed everybody was entitled to one dumb mistake—as long as nobody got hurt by it. Wazzen just had his one. Daly would tell him when they got back onboard ship. For now, he had more immediate concerns.

The multiple canopies of the Samlan didn't only block satellite observation and surveillance of the ground, they also blocked secure low-power communications from the ground to orbit—it was something in their chemical makeup. And they blocked reception of string-of-pearls downlink GPS data; the Marines had to rely on their helmets' inertial guidance system to keep track of where they were.

Every Marine who'd served long enough to have had to rely on his helmet's integral inertial guidance system knew how unreliable it could be over long distances with many turns and no obvious reference points. First squad had gone a long distance with *very* many turns.

An hour after Wazzen startled the dreer and after avoiding another SLA patrol, Daly called a rest at dead tree with a hollow bole that wasn't being used by a denning animal. The first thing he did after calling the halt was to send Corporal Nomonon up one of the trees to get a GPS reading. The GPS said they were more than half a kilometer off where their inertial guidance systems showed. They made the necessary adjustments to the systems.

After they ate a cold meal, Daly took his men into the hollow bole and put them on a 25 percent alert; one man awake while the others slept, one-and-a-half hour shifts. Six hours after entering the bole, they ate another quick meal and moved out again.

It wasn't long before they found another trail made by human feet. This one also showed vehicle tracks. Daly was sure they were getting close to their objective. He moved the patrol to the side of the trail, as far off as they could get and still see it, then parallelled it.

Three hours and five patrol evasions later, they found the Silvasian Liberation Army's headquarters.

Near the Headquarters of the Silvasian Liberation Army, Samlan Forest, Silvasia

General Leigh, the SLA commander, had picked a location under five levels of canopy, where the infrared signals of his people were shielded from orbital detection.

It was a large camp. Judging from the number of sleeping and mess tents, there were probably more than two thousand soldiers, support personnel, and others—they saw more children than could be expected in a purely combat unit in a guerrilla army, so some of the women must be wives. Which didn't mean the wives didn't also have official functions in the headquarters—and all the women they saw who weren't watching children seemed to be moving about on business of one sort or another.

Daly drew his men in close where they sat in a circle back-to-back so they could watch in all directions. They tipped their heads back so their helmets touched and they could talk via conduction without emitting radio waves.

"Where are we?" Daly asked. "Give me your inertial readings."

They all transmitted their inertial location readings to

him. He compared theirs with his own, there wasn't more than a twenty-five-meter difference among them. It was close enough, he wasn't going to call in air or naval gunfire strikes. He thought for a moment to decide their next course of action.

They had to report the location of the headquarters, that was a given. But communications were blocked by the multiple canopy. Obviously, just as every army recon patrol had done, someone had to climb a tree to call in the report. But climbing left marks on the trees, which might have been what caused some of the army patrols to be found.

SLA patrols had become more frequent as the Marines neared the headquarters—Daly had one in sight right now. There could be more; the SLA didn't have chameleons, but their uniforms were well camouflaged, making them very difficult to see visually in the permanent dusk under the multiple canopy, and their uniforms had enough infra-damping capability that their signals weren't easy to spot at a distance through trees.

Still, Daly was confident of his squad's ability to evade the SLA patrols, even if the security patrols discovered signs that told them that someone had located their camp. He was also confident that his squad could follow the headquarters with ease if it moved.

But he'd rather not be discovered in the first place. So, how to climb a tree without leaving marks that one of the many patrols would spot?

"I have one patrol in sight, two hundred meters, moving from near right to upper left," he said. "Any others in sight?"

"I have one at two fifty, near left to upper right," Sergeant Kindy, directly to his rear, reported. The distances were approximate, they didn't risk using range finders, which could be detected.

"Nomonon? Wazzen?"

"Clear," Corporal Nomonon answered; he was facing deeper into the forest.

"Nobody coming out," said Lance Corporal Wazzen; he was facing the headquarters camp.

"Let's watch, see if there's a pattern."

Unmoving except for their eyes, they sat for more than four hours; they didn't move even when a patrol came within fifteen meters of their location. One of the six guerrillas in the patrol held what looked like a motion detector; another had an infra detector. Neither spotted the Marines.

The patrols *did* have a pattern. In the segment of the camp's perimeter that they could observe, patrols went out at approximate half-hour intervals, two at a time, from spots three hundred meters apart; the departure spots rotated counterclockwise, a hundred meters at a time. The Marines couldn't tell how far out the patrols went, but they came back on different routes from those on which they'd gone out. Neither could they tell if the patrols they saw coming back were the same as those they saw go out, only that two hours after a patrol departed another returned about seventy-five meters counterclockwise from where a patrol had departed two hours earlier.

"Here's what we're going to do," Daly said when he had seen enough.

Half a Kilometer Farther from the SLA Headquarters

They were good, the Force Recon Marines. They stepped softly and kept to the hardest ground they could find; their boots made almost no imprint on the ground. Even if the SLA had trackers good enough to spot their traces, it was unlikely the one or few good enough would come across their trail, less likely they'd be looking for such slight traces.

Willing just one time to make footprints, Daly faced an

appropriate tree and planted his feet firmly less than a meter in front of the trunk and leaned into the tree, bracing himself against it with his hands. He was the biggest man in the squad; the heaviest and strongest, though not the tallest.

Corporal Nomonon was the tallest. He climbed up Daly's back and stood on his shoulders. Lance Corporal Wazzen scrambled up to stand on Nomonon's shoulders.

Sergeant Kindy, the smallest man in the squad, clambered to the top of the human spire and sank two anchor spikes into the tree trunk above his head. Securing himself to the anchor spikes with a short length of rope, he lifted his feet from Wazzen's shoulders; the Marines below him collapsed their spire while Kindy affixed climbing spikes to his boots and gloves. Then he began climbing.

As soon as everybody was off him, Daly squatted down and brushed away the worst marks of his footprints. Then, while Nomonon and Wazzen kept watch, he methodically picked up the chips of bark that dribbled down from Kindy's climbing.

It was a tall tree, and Kindy had to climb high to get above enough of the canopies to establish communications with a satellite. When he was finally high enough, he dropped two weighted lines, camouflaged to conceal themselves against the tree.

Daly grabbed one line, removed the weight, and plugged the line into a jack in his helmet. A moment later, he was talking to the duty communications officer of the 104th Mobile Infantry Division.

"Homeboy, this is Rover One," he reported. "We have them." He gave the coordinates he got from Kindy's GPS. "They have not detected us. When can we expect you? Over."

"Rover One, are you positive you've located the quarry and that you haven't been detected?" The comm officer sounded doubtful.

"That's a double affirmative, Homeboy," Daly replied flatly.

"How secure is your position, Rover? I'll have to get back to you."

"They aren't going to find us, but we have to go potty, so don't take too long." The very expressionlessness of his voice made it sound sarcastic.

"I'll be back, Rover. Homeboy out."

Daly unplugged the line to the satellite link and plugged in the other, which was connected to Kindy's helmet jack.

"Bad news," he told the assistant squad leader. "We have to wait in place until the army pulls its thumb out of its ass and decides to do something."

"You mean I got to stay up here?"

"With the birdies for the duration."

"There aren't any birdies here."

"Count your blessings. No birdies means they can't join the army in shitting on you."

Kindy snorted. "With my luck, the birdies would be the size of cows."

"So it's a good thing there aren't any birdies."

It was almost two hours before Homeboy got back to them. He sounded almost surprised that they were still in position and nothing had changed. Homeboy said a squad from the division's recon battalion was on its way to confirm their report.

"Recall that squad, Homeboy," Daly snapped. "If that's all that comes, we'll have to save their asses, and then follow the target to tell you where your recon scared them off to. And that'll piss me off, because I really have to go potty. You won't like it when a pissed off Marine who has to go potty shows up in your face."

Homeboy didn't reply for a moment, then said, "Rover, say again target strength."

"About two thousand, Homeboy. At least half of them are security or combat. I recommend a brigade to encircle the target."

"Rover, are you positive?"

"Have I ever lied to you, Homeboy?"

Homeboy wisely didn't reply to that, instead he said, "Rover, wait one."

"Wait one" in radio parlance normally means a short time, anywhere from a few seconds to a few minutes. In this instance, it meant an hour, during which Daly and his two men on the ground had to move away from the tree to let an outbound SLA patrol pass by.

When Homeboy finally came back he said three battalions were on their way and for the Force Recon patrol to go to ground.

Kindy gratefully came down from the tree and the squad returned to where it could keep an eye on the SLA headquarters.

Three hours later they saw patrols running back into the camp, and soldiers and others bustling about breaking camp.

The three battalions of the 104th Mobile Infantry Division arrived from as many directions before more than a few elements of the SLA headquarters left.

General Leigh was one of the many who were caught in the trap. There was a short, fierce fight before the defenders surrendered—the general didn't want the children to get killed in the fight.

"Mission accomplished," Daly said to his squad. "Let's go take a dump and head for home."

"Well done, Marines," General Fitzter said when the Force Recon squad, bathed, purged, and dressed in clean—and visible—dress reds reported to him in his office. "I don't know how you did it, but if you ever decide to change services, I guarantee you a job with me."

"Thank you, sir," Daly said politely. "That's very generous of the general."

Lieutenant Colonel Kevelys looked at them with a mix of resentment and awed respect. He looked at the array of ribbons on Daly's chest, indicating the numerous campaigns and operations he'd participated in, and couldn't help noticing the first two ribbons represented Marine Corps medals for personal heroism. He unclenched his jaws and said, "I believe the term you Marines use for a job well done is 'outstanding.' Now I think I have an idea of why."

"Thank you, sir," Daly said with a nod. "It's all in a day's work for Force Recon."

Fitzter's eyebrow twitched, Kevelys's jaw reclenched.

"I will write a letter of commendation to your commanding general," Fitzter said, then added wryly, "But he probably expected you to perform as well as you did."

"Thank you, sir. I'm sure he did."

"You're dismissed."

"Thank you, sir," Daly said smartly. "Good hunting on the rest of your campaign, sir." He and his men about-faced and marched from the general's office.

Kevelys opened his mouth to admonish them for not saluting, but Fitzter held up a hand to stop him. When the door closed behind the Marines he said, "The sea services don't salute indoors."

"Right," Kevelys snarled. "Arrogant bastards—I mean what he said about 'all in a day's work.'"

Fitzter nodded. "I agree. But when you're as good as they are, you can get away with a bit of arrogance."

CHAPTER
SIX

Unified World of Atlas

Atlas was a flourishing world.

When the first explorers arrived they were very pleasantly surprised to find a planet that seemed created for colonization, teeming with fauna and flora, none of which proved inimical to mankind. The life-forms native to Atlas sustained the original colonists for years, and a distinctive cuisine developed around native foodstuffs.

The seas on Atlas abounded with marine life, much of which was highly delectable to the human palate, and crops of all kinds flourished in the hospitable soils. Those early settlers established a self-sustaining colony and eventually their descendants transformed Atlas into a member of the Confederation of Worlds known for its agricultural products. Grains that had become almost extinct on Earth thrived on Atlas, as did the industry that distilled alcohol from corn, mash, and rye—old-fashioned bourbon was one of Atlas's leading exports.

The Atleans sustained themselves by growing and raising things. Hunger was unknown, and despite several wars over the recent decades, the granaries of Atlas had never run out. Atlas was the breadbasket in its quadrant of Human Space, and its exports were highly prized.

The Atleans were, of necessity, very careful to guard against the import of plant and animal species that could upset the balance of nature they'd achieved on their world. Thus all off-world arrivals and their baggage were subjected to thorough inspection and decontamination. Imports were likewise subjected to rigorous irradiation before being released to their markets. Ships and their crews transiting Atlas for whatever reason were simply quarantined at their ports of entry and the Atleans who worked there submitted to decontamination before going home at the end of their shifts. As is true anywhere, customs could be bypassed as officials looked the other way, but irradiation could not, and the penalty for trying to avoid it was death. These harsh rules were strictly enforced, but again and again they had successfully prevented alien infestations that might have ruined the crops and livestock so necessary to Atlas's economic viability.

Because Atlas was primarily an agricultural world with not much heavy industry, and what industry it had was stringently regulated, the natural environment remained largely undisturbed. The planet's beaches, mountains, lakes, oceans, and national parks were renowned throughout Human Space for their pristine beauty. The cities on the planet were small, clean, and comfortable places to live, and people came to Atlas just to get away from the hubbub of their native worlds, to enjoy the good food the Atleans were so proud of, and the natural wonders of the planet. Tourism flourished on Atlas.

Ramuncho's Restaurant, New Granum, Union of Margelan, Atlas

Ramuncho served the dalmans right out of their shells, piping hot just the way Jorge Lavager liked them, but they were also excellent cold and in salads, served as a main course with side dishes, or as appetizers.

Dalmans (*Dalmanantes postii*) were arthropoid creatures resembling the trilobites that once swam in Earth's Paleozoic seas. Dalmans lived in the littorals in the Great Northern Sea a few hundred kilometers from New

Granum. The Atleans raised them in huge seawater lakes and exported them to other worlds where they were highly prized delicacies. But Ramuncho bought his dalmans right off the docks from the fishing fleets and Lavager ate only those, freshly caught in the ocean. Ramuncho had a special arrangement with Lavager to inform him first when a new shipment of dalmans arrived in his kitchens.

A mature dalman could provide up to two kilos of indescribably delicious meat while their larvae, harvested in vast quantities, added an ineffable flavor to salads and soups. The Union of Margelan had for many years enforced a policy of restocking the dalmans in their natural habitat, which insured a virtually inexhaustible supply of the creatures, much to the delight of gastronomes throughout Human Space. A half kilo of dalman meat on Earth could fetch up to a thousand credits, a bargain, and connoisseurs were delighted to pay it.

Craaack! Lavager broke the carapace with a small hammer and then pried it open with a special set of tongs, essential tools for a dalman meal. The most delightful aroma filled the small back room as the steaming meat inside the shell was exposed. "Ahhhh," Lavager said as he inhaled the sweet essence, "this is living, eh, Locker?" He sprinkled the meat with pepper and a special hot sauce created from Ramuncho's own secret recipe.

"You use too much of that stuff, Jorge, and you won't be able to sit down for a week," General Ollwelen laughed.

"If you finish off that dalman, you won't be able to stand up for a week," Lavager countered. Locksley picked up his own hammer and deftly cracked his dalman open. The pair applied their forks in contented silence for a long while, occasionally drinking from iced schooners of ale.

"Damn!" Lavager exclaimed at last, shoving the remnants of his meal toward the center of the table and producing his portable cigar humidor. "Now don't tell me, old buddy, that we aren't living high!" Chuckling, he offered General Ollwelen, who had also just finished his meal, one of his cigars.

"My God, Jorge, when did you get these?" Locksley admired the cigar. "Davidoff Series Millennium DCLVIS! I can't believe it!" Lovingly, he clipped the end and accepted a light. He sucked the smoke in, then let it out slowly, very slowly, to savor to the utmost the exquisite flavor of the tobacco. "A dalman and a Davidoff, tonight I can die a happy man!"

They smoked in silence for a while, savoring the cigar's easy draw, the rich, full-bodied earthiness of the tobacco in its oil-saturated dark-brown wrapper—a truly classic smoke, the crowning achievement of a company that had been making crowning achievements for five hundred years. At last Locksley said, "Jorge, a matter of business?"

Lavager nodded his assent. He reached for and took a long draft from his beer schooner.

"We've got to increase security about what's going on out at the Spondu facility."

Lavager looked inquiringly at Locksley. "We already have a full platoon of infantry assigned to security out there. Why do we need more?"

"Top secret research facilities always require tight security, you know that, Jorge. But yes, we need to tighten things up out there and everywhere else, especially everywhere else—and that means right inside your own government." He paused for a moment and then came to what was really on his mind, "Gustafferson's been snooping around out there. He knows it used to be a weapons research facility."

Lavager groaned at the mention of the correspondent's name. "Can't I enjoy a meal without someone bringing up that fool's name? And we all know what the Cabbage Patch is today, what it used to be doesn't matter."

"To Gustafferson, it does," Ollwelen said. When

Lavager didn't respond to that he continued, "Gutsy may be a lot of things, but he's no fool. Besides, New Granum is swarming with agents from the Solanums, Oleania, Satevina, and the Confederation's CIO. Everyone knows we're up to something out there and they're all snooping around. But of all of the snoopers, Gustafferson's the most dangerous. You know how he'll manufacture news if he can't get anything legitimate. Look at the scandal he caused on Willis's Venue over that case of alleged child abuse in the school system, and I don't think you've forgotten how he was the willing press agent for the mob on Havanagas with all the puff pieces he wrote about the place before the Confederation cleaned it up. If Gustafferson smells even a whiff of what we're doing out at the Cabbage Patch, the whole operation will be exposed and everything we're planning to do will be compromised. We can't afford that, Jorge. You ought to have him shot. You'd do everyone a favor if you did."

Lavager snorted and waved a hand. "Well, I'm not going to have the bastard executed, if that's what you're driving at, Locker. How does such a phony stay in business?"

Locksley drank some beer. "I guess he stays in business because muck sells, and he's the biggest muckracker in Human Space. You know, he's like a lot of these media people, he rushes in, scrapes together a sensational story with no depth, and rushes out to go screw up someone else. The public only has a ten-second attention span anyway, so before the slipshod reporting is exposed, they're absorbed in the next scandal and they lose track of the ones that came before."

"Do you think someone in my cabinet, or one of the scientists out at the Cabbage Patch, is leaking information?"

"Yes. I've got army security on the job. We've been tailing Gustafferson. We don't think any of our people are talking to the other members of the League of Nations; they're not traitors in that sense. But we think with all the money Gustafferson has to toss around he's been able to get some disaffected souls to talk. Nobody quite on the inside of the operation, but we think he's gotten enough information to know there's a story out at Spondu. And something else, Jorge."

Lavager raised an eyebrow. "Somehow, old friend, I don't think I'm going to like this 'something else' very much."

"We're convinced Gustafferson is really a deep cover intelligence agent for the Central Intelligence Organization, using his reporting career, sensational as it is, as his cover. It's a perfect arrangement."

Lavager looked steadily at his old friend for a very long moment. "Then get rid of him," he said at last.

Traveler's Roost, Kraken Interstellar Starport, New Granum Terminus

Every metropolis has its seamy side and that was as true of New Granum as anywhere else in Human Space. That seamy side was the New Granum planetside terminus for Kraken Interstellar Starport, which serviced the capital and the other cities and regions that composed the Union of Margelan. The tourist or businessman visiting Atlas via New Granum saw only the sparkling facilities of the port and remained in them only long enough to make connection with transit to their hotels. But the crews of transient vessels and the human flotsam of the spacelanes that always drift into planetside terminals needed someplace to call home, even if only for a few hours, and that place was a district of flophouses, bars, cutthroat casinos, and other low-rent establishments that weren't particular about their clientele. The district was known unofficially as "Downside." Besides, men on long voyages don't turn into plaster saints. The law enforcement community of New Granum understood that and for the most part didn't interfere with the goings-on in Downside.

"I don't know why you insisted we should meet in this,

this, place." The pudgy little man sniffed and looked around the bar disdainfully. "We could've met uptown, in a nice restaurant."

It hadn't required much effort to discover that this little man had some bad habits that required a steady infusion of cash. That was all that Gus Gustafferson needed to get him into the Traveler's Roost at Downside.

"It's important nobody see us together, Ronald," Gustafferson said calmly, as if he were talking to a petulant child, because that was just what Dr. Ronald Paragussa looked like, an overgrown six-year-old. "I can't take a chance on getting scooped, and you, of course, might get in serious trouble if you were seen talking to me. So we meet here." Gustafferson smiled. "Besides, this place has atmosphere, don't you agree?" For Downside, the Traveler's Roost was almost respectable, a place where spacefarers came to eat and drink and be on their way—to the rooms upstairs where whores and stimulants were discreetly available, or back to their ships.

"Y-You mentioned—?" Paragussa rubbed two fingers together.

"Ah, yes, doctor, I did mention—" Gustafferson also rubbed his fingers together, and with the other hand passed Paragussa a small chip. "Pop this into your reader. And remember, I absolutely guarantee your anonymity, as I do all my sources, the real ones and the ones I make up."

Paragussa's eyes widened when he saw the figure GNN was offering him through its reporter for the information they wanted. He smiled and relaxed. "What is it you wish to know, sir?"

"You are a scientist. You work at the secret facility at Spondu. But you're a well-known agronomist, and the Spondu facility is thought to be a weapons research center. What does a man in your specialty do at a freaking weapons lab? I smell a story here, doctor."

"Well. I specialize in synthetic fertilizers, particularly

the process known as hydroscopy—the absorption of water. It's my job to develop fertilizers that do not absorb water."

Gustafferson wondered if this fool was putting him on. Fertilizer? "What the hell is a fertilizer man doing in a weapons lab?"

Paragussa shrugged. "There are a number of experiments being conducted at the Cabbage Patch—"

"The *Cabbage Patch* you say?" Gustafferson laughed. "That's the name of the facility?" He shook his head, amused. "Someone must have a sense of humor." When Paragussa looked confused, he added, "It's an old children's tale. Once upon a time young children were told that babies were found in cabbage patches. The name, Ronald, is a sardonic admission that the 'Cabbage Patch' is a cover for something else."

The agronomist looked at the reporter as though he was being put on, then continued, ignoring the business about "cabbage patch" being an obvious cover. "The nature of the activities at the Cabbage Patch is a closely guarded secret. Everyone's work is compartmentalized. Only the director and a few government officials, presumably, know the whole picture, where all this research is directed. My part of the project is very small, and frankly I do not know how it fits in with what the other scientists are doing out there. That's a normal security precaution at any top secret facility. Have to guard against espionage and curious reporters and all that, you know." He snickered.

Gustafferson nodded his understanding. "Fertilizers?" he mused. "You can make a bomb out of that stuff, can't you?"

Paragussa laughed. "Yes, with the proper mixture of ammonium nitrate, explosives, fusing. But to make a bomb of any significance," he held out his hands, "you'd need literally thousands and thousands of kilos of fertilizer and then how'd you transport something so huge to its target, and who'd resort to such a thing given the kinds of weapons we have today?" He shook his head. "No, we're not building a bomb out there." He laughed again.

"So what are you doing?"

"I have a theory." Paragussa held up the chip and smiled.

"All right, Ronald, I'll triple the figure if you can find out for me. But before I'll give one more decicredit, you give me something, right now."

"Very well," Paragussa leaned across the table and whispered, "I believe we're developing a fungoid strain that, once released, will have a devastating effect on all varieties of food crops, wipe them out." He leaned back, a smug expression on his face. "You see," he continued, "people can fight armies, resist invasions, win wars—but how do you fight starvation?"

"With food!" Gustafferson snapped back, sitting up straight in his chair. "With food! Destroy a society's food production and the power that can feed the people rules the world! So that's what Lavager is up to. Mohammed's uncircumcised prick!" He slapped the table and heads turned in their direction. His eyes flicked around, and he leaned forward to whisper, "It's brilliant! Hell, Atlas is already a breadbasket. If Lavager could destroy crop production on other worlds, they'd naturally turn to Atlas for relief. The next thing you know, he's dictating their foreign policy, like the old Arab oil sheiks did to the North Americans back in the twenty-first century. And once they find out what's going on, what are they going to do? Bomb Atlas? Destroy their source of food? Ronald," Gustafferson snapped his fingers, "I need confirmation. Can you get that for me? If you can, why GNN will gladly quadruple the figure on that chip."

"I think so."

"Good! How long will it take?"

"Umm, a week, maybe ten days? I'll have to do some discreet snooping of my own."

"We'll meet back here in a week, then. Excuse me now,

Ronald, I have a prelim to file." Gustafferson went to the nearest communications terminal, chuckling to himself about the irony of the name of the Spondu facility, and placed the chip he'd used to surreptitiously record his conversation with Paragussa into the transmit slot. He punched in a number at the Confederation embassy. Now his controller would know what was up. Gustafferson almost laughed out loud. He'd scored two huge scoops in less than fifteen minutes, the vital intelligence the CIO needed, and a story that once it broke would earn him a Hillary, the most prestigious award an investigative reporter could hope for.

Outside it was dark and raining slightly. Gustafferson hunched his shoulders against the drizzle. A damp wind sighed between the buildings. The street was empty and dimly lit. Off in the near distance the bright lights of the port glowed warmly. He started walking in that direction.

His badly beaten body was found in an alley several days later. Dr. Ronald Paragussa never got his money. He met with a fatal accident at the facility called the "Cabbage Patch," something to do with breathing too much ammonia.

Somebody had just made a serious mistake.

CHAPTER
SEVEN

Office of the President of the Confederation of Human Worlds, Fargo, Earth

"I always get sick to my stomach when we meet with those bastards," Madam President Chang-Sturdevant complained to her Minister of War, who had heard it before.

"I presume you're referring to our illustrious CIO director and his deputy? Steel yourself, Madam," Marcus Berentus said, grinning. "Actually, I knew Adams's parents. Very decent people, I must say. Old money, blue blood. Did I ever tell you I once dated his younger sister? I was in pilot training at the time and our base was near their summer home on—"

"Well, Marcus," Chang-Sturdevant interrupted him, "I've never trusted those two. Never. Thirty years ago, when I was on the intelligence oversight committee, they ran the CIO a lot differently. I should have removed Adams when I came into office. Not only is his intelligence faulty—how come they never knew what was going on on Kingdom, with this—what was his name?"

"De Tomas, Madam—"

"Dominic de Tomas, thank you. But I don't trust them because they have their own agenda, Marcus. Take it from someone who's spent her whole life in politics, private agendas lead to disaster."

"I may not have been in politics my entire life, Suelee,"

Berentus said softly, "but my time in the army taught me about private agendas."

Cynthia Chang-Sturdevant stopped with her hand halfway to her head and stared at him for a moment. As long as they'd known each other, and as close and trusted an advisor as Berentus was, this was the first time he'd ever called her by the name used by her family and closest friends. She shook herself, and ran her hand along the single, thick lock of gray hair that lay at the center of her coiffure. That single gray lock had started a fashion craze among well-to-do ladies since Chang-Sturdevant had been in office.

"Private agendas are what's given me this gray hair, Marcus," she said with no acknowledgment of the slight intimacy of his use of her first name. She brushed her hair into place and adjusted her blouse. Despite her years, she was still a very handsome woman. And somewhat younger than Marcus. "Adams asked for a private interview with me, Marcus, but I'm not that stupid. I invited you, the Chairman of the Combined Chiefs, and the Attorney General. I'm not going into the snake pit without my charmers."

"Umm. The AG will ensure a lively discussion; he despises the CIO people." Hugyens Long, known as "Chief," because of his long years as a policeman, was also known for his directness and acerbity and the fact that even though he was Attorney General for the Confederation of Human Worlds, he was not a lawyer. Chang-Sturdevant considered Long one of her wisest appointments, and along with Berentus, he was one of her most trusted advisers.

"Well, let's go, Marcus."

"Yes, Madam."

They headed for the door leading from Chang-Sturdevant's private office to the conference room where her cabinet usually met. Just before the door, she stopped

and turned to Berentus. "Marcus, about Adams's sister.
What ever came of your date with her?"

"Nothing. I took her home well before the witching
hour. Never saw her again. I shipped out the following
week. I understand she married well, as all the Adamses
did. But her parents were very decent to me."

"Umpf. Well, let's hear what J. Murchison Adams and
Palmer Quincy Lowell have to tell us that's so damned
important. I tell you this, Marcus, when blood stains their
hands it's red, not blue."

Chang-Sturdevant's parents had run a laundry.

The four men stood as the President entered the conference chamber. "Jay! Palmer!" Chang-Sturdevant greeted
the CIO director and his deputy warmly, as if they were
friends and welcome guests. Chang-Sturdevant was a
consummate politician, after all. "Chief," she nodded re-
spectfully at Hugyens Long. "Admiral Porter," she addressed the recently elevated Chairman of the Combined
Chiefs, who stood at attention until she indicated everyone should be seated.

"Seems to me, Madam President," Long said, easing his
bulk into his chair, "that every goddamned time I come
down here to see you it snows. Remember the last time? I
came here with Nast about the Havanagas operation.
Some sonofabitch tried to kill us downstairs in the plaza.
It snowed so hard that day that—"

"Yaass," J. Murchison Adams drawled, casting a disparaging glance at Long. "We actually had to take under-
ground transport to get here, Madam President. I'd have
asked for a postponement except that what we have to tell
you is just too important to be delayed by the weather."

"They're saying it's the worst storm in a century," Admiral Porter said. "I had to call a starship to get over here."
Long grinned but nobody else seemed to have caught the
joke.

"Well, let's get down to business, gentlemen. I don't

want to sit around here until the snow melts." Chang-Sturdevant indicated Adams should proceed.

An image of Atlas as seen from orbit flashed onto the screens in the consoles in front of each participant. Palmer Quincy Lowell explained the background of events on Atlas, emphasizing its strategic position along the spacelanes that connected many different worlds to the Confederation. He explained who Lavager was, what he had done, how under his influence the rival nations on Atlas had formed a League of Nations.

"Someone assassinated his wife?" Berentus interjected.

"Yes, very unfortunate accident. The assassin was after Lavager." Adams shrugged; to him, Annie Lavager's death was inconsequential.

Long grimaced.

"That daughter, she's his only child?" Chang-Sturdevant asked. Candace Lavager's image floated on the screens. "Beautiful child," she murmured. "So aside from conquering worlds, he's raising this daughter on his own. I wouldn't think he'd have time for conquests with a teenage girl on his hands."

"Who tried to kill him?" Long asked.

"Well, there are many disaffected groups on Atlas," Lowell answered, plainly annoyed by these questions, which he considered off the point. "Jorge Lavager is," he rushed on, "by all accounts, an intelligent, capable, and ruthless opponent. One of our best analysts even knows him," he concluded.

"Then why isn't he here with us, if this guy, Lavager, is so dangerous?" Chang-Sturdevant asked.

"She, Madam," Adams interjected. "What we have to discuss is, ah, a bit above her level, as good as she is. Um, she is an analyst, Madam President," he concluded, as if that explained everything.

"Proceed, then."

A satellite image of Spondu and the surrounding area

flashed onto the screens, then shifted to a complex a few kilometers from the town.

"This is a former weapons lab Lavager contends he's converted into an agricultural research laboratory. Agricultural research may in fact be going on in what they so quaintly call the 'Cabbage Patch,' but we believe it's a cover for the real purpose, which is the development of a superweapon that will give Lavager complete control on Atlas and put him in a position to interfere with the economies of the different member worlds in his quadrant of Human Space."

"'Today Germany, tomorrow the world'?" Long interjected.

"What?"

"Nothing." Long sank back into his chair, a sour expression on his face.

"It is very important, Madam President," Adams said, "that the nation-states of Atlas not be unified under the leadership of this man. It is bad enough for the people of Atlas that they have differences of their own that have led to several wars, but if they are unified under the leadership of a man like Lavager, we see a prominent threat to other worlds of the Confederation and that cannot be permitted. Of course," he added quickly, "what happens among the nation-states of Atlas is not our concern."

"What evidence do you have that Lavager intends to extend his reach?" Berentus asked.

"His public statements, for one. You may read them on your consoles, but I would like to play only one of them for you now." Lavager's image flashed onto the consoles and his strong voice filled the room.

"A people must have room to expand. If we are to be a great people we must not confine ourselves to our cabbage patches and think that by doing so we are preparing this world for our children and their children. No. We must move outward, expand our horizons to other worlds yet unconquered and assure the continued propagation of our people for untold generations into the future."

"The trailer on this speech says it was given before the Atlean Thirtieth Congress on Land Reform," Long said. "How do you get some kind of interplanetary invasion out of something like that?"

"Jay?" Chang-Sturdevant asked.

"We believe that is just what he's announcing, a master plan for conquest," Adams answered tartly. "Dictators, swept up in the power of their own myths, have done that before. Look at Hitler, who laid out his plans in *Mein Kampf* years before he came to power." He shot a disparaging glance at Long as he spoke. "Lavager is preparing the Atlean League of Nations for invasion, once he's totally subjected them to his control. The term 'Cabbage Patch' is a cynical joke, Madam President, a reference to the weapon Lavager is developing at that facility."

"I think you're stretching it a bit, old boy," Admiral Porter spoke for the first time.

Adams did not bother to respond to Admiral Porter's remark, but rushed on. "Here is a list of the staff at the Cabbage Patch. Note the explosives and delivery systems specialists on the list."

"But there are also quite a few agronomists there too, Jay," Chang-Sturdevant objected.

"That is part of the cover," Adams responded. "We've had all those scientists tailed, and the agronomy specialists spend most of their time on the golf links."

"So what do you recommend?"

Adams didn't answer immediately but after a short pause, "Neutralize Lavager," he answered.

"You mean kill him?" Long blurted, incredulous.

"I mean remove him, Mr. Attorney General."

"No, you mean assassinate him," Long shot back.

"I mean eliminate him as a threat to the Confederation."

"You mean kill the poor bastard. Come out and say it,

Adams," Long thundered. "You're not with the damned Diplomatic Service anymore, you're in the dirty tricks business. Tell us what you mean in plain language."

"You mean assassinate him, don't you, Jay?" Chang-Sturdevant inquired gently.

"Yes, ma'am," Adams answered at last.

"Hugyens?" Chang-Sturdevant turned to Long.

Long blew out his cheeks and leaned forward. "If he has to be 'removed,' then why not let one of those supposed disaffected groups on Atlas do it for us? They've tried before—that's how his wife was killed." He gave Adams a look that suggested he thought the CIO might have been involved.

Adams sniffed, "They are not reliable. Yes, they've tried before and, as the attorney General pointed out, look what happened when one did try to kill Lavager. Our assets are much more efficient, I assure you. And they will not talk."

"I suppose it wouldn't have upset anybody out at Hunter if they had gotten Lavager's whole family, as long as they got him, eh, Adams?" Admiral Porter said.

"Surely, Admiral, you as a military man understand the unfortunate incidence of collateral damage in certain operations," the DCIO replied impatiently. He saw where this meeting was going and regretted the presence of the other councillors. He'd been very disappointed when he learned others besides the President would be in attendance.

Long leaned back. "Sanctioned assassinations have been done, ma'am. It's not illegal if it's done for the right reasons. Which, of course, is what the DCIO is saying, to protect the lives and interests of member worlds. But it can only be done via presidential authority. And if you're asking for my advice, *no*!" He slammed a fist down on the table, making the image on his console jump crazily. "The DCIO hasn't presented convincing evidence for an assassination operation against Lavager and if you agree to this, Madam President, you'll be guilty of ordering a murder."

"Mr. Long!" Berentus exclaimed.

"That's my opinion, Madam President, and I don't give a damn who knows it! I believe in the due process of the law." Long shrugged but glared ominously at Adams and Lowell.

"Oh, yeah?" Lowell responded, his face reddening, "I suppose that's what you mean, 'due process,' when you ship some poor bastard off to Darkside without a trial? Your hands are just as dirty as ours, Long."

"Goddamnit, that's different!" Long shouted back.

"Gentlemen! Gentlemen!" Chang-Sturdevant held up her hands. "Thank you, both of you, you've finally come straight to the point. Gentlemen," she nodded at the Director of the CIO and his deputy, "the answer is 'no.' Come back when you have more concrete evidence than you've presented this morning. Admiral Porter? Confer with the service chiefs and prepare a plan for a military intervention on Atlas. Be prepared to present it when DCIO comes back here with more evidence. We very well may have to 'neutralize' Lavager, but as I see it now we'll do it the old-fashioned way—legally and in full public view." She stood up, indicating the meeting was at an end.

"Madam, may I just mention two other things?" Adams asked as he rose to his feet. "One, weapons research isn't something new on Atlas. A few years ago one of the other nation-states, a South Solanum, developed a laser rifle for military use."

"A laser rifle!" Long barked a laugh. "That's old technology, nobody's used laser rifles in a couple of centuries."

Marcus Berentus nodded solemnly. "Armies stopped using lasers because the technology to deflect and disperse the beams became inexpensive, making the lasers ineffective as military weapons." He paused and looked around the room. "Nobody uses that deflection and dispersal technology anymore, either, so that makes lasers viable military weapons again."

Inside, Chang-Sturdevant made a face, but didn't show

it to the people in the room. "What's the other last thing you wanted to mention?" she asked Adams.

The DCIO gave her a smug smile. "Two, Madam, we have a very reliable agent on Atlas who will be making a report soon. That report should convince you our option is justified."

Chang-Sturdevant felt a mighty surge of anger, but her long years of experience in public life allowed her to suppress it. How, she raged inwardly, could Adams know the report would convince her to authorize an assassination before it had even been submitted to the CIO for evaluation? "Well, Jay, let me see it, then, when it's fully evaluated," she responded coolly and swirled out of the room.

"Madam," Berentus closed the door to Chang-Sturdevant's private office behind him, "did you hear what old stuffed-shirt Porter said? Because of the weather he had to call for a starship to get over here this morning?"

Chang-Sturdevant looked at her Minister of War blankly for a moment and then burst into laughter. They both laughed. "Marcus," she exclaimed, slapping her thigh, "the old boy does have some life in him after all! Now," she plopped into the nearest chair, "I've some free time before I meet with the," she waved a hand vaguely, "the Great Wazoo of Tubegador or whomever, so let's have a cuppa java."

"That is very presidential of you—Suelee," Berentus smiled, taking a seat opposite Chang-Sturdevant.

She smiled at him, deciding she liked having Marcus call her by that name, then said, "One final thing, old friend. That analyst. The one who knows this Lavager. Find out who she is for me, would you? For her I might grant a private interview."

CHAPTER
EIGHT

Office of the Director, Central Intelligence Organization, Hunter, Earth

J. Murchison Adams cursed so foully once they were back in the privacy of his office at CIO headquarters that Palmer Lowell actually winced. When Adams was upset he resorted to gutter language using words not even the crustiest drill sergeant would employ with the dumbest recruits. Where he'd learned to curse so eloquently was a mystery to Palmer, considering the DCIO's upbringing by people who wouldn't have said "garbage" if they'd had a mouthful of it.

"That rotten sonofabitch, useless goddamned—" Adams paused to catch his breath.

"Well, Gustafferson's report will clinch matters for us, old boy," Lowell volunteered, hoping to calm the director down.

Adams gasped and wiped his forehead. He was quiet for a moment, trying to get a grip on himself. Then his face reddened again and he slammed a fist onto his desk. "And that goddamned bitch!" he screamed. "I asked for a private meeting and she went and brought in those, those—" He broke into a fit of coughing.

"Ah, you refer to our illustrious Madam President Chang-Sturdevant and her advisors, old man? Quite distressing, the whole affair, I must admit. Have some of this Paté Munchausen, old chap? Settle you down a bit."

"Goddamnit, I don't want any Paté Munchausen!" Adams shouted, but he made a visible effort to get a grip on himself. He drank a mouthful of the Club Klinko '76 the servo had just poured. "Who ordered this vinegar?" he asked, then said, "Pretty good for vinegar, though." He drained the glass and the servo poured another. He was getting back in control of himself now. "Gustafferson. Yes, Palmer, quite, quite. He's on to something out there, you can bet on it. Yes, his report will be decisive." He spooned up a bite of the Paté Munchausen. "Umm. Very good, Palmer." He activated the intercom on his desk. "Get Somervell in here, would you?" he ordered his secretary.

As he entered the director's private office, Somervell P. Amesbury, CIO Chief of Staff, exchanged a rapid glance with Lowell, who shook his head ever so slightly, indicating the blowup was over and didn't concern anyone at Hunter. The rest of the director's immediate staff had heard the row coming from his office and everyone was walking on eggshells. Good people were known to have been summarily fired when the director got into these moods.

"Somervell, old boy," Adams began, "what's the name of that analyst, the one who served on Atlas and knows Lavager personally? Odd sort of name. You know her?"

"Yes, sir. Anya Smiler. She's been with us a long time and is a very good—"

"Yaass, I'm sure. Have her taken off the Atlas desk, would you? Assign her somewhere else. When the next agent report comes in from Atlas, I want it sent directly to me. I don't want anyone else messing with it. Particularly not her. Is that clear?"

"Very clear, sir," Amesbury nodded. "Will there be anything else, Jay?" He did not need to ask how the meeting with the President had gone.

"No, no. Take care of that little matter at once and then join us back here for lunch, will you? You really should sample this Paté Munchausen. Delightful."

"Palmer," Adams began after Somervell departed, "I am not going to let this go. Lavager is a threat to the Confederation, pure and simple. This government's policy must rigorously follow the rule of balkanizing certain member worlds into nation-states so they can pose no threats to the Confederation's vital interests. I do *not* understand why this woman cannot see that."

"Well, Gustafferson's report will swing things our way, I'm sure."

"Yaass," Adams drawled. He finished his wine and refilled his glass. "But if it doesn't?" He held his hands out toward Lowell.

This was no rhetorical question and Lowell knew what the answer was his chief wanted, but he paused before answering. "If it doesn't, then, um, ah, we do it on our own?"

Adams smiled broadly and leaned back comfortably. "You said it!"

Analysis Directorate, CIO Headquarters

Anya Smiler sat at her console, reviewing incoming intelligence reports. They were voluminous and full of detail, mostly analyses submitted by agents on the scene reporting the latest political gossip, changes in government personnel and policy, economic statistics, evaluations of military force structures and so on. But over the years she had learned how to winnow out the important material in these reports and to condense it into a few succinct paragraphs that would give busy intelligence bureaucrats what they needed to know. She and her colleagues were always available to give full briefings if asked for more details.

Anya was involved in a report from the station chief on Wyndham's World about the sexual escapades of various members of a prominent Wyndhamian religious sect when her console bleeped that a very important, highly classified message was being relayed from the communications center. Her screen went dead and then the incoming message flashed across it. It was from the station chief at the embassy in New Granum on Atlas. It was a verbatim transcript from a report filed by Gus Gustafferson and it concerned the Cabbage Patch, the alleged weapons facility. Anya caught her breath as she read it. She had just gotten to the last paragraph, a standard element in these messages where the local station chief added his own interpretation of his agent's report, when she sat bolt upright at what was written there. Impossible! They hadn't lost an agent since—The screen went dead again and then the following message flashed across it, COMMUNICATION WITHDRAWN. ACCESS DENIED. SPA

"SPA" were the initials of the CIO Chief of Staff, Somervell P. Amesbury. "What the—?" Anya muttered. She knew that the recent meeting with the president over the Atlas situation had not gone the way the director had wished. Some things just weren't kept secret around CIO headquarters. She also knew how the director would use this report. She had a sinking feeling in the pit of her stomach.

Office of the Chairman, Combined Chiefs of Staff, Fargo

"Gentlemen, I give you the staple of the North American peasant for centuries—the hot dog!" Admiral K. G. B. Porter announced, holding a steaming sample of what naval personnel called "tube steak" on his fork. He popped it into a bun, doused it with condiments, and took a huge bite. "Umpf!" He shook his head with pleasure and chewed vigorously. The other three officers, members of the Combined Chiefs, unenthusiastically regarded their plates as the Chairman swallowed and followed the mouthful with a long draft of ale. "Come on, come on, eat up! It'll be a long afternoon, gentlemen!"

White-garbed messboys stood at attention around the

small dining room, the Chairman's private mess. He refused to use servo-robots but instead employed selected navy ratings as stewards to attend his meals.

"I prefer the cheeseburger," Army Chief of Staff Blankenship remarked, taking a tentative bite of his "hot dog." "Umm, well, not bad," he said.

"Cheeseburger?" the chairman exclaimed. "Capital idea! Sibuco," he turned to the senior messboy, a first-class rating, "put cheeseburgers on the menu for tomorrow's lunch, would you?"

"I like spaghetti," General Anders Aguinaldo, the Commandant of the Confederation Marine Corps said. "But hot dogs are good too." He took a bite of his.

"They're a bit, um, 'plebian,' though, aren't they, General?" Admiral Sela, who had replaced Porter as Chief of Naval Operations, said.

"Everything I like is," General Aguinaldo replied. "That comes from living on field rations most of my life." The other officers laughed politely.

"Gentlemen, the hot dog has a venerable history. Actually, they were originally a sausage called 'Frankfurter' or 'wienerwurst' in German. Some referred to them as 'dachshund sausage,' after a breed of dog with short stubby legs and an elongated body, because the animal somewhat resembled the hot dog, but also because Americans, with their zany sense of humor, implied the sausages were actually made from canine meat, ha, ha. But the Americans of the early twentieth century liked them. They became the 'national meat dish,' if you will. They were actually made of pork and beef, though."

"What are these made of?" Aguinaldo asked. "I've eaten dog meat. When I was a corporal, on Katusa. These sure don't taste like dog." He stuffed the remainder of the roll into his mouth and smiled around it. "Those Katusas really know how to slice and dice a dog for chow. Ummm." He winked at the army general.

The two admirals quickly put down their utensils and

reached for their beer. "Well, Commandant, ah, these hot dogs are vegan, actually. If you want hot dogs with real meat in them you'll have to go some place like Atlas, where they have vast herds of meat-producing ungulates. And that brings me to the subject of our meeting with the President this afternoon. You've all been furnished read-ahead reports on the situation there. Comments?"

"Ah, those drips at CIO are always trying to dip their oars into the water," General Blankenship snorted. "As far as I can tell, there's no threat to us from this Frank-furter guy, er, I mean Lavager, isn't that his name?"

"Well," the CNO interjected, "it's high time we invaded somebody, otherwise the fleets are likely to get rusty. The last time we had a full-scale combined operation was that operation on Diamunde."

Aguinaldo snorted, "Yeah, and on that operation the army general in command proved incompetent. No of-fense, General," he added in an aside to Blankenship. "And the admiral in overall command was so stupid he couldn't even spit unless he had a senior chief standing by to shove a rag in his mouth. It was my Marines who had to save everybody on that one and I'm against another bloodbath like that." He didn't mention that it wasn't until he, a lieutenant general at the time and in command of the Marine forces in the command, was placed in command of ground operations that the Diamunde campaign turned around and the Confederation forces began winning. "I agree with the army on this one," Aguinaldo said. "Be-sides, we've got a lot of fish to fry as it is, and you gentle-men all know what I mean. We can't be sending an expedition to this place without a compelling reason, and I don't think the intelligence that CIO has gathered on events there is all that compelling."

"Lavager, from what I can tell, is what the early Ameri-cans would have referred to as a 'hot dog,' gentlemen," Admiral Porter said. "In the slang of the day that meant anyone who was exceptionally capable, outstanding in his field, et cetera. Well," he wiped his lips, "J. Murchison Adams claims to have fresh intel that will change our minds, thus this emergency meeting with the President. Before we go over there, cigars, anyone?" They all rose to follow Admiral Porter into the lounge. On the way out the door he turned to Aguinaldo. "Andy, you mention eating dog. Ever eat a kwangduk? Well, I did once, when I was an ensign on the CNSS *James Aspby*. Didn't know what it was at the time, of course. Damned thing was pretty tasty, actually. We were on liberty on . . ."

Office of the Director, CIO

"So they think we're 'drips,' do they?" J. Murchison Adams laughed and shook his head. First Class Sibuco had wasted no time making his report after the chairman and his party had moved from his private mess into the lounge. Adams had trusted agents in almost every government office and all had his direct number to call when they had information that might be of importance. "Human intelligence, Palmer, that's always the most reliable! Hang all these technical devices anyway." He changed the subject. "How long before Sibuco's enlistment is up? We can't afford to lose him over there." He arose from the table, finished the glass of La Gran Chateau-du-Vichy '42, and reached for his tunic.

"We'll increase his stipend out of our agent fund, Jay, boost his pay up to the equivalent of a navy full commander. That'll keep him around a while longer, I'm sure." In former years the CIO had recruited agents from among young people who wanted to serve the Confederation; now they were recruited from those who wanted to be served *by* the Confederation.

"Palmer, let us make haste! Madam President awaits our imminent arrival and we await the presentation of the late Gus Gustafferson's report. Ah, fortuitous indeed, my dear Palmer, that someone murdered him, because that act is the final nail in Jorge Liberec Lavager's long overdue coffin!" He shrugged into his tunic. "Damn, Palmer, when are we going to get someone on the inside in Chang-Sturdevant's office, eh?"

Office of the President, Fargo

"You," Madam Chang-Sturdevant addressed a scoop of rich chocolate ice cream, "are my one indulgence." She smiled and put a spoonful into her mouth. "Marcus, a world without ice cream is a world without a soul."

"Speaking of things without souls, Suelee, we meet in twenty minutes with Adams and his deputy. They really think they're on to something this time, otherwise why did they ask for the Combined Chiefs to be present, as well as the AG and 'anyone else you deem interested in affairs on Atlas.' They're about to make an announcement, is what it is."

"Your ice cream, Marcus, you haven't touched it!"

"Ah," Marcus regarded his melting scoop of strawberry, "no appetite, I guess. Look, the news is full of Gustafferson's murder. You know how the media is, they report the massacre of a million souls with total equanimity but let one of their own get killed and they go into a mourning frenzy. GNN's been broadcasting Gustafferson's face and biography all over Human Space. There'll be a call for an inquiry in the Senate, you can bet on it. If it develops that Lavager had anything to do with it, and you can be sure the CIO is going to leak that to the media, there'll be a call for a full-scale invasion of the planet. It's happened before, you know? 'Remember the Maine!' and all that. Well, I have pretty good information of my own that the late media maven Gus Gustafferson was one of CIO's agents. I really think we're going to have to take CIO's views on Atlas seriously this time, and we should be prepared to consider their request for—"

"Your ice cream? If you won't, Marcus, then—?"

"Help yourself, Madam President." He nodded indulgently.

Chang-Sturdevant scooped the strawberry into her own bowl. "All these carbohydrates will ruin my girlish figure, Marcus. I'm really disappointed that you aren't protecting me from them."

"Well, madam, the fact of the matter is, the fatter you get the more I like it, because the more of you I see the better."

"Marcus, I'll give you precisely one hour to stop flattering me like that!" Chang-Sturdevant laughed. She finished her—and Marcus's—ice cream and wiped her lips. She stood. "Well, Marcus, let us go into the lion's den and see what the beasts have cooked up for us." Berentus bowed deeply and gestured toward the door. Before going out Chang-Sturdevant paused and turned to her Minister of War. "Marcus, do you know why I love luxury food like ice cream so much?" Marcus shook his head. "Because when I was a girl, growing up, you know what we had to eat most meals? Hot dogs and boiled potatoes, Marcus, that's what the Changs ate. And now that I'm President of the Confederation of Human Worlds, I am never again going to eat that slop!"

Office of the Chief of Staff, CIO

"Anya, my dear! Come in, come in! Please have a seat." Somervell Amesbury stood, a beaming smile on his face, gesturing toward an empty chair. "I have some extraordinarily good news for you!"

Anya took the offered seat.

"How long have you been with us at the headquarters now, Anya, ten years?"

"It'll be ten years this summer, sir. I've been with CIO for a little over twenty years."

"Yes, yes. I've been reviewing your performance appraisals recently, Anya. You've never fallen below 'Exceeds' in all your Critical Elements. A record you can be proud of." "Exceeds" was the highest rating a CIO employee could get on their efficiency reports. "You're a grade twelve, Step—" He fumbled with her personnel record.

"Step ten, sir."

"Ah. Yes." There were fifteen grades in the general schedule for CIO employees. "Steps," there were ten of them, were within-grade pay increases similar to the longevity pay military personnel received, and Step Ten was the highest within-grade pay increase authorized. Grades higher than fifteen were classified as "Senior Executive Service," the equivalent in pay and protocol to general or flag officers in the military systems. The Director and the Deputy CIO were political appointments, confirmed by the Confederation Senate; the CIO Chief of Staff and the various Directorate heads at the headquarters and certain station chiefs were Senior Executive Service appointments filled by career civil service personnel. "Well, it's time you stepped up. We have a thirteen position coming open and I've recommended you to fill it." A grade thirteen was the equivalent in pay and protocol to a lieutenant commander in the military service.

Anya smiled. "Where, sir?"

"Um, the R-76 Quadrant Desk. You know that Hammond Means is retiring, don't you? Today's his last day. Will you accept the position? You'd be senior analyst on that desk, Anya, and if you do as good a job there as you've done in your present position, I see a directorship in your future, perhaps even station chief somewhere, if you wish to go back into the field."

"I'm very honored, sir, but—"

"But what?" Amesbury knew what was coming.

"Well, there's a lot going on just now regarding Atlas and I thought with my experience I might be more valuable to you on that desk. I saw the dispatch that just came through. Can't I stay in my present job until the business there is resolved?"

Amesbury cursed to himself. The director hadn't wanted any of the analysts to see that message. "I appreciate your concern, Anya." He smiled benevolently. "You're a true professional and that's the reason we're transferring you to R-76." It was not lost on Anya that now she was being ordered to accept the new position. "The director has decided to handle the Atlas case personally," Amesbury continued. "No reflection on you or your colleagues, of course. You start in R-76 tomorrow morning. Take the rest of the day off." He rose and extended his hand. "Congratulations, Anya."

Anya took Amesbury's hand. "Thank you, sir." She knew it would do her no good to argue. She also knew she was being offered the plum assignment to keep her quiet. The director was about to pull something. What Anya Smiler did not know was what she would do about it.

CHAPTER
NINE

Jorge Lavager stared intently at the Army Chief of Staff. "I want you to tell me, General Ollwelen, that you had nothing to do with this," he said, in a deceptively quiet voice. Ollwelen knew that when his friend talked that way he was consumed with ice-cold anger. Lavager shoved a set of 2-D images across the table. Ollwelen recoiled. They were of the badly beaten body of Gus Gustafferson, the GNN correspondent and CIO agent.

"I swear to God, Jorge, on my honor as an officer, that I had nothing to do with this!" Ollwelen croaked.

"I didn't say to kill him, I said to 'get rid of him,' General," Lavager gritted.

"Y-Yessir!" Ollwelen stuttered. "I spoke to your public affairs minister, Jorge, after what you said at dinner, and told him it was your desire to declare G-Gustafferson persona non grata and deport him. I swear! You can ask the minister."

"What about this Paragussa out at the Cabbage Patch? I suppose that was an accident?"

"Goddamnit, sir, I've told you once and I won't tell you again, I had nothing to do with either of those deaths! Gustafferson was the victim of a mugging and Paragussa met with an unfortunate accident. Now if you really believe I had those guys murdered, Jorge—" Ollwelen's face had turned red and his eyes flashed with anger.

Lavager raised a hand. He believed his old friend. "Locker, who was the English king who had the Archbishop of Canterbury assassinated?"

Ollwelen thought for a moment, "Henry II, I believe." He slumped in his seat and passed a hand over his forehead.

"Yes. He just happened to wish out loud in the presence of some henchmen that he wanted someone to rid him of the Archbishop and the fools went out and murdered the old boy, thinking they were doing the king a great service. Henry had to do penance for his loose talk, didn't he? Well," Lavager sighed, "this," he gestured at the grisly images, "will be blamed on me. You can count on it."

"Well, I don't see how—"

"You don't? That's why I know you didn't order it, because nobody could be so dense they could possibly miss the implications! Look. Gustafferson was an agent of the CIO, Paragussa was a source, they met just minutes before Gustafferson was murdered, and next day Paragussa was found dead out at the lab."

"Um." Ollwelen swallowed nervously. "Well, we're presenting Gustafferson's murder as a simple robbery gone wrong, and so far the media hasn't picked up on Paragussa's death."

"Yes? Are you sure? Nobody robs a person and then beats him into an unrecognizable pulp. And the media doesn't matter here, you'd better believe the CIO knows all about Paragussa too." Lavager ran a hand nervously across his own forehead. "How much did Paragussa know?"

"Not much, I'm sure. Everything's so compartmented at the Cabbage Patch that no one person knows everything except the director and a handful of others, all of whom have been thoroughly checked and are under constant surveillance. He could only speculate."

"Wars have started over speculations too many times to count. How much could he have speculated, Locker?"

Ollwelen shrugged. "He might have been able to make some shrewd guesses, Jorge, but as to what we're really up to out there, no, he could not have figured it out. He might have concluded we're building some kind of powerful weapon but—"

Lavager thought for a moment. Something was not right here. He did not believe Gustafferson was the victim of a robbery any more than he believed Paragussa met with an accident. But if his people didn't commit the murders, then who did? Was he being set up? Why? By whom? He shook his head.

"'Building some kind of powerful weapon' you said? That's all Gustafferson would have needed for a great story. Everybody's wondering what we're doing out there, chief among them the Central Intelligence Organization. Now their spy and his informant are dead. Voilá! We had them murdered to shut them up. And once people begin to believe that, then why did we shut them up, they'll ask? Yes," he nodded, "we're working on something really big out at the Cabbage Patch and it isn't a new brand of fertilizer, it's some kind of damned doomsday weapon, that's what they'll all conclude. I mean after all, nobody's going to believe anyone killed that little muckraker over something small, Locker; in very high places they'll be thinking he was killed to hide something."

Cabinet Room, Office of the President, Confederation of Human Worlds, Fargo, Earth

Madam Chang-Sturdevant recoiled in horror at the images of Gus Gustafferson's mutilated corpse.

"Do we really have to see this?" Marcus Berentus snorted, gesturing at the gruesome images before them.

Privately, J. Murchison Adams was very pleased with the graphic display of the murdered agent's body and the effect it was having on the President. The images were creating just the atmosphere he wanted.

"Umpf," Attorney General Long grunted. He'd seen worse in his long career in law enforcement. "This guy didn't die in a mugging, you can bet your ass on it."

"Madam, I do sincerely regret that I must show you this horror, but after you've heard Mr. Gustafferson's report, you will see that all is not well on Atlas and we must do something about it."

"Gustafferson was working for you?" Commandant of the Marine Corps Aguinaldo asked. "Mr. Adams, isn't that a little damaging for the image of your agency as an objective intelligence agency, recruiting members of the media as agents?" Aguinaldo grinned. Everyone knew GNN's reporting was just about the most biased in the galaxy.

Adams's lip twitched in the tightest smile as he nodded affably at Aguinaldo. "General, we get our intelligence any way we can. Besides, who ever believed the media isn't above a little spying of their own? Surely no intelligent person believes they're above bias. Gustafferson didn't have an unbiased bone in his body, but he was a damned fine agent."

"He doesn't have an unbroken bone in his body, either, judging from those pictures," Long commented sourly.

"I was wondering when someone was going to get him," said Army Chief of Staff General Blankenship. The President threw him a sharp glance, his ears reddened, and he slumped disconsolately down into his seat.

"Gentlemen! No more of these remarks, please. Now, Jay, get on with your presentation," the President said sharply.

"Madam President, you've seen the pictures. The New Granum police are handling the investigation of Gustafferson's murder as a mugging gone wrong. But we have incontrovertible evidence it was a planned execution. He was executed because he knew too much about Jorge Lavager's plans and Lavager had him murdered. I beg you to listen to a recording of Gustafferson's report made shortly before he was killed. It arrived only yesterday via Beamspace drone."

"Is this going to make me lose my lunch, Adams?" Chang-Sturdevant asked sourly.

"It is very upsetting, Madam President, but no, it's nothing like—like—the images. But please, everyone listen carefully."

For the next few moments Gus Gustafferson's voice, along with that of the CIO station chief on Atlas, filled the Cabinet Room. When the transcript was done everyone just sat there quietly for a long moment. Chang-Sturdevant broke the silence at last. "All right, gentlemen, what do we do about this?"

"Ma'am." Admiral Porter sat up straight in his chair. "We have come prepared with a plan to put a stop to these shenanigans—"

"They're hardly 'shenanigans,' Admiral," Chang-Sturdevant interjected.

"I mean these hideous plans of Lavager's," Porter went on quickly. "We favor an immediate and direct response, Madam President. We have a corps-sized army unit standing by, and the ships to get it to Atlas within a few days. We'll swoop right down on New Granum and put a screeching halt to Lavager's government. Turn him over to the AG for the administration of justice. My staff has prepared the following brief, ma'am, which I would like to present—"

Chang-Sturdevant held up a hand. "Mr. Berentus, when was the last time the Confederation mounted an invasion force against a member world?"

"Diamunde, ma'am," Berentus answered immediately.

"Diamunde. Yes, that was several years ago, wasn't it, Admiral Porter?" It was obvious to all that she considered the chairman's plan for an invasion of Atlas little more than his looking for an opportunity to exercise military force, something admirals and generals loved to do, like surgeons who'd gladly perform a major operation to correct a hangnail just because they just loved to cut on people. Besides, a successful planetary invasion would "wet down" Admiral Porter's recent promotion from Chief of Naval Operations to Chairman of the Combined Chiefs. "General Aguinaldo, are you in favor of this invasion plan?"

General Anders Aguinaldo glanced over at Porter and said, reluctantly, "No, ma'am, I am not. But we discussed it, all the Chiefs did, and the consensus was to ask for an invasion. I did not think at the time, nor do I think even after what we've just been presented, that the evidence for a full-scale military intervention is compelling. But I'll support Admiral Porter if that is your decision, ma'am, even though my Marines are really spread pretty thin right now." He paused, reflecting.

"Well, Anders, we weren't going to rely on the Corps—" Admiral Porter began, but Chang-Sturdevant cut him off with a wave of her hand.

"Do you have something more to add? she asked Aguinaldo.

"Ma'am, Mr. Gustafferson's report said the Cabbage Patch facility is being used to develop a crop-killing fungus. But what I can't get out of my mind is the facility's history as a weapons research center. Gustafferson as much as said his conclusion wasn't confirmed yet. In whatever we do, we have to take into consideration the fact that the Union of Margelan might have a new weapon we know nothing about and have no effective defense against."

"I understand," she said, then turned to the Attorney General. "Mr. Long?"

"No, no, no, Madam President. A covert action is what we need here, not an invasion force. General Aguinaldo is right, there's not enough evidence to support the Admiral's plan. We need to know more—particularly if there are new weapons involved."

"Jay?"

Adams smiled to himself before he gave his opinion. He really didn't care how Lavager was removed, so long as he, as Director of the CIO, got the credit for starting the operation. He gave a mental shrug and thought, *Sometimes you've got to goose the goose.* "I think something must be done and soon, Madam President. Lavager must be neutralized, and however that is done is fine by me. I would urge discretion, however. Perhaps breaking down the door, as Admiral Porter recommends, is a bit too much."

"Marcus?"

"Send someone in there to find out exactly what Lavager is up to. I think this is a job for Marine Force Recon."

"Gentlemen?" she asked her advisors. They all began talking at once. She held up her hands. "All right, gentlemen, all right, that's enough. Here is what we will do. General Aguinaldo, send a Force Recon team to Atlas to conduct up close reconnaissance of the Cabbage Patch. Find out what they're doing there. If Lavager is preparing to extend his power by starving the member worlds of the Confederation, I shall authorize any, I repeat, any, operation to remove him, up to and including assassination.

"Admiral Porter, keep that corps-size force at the ready. General Aguinaldo, send out the word. AG, see what precedents we have for filing murder charges against a head of state. Gentlemen, thank you all for your hard work, you in particular, Jay. CIO has come through again. Good morning to you all."

R-76 Desk, a Week Later

So that's the plan? Anya Smiler wondered, sitting at her cubicle and reading the report Murchison had filed on his meeting with the President. They were going to send in a reconnaissance team to see what Lavager was doing. The Chief had generously offered the expertise of the CIO's laboratories to analyze whatever the team found. It was nearing the end of the day. Well, she didn't feel like going home. She opened the file of recent dispatches from the R-76 Quadrant. It was the usual stuff: recent economic statistics on the various worlds in the Quadrant, analyses of recent political events on different worlds. Nothing she wasn't familiar with. She exited the file and sat staring at her console, wondering what was happening back on Atlas.

Anya Smiler possessed not only a very brilliant mind but also a photographic memory, an invaluable tool for an intelligence analyst. She had the highest security clearances and sat on a good number of task forces so she had access to a lot of extremely sensitive intelligence information. She wondered if she knew any of the current staff at the embassy in New Granum. Using passwords and codewords from her Atlas assignment, she called up the personnel roster for the embassy. And got in! Someone had forgotten to remove her from the access list. Each CIO station chief reported regularly on the embassy staff and official visitors; information about their personalities, their shortcomings as individuals, their assignments, the purpose of all official visits to embassies from off-world government officials. Often the information contained in these reports could be used to get unwilling staffers to cooperate in clandestine operations, but it is the very nature of intelligence types to collect information for its own sake, because one never knew, even the most inconsequential fact could some day prove useful.

Names and faces flashed across Anya's screen. She didn't recognize any of them. She scrolled down to the listing of recent notable arrivals and departures. Suddenly she saw a face she recognized among the recent visitors. It

belonged to someone calling himself Heintges Germanian, "courier." He had arrived the day before Gustafferson's murder and departed the day after. The face was an
ordinary one, but she recognized it at once because it belonged to someone she'd seen before, a man named
Wellers Henrico, not Germanian. He'd visited the embassy at New Granum when she was assigned there and
that time, too, his visit had been a very short one. He had
arrived at New Granum just before the bungled assassination attempt on Lavager, the one that had resulted in the
death of Lavager's wife, and he'd left immediately afterward. On that occasion "Henrico" had also been a courier
sent to deliver high-priority messages that could not be
left to an FTL drone so his brief stay had seemed perfectly normal. But why the name change? Was it coincidence that twice he had arrived just before and then
departed just after an assassination? That sinking feeling
that had been sitting on her stomach for days suddenly became very acute.

Anya exited the Atlas file and, hands shaking, entered
her password to open an Ultra Secret listing of "special
agents" assigned to Atlas. Henrico was a contract assassin.
So that was it: The military would send in a deep recon
team to penetrate the secret lab and find out what was going on. Meanwhile, CIO would infiltrate an assassin who
would stand by for word from headquarters, probably
based on what the lab analysis revealed, but maybe only
on the whim of Adams, and then Lavager would be assassinated. Or maybe he would be murdered anyway, because
the Director thought he knew better than anyone else in the
Confederation how to solve problems among the member
worlds. She controlled her stomach only with difficulty.

Anya got unsteadily to her feet. She took a few moments to compose herself and then headed for the CIO
laboratory facility.

Office of the Director, CIO Laboratories

Dr. Blogetta O'Bygne, director of the labs, was a heavy-set, middle-aged woman who made a show of wearing very thick lenses in her spectacles. She could easily have had her vision corrected through minor surgery but preferred the old-fashioned glasses because she thought they added a scholarly air to her appearance. But over the years, as one pair after another of her spectacles had gotten lost or broken, Blogetta had wondered if she should have the surgery after all and just keep the spectacles as props. As Anya Smiler came through the security door into the inner sanctum of the labs, Dr. O'Bygne was silently considering that possibility. Her health insurance would cover the cost of the procedure.

"Annie!" she exclaimed, noticing Anya.

"Bloggie!" The two women embraced warmly. They had known each other for years and got along famously.

"Well, my dear, you certainly look glum. Has Annie taken Atlas's job and put the world on her shoulders?" She laughed enormously at her pun.

Anya smiled wanly. "It sure feels that way, Bloggie, it sure does." She took a stool beside her friend's workbench and sighed. "Not much going on down here today," she commented. Usually the labs were crowded with industrious technicians, analyzing specimens, testing new devices, or whatever else technicians did.

"Yes, it's a slow day." O'Bygne grinned. "I let everybody go early to get a jump on the weather. Don't tell old Adams." She put a finger to her lips.

Anya laughed. She felt better. "Bloggie, can you do me a favor?"

"Anything." She nodded.

"In a while you'll be receiving samples from a presidentially authorized operation we're conducting on Atlas. Would you let me know when the stuff comes in and would you—," she hesitated, "—let me know what you find out?"

"Ummm, 'presidentially authorized,' eh? Ohhh, Annie! What are you up to now? You old field officers positively scare the joss sticks right off my mantelpiece."

Anya grinned. "The usual, but as desk officer I want to know what you find out first."

"I'll bet you do." O'Bygne made a disparaging noise. "But hey, anything as long as it stands a chance of putting the screws to Adams. Count on me." She held out a pudgy hand and they shook.

R-76 Quadrant Desk, CIO Headquarters, Hunter, Earth

Back in her cubicle Anya sat at her station and tried to calm herself. Her hands were shaking and she was nearly in tears. She took several deep breaths. Okay, okay, she told herself, take it easy! With effort she managed to control her breathing. After a few moments her hands stopped shaking. What to do? Well, first priority was get out of the CIO! But not before she got to the bottom of what Adams was up to on Atlas. She had a friend at the Ministry of War. That ministry hated the CIO. But not yet, not yet.

On her way home Anya Smiler stopped at an FTL Union office and paid a week's salary to send a private message to Jorge Lavager on Atlas.

Tim Omix called her that night, she put him off, something about a headache.

CHAPTER
TEN

**Operations Division, Fourth Fleet Marines, MCB Camp
Basilone, Halfway**

The call for the commander of Fourth Force Recon
Company to report to the Fourth Fleet Marine G3 was
routine enough, right down to the "... at your earliest
convenience ..." which is military politesse for "Drop
whatever you're doing and get over here right now!"

Commander Walt Obannion, CO Fourth Force Recon
Company, dropped whatever he was doing and called for
his driver. Five minutes after receiving the call, he
walked into the innocent-looking, but nearly impregnable
building that housed Fourth Fleet Marines' Operations
department.

"Good morning, sir," Commander Ronzo, the assistant
G3, greeted him. "Th—He's waiting for you."

"Thanks," Obannion said, and headed for the private
office of Colonel Lar Szilk, the G3. Had Ronzo begun to
say "*They're* waiting" and changed his mind? Obannion
wondered. Never mind; he'd find out soon enough.

"Come!" Szilk said when Obannion knocked on the
frame of his office door. He gestured for Obannion to
close the door behind him.

"Good mor ..." Obanion saw that Szilk wasn't alone
and came to attention, facing the Marine sitting on the
sofa to the side of the G3's desk. "Sir!"

"At ease, Walt," Lieutenant General Indrus, the commanding general of Fourth Fleet Marines, said mildly. "Sit down, get comfortable. This is informal, that's why I sent for you to come here instead of to my office."

"Very good, sir." It might be an informal meeting, but a lowly commander still called a general officer "sir" no matter how much the general first-named him.

"Have you ever run an operation by presidential special order?" Indrus asked casually.

"None that were presented to me as by 'presidential special order,' nossir."

"I didn't think so. I've been a Marine for forty-five years, and this is only the third one I've seen." He paused and looked inward, wondering if he should restate that; one of the other two orders had to do with whatever it was that was going on with 34th FIST, and he'd only *heard* of that one, he hadn't actually seen it.

Indrus leaned forward and handed over a sheet of paper.

Obannion raised his eyebrows. Force Recon missions of whatever classification were always need-to-know, some even Ultra Secret, need-to-know. But what kind of mission was so secret that it had to be hand-delivered by a top-level Marine general, so secret that it had to be committed to easily destroyed paper rather than crystal? He gingerly accepted the sheet and read.

```
FROM: The President of the Confederation
of Human Worlds
TO: Commanding General, 4th Fleet Marines
RE: Special Orders
CLASSIFICATION: Ultra Secret Eyes Only
1. Fourth Force Recon Company will deploy
Force Recon resources to the geopolitical
entity called the Union of Margelan on At-
las for a classified mission. See Annex 1.
2. Appropriate transportation will be pro-
vided from Halfway to Atlas and for the
```

Force Recon resources' return. See Annex 2.

3A. The nature of Objective One is twofold:

a) To determine whether or not the facility near the mountain town of Spondu, called the "Cabbage Patch," forty kilometers from New Granum, the capital city of the geopolitical entity called the Union of Margelan, is a weapons research facility or manufactory, or in fact an agricultural research center.

b) If the facility is determined to be a weapons reasearch facility or manufactory: To conduct a raid to destroy it and, if possible, secure evidence of weapons research or manufactory to bring back to Fourth Fleet Marines HQ.

c) If the facility is an agricultural research station:
To collect specimens of what is being developed and analyze said specimens using equipment to be provided to the Force Recon resources tasked with the mission. See Annex 3.

4A. The Marines participating in this mission will:

a) Make planetfall via surreptitious means to be provided by the Confederation Navy;

b) Wear appropriate uniforms and conduct themselves at all times as in hostile territory;

c) Do their utmost to avoid all contact with locals with the single exception of the raid, if necessary, on the facility.

5A. The Marines participating in this mission will, upon completion of the mission, whether or not said completion neccessitates a destructive raid on the "Cabbage Patch" facility, depart Atlas in a surreptitious manner so that no one on Atlas will know they have departed.

Annex 1. Personnel:

1. The mission is to be conducted by one Force Recon Platoon, plus one navy corpsman, minus its sniper squad.

Annex 2. Transportation:

1. Transport from Fourth Fleet Marines Headquarters to Atlas.

   a) Personnel will depart Fourth Fleet Marines Headquarters on the fast frigate CNSS *Admiral Nelson*, currently en route to Halfway.

2. Transport from Atlas to Fourth Fleet Marines Headquarters.

   a) The CNSS *Admiral Nelson* will remain in orbit around Atlas until completion of the mission. Marines from Objective One will rendezvous with CNSS *Admiral Nelson* for return transport to Halfway.

Annex 3.

1. A compact genetic analysis machine will be provided to the Force Recon resources conducting Objective One with which to analyze organic specimens from the so-called "Cabbage Patch."

by Special Order,

Madam Cynthia Chang-Sturdevant,

President,

Confederation of Human Worlds

Obannion looked at the back side of the paper after reading the orders, then at Indrus. The orders didn't contain anything so far out of the ordinary that they required a special presidential order, or hand-delivery by a lieutenant general. But there was that puzzling "Objective One" without an "Objective Two" mentioned, plus paragraphs 3A, 4A, and 5A without "B" paragraphs. "Sir?"

Indrus looked at Szilk. "I'm sorry, Lar. Need-to-know. Would you excuse us, please."

"Certainly, sir." It may have been phrased as a polite request, but Lieutenant General Indrus had ordered Colonel Szilk to leave his own office. The colonel obeyed the general's order.

"There's more," Indrus said when he and Obannion were alone. This time he handed over two sheets of paper.

Obannion read the first page, which was exactly the same as the first page he'd read. Then he read page two.

"Allah's pointed teeth," he breathed when he finished reading. He looked up at the commanding general and, before he could think about it, blurted, "Has this been authenticated, sir?" Had he thought about it, he might not have asked.

Indrus looked at him with approval. "I'm glad you asked that, Walt. That was my first reaction, too. I sent a back-channel to Marcus Berentus, asking for verification."

Obannion fleetingly wondered how many regulations Indrus had violated, bypassing the chain of command and going directly to the Minister of War for verification of orders.

"I've never seen orders with a Darkside penalty attached to them before."

"I have, Walt. You do know what that means." It wasn't a question.

"Anyone who says anything . . ."

"If anyone who knows about Objective Two says anything to anyone who doesn't, everyone who knows about it goes to Darkside."

To most citizens of the Confederation, Darkside was a mythical place; a bogeyman used by frustrated parents to frighten misbehaving children into good behavior. But it was real, very real. Nobody who didn't need to know where it was knew its location. A sentence to the penal world called Darkside was for life; nobody committed to Darkside ever left, not even in death for burial on their home world. If everyone with the need-to-know about the mission was under threat of sentence to Darkside, that explained why Obannion had never heard even a whisper of an assignment like the one before him carried out by Force Recon—if there ever had been such a mission.

Indrus gave Obannion a moment to absorb the implications of the penalty, then got briskly back to business.

"I know that all of your Marines have high enough security clearances for the mission on the first page of these orders, and I believe you have snipers who have high enough clearances for the second mission. Is that right?"

"Yessir." That business about the personnel on the page-two orders. Very curious. He'd have to check with Sergeant Major Periz to be positive, but he was certain that Lance Corporal Dwan had an Ultra Secret clearance. "But, sir, while the main mission is a routine enough mission for Force Recon, that second mission—it's an assassination, and *that* is nowhere near a routine assignment." Obannion paused in thought for a moment, then said, "Offhand, I don't think I've ever heard of an assassination mission being given to Force Recon."

Indrus looked at Obannion for a long moment, considering what he should say. He decided and abruptly leaned forward. "Walt, we both have Ultra Secret clearances. You have one, I have one. There are things we are both cleared to know, things known to almost nobody else in the entire Confederation of Human Worlds. But neither of us knows everything Ultra Secret; most of that knowledge is restricted to those few who need to know it. A general, especially at my level, has a need-to-know that a commander doesn't.

"You don't know what I'm about to tell you, you don't have the official need-to-know. But I'm a Confederation

Marine Corps Lieutenant General, and *I* think you need to know more than you do.

"I happen to know of four assassinations carried out by Force Recon—and I'm morally certain there have been many more."

Stunned, Obannion simply stared at his commanding general. The Force Recon community was tight-lipped; it had to be, most of what Force Recon Marines did was classified. Nonetheless, word of out-of-the-ordinary missions, particularly difficult missions, extremely hazardous missions—in short, anything truly unusual—got around regardless of their level of classification. Force Recon Marines believed they all had to know about the particularly unexpected or unusual, that such knowledge might save Force Recon lives and increase the odds of mission success. How did it happen that a Force Recon company commander didn't know about assassination missions?

That was the real reason for Indrus meeting Obannion in the G3's office rather than his own; if the commander of the Force Recon company had been called to the office of the CG, Fourth Fleet Marines, it would be unusual enough to attract attention, and people who didn't have the need-to-know might try to find out what the mission was. Obannion almost wished he didn't know about it himself.

It was as though Indrus read Obannion's mind. "Those missions were Ultra Secret, need-to-know, with a Darkside penalty, the same as this one," he said. "The only people who will know about this mission are the two of us, the sniper team that gets the assignment, and the platoon commander and platoon sergeant who will give the final go-ahead if Objective Two proves necessary. Now do you understand why you've never heard about these missions?"

Again, Obannion felt as though Indrus was reading his mind. "Yessir, I guess I do."

"You've got the people who can pull this mission off—including Objective Two. Now, do you have a problem with it?"

"A problem? Let's say rather, I have a discomfort with it." Obannion leaned forward. "But you checked this out with Minister of War Berentus, and he said this is what the President wants?"

"Yes, I did. And he said she wants it."

"We're Force Recon, sir. The merely difficult, we do immediately. The impossible may take a little longer."

"Good. Lar will develop a cover story for the primary operation; nobody not directly involved in the planning and running of the op has the need to know about it. I'm talking about the page one mission now. Understand?"

"Yessir."

"Don't draw plans for the page two mission, that's already been done. It came directly from the Office of the Chairman of the Combined Chiefs." An expression of disgust flickered across his face. "I'm afraid I can't show it to you yet, not until your platoon is ready to embark on the *Admiral Nelson*. Then you'll have to brief the platoon commander and platoon sergeant. You'll have a little time after that to brief your sniper team and get them on their way. You'll have noticed that page two of the orders I showed you is missing its Annex Two. The specific personnel details of that mission are in that annex."

"When you've got your main operation plans drawn up," the general said as he stood, Obannion jumped to his feet as well. "Lar will pass them on for my approval. You've got three days. Lar should have your cover story ready by then as well. You will tell *no one* about page two. Understood?"

"Yessir."

"Good day, Walt." Indrus turned and left the office via a rear exit. Nobody in Operations knew he'd been there, except for Colonel Szilk—and probably Commander Ronzo.

Fourth Force Recon Company, Fourth Fleet Marines, Camp Howard, MCB Camp Basilone, Halfway

"What kind of clearance does Bella Dwan have?" Obannion asked Sergeant Major Periz as soon as he returned to his office.

"Ultra Secret." Periz didn't have to check, he knew these things. "So does Sergeant Gossner." If the skipper wanted to know about Lance Corporal Dwan's clearance, Periz reasoned, he'd also need to know her team leader's clearance.

"Thanks, Sergeant Major. I don't want to be disturbed for a few minutes." Obannion went into his office, closed the door behind him, and sat down to read the orders again—especially the second page, the one he couldn't show any of his people.

```
FROM: The President of the Confederation
of Human Worlds
TO: Commanding General, Fourth Fleet
Marines
RE: Special Orders
CLASSIFICATION: Ultra Secret, Eyes Only,
Darkside penalty
1. Personnel: One sniper team to consist
of: one male and one female.
2. The mission to Atlas has a second ele-
ment (Objective Two), to be conducted by
one Force Recon sniper team from the Force
Recon platoon assigned to the primary mis-
sion.
3. Objective Two is contingent on the find-
ings of the primary mission.
   a) Should the primary mission determine
that the Spondu facility known as the
"Cabbage Patch" is a civilian research fa-
```

cility or manufactory, the snipers will take no action, instead they will return to Headquarters, Fourth Fleet Marines as per instructions in Annex 1.

b) Should the primary mission determine that the Spondu facility known as the "Cabbage Patch" is a weapons research facility or manufactory, or is developing a crop-killing fungus, they are to neutralize President Jorge Liberec Lavager of the Union of Margelan at a place and time they will determine. (See Annex 2)

4. The Marines involved in Objective Two will:

a) Make planetfall via civilian starship transport (see Annex 1);

b) Wear civilian clothing throughout the entire deployment;

c) Do their utmost to appear as civilian visitors on holiday (see Annex 2).

5. The Marines participating in Objective Two will, upon completion of their objective, whether or not that completion necessitates neutralization of President Jorge Liberec Lavager, depart Atlas as scheduled on civilian transportation (see Annex 1).

Annex 1

a) The Marines involved in Objective Two will transit from Halfway to New Genesee via civilian cargo freighter, where they will meet and embark on the SpaceFun Lines tour ship *Crimson Seas* for transport to Atlas. Tickets will be provided, as well as a stipend for housing, food, and necessary cover travel and entertainment while on Atlas. (See Annex 2)

b) The Marines involved in Objective Two
will return from Atlas to New Genesee via
SpaceFun Lines tour ship *Blue Ocean* and
transfer to the next available civilian
freighter heading for Halfway.
by Special Order,
Madam Cynthia Chang-Sturdevant,
President,
Confederation of Human Worlds

Obannion sighed; the orders read exactly the same as
when he first read them. Particularly that "one male and
one female" on the second page. Lance Corporal Bella
Dwan was the only female sniper in Fourth Fleet Marines,
the Office of the Chairman of the Combined Chiefs had
to know that. And if it didn't, the Commandant's office
should have told them. He had an idea of what the cover
story in Annex 2 said, and feared Bella Dwan would rebel
at it. He wouldn't find fault with Ivo Gossner if he re-
belled at it as well.

Then he finally faced a facet of the assignment he'd
been avoiding. Bella Dwan was the only female sniper in
Fourth Force Recon Company—there wasn't another
woman sniper available to pair her up with as her team
leader. Obannion wasn't positive, but he was pretty sure
there wasn't another mixed-gender sniper team in the entire Corps; women snipers were normally paired with
women team leaders. That was because of the normal
hormonal response to the aftermath of violence and
death—people who'd just come out of violence and death
had to somehow reaffirm life, and there's nothing more
reaffirming of life than sex.

It could be very bad for the morale of others in the platoon if a sniper team leader and sniper fucked right after a
kill, even if they held off until they got safely away; those
two got some, what about the rest of us? Moreover, what
would happen to discipline once a sniper team did have

sex? What if one wanted to continue a sexual relationship and the other didn't? What if one took advantage of such a relationship to get out of duties, or to get other favors? That would be bad for overall morale and unit effectiveness. This was directly linked to the reason that no branch of the military allowed married couples to serve in the same unit; if both were in the Marines, or the army or the navy, they weren't always assigned to the same stations, and when they were they were assigned to different battalions or equivalent.

Obannion almost felt safe having Bella Dwan paired with Ivo Gossner. Nobody in the company would dare try anything sexual with the Queen of Killers, and Gossner was one of the steadiest Marines in the company.

He touched the intercom and said, "Sergeant Major, get Captains Qindall and Wainwright for me, please. You come in with them."

The company's executive officer and operations officer arrived in two or three minutes. Periz ushered them in.

"Come on in, gentlemen, have a seat." Obannion gestured for someone to close the door behind them.

"What's up, boss?" Qindall asked as he sat.

Wordlessly, Obannion handed him the single-page orders. Wainwright and Periz leaned forward to read it over the XO's shoulders.

"I believe everyone in the company has high enough clearance." He looked at Periz for confirmation. Periz nodded. "So the first question is, who gets the call?"

Wainwright didn't hesitate. "First platoon still has three months to go on Carhart's World. Half of third platoon is on missions and won't be intact for at least two months. Second platoon only has one squad deployed, and it should be back within the next two weeks, standard. That leaves second platoon as the only one immediately deployable."

"Do you think Tevedes is up to it?"

"He ran a couple of successful detached platoon missions when he was with a FIST," Qindall said.

"Also, he's itching to run a platoon-size FR op," Wainwright added.

Obannion looked at Periz, but the sergeant major had nothing to add.

Obannion considered for a moment. What his top officers said was true. He added in the fact that Tevedes had been an outstanding squad leader during his first Force Recon tour, and probably would have been moved into the next available section leader slot if he hadn't opted for officer training and gone to a FIST after getting his commission. He'd acquitted himself well since his return to Force Recon. Obannion couldn't think of a reason to deny him this opportunity.

"Second platoon it is then," he decided. "Get started on some plans, we'll bring Tevedes and Gunny Lytle into it tomorrow."

Obannion and his primary staff began studying up on Atlas.

Company Commander's Office, Fourth Force Recon Company

Commander Obannion finished outlining the operation to second platoon's commander and platoon sergeant, then added, "Don't tell your Marines—don't tell *anybody*—about this. We'll give you a cover story to tell them for now. Your Marines don't get told the real mission until you're in Beamspace on your last jump before Atlas. Understand?"

"Yessir," Tevedes replied. He was giddy about taking his platoon on a mission, but not so giddy he didn't understand what his company commander said, or the need for secrecy.

Gunny Lytle also said, "Yessir," but his reply was far more restrained. He wondered why this relatively routine mission was being kept so secret within the platoon.

Second platoon squadbay, Fourth Force Recon Company

Preparations for mounting out on a mission were always the same whether one squad or an entire platoon deployed, only the details changed.

The Marines double- and triple-checked their weapons to make sure they were in proper working condition, and replaced any parts they even suspected might fail. They did the same with their uniforms and gear. Then they checked their weapons again.

They studied the operation plan and rehearsed whatever actions they were going to perform. And checked their weapons yet again. They read up on their objective area and studied maps of the area of operation and the surrounding territory. And rechecked their weapons.

Lance Corporal Wazzen noticed a glaring discrepancy: The operations plan didn't quite match the maps, and the maps and area studies had obviously false names on them. He pointed that out to Sergeant Daly.

"No kidding," Daly said. "Did you happen to notice the classification level of this operation?"

"Ultra Secret. So?"

"Ultra Secret. That means this operation plan is probably a dummy, just in case somebody who doesn't need to know what we're doing gets hold of it."

Wazzen looked at him blankly. "Then what are we really going to do?" This was his first Ultra Secret, need-to-know mission.

"We'll find out when we really need to know."

"When will that be?"

Daly gave a nonchalant shrug. "Before we get where we're going."

Wazzen looked like he was trying to come up with another question to ask, but Daly had another piece of information for him first.

"Something else it means is, you're confined to the

company area until we mount out, and can only go to chow with someone from the squad."

"What!" Wazzen squawked. "Why?"

"To guarantee you don't say anything about a dummy plan where someone who doesn't need to know can overhear you."

They checked their weapons and gear again.

Office of the Company Commander, Fourth Force Recon Company

Commander Walt Obannion didn't bother looking at page two of the orders again before he sent for Lieutenant Tevedes and Gunnery Sergeant Lytle. As much as he might wish it otherwise. Unlike data stored on crystals, which could be changed, he knew the page would say the same thing it did the last time he looked at it—once words were on paper they tended to say the same thing until the paper was destroyed.

He stood when he heard Tevedes and Lytle enter the outer office and met them at the door of his inner sanctum. He gave Sergeant Major Periz an apologetic shake of the head when he closed the door, shutting his top enlisted man out of the loop. Neither Tevedes nor Lytle missed the significance of the absence of the company's top dog. Wondering what was about to come down, they both stood a little more erect.

"You both better sit down for this one," Obannion said as he brushed past them to his desk. The two paused just long enough for their commander to sit before they followed suit.

Obannion looked at the two leaders of the Atlas mission levelly, then shook himself as though breaking out of a paralytic grip. "I think you better take a look at this," he said, handing Tevedes the two-page order.

Lytle leaned over to read along with the lieutenant.

When each finished reading page one, they looked up. Tevedes said what he was thinking:

"What's so important? We've seen this before."

Lytle knew the important business was on page two. "Turn the page," he said.

Tevedes did, and the two read.

Tevedes stopped reading before he got to the details and raised his eyes. "Assassinate the President of a nation-state on a Confederation member world? Is that *really* what this says?"

Obannion nodded solemnly. "General Indrus verified the orders, that's what it says."

"And the Darkside penalty for everyone who knows?"

Obannion nodded again. "They're very serious about the secrecy of this mission."

Tevedes sucked in a breath and blew it out. He looked Obannion in the eye and said, "I know about this mission. So even if I turn it down, I can be sentenced to Darkside if anybody divulges information about it."

"Me too." Obannion looked at Lytle.

Lytle had read the entire page. "Where's Annex Two?" he asked.

Obannion shook his head. "I haven't seen it yet."

"How are we supposed to communicate with the sniper team?" Lytle asked.

"I believe there will be encoded instructions for you to open before you make planetfall on Atlas. I'll know for certain later today."

"With the Lieutenant's permission," Lytle said, looking at his platoon commander, "I think we better accept this mission, if for no other reason than to limit how many people know about it—and so we can have some control over those who know."

"I think that's wise," Tevedes agreed.

Obannion didn't show the relief he felt as he nodded.

"Thank you for your confidence in us, I guess," Tevedes said.

"I know second platoon can execute the primary mission, Gott. And I trust your judgment, both of you, on the secondary objective—and I know that you've got a sniper team that can execute that mission and keep their mouths shut about it."

Tevedes flinched at the second "execute," because that's what it was, an execution. "Which team?" he asked, then shook his head. "You mean Gossner and Dwan, don't you?" It couldn't be anybody else.

"Can you think of anyone better?"

Tevedes slowly shook his head. "Nossir, I don't think I can." He paused a beat, then continued, "If Dwan's willing to do it. I know she talks and acts tough, and she's an outstanding sniper. But assassinating a civilian leader isn't the same as sniping at an enemy soldier. I strongly suspect that somewhere deep inside she's got scruples. She could draw a line at the assassination of a civilian."

"There's only one way to find out."

"Yessir, I guess there is. Do we have a cover story for where they're going?"

"That's part of their operational plan, which has been drawn by higher-higher. I haven't seen it yet." Obannion made a face. "Certain elements of this mission are being divulged only when they have to be known. I'm not sure yet whether I'll be privy to those details."

Tevedes shook his head; matters seemed more serious every time he heard something new. Lytle showed no reaction; matters were every bit as bad as the worst he'd imagined.

"Any other questions?"

"Nossir."

"Is the platoon ready to mount out?"

"On about one minute's notice."

"Then, gentlemen," Obannion rose to his feet and held out his hand, "good hunting."

Obannion followed them to his office door and watched until they left the outer office. He turned to Periz.

"Sergeant Major, I'm sorry, but they're very serious about this." He left the door open as he returned to his desk. When he sat he saw Periz standing in his doorway looking as stern as he'd ever seen him. "Sergeant Major, this is an instance where I think you really are better off if you don't know what's going on." He called up the status report on the deployed elements of the company so he could look busy.

Periz continued to stand in the doorway for a moment, staring at his company commander, then snorted and returned to his own desk, muttering about, "There's *nothing* a sergeant major is better off not knowing about what his Marines are doing." He sat at his console and got busy. One way or another, he *was* going to find out.

CHAPTER
ELEVEN

Fast Frigate CNSS *Admiral Nelson*

Second platoon, Fourth Force Recon Company, shipped out on the fast frigate *Admiral Nelson*. The only contact the Marines had with the ship's crew was with the bo'suns who conveyed them to their compartments, and messmen during their mealtimes—the rest of the ship was off-limits to them, except for the library and one gym, which were designated for their exclusive use during specific hours.

The Marines didn't chafe under the confinement, they were too busy tending to their weapons, uniforms, and gear, studying the operation plan and keeping themselves physically fit with isometric exercises in their cabins. And the *Admiral Nelson*'s sailors were just as glad they didn't have to deal with the Marines. The Force Recon Marines projected an even more calm dangerousness than the Marines of a FIST did—if such a thing was possible—and most sailors thought ordinary FIST Marines were entirely too dangerous to have around.

When the Marines hit the ship's library, they were particularly interested in maps of their area of operations. Atlas, they found out once they were given their destination, was almost unique among members of the Confederation of Human Worlds in that it didn't have a globe-girdling satellite system other than its orbital port, Kraken Interstellar. Because, again almost unique among Confederation member worlds, Atlas didn't have a planetary government, but rather a number of independent and often antagonistic nation-states. No nation-state was willing to allow satellites belonging to another to overfly its territory. And nobody in the Confederation congress thought Atlas was significant enough to press the issue, so when Atlas's most powerful nation-states jointly requested that visiting Confederation navy ships not deploy their string-of-pearls satellites, the congress so ordered.

The navy wasn't happy about that order, and the Marines less so; for one thing, the lack of a string-of-pearls meant there were no up-to-date military-quality maps available. But there were other recent maps, and the Marines of second platoon endeavored to commit them to memory. Additionally, everyone from squad leader up downloaded the maps to their personal comps to carry along on the mission.

Company Commander's Office, Fourth Force Recon Company, Fourth Fleet Marines, Camp Howard, MCB Camp Basilone, Halfway

Commander Obannion had to wait until the *Admiral Nelson* made her jump into Beamspace before he got Annex 2 of the second page of the orders.

```
            Special Presidential Order,
                  page 3, Annex 2

    Annex 2
      a) Cover: The Marines, one male and one
    female, assigned to Mission Objective Two
    will travel as a recently married couple.*
    All relevant documentation (see section b)
    will be provided to them in sufficient time
    prior to their departure from MCB Camp
    Basilone, Halfway, for them to memorize the
    necessary details. They will travel in
```

civilian clothing (provided, see section c), under civilian passports (provided, see section b). They will not carry any Marine Corps identification, uniforms, or insignia. They will leave their identification bracelets behind.

*Neither the President of the Confederation of Human Worlds nor the Commandant of the Marine Corps expect the Marines assigned to Mission Objective Two to maintain the cover of being married when they are in private, that cover is directed to be maintained for public consumption only.

b) Documentation: The Marines assigned to Mission Objective Two will be provided with: 1) civilian passports in their names and with their likenesses issued by the Foreign Ministry of New Genesee (see attached package*); 2) travel permits and passport stamps issued by the Ministry of Tourism of The Union of Margelan, Atlas; 3) a marriage certificate issued by the Home Ministry of New Genesee (see attached package*), and 4) up-to-date health and innoculation certifications issued by the Ministry of Health of New Genesee (see attached package*); 5) employee identification cards from Imperial Industries and Starcraft Crafts bearing the names and likenesses of the assigned Marines are included in the clothing packages en route to MCB Camp Basilone.

*If the referenced package is not attached to this annex, notify the Director, Central Intelligence Organization immediately and directly. Do not go through the normal chain of command.

c) Clothing: Appropriate civilian attire is en route, in parcels addressed individually to the Marines assigned to Mission Objective Two.

d) Tickets (tourist class) for passage to and from Halfway and Atlas via civilian freighters and cruise ships are enclosed with the clothing allotment en route. A reservation in the married name of the Marines assigned to Mission Objective Two has been made at the New Granum DeLuxe Inn in New Granum, Union of Margelan, Atlas.

e) Credits: Open-limit cred-sticks* are included in the packages (see section c) en route to the Marines assigned to Mission Objective Two.

*It is understood that although the assigned Marines will make all expenditures necessary to maintain their cover as recently married individuals on holiday, they will not undertake to make unnecessary or frivolous expenditures.

f) Weapons and special equipment: Surveillance device detection units are provided, along with instructions for their use. (See attached package*) An M14A5 maser sniper rifle will be secreted in a location marked in the *Tourist and Visitors Guide to Atlas* (see attached package*) to be found in the cabin assigned to the Marines assigned to Mission Objective Two aboard the *Crimson Seas*, along with a P6 radio to be used for oneway communications with the command element of Mission Objective One.

*(See note to section b.)

Commander Walt Obannion read Annex 2 behind a closed and locked door, which would have been a very good thing if anybody had looked in when he reached section b of Annex 2. The documentation in the names of the Marines assigned to the mission had to have been made out before the orders had even reached Camp Howard. Yet the assigned Marines weren't named in the orders. That had shaken him. The orders were over the signature of the President of the Confederation of Human Worlds, but the annexes were attached and not over the president's signature. Who could have determined who was going on the mission before he—or even Lieutenant General Indrus for all he knew—had received the orders? The Commandant of the Marine Corps and his staff could have easily determined that there was only one woman sniper in Fourth Force Recon Company. But surely they wouldn't have made a personnel assignment without somehow notifying the commanding general, if not the company commander. The Combined Chiefs and their staffs would have had access to that information, but they also weren't likely to make a personnel assignment without informing the office of the responsible commanding general—and he thought it equally unlikely Lieutenant General Indrus would have failed to inform him if he'd known.

There was that reference to the Director, Central Intelligence Organization, in the footnote to section b. *That* told him where the annex had to have originated, and why the CG Fourth Fleet Marines hadn't alerted him. He wondered what the CIO knew about his Marines, and why they knew it. For that matter, why couldn't the CIO do its own dirty work?

But his wasn't to reason why, his was to do or . . . Well, he was a Marine. Marines don't do or die, they simply *do*.

He opened the attached package. All the documents specified in section b were there, in the names and likenesses of Sergeant Ivo Gossner and Lance Corporal Bella

Dwan. Of course, their ranks appeared on none of the documents. The parcel also included two wigs. One, shorter-haired, was obviously for a male, the other, longer-haired, was just as obviously for a female. Something about the wigs felt odd.

Obannion looked in the package and found another sheet of paper. He shook his head; he'd never before seen a mission on which so much was consigned to paper. For all he knew, he had the only copies of the Mission Two orders and annexes in existence. If so, it would be easy to burn the orders to ash and scatter the ash, leaving no evidence they had ever been received.

The latest sheet of paper was instructions for use of the surveillance-device detection units, one slender, flexible, wand hidden in each wig, which explained why the wigs felt so odd. The instructions also claimed the wands were not detectable by "any electronic means known to be available to the authorities on Atlas." That gave Obannion pause. Finally he decided that if the wands' cloak of invisibility did not work, Gossner and Dwan could always take their failings up with the manufacturer. After they got out of jail.

Obannion's office had two visual and four audio recording devices, which he could activate at will to make a record of anything that took place in it. He routinely turned them on when he left for the day and off when he returned. Following the detector's instructions, he was able to find all that spyware even when the units were turned off.

He replaced the wands in the wigs and looked in the box again. One item remained, a copy of the *Visitor and Tourist Guide to Atlas* on crystal. Yet another sheet of paper was attached to it. The sheet gave specific instructions for finding data hidden in the book. *Who is going to put an exact copy of this crystal in their cabin on the* Crimson Seas? he wondered. According to the instructions, when the crystal was inserted into a standard reader, certain pages would show additional information in ultraviolet. He could put the crystal in his reader and look at it through his helmet to see the UV, but Gossner and Dwan wouldn't have a Force Recon helmet with them, so there must be some other way for them to see in ultraviolet.

An ultraviolet viewer was the last item in the package. He opened his office door. Sergeant Major Periz was at his desk, busy at his console. "Excuse me, Sergeant Major."

Periz looked up at him, quickly toggling his console to a different display. Obannion noticed but said nothing; he knew that Periz had to be deeply offended by his exclusion from what was going on. Someday, he vowed, he would find a way to make it up to the Sergeant Major.

"Yessir?" Periz gave him a blank look.

"Have Sergeant Gossner and Lance Corporal Dwan report to me immediately, please."

"Aye aye, sir." Periz returned to his comm and Obannion to his office.

Ten minutes after Obannion sent for them, the intercom buzzed and Periz's voice growled, "Sergeant Gossner and Lance Corporal Dwan are here." Obannion noticed the lack of a "sir."

"Thank you, Sergeant Major. Send them in if you please." The two snipers marched into his office and stood at attention in front of his desk.

Obannion leaned back in his chair and studied the pair. What did the CIO know about them? Did they know anything more about Dwan than that she was a woman? Why would they think she could successfully pull off a masquerade as a newlywed bride? Sergeant Gossner as a new husband, sure; he could have been the model for a Marine Corps recruiting hologram. He didn't have the steely, blood-freezing eyes that Dwan did. No, despite her elfin face, Bella Dwan definitely didn't look like a blushing bride—or anybody's kid sister.

He took a different tack than he had with Lieutenant Tevedes and Gunnery Sergeant Lytle.

"Lance Corporal Dwan, it is my understanding that you consider yourself the best sniper in the Confederation Marine Corps. Is that true?"

"Yessir. Nossir; I *am* the best sniper in the Marine Corps."

"What about you, Sergeant, do you think she's the best sniper?"

"Well, sir, I haven't seen every sniper in the Corps, but she's the best I've seen."

"And you're willing to be her team leader on any sniping mission she's assigned to?"

Gossner's lips hinted at a smile. "Sir, Lance Corporal Dwan is a, ah, an enthusiastic sniper. She does better when I'm there to help her keep calm and focused."

Obannion noticed that Dwan's jaw clenched at that. "Then the two of you are willing to take on a most unusual assignment, one that has more than the normal complement of hazards, and—most importantly—one that you'll never be able to brag about on penalty of Darkside?"

"Sir?" Gossner said.

"If you've got a tough one, sir, I'm your sniper," Dwan said flatly. "I'm the best in all of Human Space."

"Did you say Darkside, sir?" Gossner said.

"The penalty for telling anybody about this assignment is summary sentence to Darkside, yes."

Gossner sucked in a chestful of air and noisily blew it out. Dwan kept her hard gaze on her company commander, but didn't say anything. The fingers of her right hand began twitching as though she was firing her maser.

"Well, Sergeant Gossner, Lance Corporal Dwan looks like she's ready to take on the assignment. What about you?"

"Sir, if Lance Corporal Dwan's going, I guess I have to go along to keep her out of trouble." He ignored the warning look she flashed him.

"Pull a couple of chairs close together and sit down."

He waited until they had done so and handed them the orders and annexes for the sniper mission.

"*This* is what you want us to do?" Gossner asked when he finished reading the first page.

"Yes it is." Obannion nodded at the orders. "Keep reading."

"This says we're masquerading as a newlywed couple," Dwan said almost immediately after she began reading Annex 2. "What's on Atlas that tourists would want to see?" Interstellar travel was expensive, both in monetary cost and travel time. Other than the idle rich, not many people could afford the time or money involved in casual interstellar travel.

"Have you ever heard of Niagara Falls?" Obannion asked. He noticed that she hadn't objected to the newlywed masquerade and wondered if that meant she simply accepted it.

Dwan looked blank. Gossner said, "Isn't that on Earth? A big waterfall or something?"

"That's right. For a couple of centuries, people thought it was a very romantic place. Many newlyweds went there for their honeymoons. There's an even more spectacular waterfall close by New Granum, where you'll be staying. It's a popular honeymoon destination for the people in that quadrant of Human Space who can afford it.

"You'll be masquerading as honeymooners." Obannion said that calmly.

Gossner kept his face blank and didn't look at Dwan. The look she gave Obannion almost made him tense to dive for cover.

"I saw that in section a," Dwan said. "Is this somebody's idea of a joke?" she demanded. "If it is, it's not funny."

Obannion shook his head. "Those are the orders as they came from Earth. I doubt the bureaucrats there have that kind of sense of humor."

"Do they expect us to, you know . . ." Gossner said uncertainly.

"No. That's covered in the note to section a. But you have to act like you're newlyweds anyplace where people can see you."

Gossner sighed and Dwan shot him a look that Obannion was glad wasn't directed at him. Otherwise, it was going better than he had feared. But how would she act once they were undercover?

"Finish reading the orders," Obannion said. He waited until they were through, then got out the package that had come with Annex 2 and opened it again. Sorting through the documents, he made two stacks, one for each.

"These are your documents." He waited while they inspected them, then got out the wigs. "Put these on." He was surprised at how well the wigs fit; Dwan hardly even had to tuck any of her own hair under hers. "Now feel them, probe with your fingers." They quickly found and withdrew the wands. He walked them through operating them. Within two minutes, they had found all the concealed recorders in the office.

"You'll need to check your hotel room, and every other place where you want to talk privately, to be certain you aren't under electronic observation." He then pointed to the two bulky parcels. "There's one for each of you, your names are on them. Open them now."

They did. Gossner whistled at the clothing his parcel held. "Do I get to keep these when the mission's over?" he asked.

"I don't know, the orders don't cover that. We'll have to wait for further instructions."

"What's this?" Dwan asked. She held up an ordinary-looking purse mirror and pressed a slight indentation on its back. The mirroring vanished and it became a clear glass.

The crystal that had come in the package with the documents and wigs was still in Obannion's reader. He opened the book to one of the pages with hidden data and took the now-clear mirror from her. When he looked at the reader through the mirror, he saw things that weren't there when he simply looked at the screen.

"This is what you use to see the hidden instructions," he said. "The indentation is keyed to the print of your right index finger and that of Sergeant Gossner. Take care not to open it in the presence of anyone not cleared for knowledge of the mission."

Dwan grunted and took the mirror back.

The comm beeped, Obannion picked it up and listened. When he put it down, he said, "The civilian freighter *Ore King* breaks orbit the day after tomorrow, bound for New Genesee. You board her tomorrow. Do you have any other questions?"

Dwan mulled over the mission orders. Whoever wrote the orders, at least the annex, was right: She and Gossner were the logical choice for this mission. "You know, sir," she said, "this isn't sniping. In the Marines, sniping is when a soldier shoots a selected enemy soldier or officer, either a target of opportunity or by selection. Deliberately shooting a civilian leader is assassination."

There it was, the thing that bothered Obannion about the mission to begin with, and even more ever since he realized who was going.

"Do you have a problem with that, Lance Corporal?" he asked.

"Hell no, sir! Not as long as it's properly authorized. Anyone who can shoot straight can be a sniper. But it takes real class to be an assassin."

Obannion didn't let his relief show, or his surprise at her reply. "Take your parcels. I'll arrange for your transportation to Cunningham Field, and a shuttle to the *Ore King*. He stood and held out his hand. "Good hunting, Marines."

"Thank you, sir," they said in turn as they shook his hand. They returned to attention, about-faced, and marched from his office carrying their parcels.

CHAPTER
TWELVE

Lakeview, New Genesee

When the *Admiral Nelson* pulled into orbit around New Genesee, rotating shore liberty was sounded for all hands—one-quarter of the officers and crew remained on duty while the rest headed planetside. Every six hours Standard, an equal number launched to orbit to assume duty, allowing those who had the duty to take a turn planetside. The sailors thought having eighteen out of every twenty-four hours planetside during the *Admiral Nelson*'s six days at New Genesee was pretty good.

The Marines of second platoon didn't have to rotate back to ship for duty; they had rooms in the Tartar Arms, a mid-level hotel, where all of them spent significant amounts of time tending to their weapons, uniforms, gear, and study. They didn't mind having to take part in the New Genesee Enlargement Day parade, not when they found out that was the price the Confederation embassy extracted in exchange for paying for their hotel rooms and two meals a day.

None of the Marines except Lieutenant Tevedes and Gunnery Sergeant Lytle knew that the reason the *Admiral Nelson* was orbiting New Genesee for a week was because they had to wait for Sergeant Gossner and Lance Corporal Dwan to arrive and board the SpaceFun Lines cruise ship *Crimson Seas*. Gossner and Dwan had to reach Atlas several days in advance of the platoon.

Gossner and Dwan made planetfall on New Genesee

only long enough to transfer from the shuttle that brought them down from the *Ore King* to the shuttle that took them back up to the *Crimson Seas*.

Room 581, The Tartar Arms, Lakeview, New Genesee

Lieutenant Gott Tevedes learned quickly that the Tartar Arms was the facility the Confederation embassy sometimes used to house visiting minor dignitaries. He appreciated the fact that the Embassy picked up the tab for the rooms; the accommodations the Marines had on the *Admiral Nelson* were cramped—they always were for Marines traveling aboard fast frigates.

"I logged you in as on TAD to the embassy to march in the celebration of New Genesee's Enlargement Day, the day the world was admitted as a full member of the Confederation," embassy Chief of Staff Raymondo Schenck explained after he handed over a sealed envelope. "Of course, that means you'll actually have to march. Do you have appropriate uniforms with you?" He managed not to look too disappointed when Tevedes didn't open the envelope in front of him.

Tevedes and Gunnery Sergeant Lytle exchanged a glance.

"Only what you see and our chameleons," Tevedes replied. He and Lytle were in their dull green garrison utility uniforms; they didn't have any civilian clothing with them.

Schenck asked, "Well then, can you look real soldierly? I mean with weapons and all, like you're about to go to war?"

"And be visible, you mean?" Lytle asked.

Schenck blinked. "Of course, visible. How else would you be?"

Neither Marine bothered to explain.

"Yessir, we can look ready to fight," Tevedes assured him.

Thus assured, Schenck returned to the embassy.

Gunny Lytle looked curiously at the envelope that Lieutenant Tevedes weighed in his hand once they were alone.

"Sealed orders," Tevedes said softly. He broke the envelope open. It contained a flimsy sheet of paper and another sealed envelope. The two Marines exchanged a glance—yet more orders. Tevedes held the sheet so Lytle could read along with him.

The reading didn't take long; the message was one short paragraph. It instructed Tevedes to open the enclosed sealed envelope shortly before making planetfall on Atlas and informed him that the written orders contained therein would self-destruct five minutes after the envelope was opened. The last sentence instructed him to eat the flimsy after reading it.

Tevedes and Lytle exchanged another look, then the platoon commander shrugged, folded the sheet, put it in his mouth, and began to chew.

On Enlargement Day, the Marines grumbled a bit about having to remove the chameleoning from their weapons and helmets for the parade, and then chameleoning them again afterward. But it wasn't serious grumbling; they had to do it anyway to properly inspect the outer surfaces of their weapons and helmets before they made planetfall on Atlas.

Kraken Interstellar Starport, Atlas

The *Crimson Seas* had a routine docking at Kraken Interstellar, Atlas's orbital starport, named after the planet's first president. Kraken Interstellar was pretty standard as second-class starports went; mid-level orbit, bays sufficient for ten starships—provided none of them was larger than Goddard Class cruise ships or a Confederation Navy light cruiser; Kraken couldn't physically accommodate the largest starships except via shuttle.

Sergeant Ivo Gossner and Lance Corporal Bella Dwan, dressed in clothing from the parcels they received in Commander Obannion's office, debarked with the rest of the passengers and followed the ship's activity director to the customs queue. They found customs quite single-minded.

"Anything to declare?" the customs agent asked Gossner.

"Not a thing," Gossner replied jauntily.

"Are you sure of that?"

Gossner nodded brightly. "I read the guidebook while we were on the *Crimson Seas*, and I don't have anything on the banned and restricted list that was in the book. I certainly don't have any agricultural products." He paused and wrapped a proprietary arm around Dwan's shoulders. "Neither does my wife," he added.

Dwan simpered and batted her eyelashes at the customs agent. "We *are* married you know." She fluttered the fingers of her left hand, displaying the wedding band circling the third finger.

"How long do you expect to stay on Atlas?" The agent didn't need to be told that they were married; nearly every couple coming to Atlas was newly married.

"Two weeks. Then we have to go back home."

"Do you have return passage?"

"We have reservations on the *Blue Ocean*." Gossner waved the return ticket crystal.

The customs agent took the crystal, examined it, and made note of the registration number, then grunted and cast an eye at their carry-on bags. "That's not much luggage for two weeks' stay."

"We have two more cases coming from the cargo hold."

Dwan smiled broadly and said, "I don't need a lot of luggage. Ivo got a promotion and big raise on his job. I'm going shopping!" She flicked a hand to her face to titter behind.

"Open them up," the customs agent said, still looking at their carry-ons. Gossner opened the bags while Dwan stood primly to the side, feet together, hands clasped between her breasts, looking more innocent than any Marine who ever served with her could have believed was possible.

The customs agent inspected the bags very thoroughly with hands and eyes, and with several biological-detection devices. Then he put them on a conveyer that led them through a swinging door into an unseen area.

"Wh-where is our luggage going?" Dwan asked nervously.

"It's all right, honey," Gossner said, putting a reassuring hand on her arm. "Remember what the *Visitor and Tourist Guide to Atlas* said? Everything has to be irradiated to make sure no contaminants are imported."

The customs agent nodded approval; his job was a lot easier when tourists had actually read the customs information in the *Guide*.

"Now if you will go through those doors and follow the instructions—" The customs agent pointed to side-by-side doors, one with the universal sign for "male" and the other with the sign for "female."

"Ivo?" Dwan timidly said.

"It's all right, dear," Gossner said, and touched her brow with a soft kiss. "We have to be decontaminated."

"A-All right. If you say so," she said softly.

They entered their respective decontamination chambers, where they stripped and were given a thorough shower with a sudsing decontamination agent and blown dry with hot air. While they showered, their clothing went into a box for irradiation.

Completely decontaminated and redressed, they returned to the customs agent.

"Welcome to Atlas. Enjoy your stay." The customs agent zapped the appropriate code into their passport logs and looked past them to the next in line. They were through. No one had examined their heads to discover the wigs with the hidden wands, or looked at the pocket mirror in Dwan's luggage.

The shuttle ride planetside was uneventful. Nobody paid any attention to them. Not even the person arriving on Atlas for a third visit, someone who would have had a great deal of interest in them had that person known the real reason for their visit.

Room 1007, New Granum DeLuxe Inn, New Granum, Union of Margelan, Atlas

The New Granum DeLuxe Inn may have rated three stars in the *Visitor and Tourist Guide to Atlas*, but no interstellar hostelery guide gave it more than two. Which meant it was clean, well-enough appointed, and vermin free, but didn't provide its guests with such amenities as the complimentary baskets of local fruits and beverages that better hotels did, or plush, real-cotton terry robes. Which lacks Gossner and Dwan expected—after all, the Confederation Marine Corps was footing the bill, and the CMC wasn't about to pay for luxury accommodations for a junior NCO and a junior enlisted woman.

Gossner and Dwan poked through their wigs and withdrew the wands, which were in fact on the banned and restricted item list in the *Visitor and Tourist Guide to Atlas*. In seconds, Dwan was waving hers over every object, electronic or otherwise, in the room and Gossner covered the walls, ceiling, and floor with his. The ersatz newlyweds murmured unintelligible words, interspersed with gasps, groans, and occasional high-pitched laughs from Dwan as they made the security check.

"Clear," Gossner shortly announced.

"Me too," Dwan said.

They stopped making lover-noises and in a moment the wands were restowed in their wigs.

Had they indeed been honeymooners, their room would

have been more than adequate: a bath with all the necessary appliances, not in any configuration either of them had ever previously encountered; a large closet sufficient for their clothing; a large bureau with mirror; chairs and a table large enough for room service meals for two; entertainment center; and a queen-size bed. Their cabin on the *Crimson Seas* had had two narrow bunks.

One bed. That could present a problem, though newlyweds sleeping in separate beds might have aroused suspicions.

Bella Dwan was ready. She plopped their luggage onto the middle of the bed, in a line from head to foot.

"That side's yours," she told Gossner, "this side's mine. We'll muss it up in the morning before housekeeping comes in so it'll look like we spent the night all over each other."

"There are easier ways to make the bed look well used," Gossner said with feigned innocence.

She ignored his remark, knowing her virtue was safe; men were too afraid of the Queen of Killers to make any kind of serious sexual advance. For that matter, most men who knew her reputation would back away from the Queen's advances if they thought they could do so safely.

"I could hardly believe that was you. Going through customs, I mean," Gossner said, oddly relieved that Dwan ignored his bed remark.

"What, you think I don't know how to make men think all I am is tits and a cunt?" She laughed at his shocked expression. "Ivo, every woman learns how to do that before she has tits or a ripe cherry, much less any idea of the power it gives her." She looked away and shook her head. "Some women never realize the power they have." She looked back at him, hard-eyed, and flexed her hands as though she was fondling a weapon. "I prefer to use power that men understand and fear."

Gossner gave her a level look, but said nothing. Inside, he was glad they didn't have any weapons with them; with a weapon in her hands, she was the most frightening person he'd ever met.

"Let's go sightseeing," is what he said.

"I'm going to change first." She disappeared into the water closet.

Pauke Falls, North of New Granum

Ivo Gossner and Bella Dwan, in the recommended water-resistant clothing, boarded a tourist airbus along with a score of other visitors for the trip to Pauke Falls. The airbus pilot tended to the driving while a tour guide kept up a steady patter and answered questions about the natural wonders the airbus flew above. The pilot moved the airbus up and down, side to side, so the passengers could better see whatever the guide was describing. The forty-kilometer trip took nearly half an hour Standard.

Well before they reached it, they heard the falls through the airbus's external audio pickups, and saw its cloud of spray when they were still too distant to see the water. When they first glimpsed the falls the tourists thought they were much closer than they were but although the airbus kept closing on them for several minutes they didn't seem to get any nearer. That was when the passengers began to realize how high Pauke Falls actually was.

The airbus landed in a parking lot more than half filled with air- and ground buses marked with the names and symbols of a half-dozen hotels and tour companies; there were even a respectable number of private vehicles. The guide led them to an observation platform from which they could see the falls, still two kilometers distant.

Pauke Falls was huge, a kilometer wide and two hundred meters high. The water at the foot of the falls boiled into spray that didn't begin to dissipate until it was a hundred meters high, and continued to rise higher than the falls. The pool the water emptied into was a very large lake. A broad river rioted south from it, past the observation platform, to a huge lake three or four kilometers farther downstream. The walls of the canyon formed by the river that flowed from the lake at the falls' foot was studded with observation platforms, most of which held people gaping at the falls or the canyon. Dartboats shot about the downstream lake like a cloud of feeding dragonflies. Even two kilometers away, the roar of the falls was loud enough to make conversation difficult. The thin mist that reached them even on the platform made it clear why water-resistant clothing was recommended for the visit.

The guide prattled for a while about the wonder the tourists were watching, and answered all their mostly inane questions. After fifteen minutes she gave them directions to the restaurants, souvenir shops, and nature walks, and finished with an admonition to be back in two hours, or they would miss the airbus back to New Granum and would have to pay another fare on a different bus.

Gossner and Dwan joined the crowd heading for the eateries—they didn't want to do anything to draw attention to themselves. After a light meal, they visited a gift shop where they bought a cased fishing rod and creel, then headed for the most remote nature trail, one that incidentally led to fishing ponds.

Away from the tourists, Gossner got out his reader. The guidebook crystal was already inserted, and he examined the map on page 148 through Dwan's ultraviolet mirror. It showed a spot a hundred meters away, at the outer side of a bend in a branching trail called "lovers' lane."

Other couples were walking along the broad path, so Gossner and Dwan held hands and walked close together, looking like any other young lovers. They were the only ones to turn onto the lovers' lane. Just where the map showed, they found a flat rock, under which was a space just the right size to hold a cased maser. Dwan reached through the foliage that camouflaged the gap and her hand fell upon the familiar shape of an M14A5 maser wrapped in a protective cover. They removed the fishing rod from its case and replaced it with the wrapped maser, then continued down the lovers' lane to a small fishing pond where Gossner pretended to fish.

It wasn't a complete charade; he caught two piscoids, ugly things that he threw back with a shudder. On their way back they secreted the rod under the rock, where it was unlikely to be found anytime soon, and returned in time to board their airbus for the ride back to New Granum.

On Board the CNSS *Admiral Nelson,* Approaching Atlas in Space-3

Lieutenant Tevedes and Gunnery Sergeant Lytle secured their cabin door before Tevedes retrieved the sealed envelope from his pack. He showed the seal to Lytle to demonstrate that he hadn't cheated by opening it early. Then he broke the seal and opened the envelope. It contained one sheet of flimsy paper, but the flimsy felt different from the one with the instructions to open this envelope hours before launch planetside. *That must be whatever's going to destroy it,* he thought.

Again, the message was brief. It contained a radio frequency and two code words. One code word was the abort signal if the Spondu facility was a bona fide agricultural research station, the other was the go signal if it was a weapons research station or manufactory. It also instructed them to make sure the platoon's noncommissioned officers knew how to use the frequency and code words if Tevedes and Lytle became casualties before they were able to transmit the proper code word to the team in New Granum.

"The tricky part," Tevedes said, "is going to be making sure they know about it without knowing what the code word means."

"They're smart," Lytle said with a shake of his head.

"Even if it doesn't come to that, if they hear later that President Lavager was assassinated during this mission, they'll know there was a connection."

Tevedes sighed. "Yeah. No matter how hard you try, some things just can't be kept secret."

Planetfall, Atlas

The fast frigate CNSS *Admiral Nelson* was under power, a day away from Atlas orbit, when a government launch docked at her larboard personnel hatch to put aboard the pilot who would supervise her insertion into orbit. Unknown to the pilot or the launch's crew, the *Admiral Nelson*'s starboard cargo hatch was already open to the vacuum of space. As soon as the clangs of the docking launch sounded in the ship, a StealthGhost shuttle was ejected through the cargo hatch, the sound of its ejection lost in the noise of the launch's docking.

The navy's stealth lander, called the AstroGhost and used exclusively for clandestine insertions, was about the same size as an Essay, the navy's standard surface-to-orbit shuttle, though its cargo capacity was little more than half that of the Essay. The AstroGhost was matte black to make it almost impossible to see in visual except as a hole in the stellar background, and surfaced with a radar-absorbing coating to avoid detection by planetary warning systems. In addition, the plates of material it was constructed with had been assembled at angles designed to scatter any radar waves its coating didn't absorb. Which made an AstroGhost nearly impossible to detect during its approach to a planet's atmosphere.

But no matter how stealthy an orbit-to-surface lander might be on approach to atmosphere, the brilliant streak it made dropping through the atmosphere was impossible to miss.

Which was why the AstroGhost's cargo space was so much smaller than that of the similar-size Essay; it had a massive, hypereffective refrigeration unit that significantly slowed the burning of the ablative coating on the exposed surfaces. That cooling, combined with kilometers-long radiator strings that trailed it, was so efficient that an AstroGhost left no more atmospheric trail than did a meteorite barely big enough to make it all the way to the ground.

The major drawback to the refrigeration unit was that its initial installation was monstrously expensive, and its cooling elements and fluids had to be replaced after every use—again at considerable expense. Which expenses were the major reasons the AstroGhosts were strictly used in clandestine operations where entry couldn't be concealed by other means.

When the pilot's launch docked, the AstroGhost was ejected with enough force to quickly separate it from the *Admiral Nelson*. In twenty minutes it was more than a hundred kilometers aft of the starship, and the coxswain fired its heavily shielded engines long enough to send it on a collision course with Atlas.

Between its own shielding and the further shield offered by the firing engines of the *Admiral Nelson,* which was directly between the AstroGhost and Atlas, the firing went unnoticed by anybody planetside or in orbit.

Shortly after the AstroGhost's course adjustment, the Atlas pilot cut the *Admiral Nelson*'s main drives and made a minor course correction to drift her into her proper slot among the spacecraft orbiting the planet. An hour later, the AstroGhost, heading directly toward Atlas, was closer to the planet than the starship, which was aimed at an angle to achieve orbit. The pilot onboard the *Admiral Nelson* was just starting to make his final calculations to slide into orbit when the AstroGhost reached atmosphere.

It may have been a different vehicle, but the ride from the toposphere to the planetary surface was just as much a "high-speed ride on a rocky road" as planetfalls made by FIST Marines in a regular Essay. The only difference was, the Marines of second platoon didn't make planetfall over open water. The AstroGhost gently touched down in a forest clearing some three hundred kilometers from New Granum and several klicks from the nearest road. The landing zone and most of the area between it and Spondu and the Cabbage Patch facility were unpopulated, so it was highly unlikely that anybody would come to investigate the "meteorite," or see any sign of the Marines as they approached their objective.

Metsa Forest, Three Hundred Kilometers East of New Granum

"Clear space under those trees!" Lieutenant Tevedes ordered.

"Move, move, *move*!" Gunny Lytle shouted.

"You heard the man, let's see some hustle here!" Staff Sergeant Suptra commanded.

"In there!" Tevedes ordered, pointing at an area where spreading boughs covered a space barren of full-grown trees.

The Marines of second platoon, Fourth Force Recon Company, boiled out of the rear hatch of the AstroGhost and raced to the cover of the nearby trees. Armed with long knives, some of them immediately started chopping away at undergrowth and low branches; others grabbed the cut growth and hauled it deeper into the forest. HM2 Natron, the corpsman assigned to the mission, pitched in and helped.

In ten or twelve minutes, the area under the spreading boughs was clear of most growth. The Marines scrambled out of the way and the coxswain drove the AstroGhost into the makeshift hangar.

The AstroGhost's navigator-radioman jumped out, carrying a small parabolic dish trailing a cable, and clambered up the closest tree. He was back down in a couple of minutes and signaled Tevedes that tight-beam comm was established with the *Admiral Nelson*, which was nearing orbit.

Tevedes reboarded the AstroGhost and climbed into the cockpit. "Aerie, the Eagle has landed and the nest is secure," he said into the radio. He waited for the doubled bursts of squelch that told him the message was received. If the *Admiral Nelson* had any reason to suspect the entry had been detected, the reply would have been a triple squelch.

He handed the radio set to the coxswain and asked for the AstroGhost's locator reading, which he compared with his own. When he saw they matched, he said, "We should be back within forty-eight hours."

"We'll be here, sir. Good hunting."

"Thank you." Tevedes left the cockpit. When he got outside he found the platoon waiting for him in rough formation; the Marines had their helmets off so he could see them. They already had puddle jumpers strapped to their backs.

"We're exactly where we should be," Tevedes told his Marines. "Our objective is two hundred and ninety kilometers that way." He pointed north of due west. "We'll jump the first two-seventy klicks and walk the rest of the way. You know what to do when we get there." He grinned. "So let's hop to it."

With a minimum of talk, the Marines headed into the clearing where squad and team leaders checked the ultraviolet locator lights on their men's shoulders as soon as they donned their helmets. Gunny Lytle and Doc Natron checked each other, and Lytle and the lieutenant did the same. On Tevedes's order, the Marines fired up the puddle jumpers and rose twenty meters into the air before switching to level flight and heading a few degrees north of due west.

The area selected for the insertion was unpopulated,

chosen to reduce the chances of anyone seeing the
AstroGhost land or the Marines fly away from it with their
puddle jumpers. There were few roads and no regular air
traffic in that region of the Union of Margelan, so they
were able to make good time for the two hundred and seventy kilometers they traveled in thirty-klick jumps. An experienced Marine could average better than a hundred
kilometers per hour using a puddle jumper, and every
Force Recon Marine had that much experience. Flying
closer than twenty kilometers from their objective, they
ran a slight risk of detection by traffic to and from
Spondu.

After three and a half hours, mostly in the air, they
dropped the puddle jumpers and hid them to pick up on
their way back. They continued on foot. Rapidly for the
first ten kilometers, then at a more normal walking pace
for the next five. The last five they took at a slower pace.
They made the entire two hundred and ninety kilometers
without being noticed by anyone—except for a few animals that startled at nearby noises made by beings they
couldn't see.

CHAPTER
THIRTEEN

Somewhere in New Granum, Atlas

The man was very disturbed about what he had to do. But what had to be done could be accomplished only by a member of the inner circle, and he was one of the most central figures in that small circle. He hadn't approached any of the others, but he knew they were too blinded by their loyalty to Jorge Liberec Lavager to see what he was becoming, had become.

Early in his presidential term—a presidency he'd won out of the gratitude of the citizens whose army he'd led during the war that led to the current preeminence of the Union of Margelan among the nation-states of Atlas— he'd been a marvel in getting the disparate nation-states to cooperate, to the enrichment of all of them. And he'd seen to it that Margelan had maintained its dominant position among the nation-states. Margelan—and Atlas at large, thanks to Lavager—was more prosperous than it had ever been in the past.

But now he wanted to unite the entire world under one central government. He said that would only strengthen Atlas as a whole, that the Confederation of Human Worlds would necessarily pay closer attention to a united world than to a fragmented Atlas, that now Confederation members saw Atlas as a backwoods world, almost a world of savages who were almost constantly at each other's throats. He said that nobody elsewhere in Human Space took Atlas or its nation-states seriously.

But what Lavager failed to see, and the other members of the inner circle were too blind to see, was that the Confederation would see a united Atlas as a threat.

Too many shipping lanes passed near Atlas. The world's near-space, the area between its orbit and the orbits of the planets sunward and spaceward from it, was used as a convenient transfer point for cargos from one starship to another. Starships on long voyages made stops at Atlas to give their crews shore liberty—and didn't have to worry about crew members jumping ship.

But if Atlas was united, it could control interstellar shipping in its area. A united Atlas could charge dockage fees in its area and build a navy to enforce payment of those fees. A united Atlas could deny planetside rights to passing starships. A united Atlas would command a strong voice in the Confederation Congress on Earth. Balances of power would be upset—the powers who ran the Confederation of Human Worlds would be upset.

If that happened, the Confederation would take action. It would send its army and navy to Atlas, to crush any possible united government and impose its own regent on the world.

Now, a number of people on Atlas had power and riches in their own nation-states. Not as much as they would have in a united Atlas, and not as many as would benefit by uniting. But none of them would have anything like the same power or wealth under a Confederation regent. And what would they do without power and riches?

A core member of the inner circle, the man knew these things very well. He had received visitors from powerful agencies within the Confederation, and they had impressed upon him the truth of these things.

There was only one way to prevent the Union of Margelan—and the rest of Atlas as well—from becoming a ward of the Confederation. Jorge Liberec Lavager had to go.

The man was very disturbed about what he had to do. Jorge Liberec Lavager was an old friend of his.

But he had to do it.

A Private Residence in New Granum

The coffee cup looked tiny and fragile in the big man's hand.

"No one saw you coming here, I hope?" his host asked nervously. He couldn't keep his eyes off the big man's hand. For its size it was delicate, almost, hairless, the hand of a man who was unused to rough labor of any kind, not the kind of hand one would imagine belonged to an assassin.

"Thank you for the coffee," the guest replied sarcastically. "I understand the beans are grown right here in Margelan somewhere? Something you're working on at your secret facility near Spondu, the Cabbage Patch?" He grinned fiercely at his host and sipped the coffee. He ran his free hand through his closely cropped blond hair.

"Very funny, Mr. Germanian, or whatever your name is."

The big man nodded. "In my line of work a good sense of humor is essential." He sipped again from his coffee and then set the cup on the table. "Do you think I'm an amateur, General?" His voice had turned hard. "We've spent a lot of money on this operation and I'm here to see that it gets spent properly, that things get done right. You, personally, have a lot riding on this, my friend. If it goes off smoothly, we will spend even more money to put you into the top slot. We've done that in other places for other clients, and we can do it again. For you. Now, what have you been able to put together for us?"

They were sitting in a back room in a big house in an exclusive neighborhood on the outskirts of New Granum.

Since his host was so well known in the city, the big man had agreed to meet at the general's home to finalize the arrangements they were discussing.

"I've put together a team of assassins, all men from other nation-states. Reliable men, professionals. They are currently occupying safe houses in the city, waiting for the signal to proceed. I will not kill him in New Granum; it's got to be done outside the city. On the way to the Cabbage Patch there's an ideal spot that we've already reconnoitered. They just need advance warning to get in place out there."

"Can you get him to go out to the Cabbage Patch?" Germanian smiled at the name of the facility.

"Sooner or later, yes. I've mentioned a trip to him several times. With all that's happened recently, especially the death of Dr. Paragussa and the murder of that reporter, Gustafferson, I think he wants to go out there just to be sure security's in place. The truth of the matter is, everyone's curious to know what's going on out there, especially our friends from South Solanum. We've been surveilling several of their agents based right here in New Granum. I'll see to it that they are arrested as soon as the job is done."

The big man smiled cryptically. "Why is the place called the 'Cabbage Patch,' if I may ask?"

His host shrugged. "Lavager gave it that name. He told me once he got it from a book by the French philosopher Voltaire. *Candide.* Did you ever read it? I didn't think so. It ends with Candide attending his cabbage patch, giving up politics. It's a dream Lavager's had for himself for years to retire and become a nobody again."

"He's your friend, isn't he?" the big man said as he reached for his coffee cup.

"Yes," his host answered, his voice heavy. "He's also one of the greatest men I've ever known. He's a greater man than I'll ever be," he added bitterly.

Germanian grinned and sipped his coffee. "This really is an excellent blend. Have you ever read the Judeo-Christian Bible, General?"

"What? I'm familiar with it, of course, but I'm not a Judeo-Christian, Mr. Germanian."

"You really ought to read one of the books in it, the Book of Job. God made a bet with the Devil that Job couldn't be turned against him. The Devil lost that bet. We're counting on winning this one." He grinned and finished his coffee. "That ought to tell you exactly whose side you're on, General." He laughed as he poured more from the silver pot sitting on the table.

"I do know about Judas," the General said softly. "All about him."

"Have you checked your off-world account lately? There's a lot more than thirty pieces of silver in it, General. Judas ended up badly. You'll die rich and in bed—if this is done right."

"I've led armies, Mr. Germanian, I can pull off a little ambush, don't you think?"

The man called Germanian looked carefully at his host over the rim of his coffee cup. *He will do it,* he thought, *but he's beginning to have second thoughts. That reference to the Biblical Judas spoke volumes about his state of mind.* Out loud he said, "I need to see a layout of the ambush site." He nodded at the reader sitting at one end of the coffee table.

"This is the main road to the Cabbage Patch. It's the one we'll use. Right here is where the team will be waiting for him. He'll be in a three-vehicle convoy, him in the middle vehicle, me in the lead vehicle. My men will take out Lavager's car and make their escape to this road here, the one on the other side of the cornfield running parallel to the main road. You'll see," he zoomed out, "there are no dwellings within kilometers of this site except those of the farmer who owns these fields. The whole thing will be over before the farmer even knows what's going on in his fields. The harvest is weeks away yet, so there's no reason for anyone to be working in that field."

"Good. Now give me the crystal."

"Wh—?"

"Give it here, General. You don't want to be caught with the damned thing. Your men have been briefed? They know the lay of the land? Escape routes have been laid out? Good. You won't need this anymore then. I presume, and I'd better be right, there are no copies." He took the crystal and slipped it into a pocket. "Let me know as soon as the team is in place." He stood up. "Well, I must be off now. Thanks for the coffee. I'll see myself out." He paused at the door, turned, and looked back at his host. "General, everything has its price. Your price to be President of Margelan is to kill your friend." He shrugged. "Read the Book of Job. Screw this up and what he went through will look like the common cold compared to what'll happen to you. I guarantee it, and you know who I work for." Grinning, he turned and left.

The man with the scar on his face held his beer mug loosely in one hand, a massive, hairy hand that was missing its little finger. He looked steadily at the big man sitting on the opposite side of the booth. To him the man looked like nothing more than a soft fairy, someone he could easily take down, if the need arose. But he was paying the bills.

"The general sends his regards and me with this," the big man said, shoving a fat envelope across the table. The man with the scarred face tore off one edge and examined the contents. He raised his eyebrows. "That's just expense money," the big man said. "When the job's done, the second half of your fee will be deposited in your accounts."

"Check."

"That farmer? Take him out and anyone else you find

on the place. Your back has to be secure," the big man said.

"Check."

"Take out all the vehicles in the convoy. There can be no survivors."

"Check."

"Your men are ready? Weapons secure? Everyone knows his job?"

"Check."

"Very well, then. As soon as the job is done send me the signal we agreed on and the rest of your money will be deposited for you."

Outside the sleazy bar the man who called himself Heintges Germanian (or Wellers Henrico on occasion, or a dozen other aliases) paused to take in the night air. What bumpkins these Atleans are, he mused. As soon as Lavager and his escort were dead, the crystal in his pocket would appear as if by magic in high places. If any of the assassins survived they would never be able to identify him. Maybe next time he could perform the hit himself. He loved the challenge of an assassination and the rush he got from the actual killing. But this time orders were to arrange the job differently. Nevertheless, he would have blood before this operation was over.

Back in his hotel room Germanian changed. He regretted having to cut his beautiful blond hair for this assignment. He removed his neck scarf. It contained the device that altered his voice. He smiled to himself. Finally, a scarf that performs a useful function. Only two people in the agency that employed him knew who he really was. Actually, he wasn't big, he was buxom. Heintges Germanian was a woman.

CHAPTER
FOURTEEN

Room 1007, New Granum DeLuxe Inn, Union of
Margelan, Atlas

Sergeant Ivo Gossner came out of the water closet already dressed. Lance Corporal Bella Dwan was in bed still asleep.

Despite what she'd said when they checked in, once Dwan had finished unpacking, she'd moved their bags to the luggage racks and they'd slept side by side, or rather back to back, with no physical barrier between them.

Gossner stifled a groan. While he was in the water closet, Dwan had kicked the covers off. She slept in a lightweight, hip-length pullover and green panties, which peeked out from under the pullover. She stirred in her sleep, and through the pullover, he could clearly see her breasts move. He closed his eyes and took a steadying breath.

Down boy, he thought. *That's the Queen of Killers.*

When he opened his eyes again, she was looking at him. She smiled and stretched languidly. "Good morning," she mumbled sleepily.

"Morning," he mumbled back.

She stopped stretching and lay still, looking at him, her body curved and her near arm curled on the bed with its hand next to her cheek. "What's the matter, Ivo?" she said in a purr that sounded to him like a happy cat about to pounce on a mouse. "You've seen me stretching before."

"Right. But not dressed like that." Her pullover had

moved up when she stretched, and a narrow strip of belly now showed between its bottom and her panties. To distract himself, he went to the kafe maker and dialed a cup for her. He almost spilled it when he turned around; she was standing barely a meter from him, hands clasped low behind her arched back, chest sticking out. Her nipples made clear bumps in her thin shirt.

"For me, Ivo?" she said sweetly, and took the cup. She continued to look at him as she took her first sip.

That was when he looked into her eyes. Any impression he may have gotten that she was attempting to seduce him, or at least signaling her availability, vanished instantly—her eyes were the cold killer's eyes he'd always seen, not those of a desirable woman.

"I'm through in the head," he said gruffly. "Get in there, get cleaned up, and get dressed, Lance Corporal. We're going out to spend the day making like tourists."

"Yes, Sergeant. Right away, Sergeant. Whatever you say, Sergeant." She turned and headed for the water closet.

Gossner stared after her. Had she really winked at him as she turned? Was she *really* twitching her bottom at him?

Government District, New Granum

After breakfast in the hotel dining room, Gossner and Dwan spent the morning in the government district, not because they were tourists, but because they were on a scouting mission. They agreed the government district was the most likely place to find their quarry. Like the governments of most worlds in the Confederation, the Union of Margelan had a tripartite government with executive, legislative, and judicial branches, each of which in New Granum had its own unimaginatively named complex.

They started at the Executive Center, a complex of

buildings that faced a flagstone-paved plaza some four hundred meters long and one hundred and fifty wide. Gardens filled the spaces between buildings.

A helpful, uniformed docent—her nametag said "Becky"—gave them a tour. "That is what some consider the center of gravity of our government," the young woman said, gracefully pointing at a massive stately building, faced, as were all the other buildings in the Executive Center, in a tightly grained pink limestone. "It's called Presidential Hall. President Jorge Liberec Lavager's office is right there." She pointed at a row of windows on the second floor of the building.

"The five windows in the middle, that's the president's office?" Dwan asked, sounding appropriately awed.

"Yes, right there in the very center of the building," Becky almost chirped. "It's symbolic of the president's being the center of the government!"

"Why are the walls blank to the sides of those windows?" Gossner asked. There were no windows on the second floor for a distance of twenty meters on either side of the five into the presidential office.

"Umm. I believe there are storage and office machinery rooms behind the walls there, rooms that don't need windows." Becky shook her head. "I don't know for certain, though. I've never been in there. I mean, I *have* been in Presidential Hall, and I've even been in President Lavager's office, I mean I've never been in the rooms next to his office."

More likely at least one of those rooms is a guard room, Gossner thought. *And the security people probably have a way of seeing through the walls to the plaza.*

Docent Becky pointed out the other buildings around Executive Plaza and told Gossner and Dwan more about the functions of the Commerce, State, War, Communications, and Treasury Ministries—each of which had its own building on the plaza—than either of them wanted to know.

The most important building, even bigger than Presidential Hall, was home to the Agriculture Department. It and its attendant gardens occupied the entire length of the plaza opposite Presidential Hall. The gardens were part of the tour. Gossner and Dwan were far more interested in the gardens than they were in the administration department buildings.

"Are all of the gardens between the buildings crops?" Dwan asked.

"Yes!" Docent Becky preened. "Atlas is an agricultural world, and the Union of Margelan is the major food producer in the whole world. Not only do we grow nearly all of our own food, we export huge amounts to the rest of Human Space. So it's only natural that our government honor farming by having crop gardens in its center." She waved a hand to indicate the gardens between the buildings.

"Many Earth-native foodstuffs have taken to the soil and climate of Atlas as though they evolved for a place just like this," Docent Becky told them in a tone and cadence that suggested she was delivering a lecture she'd already given too many times. "They don't just thrive here, often they prosper better than in their native lands. Wheat and the whole broccoli family grow almost twice as big on Atlas as on Earth, and are even more nutritious, which is why they are major exports, highly regarded and desired imports on longer-settled worlds. Our tubers and legumes are also highly prized on many worlds, as are our nuts.

"Some of the vegetables have made adaptations that are simply amazing. The most amazing adaptation is corn. Ten thousand years ago, hunter-gatherers reached South America on Earth, where they found a grain with a head only slightly larger than wheat. For reasons nobody can even guess at, they cultivated that unassuming grain and over centuries its head grew larger and larger until it became what was called maize. By a thousand years ago, when the first Europeans arrived in what they called the

New World, maize had become so totally domesticated it couldn't grow on its own anymore, it could only grow if it was cultivated—deliberately planted.

"On Atlas," her voice abruptly became sprightly, "corn is beginning to grow wild again. Not as a small grain like the first hunter-gatherers found, but with the large ears we've been used to for the past millennium or longer."

Bella Dwan *ooohed* and *aaahed* at that. Docent Becky beamed.

"Other worlds are very interested in our strain of corn," Becky said proudly, "and want to see if it will grow in their farms. They think corn that doesn't have to be meticulously planted will be more economical to grow and feed their populations!"

"You keep talking about crop-foods," Gossner asked. "What about meats or fish and fowl?"

"We have all the major Earth-native mammal and avian food animals, but there's nothing special about them compared to the animals grown on other worlds," she said. "And we have the Atlas-native rambuck and lambhawk, but they aren't domesticated enough to have sufficiently large herds and flocks that we can export them. Crops are our main export foods, though some seafood, such as the arthropoid called the dalman, are prized as gourmet foods on other worlds."

She went on to tell them about the Earth-native fruits and nuts that grew on Atlas, for each pointing out a sample tree or bush growing in the gardens. From there she went on to a brief catalog of Atlas-native fruits, vegetables, and nuts that were suitable for human consumption.

"If you haven't yet," she said, "you really must go to a local restaurant and try some dishes made from native foodstuffs. Some of them are really delicious." Her face briefly saddened as she said, "Unfortunately, we haven't had much success in exporting our native foods, other than a few gourmet items."

Gossner spoke up for only the second time since they entered the gardens. "Maybe that's because they're exploiting their own native crops, and aren't ready to introduce exotic foods from other places."

"You're probably right," Docent Becky said, resignation in her voice.

What Gossner had really been doing during the tour of the gardens, of course, was examining them and the area close behind as possible locations for Dwan to ambush President Lavager—and then make her escape. In chameleons, it would be a snap—provided they could get the unchameleoned maser rifle into and out of the spot he and Dwan picked for her to fire from without raising any suspicions. Dwan had also studied the gardens with a sniper's eye, but was able to give enough attention to the docent's presentation to keep Becky happy and feeling fulfilled in her job.

They volubly thanked her for the marvelous tour of the gardens and moved on to the Judicial Center.

It was a repeat of the Executive Center, though writ smaller and its buildings were faced with orange limestone rather than pink. Crop gardens grew between the buildings there just as they had in the Executive Center. They didn't bother with a tour.

They headed on to the Legislative Center, which was half again as large as the Executive Center.

Gossner suddenly stopped in the middle of Legislative Plaza and asked, "Have you ever been in a capital city before, Bella?"

It took a conscious effort for Dwan not to shoot Gossner a glare for asking such an irrelevant question, but she remembered her role in time and simpered at him. "No I haven't, Ivo. But this one certainly looks very impressive."

Centered on one side of the six-hundred-meter-long plaza was Congress Hall, which took up nearly half the plaza's length. The Legislative Gardens flanked the building for most of the rest of that side. Opposite Congress

Hall was a row of well-spaced, imposing buildings—separated by more crop-growing gardens—which contained the offices of the legislators and all the staffs of the legislation. The windows of the facing buildings, including Congress Hall itself, began well above ground level, giving them something of a fortress appearance; most of the buildings in the other two governmental centers also had windows that began above ground level. A pyramidal tower was at one end of the plaza and an incongruously globular building, neither with windows, at the other. They were faced with white limestone.

Gossner stopped in the center of the plaza and slowly turned about. Dwan, her arm linked in his, of necessity also stopped. When he turned, their linked arms moved her around him like a satellite.

"I've been in a few," he said. "And you know what?"

She gave him a look that to any casual observer looked like admiring expectation, but up close carried a threat. "No, Ivo. What?"

"They all look alike." He stopped turning and shook his head. "It doesn't matter what architectural style they are in, the buildings are always massively imposing and widely spaced. It's like they're trying to impose themselves on all who see them, to impress everybody with their importance and power."

Dwan's eyes widened, as though she was thinking how smart and perceptive her new husband was. In reality she was thinking, *You turned me around you like some empty-minded bint to tell me the obvious?* But she said no such thing. Instead, she looked from him to the buildings and used their linked arms to turn him around her as she had just been turned—the turn was facilitated by her free hand, which she used to grip the thumb of the hand at the end of the arm with which hers was linked and lever it in a modified come-along. She made a show of looking at the buildings with newly enlightened eyes.

"You're right, Ivo!" she squealed. "They *do* look deliberately impressive and imposing." She gave his thumb a little extra jerk, then released it and patted his hand before raising hers to flutter at her throat.

Gossner managed to not flinch or otherwise show pain. When she released his thumb, he half-turned and leaned close, as though to kiss her cheek. "Sorry, Bella," he murmured, "I didn't spin you around on purpose."

She smiled and nuzzled his cheek. "Don't do it again," she whispered. Then more loudly, "Ivo, I'm getting hungry. Let's go and have lunch someplace. Can we do that?"

"Anything for you, my love," he said as, under cover of patting the hand linked through his arm, he put her in a wrist-cracking come-along. Leaning close, he whispered, "You may be nasty, Bella, but I'm bigger and stronger. Besides, I outrank you."

Dwan showed her teeth when she smiled up at him and asked, "How fast can you wake up and defend yourself when somebody crushes your larynx while you're sleeping?"

Gossner remembered something someone once told him: "The greatest sign of trust you can display in someone is to fall asleep next to that person." He released the come-along with a murmured apology.

Scott Park, New Granum, Union of Margelan, Atlas

They didn't head straight toward the entertainment and dining district, but made a brief digression to a small, empty park just off Central Boulevard and sat on a tree-shaded bench. They sat close, with their heads together, looking to any casual observer like lovers.

"So what'd you think?" Gossner asked.

"Give me a set of chameleons, and maybe," Dwan answered. She didn't look totally sure of herself when she said it.

"We don't have a set of chameleons. Even if we did, the

maser we have isn't chameleoned, we'd have to find another way to get it in without anybody noticing and raising an alarm." He looked up at nowhere in particular for a moment's thought, then turned his face back to hers. "Even without chameleons, you could get into the gardens and hide well enough that nobody would know you were there."

She grimaced. "There're a couple other problems with doing it there."

Gossner didn't ask, he was pretty sure he knew what one of the other problems was. He was right.

"Did you look at the windows in his office? There was something off about the way they reflected light. I think they're reinforced with something. They're probably resistant to projectiles. I don't doubt they'd also deflect microwaves."

"Yeah," he agreed. "I wouldn't be surprised if they could resist a sustained burst from a plasma assault gun—at least for long enough for anybody inside to get out of the line of fire."

Dwan nodded.

"So what's the other problem you see?"

She grimaced again. "I'd have to do it when Lavager is entering or leaving the building, and that would make it a tough kill. He's sure to be surrounded by guards and aides when he goes out, which might make it hard to get a good sight picture on him."

Gossner raised an eyebrow. Bella Dwan was admitting to the possibility she couldn't get a good sight picture?

"More important, he'll be moving. That'll make getting a three-quarter-second lock on him very difficult, if not impossible, even for me."

Gossner didn't even need to think about it. "So we scratch doing it in the government district. We'll have to check out the Presidential Residence; maybe that'll be easier."

"Is he giving a speech someplace any time soon? If he's standing on a stage out in the open, that would be easiest."

"We can find out. Still hungry?"

"Yeah." She said it without enthusiasm.

"Hey, we don't know yet, we may not have to do it."

"Maybe not," she said softly. "But I want to."

Gossner gave her an encouraging squeeze—he didn't dare think of his gesture as comforting.

"Thank you," she murmured. They got up and left the park, heading down Center Boulevard, the main thoroughfare in New Granum's entertainment and dining district—where, by chance, they happened on Jorge Liberec Lavager's favorite restaurant, right there on Center Boulevard, not far from the hotel where they were staying.

CHAPTER
FIFTEEN

Ramuncho's Restaurant, New Granum, Union of Margelan, Atlas

A few blocks from the park, they stopped in front of a discreet sign that bore the name "Ramuncho's Restaurant" and looked at the menu mounted on an easel next to the entrance.

"Are those local dishes, or did the printer have a bad case of speaking in tongues when he programmed it?" Dwan asked.

"At this point, your guess is as good as mine," Gossner replied. They'd only been on Atlas for two days and hadn't yet experimented with the local cuisine. At Pauke Falls they'd simply pointed at 2-D pictures of the food they ordered, and otherwise had eaten at their hotel, which served more or less standard Confederation fare that could be found in nearly every chain hotel in Human Space.

"Do you want to go in and find out?" she asked.

"One reason I signed up was to go to strange places, eat strange foods, and meet strange people," he said softly.

"And kill them," she added even more softly.

Gossner's eyebrows twitched up. "That too." He glanced around, but no one was close enough to have overheard.

The interior of Ramuncho's was muted: dim lighting,

green-on-green damasked wallpaper above dark wood wainscotting; thick, sound-absorbing carpet covered the floor; folding screens placed here and there that could be opened to provide a modicum of privacy. A diminutive and graceful fluted flower vase with blossoms neither of them recognized stood on every table. The task light centered on each table was so soft that even the snow white cloths that covered them seemed muted.

The maître d' gave them a moment to look, then was happy to seat them without a reservation; it was past the lunch rush and many tables were available. He began ushering them to a table to one side of the main dining room, though not against the wall.

"Oh, could we have that table, please?" Dwan smiled sweetly.

He looked where she pointed, a table with a discreet "reserved" sign in front of the windows onto the street, and cocked his head for a moment's thought before saying firmly, "Most certainly, madame."

"I bet a lot of famous people walk past these windows," Dwan gushed.

"They assuredly do," the maître d' confirmed. "And come in, as well. Why, at this very table," he said as he held a chair out for her, "our President, the great Jorge Liberec Lavager, sometimes dines." He deftly removed the "reserved" sign.

"Really?" Dwan squealed, eyes wide.

"Sometimes. Ramuncho's is his favorite restaurant, you know, though most often when he comes he dines in a private room in the back."

"Do you, do you think he'll come in today?" Dwan said so rapidly her words ran into each other. "Could I meet him?"

"Ah, but no, madame. I had to pause before allowing you this table, as I had to remember whether he was in New Granum at this time. But I remembered that a member of his staff called to say he wouldn't be dining here today as he is away on government business. The President must often go to other parts of the country, you understand."

"So you're saying," Gossner said with casual-seeming interest, "that you normally keep this table reserved for him?"

"Indeed, sir." The maître d' nodded. "As well as the private room he often uses."

"Really!" It didn't seem possible, but Dwan's eyes opened even wider. "That's amazing." The words came out in an awed whisper.

"The President eats here often enough to have both a table and a private room reserved for him," Gossner said, sounding impressed.

"It's true, madame and sir. We at Ramuncho's are quite proud of having our President's patronage."

"I believe it."

A moment later the maître d' left them. A human rather than robot waiter took their drink orders and left them with menus. They sat at adjoining sides of the table rather than opposite each other.

Dwan leaned toward Gossner and her eyes flicked toward the maître d', who was back at his podium. "How do you think he manages that?" she whispered.

"Manages what?"

"To be officious and obsequious at the same time."

Gossner managed to look at her with a straight face. Sometimes the Queen of Killers surprised him, and that was the second time of the day. Who would have thought Bella Dwan even *knew* the word obsequious, much less was able to use it correctly?

"I think they program that into maître d's at the factory," he finally whispered back.

She giggled and returned her attention to the menu.

Damn, but her giggle sounded downright girlish. If Gossner hadn't known her so well he would have thought . . . No, it wasn't possible for the Queen of

Killers to turn human just because she was on an independent assignment, away from other Marines.

One leaf of the menu had the standard fare found throughout Human Space, the facing leaf was local dishes, presumably made from native foodstuffs.

Suddenly, Dwan leaned in again, her eyes glittering. "What do you think 'Alborda Tag Bika Here' is?"

"Where?" Gossner searched his menu, narrowed his search when she said, "Halfway down the local menu," and found it. He shook his head. "I have no idea, there's no description."

She leaned close and said under light giggles, "It looks like somebody who doesn't know the language tried to write 'false large bull balls' in Hungarian."

Gossner couldn't manage a straight face this time, he had to blink in surprise. "Hungarian?"

"You know, Hungarian. The old European language? From Earth?"

"I know what Hungarian was."

She smiled sweetly. "But you didn't think I did."

"I'm surprised you can read it."

She grinned impishly. "I can do a *lot* of things you don't know about." She wiggled on her seat, as though pleased at scoring a point.

He twitched his eyebrows—that wiggle reminded him too much of her twitching bottom as she headed for the water closet that morning—and said "I guess so," then returned to the common foods on his menu. After a moment he said, "It's probably not a good idea to order the reindeer steak here."

"Oh? Why not?" Dwan looked honestly interested. They spoke in soft voices so they couldn't be overheard by the staff.

"It's a Thorsfinni's World dish. This far from Thorsfinni's World, there's no telling what kind of meat they might use. For all we know, it'd turn out to be a cut of kwangduk." He shuddered.

"Have you ever had kwangduk?"

He nodded. "Once. In a stew. It's not an experience I care to repeat."

She laughed lightly and whispered, "And here I thought you were a tough Marine."

He grunted, then continued examining the menu. After another moment, he said, "We're on a strange world with its own cuisine, what am I doing looking at the items I could get anywhere? I'm going to just ask the waiter to recommend something made from local ingredients." He shook his head. "They've got 'Grande Milho Bolo' listed as an entrée. I think that's Portuguese, and it sounds more like a dessert than an entrée."

Dwan gave him a gracious nod. "I'm surprised you can recognize Portuguese. I think asking for the waiter's advice is an excellent idea."

"I've been around," Gossner muttered, and started to look for the waiter; the waiter was at his elbow before his head made more than a quarter turn.

"Yes sir, are you ready to order?"

"Listen," Gossner said, stifling his surprise that the waiter could reach him so quickly without him noticing his approach, "everything on the menu sounds so good that I don't know what to order." He stopped and shook his head. "No, they don't. My wife and I," he put a possessive hand on Dwan's; she turned her hand palm up and interlaced her fingers between his, "we just got here and really don't have any idea of what the local foods are. But we want to try them. What do you recommend?"

"Oh, sir and madame! May I recommend—" The waiter began spouting words in no language Gossner knew, but he recognized the "dalman" in the description of appetizers, "rambuck" and "lambhawk," and the word "sauce" somewhere in the middle, and the final description concluded with, "—to perfection." The waiter looked at them with proud expectation.

Gossner and Dwan exchanged a glance, she gave a

nearly imperceptible nod. He turned to the waiter and
said, "Thank you, that sounds—very interesting. We'll
start with the dalman appetizer, and share the rambuck
and lambhawk entrées." He also ordered a half-bottle of a
local vintage.

"You will be delighted, sir and madame." The waiter
took the menus, dipped his head and shoulders in a bow,
and glided away to place their order.

Once he was gone, the sniper and her team leader
leaned in close enough their shoulders touched and their
heads nearly did as well, and looked at Center Boulevard,
the buildings across the way, and the byways between the
buildings. Gossner didn't say anything at first, he was still
a bit shaken by the way the waiter had appeared as soon as
he began to look for him. He wanted to be *very* careful of
what he said in the vicinity of people who could move that
stealthily. Dwan picked up on his unease and touched the
corner of her brow to his.

"Listeners?" she asked in the soft voice combat troops
develop that is clearer than a whisper, but doesn't travel as
far.

"Possible," Gossner said back.

She left her head where it was, they'd look more natural
if they were in intimate contact while not speaking than if
they sat silent while not close. They studied everything
they could see without turning their heads, committing
everything to memory—a sniper's memory.

The waiter came back with a trio of dishes and, with a
flourish, placed one in front of each of them. One held
two shelled arthropoids, the dalmans, and another a sauce
neither of them recognized. The waiter showed them how
to crack the dalman shells and pluck the meat from them.
The third dish, he demonstrated, was for the empty shells.

They'd barely had time to finish the dalmans when the
entrées arrived, delivered by four waiters; one controlled
the cart, two placed empty plates in front of them, then set
plates with the food within easy reach of both, the fourth

opened a bottle of wine and poured for Gossner to approve, then filled both their glasses. Gossner said, "Thank you," and the quartet bowed themselves away.

Neither Gossner nor Dwan had any idea what it was they were eating, but both enjoyed it tremendously.

"Thank you, Mother Corps," Gossner murmured when they were finished.

Dwan cocked an eyebrow and gave him a simpering smirk. "Already?" Then she turned to the original waiter who was approaching with the dessert tray.

Gossner groaned when he saw the tray; he hadn't considered the possibility of dessert while he was eating most of the two entrées served to them. Even so, he managed to eat a slice of pie filled with some local fruit that vaguely reminded him of apples, while Dwan had something that looked fatally chocolate.

"*Now* you can thank Mother Corps," Dwan said softly when they finished their desserts and coffee and the bill had been presented.

Gossner looked at the total and nearly blanched. He could never afford prices like that on his own income, and he hoped the Marine Corps's accountants didn't challange this particular expense too vigorously. He paid, including an appropriate gratuity, with one of the creds they had been given to cover expenses.

On the way back to their hotel, Dwan said, "When we get back to our room, it'll be *your* turn to strip down to your skivvies and take a nap while *I* watch."

Gossner tightened up and stared straight ahead, not daring to speak or even look at her.

She laughed aloud at his discomfort.

Room 1007, New Granum DeLuxe Inn

The first thing they did when they got back to the hotel was to scan for observation devices. When they didn't find any, Dwan checked for messages from the *Admiral Nelson* while Gossner lay down for a nap, but he didn't strip to his skivvies. Dwan giggled at him once—damn, but if he didn't know who that giggle came from—then reverted to the professional she was.

The *Admiral Nelson* had no messages for them.

He'd eaten enough that he didn't feel like going out again right away when Dwan woke him after a short nap, but she had other ideas.

"Up and at 'em," she said, poking him in the ribs when he rolled over after her first attempt to make him get up.

"I rank you," he mumbled, "you don't tell me when to get up."

"Do you remember what I told that customs agent at Kraken Interstellar when we got here?" she asked.

"What?"

"I said I was going shopping. We've got all those creds, and I intend to spend my share of them on things other than fine dining."

"So go shopping." He snuggled more comfortably into his pillow.

"Ivo," she said sweetly, "do you know what a newlywed husband's job is when his new bride goes shopping?"

"What?" he asked suspiciously.

"Pack animal. Now get up and come to lug and tote for me. It'll look very suspicious if anybody notices a brand new bride shopping without her hubby to carry for her."

Gossner groaned, but he knew she was right. He rolled over and sat up. "Yes, dear. Give me a minute to wash the sleep out of my eyes."

She looked at her wrist. "One minute. I'm timing you."

"I never would have guessed you'd turn into a nag as soon as you got married," he grumbled as he made his way to the water closet.

She laughed.

* * *

They got back to the hotel four hours later. Sergeant Ivo Gossner was loaded down with parcels. The parcels weren't heavy—after all, they only contained a few souvenirs and lots of clothing, mostly women's clothing, souvenirs which were lighter than a similar amount of men's clothing would have weighed—but there were so damned *many* of them. Gossner felt like he'd been dragged around to more stores than there could possibly be in downtown New Granum, and something was added to his burden in each of them.

Lance Corporal Bella Dwan, on the other hand, carried only one oversize handbag slung over her shoulder containing two small packages with what she referred to as "female necessities that you needn't worry your sweet little head about."

Gossner dropped his burden on the bed and they chatted inanely about the shopping expedition while they scanned the room for bugs.

When they didn't find any, he said, "You're going to get yours when we get back to Camp Howard, Lance Corporal."

"All these new clothes! Would you like me to model them for you, sweetheart?"

He tried to glare at her, but was distracted by an odd crinkling at the corner of her eyes. What was that? If those weren't the eyes of the Queen of Killers . . .

"I'm going to find a way for us to get out of here without being seen," he said gruffly, and left.

"Don't be long," she said. "I'm hungry after all that shopping." She turned to her purchases and went through them while he was gone.

He was back in less than twenty minutes and nodded his approval at how she was dressed. The colors of her shirt and pants were muted, matte grays and blacks, yet their pattern was festive. They looked like they'd been designed for a conservative dresser who nonetheless wanted to look filled with gaiety. She had laid out similarly patterned and colored garments for him. The patterns and colors would make very good camouflage at night.

"At least the whole shopping trip wasn't a waste," he said as he picked up his clothes and headed for the water closet to change. She made a face at his retreating back.

After eating they returned to their room, and slipped back out a few minutes later.

Near Ramuncho's Restaurant, New Granum

The streets were brightly lit and noisy with lively vacationing tourists and locals out for an evening of theater, dining, or partying in nightclubs. People constantly brushed against and bumped into each other in the boisterous crowds and had to shout for their companions to hear them. But in the service and access alleys behind and between the buildings, it was quiet and dark. There was nobody to note the two shadows that occasionally seemed to hump bigger than they had been and move from here to there, and nobody could have heard the shadows, because they were as silent as shadows should be.

Gossner and Dwan moved slowly and carefully, sliding soft-shod feet over the pavement, searching for obstructions and objects that might make noise when they stepped. They probed ahead and to the sides with their hands for obstacles their feet wouldn't encounter. The pavement seemed to hold the usual amount and assortment of detritus to be found on city alleys, haphazardly lined with frequently overflowing trash receptacles. Almost anybody could be excused for tripping, kicking, or bumping into noisemakers while negotiating them in the night—or during the day, for that matter. But Gossner and Dwan weren't almost anybody, they were Force Recon Marines, and knew how to move silently though worse places than this; unlit city alleys posed no problem for them. They didn't speak until their reconnaissance was complete, and they vacated the shadows of the alleys for the shadows of a nearby park, where whispered male and female voices from the bushes wouldn't cause comment.

"Two places I can do it from," Dwan said when they were huddled close in a clump of low-lying bushes. Their backs were to a windowless wall and they could see all approaches to the bushes. "But in one of them, I have to be too close to the street, there's too good a chance someone will spot my mazer."

Gossner grunted softly in agreement. "Civilians bother me," he said back. "If there are people on the street, someone might walk into your line of fire while you're shooting and block enough of your shot to just make the target sick."

Now that they were really planning it, Jorge Liberec Lavager was no longer President Lavager, he wasn't even a person; he was simply "the target."

"I need a higher place. Maybe farther back."

"I thought I saw something while we were at lunch. Let's go and check it out."

"Lead the way."

They went back into the service alley, to a building that backed onto it opposite one of the access alleys that gave a view of the front of Ramuncho's Restaurant. During the day, Gossner had gotten the impression it was vacant. A broken ground-level window gave them access to the building's basement. They had to move by touch in the darkness, but that was not difficult because the basement seemed to be empty. The stairs to the ground floor were sound and the door at their head ajar; it squeaked slightly when Gossner eased it open, but he lifted up on it and the squeaking stopped. They inspected the ground floor, which was easier than finding the stairs in the basement because of the street light that came through the front windows. The ground floor was empty. The second floor was also empty.

Gossner squatted and brushed his fingers against the

floor. "It hasn't been vacant long," he whispered. "No dust."

Dwan nodded, and went to look out the back windows. Right away, she found one she liked for the mission. Then she wanted to check the third, top, floor. As they expected, it was vacant as well.

Their inspection of the spaces behind Ramuncho's wasn't as successful, even though they found several spots from which a sniper could fire through the windows of the back rooms—they didn't know *which* windows were to the private room Lavager normally used.

Reconnaissance complete, they returned to the hotel.

CHAPTER
SIXTEEN

Near the Cabbage Patch, Forty Kilometers northeast of New Granum, Union of Margelan, Atlas

Clouds were gathering in the east when second platoon, Fourth Force Recon Company, went to ground in a dense stretch of forest one and a half kilometers from the suspected weapons research facility-manufactory.

Lieutenant Gott Tevedes transmitted a directional burst message: "First squad, you know what to do?"

Sergeant Jak Daly clicked his transmitter twice for "Yes."

"Any questions?" Tevedes transmitted.

Daly clicked once; he had no questions.

"Second squad," Tevedes radioed, and asked the same questions of Sergeant Wil Bingh. Bingh replied with the appropriate clicks; he also knew what to do and had no questions.

"Do it."

Daly and Bingh signaled their men, and the eight Marines rose to their feet and headed for the former weapons factory now called the "Cabbage Patch." Second squad followed behind first squad, fifty meters to its left. Daly carried a passive mapper; it would scan everything he pointed it at, but didn't use a range finder so its depth perception wasn't totally reliable. Bingh carried a scope with face recognition capabilities to take a census of the personnel in the Cabbage Patch. The only data they had on who was in the compound was a rough head count of the military garrison, but that count probably wasn't reliable. The identifier would make a record of every individual it saw and prevent any of them from being counted twice.

Until they returned to the AstroGhost, they were on full combat footing; it took more than an hour for the two squads to cover the 1,300 meters to their first observation location.

The Confederation Navy string-of-pearls-generated topographic maps the platoon used weren't the most up-to-date maps available to the Marines, but they were the most detailed. The map of the Cabbage Patch and its environs showed a shallow dip in the side of a hill two hundred meters east of the facility and above it. The buildings and roads shown on more recent maps were superimposed on the topo map. The hollow was shallower than the decades-old topo map indicated, and many of the game trails marked on it no longer existed; the trails that were still there showed scant sign of recent use. Nor did all the buildings in the Cabbage Patch complex appear on the map. Several of them looked to be of very recent construction.

Daly was glad the hollow was shallower than the map showed; the Marines would be able to lie comfortably on its slopes and watch in all directions with nothing but their heads exposed outside it; if it had been deeper, they might have had to cling to the sides.

Using touches, Daly positioned everybody. He placed Corporal Nomonon to watch the rear; Sergeant Kindy and Lance Corporal Wazzen had the flanks. He took his own place overlooking the Cabbage Patch complex after Bingh signaled that second squad was in its observation position to their south.

President Lavager of the Union of Margelan publicly claimed the Cabbage Patch was an agricultural research station. Force Recon was sent in because it was known to have been a weapons factory, and now its security was tighter than could be accounted for by its claimed use—it was more like the security one would expect in a top-secret military research station. The visible and easily-detected-by-other-means security the Marines observed was even tighter than intelligence reports had led them to believe.

The compound was a rough rectangle with its northwest corner chopped off, truncated by the New Granum road, which ran southwest to northeast. Inside the main gate off the road was the administration building. To its right was a cluster of small buildings that looked to be housing; a probable dining hall was adjacent to them. On the admin building's left was a vehicle barn—at least that's what the map said. During the time Daly watched, he saw several ground cars and lorries enter and not leave, so the map legend was likely right.

Those buildings and a multistory structure behind the admin building were the original buildings in the compound, and were oriented on the road.

The rest of the buildings were laid out on an east-west or north-south axis, though "laid out" wasn't an accurate term—they seemed to have been thrown up wherever there was space as the need for them arose. According to the map, the building directly south of the original lab was another laboratory, the building to the south of the garage was labeled a barracks. Judging by the uniformed people Daly saw entering and leaving it, he thought that was likely. A small mess hall was south of the barracks, with a military office building to its east. To the east of and between the two labs was a large power plant; the map said so, and it looked like one. Daly wondered what kind of agricultural research could require a power plant that big.

Then there were buildings not on the map. A barracks was southwest of the second lab, another lab was east of the power plant, an unidentifiable building was in the southwest corner, and a foundation for another building had been laid to the barracks' east. North of the new foundation was a field on which a platoon of soldiers was running combat-maneuver drills. North of the drill field was a short-takeoff-and-landing airfield with hangar and control tower. A tall communications tower stood in the center of the compound.

The entire complex was surrounded by a razor-wire fence of alternating aprons and tightly wound coils. The fence would be very difficult to penetrate without explosives or sustained bursts from a plasma-firing assault gun. The platoon didn't have any assault guns, but it did have explosives. Unfortunately, the platoon carried little more than the exact amount of explosives they would need to blow up the suspected weapons buildings intelligence knew to be in the Cabbage Patch when the orders for the mission were drawn; there wasn't any spare to use to blow holes in the defensive fence. To make matters worse, there was a trench outside the wire. From his vantage on the hillside, Daly could see the trench was filled with sharp stakes, making it extremely difficult and dangerous to traverse as well.

It's too bad we left our puddle jumpers behind, Daly thought, *we could use them to get over the trench and wire*. The defenders would be able to see the puddle jumpers themselves, but would likely hesitate before opening fire on the unidentified and apparently unmanned objects. When they did open fire, they probably wouldn't be able to shoot many—maybe none—of the invisible Marines during the short time it would take them to jump over the trench and wire.

The perimeter fence was backed up with fifteen reinforced guard towers and at least fourteen bunkers. Later, after his squad had made a complete circuit of the compound, he found there were eighteen bunkers in all. Each of the towers housed an assault gun.

Now, if we could manage to get the towers to fire on the fence and trenches, they could open paths for us, he thought, though he couldn't think of a way to get the defenders to destroy their own first line of defense.

A quick calculation told him the garrison had to be perhaps two companies strong, allowing for four soldiers per tower and bunker, plus command and communications, and allowing for a reserve. It could easily be larger if the bunkers held more than four men each, or the commander had a rapid-maneuver force in addition to a reserve.

He didn't see any communications trenches inside the compound, but that didn't preclude the existence of tunnels for reserves and maneuver forces to move through.

Daly drew his men together and told them what they were going to do next. Then he and Wazzen headed south while Kindy and Nomonon went north. They'd move a hundred meters closer to the perimeter and circle the compound to get a closer look. They would rendezvous on the other side of the road opposite the main gate.

On the way around the perimeter, Daly stopped to check on second squad. Fortunately, Bingh had positioned his men exactly where they'd planned; between the chameleons and their skillfully hidden positions, second squad might otherwise have been impossible for Daly to find.

Daly touched helmets with Bingh so they could talk without using their radios and asked, "How many have you seen?"

"So far we've identified seventy-five different soldiers walking around or on the drill field," the second squad leader answered. "I saw a major, maybe he's the commander. And eighteen different people in lab coats, though I wouldn't swear all of them are scientists—some of them are probably lab techs, and I think at least one was a cook or messman."

"What about admin or other civilians?"

"Two drivers parked their lorries in the garage and went into the admin building. Nobody else went in or came out."

"Guard towers?"

"The light's too poor for identification, but it looks like there are four people in each. I couldn't detect anyone in the bunkers."

Seventy-five on the ground and sixty in the towers, a hundred and thirty-five. That accounted for two-thirds of the minimum number of soldiers Daly thought were in the garrison. *If* the garrison had equal-size watches, there were probably another sixty or seventy asleep or otherwise off duty or out of sight. Not counting any who might be in the bunkers.

"What about the main gate?"

"It's too far away to make out enough detail. There are eight individuals, but the scope couldn't pick up enough data to identify them."

"Good job. Keep looking." Daly told Bingh what his squad was doing, then clapped him on the back and touched Wazzen to let him know to continue the circuit.

Detectors the Marines carried showed them the locations of mines, both antipersonnel and antivehicle, that were buried just under the surface of the ground between the forested hillsides and the trench, as well as a variety of telltales to detect infrared radiation and motion. The infrared detectors didn't cause them any problem, but the motion detectors forced the encircling Marines to keep farther inside the trees than Daly wanted to. He plotted all the mines and detectors on his map.

Kindy and Nomonon were waiting for them in the trees across the road, two hundred meters from the main gate.

"The bunkers on my side all seem to be unmanned," Kindy reported as he touched helmets with Daly. That jibed with what Daly and Wazzen had seen on their circuit.

"Secondary gates?" Daly asked.

"None that are obvious."

Daly hadn't seen a back gate either. He found it curious that the compound wouldn't have any way in or out other than the main gate. Every military installation he'd ever seen had at least one back gate. So did nearly every civilian complex he'd ever seen.

"Any activity here?"

"Nothing."

"Let's watch for a while."

The four Marines settled in to observe the road and the entrance to the compound, and the admin building just inside it. Daly checked the time. It was a few minutes shy of 16 hours. Most government and military installations had a shift or watch change at 16 hours. Maybe they were about to see some activity.

Nobody came out of the admin building's front door, but at 1615 hours, a group of people in civilian clothes exited the side of the building and headed for the housing area, and a second group exited on the east side. They joined other people, who were probably coming from the labs behind the admin building, in entering the vehicle barn. Minutes later an air-cushion passenger carrier drove out of the garage, through the main gate, and headed northeast, the direction of Spondu.

No night shift, Daly thought. *Not unless the night shift lives in the housing units.* He could only see half of the housing area from his position.

A few minutes after the bus left, a guard sergeant marched eight soldiers up the road along the east side of the admin building to the main gate where they relieved the guards on duty. The guard sergeant marched the relieved guards back the way he'd come.

Not long after that, four lorries came from the southwest, the direction of New Granum. The guards at the gate made them wait outside until the officer of the guard came out to admit them. The officer directed them to follow the road to the west of the admin building, then returned to it. He was the only person they'd seen enter or leave the building through its main entrance.

When nothing else happened for a half hour, Daly decided they'd watched the front long enough.

"Look for a tunnel entrance on the way back," he told Kindy and Nomonon. The squad again split into two-man teams to return to the shallow hollow where they'd started watching.

Daly stopped to check with second squad again. He and Bingh touched helmets.

"We identified another hundred and fifteen soldiers, including the gate sentries during the changing of the guard," Bingh reported. "We'd already identified some of the guard sergeants, and we didn't get face shots of all the soldiers who were heading to the gate."

"That's two hundred and fifty positives on the garrison, plus others not positively identified."

"Right."

"Tell me about the tech shift change."

"We identified thirty-six individuals coming out of the labs. There were more, but we couldn't ID all of them because they were too far away, or we couldn't see their faces. We didn't ID any of the people who went from the admin building to the housing area. Do you want to know about the thirty-three who left on the bus?"

"I don't think that'll be necessary," Daly replied. "Whatever we do here will be done before they come back. Anything else?"

"Yeah. Nobody entered or left the power plant."

Corporal Musica, who was using the scope while the squad leaders conferred, poked his helmet in and said, "Six more."

Daly and Bingh looked at the compound. Soldiers were walking from the barracks to the mess hall.

"Another five," Musica said.

There were at least two hundred and sixty soldiers in the compound, and only one way in or out. The platoon didn't have the equipment or materials it needed to breach the outer defenses. And the compound didn't look anything like an agricultural research station—there wasn't a greenhouse to be seen.

"Give me what you've got," Daly said.

Bingh used his hands to orient himself with Daly, then tight-beamed the scope's data to the first squad leader's comp.

"Give it one more hour," Daly said when the data transfer was finished, "then return to the hollow. Look for a tunnel entrance on your way back. I just can't believe there's only one way in and out of that place."

"You got it," Bingh said.

On the way back to the hollow Daly divided his attention between looking for a tunnel entrance and preparing the data the recon had collected into a packet he could send to the *Admiral Nelson* via burst transmission for relay to the platoon.

CHAPTER
SEVENTEEN

In the Trees, North of the Cabbage Patch, Union of Margelan, Atlas

Sergeant Kindy and Corporal Nomonon didn't return to the hollow by the same route they'd followed on their first circuit; they followed a route seventy-five meters farther upslope and deeper into the trees. They did that partly because good troops never follow the same route returning as going out, and partly because Kindy wanted to see if there were mines and detection devices farther out from the fence and trench.

And partly because he and Nomonon hadn't seen anything that might be a tunnel or cave entrance the first time around. He'd looked. He hadn't spent as much time observing the compound as Sergeant Daly had, but he'd noticed the lack of an obvious back gate and, like Daly, couldn't accept that there wasn't another way out.

Halfway from the New Granum road to the hillside where the hollow was, he spotted an anomaly. He and Nomonon were paralleling a game trail that was just as neglected as every other game trail in sight of the fence; the game trails so close to the Cabbage Patch didn't show as much use as the trails he'd seen farther away from it. The anomaly was, the trail abruptly seemed to have slightly heavier use.

"Where'd they go?" he murmured, unheard inside his helmet.

He stood erect and Nomonon came close behind to touch helmets.

"Where'd they go?" Kindy repeated, this time to the other Marine.

Nomonon looked around and saw the same slight-but-abrupt change in the game trail. "Maybe they saw something they didn't like and turned back," he said facetiously. He kept looking around.

Kindy in the meantime had concentrated his attention on a slab of rock right where the game trail changed.

"Look for a camera," he told Nomonon as he squatted for a closer look at the rock slab. He was careful not to touch anything, though he wanted to brush dirt off the rock's surface. He slid his light gatherer and magnifying screens into place.

And saw faint scrape marks on the ground where the slab of rock had been swiveled aside.

Nomonon bent over to touch helmets and said, "I have a camera."

Kindy slowly rose to his feet, careful not to move his feet so they wouldn't disturb the ground under his boots. Nomonon put his arm around Kindy's shoulders and turned him to face the tree where he saw the camera. "Three meters up," he said.

Kindy looked up and spotted the camera. It was small, camouflaged to look like a leaf dangling from a branch close to the tree's trunk. But the camouflage wasn't well maintained; if it had been, a visual search from ten meters away wouldn't have spotted it. The camera was aimed at the slab of rock. Unless it was a wide-eye, except for Kindy's feet they were outside its field of vision.

"Keep looking," Kindy said. He and Nomonon stayed in position for another ten minutes looking for another camera without seeing one. Either the others were better camouflaged, or there was only the one. From the state of the camouflage on the camera they saw, Kindy's guess was there wasn't another.

A Hillside East of the Cabbage Patch

Sergeant Daly and Lance Corporal Wazzen reached the hollow first, even though Sergeant Kindy and Corporal Nomonon had a shorter distance to cover. Daly assumed it was because they'd found the tunnel, or something else of interest. Time was passing and he had to make a report, he didn't have time to wait for them to come back. He climbed a tree to establish a comm connection with the orbiting *Admiral Nelson*.

The navy starship hadn't remained docked at Kraken Interstellar, but trailed it in the same orbit by two hundred kilometers in order to facilitate communications with the covert operation of the Force Recon platoon on the ground. Nobody on Kraken gave the separation any thought; it was Confederation Navy policy that ships of the line didn't remain docked to civilian starports any longer than necessary. The difference was the degree of separation; single navy starships normally didn't remove themselves much more than one hundred kilometers from an orbital port, but Kraken didn't know that—Atlas was seldom visited by an unaccompanied ship of the line.

Kraken Interstellar was barely visible to the naked eye, nearing the horizon when Daly climbed the tree, and the *Admiral Nelson* was only a few degrees higher. He didn't have much time to make his report, but it was long enough for a burst transmission.

He found the *Admiral Nelson* in the sights of his point-transceiver and activated it to lock onto the starship. When the transceiver signaled it had a lock, he touched the contact that sent the one-and-a-half-second burst. As a failsafe, he had the transceiver programmed to send the burst automatically five seconds after it registered it had a lock. A much longer delay, and the lock might be broken.

Before descending the tree, Daly studied the clouds headed toward them from the east. They looked like they were dropping rain, but the rain didn't look so heavy that

it would have an effect on their operations even if it
reached them. He was on the ground minutes before
Kindy and Nomonon returned with their surprise.

Five Kilometers East of the Cabbage Patch

The radiomen in the *Admiral Nelson*'s comm shack were
every bit as alert as the Marines needed them to be, and
they relayed Daly's burst in plenty of time.

"Sir, we got a burst," Gunny Lytle reported.

Lieutenant Tevedes sucked in a deep breath. He accepted the packet Lytle tight-beamed to his comp and
called the data up on his HUD. "Are you looking at this,
Gunny?" he asked.

"Yessir."

"No crop fields, no greenhouses. What kind of agricultural research station is this?"

"One with a lot of soldiers," Lytle said pensively.

"Too many soldiers."

"Guard towers, bunkers, razor wire, stake-filled
trenches, peepers and mines all around. It looks like
they're ready to repel a major assault."

"What kind of agricultural research station expects a
major assault?"

Lytle didn't bother answering, Tevedes knew the answer as well as he did.

"Have the men saddle up, we're moving in."

"Aye aye, sir."

Near a Game Trail, Four Hundred Meters North of the Cabbage Patch

"Let's go," Sergeant Kindy finally said.

And froze before he took a second step.

A *click* had come from the rock slab.

Kindy put out a hand and gently swept it in an arc until
he found Nomonon. Using a series of taps and arm

squeezes, he told him what he wanted to do. Nomonon replied with a return touch. Normal communication between men who must maintain silence, even radio silence, and can't see each other except as the faintest of smudges even in infrared, is impossible; Force Recon had a vocabulary of touches and squeezes to use in those instances when they couldn't even touch helmets.

Kindy and Nomonon watched the rock lift a few centimeters, then pivot to expose a meter-wide hole. A head popped through the hole and looked quickly around, then was followed by the rest of a man in an unmarked military uniform. He was unarmed. The man didn't bother looking around again after climbing out of the hole, but went straight to the tree with the badly camouflaged camera and flipped a chunk of rugged bark aside to reveal a small control panel. The control panel's cover was far better concealed than the security camera was.

Kindy watched closely as the man tapped a five-touch pattern on the control panel, and was certain he could repeat the sequence.

The rock slab pivoted back over the hole and settled into place. Again without looking about, the man stepped onto the better-used part of the game trail and headed northeast. Kindy touched Nomonon and the two Marines soft-footed after him.

In fifty meters, Kindy judged enough trees were between them and the tunnel entrance to be completely out of sight of the security camera. He touched Nomonon's arm and the two Marines sprang forward. They were on the man in the unmarked uniform before he was fully aware of the footsteps running behind him. Nomonon took him at the shoulders, bending him forward, while Kindy threw his shoulders into the back of the man's knees, buckling his legs. They hit the ground hard. The force of the landing, and being sandwiched between the ground and Nomonon, knocked the air out of the man's lungs—he couldn't even gasp, much less yell, before

Nomonon had him in a choke hold. In seconds his eyes rolled up and he went limp, unconscious.

"Grab him and go," Kindy ordered, touching his helmet to Nomonon's.

Nomonon got up, then hoisted the unconscious man onto his shoulders in a fireman's carry. The two Marines sprinted.

After fifty meters they slowed to a pace Nomonon could maintain indefinitely with his burden, then came to a complete stop a hundred meters later when the prisoner began to regain consciousness.

Kindy unsheathed his combat knife and held it to the man's throat. "Make noise and you're dead," he said harshly through his helmet speaker. "Do you understand?"

The prisoner's eyes darted about, trying to see the source of the voice, then looked down to see what was pressing against his neck. He couldn't see the talker, but the blade of the knife that pressed against his throat was highly visible. He tried to nod, but was afraid of cutting himself. "Yes," he croaked softly, not wanting to cut himself by speaking, either.

Inside his helmet, Kindy smiled—he had the back of the blade against the man's throat, he also didn't want the prisoner to get cut accidentally.

"We're going to tie your hands and take you with us. Do we need to gag you, or can you keep quiet on your own?" He eased the pressure of the blade.

"I-I'll be quiet."

"Good. Then maybe you don't have to die." Kindy jerked the knife away as the man's eyes popped and he began to tremble violently. He stood and yanked the prisoner to his feet. Nomonon secured his hands behind his back and tied a length of cord snugly around his neck, but not so tight it cut off his air.

"We're going to move fast," Kindy said. "Keep up or it's going to hurt."

The prisoner's eyes widened even more and he fish-mouthed, unable to speak. They searched him before they set out. He had a wallet with civilian identification and cred chips, but nothing else. Certainly no military documents or weapons.

Kindy set a fast enough pace to keep the prisoner worried about keeping up, but not so fast he was in real danger of falling.

A Hillside, East of the Cabbage Patch

A *click* announced the return of Kindy and Nomonon. Daly whistled in surprise when he saw the bound prisoner stumble out of the trees.

"That's the best birthday present I've gotten all year," he said through his helmet speaker so the prisoner could hear him.

"We caught him coming out of a tunnel," Kindy said, also through his helmet speakers.

The prisoner looked wild-eyed for the sources of the voices, visibly upset by so many invisible men.

"What's your name?" Daly demanded.

The prisoner's mouth worked, but he couldn't form any words.

"Answer the man," Kindy demanded.

The prisoner flinched from the harsh voice next to his ear. He tried again and managed to gasp out, "Nijakin—Lucyon Nijakin."

"What's your rank, Lucyon?" Daly said with a glance at the unmarked uniform.

"N-No rank. I'm a-a c-contract worker."

"What are you working on?"

"M-Machinery."

"What kind? What do you make with it?"

"Tools. T-Tools and p-parts. I-I'm a m-machinist."

"What kind of machines do you make parts for?"

"I d-don't know."

"You can't be a very good machinist if you don't even know what kind of machines you're making parts for."

"M-Manufacturing."

"What kind of manufacturing?"

Kindy poked him and whispered harshly, "Stop wasting time."

Nijakin flinched again and looked around wildly. "Th-they make t-tubes. Tubes and bl-blades."

"Tubes like barrels? Blades like knives?"

Nijakin looked uncertain, like he didn't understand the question.

Wazzen reached in and gave the prisoner a sharp but light tap on the back of the head. "Speak up," he snarled. "The tubes, are they barrels for weapons?"

The man jumped and looked even more frightened at being questioned by yet another unseen person.

"Y-Yes. I-I d-don't know. Th-They could be." He nodded vigorously. "N-Nobody t-told me."

This could be it, Daly thought. "How big are the barrels?"

Nijakin's shoulders twitched as though he was going to lift his hands to show him. His expression went from frightened to resigned sadness. "Some are two hundred centimeters in diameter." He also stopped stammering.

Daly shook his head. Lucyon Nijakin now believed they were going to kill him. He decided to reassure him.

"All right, everybody leave him alone, he's cooperating. Listen to me, Lucyon—right, your name is Lucyon? Relax, nobody's going to hurt you. We just want to know what's being done at the Cabbage Patch. You're being very helpful, and I appreciate that. When we're finished here, you'll be free to go. Do you understand?"

"Yes." Nijakin's voice was flat, obviously he didn't believe Daly.

Daly sighed softly. "I'm telling you the truth. Now, those two-hundred-centimeter tubes, how long are they?"

"Ten meters. Maybe longer. I don't work on them, they're made in a different lab. I don't see them very often."

"What were you doing coming out of the tunnel alone?"

His mouth twitched. "There's a woman, she's a tech, she lives in Spondu. I was going to see her."

"Is she going to call someone and ask where you are when you don't show up on time?"

Nijakin hung his head and shook it.

"Why didn't you leave through the front gate with everybody else?"

Nijakin sighed. "They think I'm a security risk. I'm confined to the compound." His mouth twisted. "That's why Mari won't call when I don't show up. She knows that sometimes I can't get out."

"Aren't you concerned about being reported when security saw you through the surveillance camera when you left the tunnel?" Kindy asked.

Daly glanced toward his voice. He knew there had to be a camera in the tunnel, but hadn't known the entrance was also covered by a camera.

"I have a friend," Nijakin said. "He puts a loop in the system when I go in and out so security doesn't see me."

"When are you supposed to go back in?" Daly asked.

"An hour before sunrise." A tear leaked out of the corner of his eye.

Now Daly knew how they could get into the compound. "Where is it?" he asked Kindyon on a tight-beam.

Kindy tight-beamed the coordinates of the tunnel entrance and the visuals he'd taken of the entrance setup. Daly examined the images on his HUD. Yes, that was how they could get in.

"What have we here?" Sergeant Bingh asked as he and his squad slid into the hollow.

"Kindy, tell them."

Kindy took the second squad leader aside and touched

helmets to catch him up on his and Nomonon's discovery of the tunnel entrance and their capture of a prisoner.

"I have to keep you tied up so you can't run away," Daly told Nijakin, "but I don't want to gag you. Can you keep quiet?"

"Yes. Nobody in the compound could hear me if I yelled anyway. We're too far away."

"Are you thirsty? I can give you a drink if you're thirsty."

"No, I'm not thirsty." Lucyon Nijakin almost laughed. He thought it ironic that a man who was about to kill him would be so solicitous.

CHAPTER EIGHTEEN

A Hillside Near the Cabbage Patch Agricultural Research Facility, Union of Margelan, Atlas

"Sorry, sir," Sergeant Daly said when Lieutenant Tevedes arrived with the rest of the platoon. "Second squad didn't bring him in until after I sent my report."

"That's all right," Lieutenant Tevedes said, eyeing the prisoner. He and Daly stood facing each other, only a meter apart, talking over tight-beam radios directed at each other's torso pickups so nobody else could receive.

Lucyon Nijakin knew more invisible men had arrived even though nobody had told him and he couldn't see anyone for himself. There were more minor sounds to tease his ears and taunt him—and it *felt* like he was in the middle of a larger crowd by then. His demeanor went from resigned sadness back to active fear.

"What have you gotten out of him?"

Daly gave the officer the short version of his interrogation of Nijakin, which amounted to little more than, "It sounds like they're making artillery or rocket components."

"What's the place look like?" Daly transmitted his map visuals and the summary of Sergeant Bingh's census.

Tevedes studied the material for a moment, then said, "I hope you don't mind, Sergeant, but I want to question him myself."

"Please do, sir. I imagine you'll come up with questions I didn't think of."

"What's his name?"

"Lucyon Nijakin."

Tevedes squatted down in front of Nijakin and turned his external speaker on at low volume.

Nijakin flinched, and pressed his back into the tree trunk he sat against. He'd been right, there were more people, this was a voice he hadn't heard before. His lower lip trembled.

"Mr. Nijakin, how big is your garrison?" was the first thing Tevedes wanted to know after he asked the same questions Daly did to establish who the prisoner was and his position in the Cabbage Patch.

"I-I'm not a soldier, I don't know exactly how many. There are more than two hundred soldiers. Maybe three hundred, that's all I'm sure of." He visibly hesitated, then added, "There could be even more, I just don't know." He tried to shrug, but it turned into a shudder. "I don't have much to do with the soldiers."

"What about scientists and technicians? How many of each?"

Nijakin thought for a moment, moving his lips as though he was naming them to himself. "There are nine scientists. Each of them has three or four lab assistants. I guess they're what you'd call techs—wait, Dr. Kabahl, I think he's the chief scientist—he's the scientific administrator, anyway—has six lab assistants. Then there are twenty-five of us machinists and other skilled trades, we've got I think twelve helpers." While he talked he got control of his expression and finished by looking at where he thought Tevedes's face was, doing his best to look helpful and cooperative.

"How are these people armed?"

"The soldiers have soldier weapons. I've never been a soldier, I don't know what—"

"I mean you people, the machinists and techs," Tevedes interrupted. "How are you armed?"

Nijakin looked shocked by the question. "Armed? We're civilians. We aren't armed; we aren't soldiers!"

Tevedes didn't reply to Nijakin's denial, not that he necessarily believed him. Instead he asked, "Administration. How many?"

"There's Dr. Truque, he's in charge of the center. Secretaries, accounting, payroll—seven or eight people altogether. I'm not sure, maybe ten. I don't have much to do with them, either, except—" He stopped.

"Except?" Tevedes prompted.

"Except—" Nijakin paused, "—there's a woman . . ."

"A woman?"

"Y-yes."

"Do you like her?"

Nijakin looked down to the side and nodded.

"Does she like you?"

"I think so," he said weakly.

"Well, Mr. Nijakin, let's try to get you back to her quickly. You're being very helpful. Now, is there anyone you haven't told me about?"

"Nossir. That's everybody I can think of," Nijakin said.

"So you're telling me there are nearly four hundred people in the facility, and more than three hundred of them are soldiers. Is that right?"

"Yessir, close to four hundred, that sounds about right."

"How many of the scientists are agronomists or biologists?"

Nijakin blinked and looked puzzled. "All of them! What other kinds of scientists would you expect to find at an agricultural research center?"

"If the Cabbage Patch is really an agricultural research facility," Tevedes asked sarcastically, "why does it need so many soldiers?"

"Atlas is an agricultural world," Nijakin blurted. "Food

production is power here. The center needs the soldiers in case some other country tries to steal our secrets. The Union of Margelan has enemies who . . ." His eyes and mouth suddenly formed large "O"s. He thought furiously, these invisible men, they spoke with some kind of accent. What was it? Did it sound like—yes it did! "You're from—"

Tevedes stopped Nijakin by pressing invisible fingers to his lips. "Where's the other end of the tunnel you came out of?"

"I-It's on the side of the power plant facing l-lab three."

"Which one is lab three?"

"It's the b-building next to the p-power plant, t-to the east of the p-power plant."

"How is the entrance guarded?"

Nijakin shook his head. "I-It's not g-guarded."

"Is it locked?"

Nijakin shook his head again. "It d-doesn't even have a d-door."

Tevedes called up Daly's map on his HUD and examined it. If the inside entrance to the tunnel was on the east side of the power plant, that put it in sight of the new barracks to the south. That shouldn't be a problem for his Marines, not with their chameleons. And it was only twenty meters from there to lab three, which meant they could easily get into the lab and see positively what was there.

"There's a communications tower in the middle of the compound, radio and microwave. What other communications are there?"

"Th-That's everything."

"No other communications? No buried wires?"

Nijakin's eyes wandered to the side for a moment, as though he was lost in thought. Then he shook his head. "No, n-nothing that I kn-know of."

"What are the dimensions of the tunnel? I mean how wide and how high?

"It's two meters high and a meter wide." Nijakin decided to seem helpful and cooperative again and his stammering stopped again. "It's made of fused lithocrete and has motion-sensitive lighting."

"Thank you, Mr. Nijakin. You've been very helpful."

Nijakin tensed, expecting to be shot or garroted.

Tevedes did neither. Instead he asked, "Are you hungry? If you are, I can have your hands untied long enough for you to eat and drink something."

Nijakin's stomach growled.

"That sounds like you missed dinner."

Nijakin couldn't help saying, "The condemned man's last meal, is that it?"

"Nothing like that, Mr. Nijakin. When we're done here, you'll be free to go."

Tevedes turned off his external speaker and toggled on his command circuit radio. "Gunny, have the Doc check the prisoner for anything obvious, then have somebody give him a meal. Keep his feet tied while he eats, and secure his hands again when he's finished. Join me when you've done that."

Tevedes made sure his UV markers were on so Lytle could find him, and went off by himself to plan the raid.

Gunny Lytle joined him a couple of minutes later and touched helmets. "What do we have, Lieutenant?"

"Call up your map." Tevedes linked Daly's overlay of the compound into Lytle's HUD and made a mark on the side of the power plant.

"From what the prisoner says, it sounds like Lavager is making advanced weapons components in this supposed agricultural research facility. If anybody wants to believe it's farm equipment, I have a solid gold asteroid I'd like to interest them in.

"We'll take the platoon in through the tunnel at two hours, everybody but the duty guards should be asleep then. This is where the tunnel lets into the compound." He highlighted the mark on the side of the power plant. "The first thing we'll have to do is destroy the communications tower." He marked it. "I'll go into lab three," he marked it as well, "with one squad from first section to collect evidence—Daly and his people have done all the hard work, they should get the job of gathering the proof of what they found. Do you agree?"

"I was going to suggest first squad if you didn't," Lytle agreed.

"Once we have the evidence, you bring the rest of the platoon out of the tunnel. The rest of first section sets the charges while second section provides security. We should be in and out in less than half an hour. Any questions?"

"It works for me."

"Good. How's our prisoner doing?"

"Doc says he's okay, just more scared than he's probably ever been before. Bos gave him a ration." Lytle chuckled softly. "He's eating like somebody's forcing him to. I believe he thinks we're going to kill him."

Tevedes snorted. "Yeah, I know. What he doesn't know is we're Confederation Marines, we only kill people who need to be killed. Mr. Nijakin doesn't need to be killed." He paused for a moment to consider what he wanted the prisoner to know. "He thinks we're from one of the other nation-states on Atlas. Let's not disabuse him of that notion."

"I like the way you think, Mr. Tevedes," Lytle said.

"Did Doc give him a sedative?"

"No. He said Nijakin would probably think it was some kind of poison pill, and didn't want to scare him any more than he already is."

"Good thinking on Doc's part," Tevedes said. He paused, looking west, toward the compound that was looking more and more like a weapons research facility. "One more thing I'm thinking about."

Lytle made an expectant noise.

"I'm wondering if we have enough yet to justify sending the go code."

Lytle had been wondering the same thing. He had a few more years, about three or four, experience as a Marine than Tevedes, but the lieutenant had more training due to Officer Candidate College. While Lytle was certain some officers would decide the strong defenses of the facility, combined with what the machinist told them, was convincing enough to justify sending the go code, they didn't have actual physical proof. Assassinating a sovereign head of state was too serious for anything less. "If the lieutenant's asking my advice or opinion, I think we need to get our hands on hard proof before you make that serious a decision."

Tevedes nodded; it was all right that Lytle couldn't see the nod, it was to himself more than to the other Marine. "I do believe you're right. I like the way *you* think, Gunnery Sergeant."

Lytle chuckled. "I'll get the platoon ready to move."

"You do that."

Lytle stood and went to check that the platoon was ready while Tevedes prepared a report to burst beam to the *Admiral Nelson* and a message for the starship to relay to the waiting AstroGhost. When the *Admiral Nelson* was overhead he climbed a tree, located her, and beamed his messages. He got the acknowledging click, then returned to the ground. All that was left now was to wait for the time to enter the tunnel.

En Route to the Cabbage Patch

Sergeant Kindy and Corporal Nomonon led the way to the tunnel, the ultraviolet markers on their shoulders allowed the others to see them to follow. Tevedes had ordered everyone to use their markers; he thought the risk of detection was less than the risk of somebody getting lost. On Tevedes's order, Kindy fingered the bark of the tree with the ill-camouflaged security camera and found the control panel cover. It flipped open easily. Too little starlight shone through the foliage for him to see, but his fingers found the keypad easily enough. He looked at the pad in infrared and saw the faint outlines of the keys. Six of the keys glowed slightly, as though they retained heat from recent use.

Kindy hesitated. He was positive Nijakin had only touched five keys to pivot the rock slab back into place, so why did six keys look like they'd been used? Did it use different combinations for opening and closing? He remembered the prisoner had said he had a friend who put a loop in the system when Nijakin used the tunnel. Maybe the sixth button sent a signal to his friend. But Nijakin was still secured to the tree behind the hollow, so he couldn't ask. He keyed in the sequence he'd memorized.

With a faint *click,* the slab rose a few centimeters and pivoted to the side.

Corporal Nomonon immediately sat next to the opening and swiveled to lower his legs into it. His feet found the rungs of a ladder and he climbed down. The hole was about six meters deep. At its foot, using his light gatherer screen, Nomonon saw a control panel like the one imbedded in the tree above. He had to turn around to face into the tunnel. He raised a hand to feel for the ceiling; it was low enough that he had to duck to keep from banging his helmet on it. He took a step and froze when lights came on ahead of him.

He peered, the lit area extended thirty meters ahead of him. He took a couple more steps and the lighting extended an equal distance ahead.

"Any problem?" Sergeant Daly asked.

"No, just checking."

"Let's move, we want to be well away from here by sunrise."

Nomonon stepped out at a brisk walking pace. The tunnel was wide enough for a man to walk without brushing the walls.

Kindy paused a couple of seconds to look at the control panel at the foot of the hole. In infrared it also showed sign of six buttons being used. It took only a five-key sequence to open and close the entrance, and he wondered again what the sixth key might be used for.

Watch Office, the Cabbage Patch

Private Second Class Handquok's head jerked up at a chime and he shook his head. He blinked at the bank of displays. Most of them showed the same unchanging views that had been boring him to sleepiness for two hours. Then he saw an unexpected red light. He checked the monitor matched to the telltale, but saw only the expected darkness under the trees of a moonless night. He leaned forward and tapped the light with a fingernail. It stayed red.

"Hey, Sarge?" he called.

"What's up?"

"Look at this. The telltale says the tunnel's outer door is open."

Sergeant Oble, the sergeant of the guard, leaned over Handquok's shoulder and looked at his displays. Sure enough, the indicator light for the outer tunnel door said the tunnel's door was open. The monitor didn't show anything because it was too dark.

"Hit the infra," he ordered.

Handquok flipped the toggle that switched the exterior security camera from visual to infra. It was long enough since sundown that most of the built-up ambient heat from the ground and the rock slab door had radiated away; the differences in radiation were too slight for Oble to tell if the slab was in place.

"Try the tunnel cameras." Oble's jaw dropped when the monitor showed the lights in the tunnel were on. The lights were motion activated, but nobody was there!

"I don't know what the hell's going on, but whatever it is, it's wrong." He rushed to his own desk and slapped the panic button.

Alarms sounded in the barracks and the officers' quarters.

The Cabbage Patch

It was just as Nijakin had said, the inner end of the tunnel was on the east side of the power plant and was unsecured. Unlike the outside end, which ended in a vertical, the inside end of the tunnel had a stairway leading up to a short corridor to the exit; eight Marines were able to stand back to belly in the corridor.

Corporal Nomonon looked both ways, then signaled all-clear into the all-hands circuit. Second squad ran past him and turned sharp left to race to the communications tower. Nomonon stepped through the door on the side of the power plant. Sergeant Daly followed him.

"Let's go," Daly said. He and Nomonon sprinted the short distance to lab three. Sergeant Kindy and Lance Corporal Wazzen followed right behind them, racing with Lieutenant Tevedes. Tevedes put on an extra burst of speed at the end and reached the door to the lab just ahead of Daly.

Tevedes turned his head and grinned at the squad leader, unmindful that his grin couldn't be seen inside his chameleoned helmet. He reached for the doorpad and pressed. The door silently swung open and he led the way inside.

Once the door was securely closed behind them, the Marines projected a combination of infrared and low level visual light to see by.

The part of lab three they were in looked like an assembly shop. Tubes of various sizes, up to seventy-five centimeters in diameter and seven meters long, were stacked against two walls—Daly didn't see any of the two-hundred-centimeter diameter tubes Nijakin had mentioned; he wondered if the machinist had been wrong or lied to him. Or maybe the bigger tubes had been removed. Rows of bins ran the length of the room's central area. Between them were matrixes, some of which held tubes and other parts from the bins in partial assemblage.

Daly sucked in a breath. The partly assembled things looked like barrels for advanced artillery pieces or rocket launcher tubes.

"That's it," Tevedes said through his speaker. "Set your charges." He headed for the exit to tell Gunny Lytle to deploy second section for security and get the rest of first section ready to set their charges. He'd have to wait until the *Admiral Nelson* was back above the horizon before he could send the go code to the sniper team in New Granum.

Daly directed his men in setting their explosives. Nomonon and Wazzen set theirs to do the most damage to the parts stored along the walls while Kindy set his to the building's main structural supports. Daly set his own under the bins in the central area.

Second squad ran to the communications tower while second section poured out to take their defensive positions; fifth and sixth squads went north to secure the area facing Lab One, the housing area, and the STOL field. Seventh and eighth squads went south to secure the approaches from the barracks.

Lance Corporal Thalia of seventh squad was the first Marine to reach the southeast corner of the power plant. He collided with a soldier carrying an assault gun and both of them crashed to the ground.

Floodlights sprang on in the guard towers and swiveled to probe into the compound. All they revealed was the compound's own garrison; the flaming bolts from the Marines' blasters didn't need the floodlights to be seen.

There was a loud explosion, followed by a drawn out crashing noise as second squad brought down the communications tower.

CHAPTER NINETEEN

"Dammit, they're after you!" General Locksley Ollwelen exclaimed after he'd read the message flashing on Jorge Lavager's screen.

"Eh," Lavager made a dismissive gesture, "since when hasn't someone been after me, Locker?"

"Dammit, Jorge, get security in here to see this thing." Lavager only shrugged. "Jorge, either you get al-Rashid in here or I'm going to do it for you! You know who this Alfa Sierra is, don't you? You know this is no hoax, don't you? Get him in here. Now!"

Lavager sighed in resignation. "Get al-Rashid in here right now," he told his private secretary. Within moments Lavager's security chief was standing in front of him. "Franklin, read this." Lavager leaned away from his viewscreen so the security chief could read the brief message blinking there: YOU'RE NEXT. ALFA SIERRA.

"FTL Union?" al-Rashid murmured and shook his head. "Is it a hoax, maybe?" He looked questioningly at both men. Lavager shrugged, but Ollwelen shook his head firmly. "A threat? This came via FTL Union using their commercial codes? They must know who sent it, sir, I'll run a check."

"Don't bother. I know who sent it. Did you notice where it came from?"

"Yes, Fargo. Is this 'Alfa Sierra' a friend?"

"Yes. Franklin, if it's who I think it is, this message comes from someone at the Central Intelligence Organization, and it means my life is in danger."

Ollwelen snorted.

Al-Rashid nodded. "We think Gustafferson was murdered. Paragussa too. Both probably by a hired assassin working alone. I sent you a memo—"

"I was copied on it. Jorge, did you read the damned thing?" Ollwelen demanded.

Lavager held up a hand. "I got the memo, gentlemen. I'm not worried about me. I can take care of myself. But what about the Cabbage Patch? If anything happens to that facility, I may as well be dead. I've been planning a visit out there all week. We agreed on today, now you seem to be trying to talk me out of it."

"The Cabbage Patch is well protected, sir. And under the circumstances," he gestured at the message, "I strongly recommend you don't take any rides in the country just now."

"Convince me." Lavager leaned back in his chair and lit a Davidoff. He could always work his way through the most difficult problem if he had the help of an Anniversario. "Have one?" Al-Rashid declined the offer but Ollwelen, still frowning, took one. Lavager nodded at a chair and the security chief sat down.

"The physical security at the Cabbage Patch is state-of-the-art, sir. We've taken into consideration the vegetation, reshaped the terrain for security, and established three-hundred-and-sixty-degree boundary barriers. The entire facility is surrounded by fencing consisting of a mix of razor wire in concertina rolls and dual-facing aprons. The concertina is five rolls high and six wide. The apron is three meters high and set at a forty-five-degree angle."

"What's the strength of the security detachment?"

"A light battalion of specially trained infantry, more than

three hundred and fifty troops at any given time, depending on training, sick call—you know, the usual excuses."

Lavager nodded as he lighted his cigar. "What do you have as anti-intrusion measures?" He offered a light to Ollwelen.

"A layered defense. First there's a two-meter-deep moat all around the facility studded with tungsten-steel spikes. Then there are infrared sensors with a minimum illumination of five microwatts per square centimeter in bands up to 1.1 microns measuring three centimeters above the ground. We have fence-mounted sensors that can detect bending of light waves caused by climbing, cutting, or lifting of the fencing materials. There is also a buried sensor line that can detect changes in a generated electromagnetic field caused by attempts to walk, run, crawl, or leap through the sensor field. There are clear zones that extend ten meters on both sides of the fencing. At the entry control point—there's only one—the same cleared zone both inside and outside the gate. No vegetation within a radius of a hundred and fifty meters outside the fence is allowed to grow any higher than twenty centimeters. Even the drains are protected, none of which offers an opening large enough for a human, and they are sealed with welded grills."

"We also have a strategically emplaced system of bunkers and towers, all with interlocking fields of fire," Ollwelen interrupted. "Then there are minefields, surveillance cameras, and anti-intrusion devices spread out around the facility up to a kilometer in every direction. The devices are under constant monitoring and maintained on a regular schedule. They're accessed by a secure system of tunnels that can be used only by technicians who know the cipher codes, which are changed daily at different intervals."

"What if somebody comes in from the air, using military hoppers or some sort of high-altitude, low-opening paraglide device?"

"No problem, sir. The grounds are studded with pylons to impale aircraft, parachutists, and the like. And the facility is also protected by continuous foot patrols of heavily armed guards, and there is always a quick-reaction force on call in case of emergencies. That facility is virtually impenetrable by a raiding force, sir. What we need to worry about is someone on the inside. But all our people out there have passed the most rigorous security checks. Nossir, the Cabbage Patch is secure. I guarantee it."

Lavager drew on his cigar. "Franklin, nothing is secure from men who are daring or desperate enough to get through your screens. There is a flaw in your system somewhere," he gestured with a finger, "and I want you to find it."

"Buddha's drooling lips," Ollwelen cursed, "that's just the point I've been making about your personal security all along! Only I already know what's wrong with it: You don't have any!"

Al-Rashid exchanged glances with Ollwelen and then said, "Very good, sir. But what about you? This message," he nodded to the FTL Union message still blinking on the screen, "is about you, not the Cabbage Patch. Can't I convince you to increase your guard, to stop these late-night visits to Ramuncho's and restrict your public travel and appearances? I could arrange for a double. It is only common sense for a head of state to take these simple precautions, sir. I'm begging you—"

"The man is speaking perfect sense, Jorge!" Ollwelen exclaimed, leaning forward in his chair and jabbing his cigar at Lavager.

Lavager regarded his Minister of War and his head of security carefully. "Locker, Franklin, I hear you. But no. I am not going to be a prisoner in my own country, in my own house. Franklin, you keep up your guard, but be discreet about it. You'll just have to adjust your security to meet my personal idiosyncrasies, that's the way I want it to work. Gentlemen, I repeat, there is no security system that can't be breached, and there is no one in any government who is indispensable either. I am expendable. You protect the Cabbage Patch and I'll protect Jorge Leberec Lavager."

"Dammit, Jorge, you're like the man who wouldn't fix the leak in his roof because it didn't rain that often!"

Lavager laughed. "I know, Locker, I know, and why bother to take a bath; you're only going to get dirty again?" He chuckled but was silent for a long moment, looking intently into the cloud of tobacco smoke in front of his head. Then: "Franklin, I'm going out to the Cabbage Patch as planned. I told you both to set this up last week. I hope neither of you called ahead and warned them I was coming. Today's the day. But I want to arrive there like anybody else, unannounced, drive up to the gate and see how alert the sentries are, that sort of thing."

"I don't understand, in light of this warning, sir. I recommend air transport if you really must go out there today."

"No. We're driving. Franklin, as a security man you should know it's always a good idea for the boss to pull a surprise inspection. I want to see things for myself. I want to see if there's a chink in your armor."

"But—?"

"Jorge! You may be right, but leave it to Franklin here to fix the problem! No damned reason for you to go running out there!"

"Yes, there is. Those inspection tunnels: They're your Trojan horse. Now gentlemen, let's get a move on."

Al-Rashid hurried off to arrange transport. "I need to go back to my office at the ministry, Jorge," Ollwelen said as he stood to go. "Need to get something there before we depart. I'll meet you outside in five minutes." Lavager casually nodded his okay.

Back at his office Ollwelen made a call.

The Medina Farm, Between New Granum and the Cabbage Patch, Union of Margelan, Atlas

Fifteen-year-old Gina Medina was alive because she wasn't home when the men came for her family in the night. They took them all, including the farmhands who lived with the Medinas, into a barn and killed them there.

Gina's love for the wilderness saved her life. She'd gone into the woods in the late afternoon with her dog, Roland, entered the secluded glade deep in the forest that was her secret refuge, and smoked thule until she fell asleep. It was long after dark when she awoke. Gina loved the forest. There were no creatures inimical to humans on Atlas except other humans, so wandering in the woods was totally safe, and the long walk home in the dark with Roland by her side was the perfect ending to her day. Her parents had long ago accepted Gina's wanderings and, as long as she pulled her weight on the farm, they let her go with a parental shrug of the shoulders. And she did carry her weight on the farm. Next to the forest, she loved growing things best.

But what she discovered when she got back to the farm that night was horror beyond her wildest nightmares. Later she could not remember much of the rest of the night, the discovery of the bodies of her parents and the farmhands, the destruction of the vehicles and the communications system. Dimly, she realized if she was to find help she would have to walk the twenty kilometers to the next farmstead. And what if whoever did this came back?

The sun was well up when she spotted the pall of smoke over her father's farthest cornfield. She knew what to do about that.

En Route from New Granum to the Cabbage Patch

It was a brilliant day in New Granum, warm, sunny, clear, blue skies. "A perfect day for a ride in the country!" Jorge

Liberec Lavager exclaimed, breathing in the fresh morning air. He looked at the gardens growing around the buildings on Executive Center. "Farmer's delight, eh, Locker?" he slapped Locksley Ollwelen heartily on the back.

"My dad was a distiller," Ollwelen said glumly.

"Yeah, I can see that by the red in your eyes, Locker. Had a bit too much of that old family bourbon last night, did you? Bad news when you got back to your office?" Ollwelen smiled weakly. He did look a bit peaked and shaky just now. "You should have invited me over." Lavager chided his minister and then laughed.

Lavager was in an excellent mood that morning, despite the warning message and the opposition of both Ollwelen and Franklin to his trip, but he'd been looking forward to it all week and the weather was cooperating beautifully. They were standing in the shade of the main entrance to the government building, waiting for Franklin al-Rashid to join them with their transportation and security detachment.

"The hell with waiting, Locker, let's take my car and just you and me, we'll drive on out to the Cabbage Patch," Lavager said suddenly.

"But—"

"Come on, we'll show up out there like tourists, lost and asking for directions. See if they can recognize us. Besides, we convoy out there and everyone'll know we're coming. We might as well make an announcement in the media."

"Jorge, you can't just, just—" He gestured in frustration.

Lavager laughed again. "I know. I'm a prisoner in my own land. Well, I thought I'd try."

Three heavily armored landcars rolled to a halt at the bottom of the steps below where the pair stood. Several burly security officers, followed by al-Rashid, piled out of the vehicles and rushed up to Lavager. "Follow us, sir," one of them said. The others surrounded Lavager, their

eyes never resting on him but roaming all over the land-
scape, looking for signs of possible danger. They protected him with the bulk of their own bodies.

"You see why I don't like this security business,
Locker? I already feel an attack of claustrophobia coming
on."

"You ride in the second vehicle, sir," al-Rashid ordered.

"Wait a minute, Franklin, do we really need all this security? Nobody knows where we're going. Dammit, I
wanted to arrive out there as inconspicuously as possible!" He gestured at the three large cars and all the guards.

"Sir, this is just standard security for a head of state."

"Well, I resign then! As of this moment I am plain Mister Lavager!" Al-Rashid looked at Lavager in astonish-
ment, his mouth half open.

Lavager shrugged. "Oh, all right. I know, I know. But
no, if I've got to put up with this farce I'm riding shotgun
in the first vehicle. If you aren't the first dog in line, the
view never changes, eh Locker? We learned that on those
long forced marches when we were lieutenants, right?"

Ollwelen started. "What?"

"Locker, what *is* the matter with you this morning?"

Ollwelen grinned sheepishly. "Well, Jorge, you riding
in the middle car is to protect you from roadblocks in the
front, and vehicle attacks from the rear," Ollwelen
protested. "I need to ride in the first vehicle to support the
fire team."

Lavager glanced curiously at his defense minister. "I
was hoping we could ride together, chat and enjoy a cigar
on the trip out." He shrugged. "But if that's the way you
want it, Locker, you can ride in the second vehicle, but
I'm riding up front."

"Oh, I'll ride with you, Jorge," Ollwelen said quickly.
"I wouldn't want to miss one of your cigars," he added,
grinning.

"That's more like it." Lavager slapped Ollwelen on the
back again and got into the first vehicle. The officer in

charge of the security detail cast a questioning glance at al-Rashid, who only shrugged as if to say, "He's the boss."

"Put the windscreens down," Lavager told his driver, "and take it easy. Keep it down to forty kilometers an hour. I want to enjoy the fresh air and the countryside. We've got all day to get there." Lavager produced his travel humidor and extracted two Davidoffs. "You get one when we arrive," he told his driver, patting the man on the shoulder, "but I don't want anything to distract you while you're driving." Despite the chances he always took with his personal security, which gave al-Rashid fits, the bodyguards liked being around Lavager. He was a no-nonsense type of person who always considered the comfort of his security detail first. They especially appreciated his late-night rendezvous at places like Ramuncho's, because he never called them out of their beds to stand watch over him on those occasions.

Beyond the city limits, the road wound through endless fields of ripening corn. The plants stood a full two meters high on either side of the road, giving the impression the convoy was driving through a green tunnel. A heavily armed security agent sat in the back of Lavager's car, monitoring various scanners that would indicate the presence of living things up to one hundred meters to either side of the road. He also had at his fingertips an array of defensive weaponry that could be employed to virtually level the corn within that one hundred meters.

"What's your name?" Lavager asked, twisting around to look at the security agent.

"Leelanu Lanners, sir."

"Are you sure you know how to use all those weapons?" Lavager asked, eyeing the man's laser rifle and sidearm.

Lanners grinned tightly. "Very well, sir. I'm a pretty

good shot with just about any personal weapon." Lanners faced Lavager and nodded, but his eyes kept moving, watching their surroundings.

Lavager noticed Lanners's constant eye movement. "Were you ever in the army?"

"Yessir, I gave it a try. Twenty-four years. Then I decided I didn't want to make a career of it."

"Pity. Another sixteen years and you could have retired."

Lanners shrugged. "My twenty-four in the army counts toward my time in the security service, so it all works out."

Lavager nodded; the army and the security service were both armed government services. He looked to the sides of the road and suddenly shouted, "Look lively back there! See all that corn? We're being 'stalked'!" He laughed enormously and thumped the driver on his back. The man grinned but kept his eyes on the road. Through his own onboard monitors he could both see and speak to the drivers of the two vehicles behind him; they were also busy scanning the terrain. With al-Rashid monitoring everything in the third vehicle, the other two cars in the convoy contained men totally alert, weapons ready to deliver immediate fire. "I feel young again!" he said suddenly. "Locker, remember that song we used to sing back in the old days? Come on, join me in the chorus," and he began to sing in a fairly decent tenor voice an old ditty that was popular in the army when he was a young officer:

"To the ladies of our Army our cups shall ever flow,

Companions in our exile and our shield 'gainst every woe;

May they see their husbands generals, with double pay also,

And join us in our choruses at Happy Hour, oh!"

They had been driving for about half an hour when the sensors on Lavager's car warned his driver of an anomaly in the roadbed just ahead of them. There were no telltale signs from the infrared monitors, just what appeared to be a slight hump in the ferro-asphalt that the computer sensed shouldn't be there. It was so tiny the car had driven over it before the driver realized what it was.

CHAPTER TWENTY

On the New Granum Road, Northeast of New Granum, Atlas

A command-detonated mine exploded under the second vehicle with a tremendous *craaak*! The concussion threw everyone in Lavager's vehicle forward in their seats while the force of the explosion lifted the second heavy armored car a full two meters into the air before it came crashing down in flames to bounce off the road and plow into the corn. When its fuel cells ignited, the explosion threw a fireball and a greasy column of smoke high into the air. Pieces of ferro-asphalt and parts from the destroyed vehicle fell to earth in lazy arcs, bouncing, smoking, and skittering over the roadway.

The driver in the third vehicle whipped around the gaping crater that appeared in front of his vehicle.

"Floor it!" al-Rashid yelled over the comm.

Ambushers who had lain hidden along the left side of the road then opened fire with lasers and rocket-propelled grenades. Instead of trying to outrun the fire, Lavager's driver turned his vehicle straight into the corn at maximum acceleration, bouncing one of the assailants off his hood and over the roof of the car. Laser beams hit the car, but most were harmlessly bled off into the earth by its armor. One lanced through the window and took the driver's head off in a spray of blood and shredded skull fragments. The dead man's hand remained grasping the accelerator lever. Lavager reached over, pried the lifeless fingers loose, unfastened his seat belt, released the door mechanism, and shoved the corpse out into the corn, which was making a thud-thud-thunking sound as the vehicle rammed across the rows. Clutching the steering column, Lavager slewed the vehicle around. Huge gouts of rich, dark earth spouted up from beneath the roaring vehicle. He applied the brakes and the car plowed to a stop. Suddenly it was quiet.

"Where are they?" Lavager asked as he released the catch to the onboard shotrifle. He checked the magazine, inserted a round in the chamber, took the safety off.

"One hundred and fifty meters to our rear," Lanners answered. "I make out—Good God!—a dozen! No, more! Coming this way." A huge explosion from the road marked the destruction of the third vehicle, the one al-Rashid had been in.

"Arm yourself," Lavager told Ollwelen, who had been sitting stiffly in his seat all the time. "Are you hit, Locker?" he asked when the man didn't move.

"N-No—I don't have a weapon!"

Lavager ignored Ollwelen. "How about your onboard weapons system? Can you use it?"

Lanners swore. "A bolt must've taken the damned thing out, sir! We'll have to use our personal weapons." Grenades began ripping through the corn over their heads and exploding behind them. "They're ranging on us!"

"Franklin!" Lavager was on the communications set now. "Report!" There was no answer. Lavager didn't expect one, because a second column of greasy, black smoke was now curling up from the road. It spoke volumes about al-Rashid's fate. And if that wasn't all, the cornfield, which was very dry, was catching fire.

"They're coming!" Ollwelen shouted. Sure enough, from a short distance ahead they could hear the sound of men crashing through the corn.

Without even considering flight, Lavager prepared to fight. "Dismount! We'll form a firing line, use this car as cover, come on, move it, Locker! Get your ass in gear! What the hell's the matter with you?" Before Ollwelen could answer, Lavager was outside in the corn using the hood of the vehicle as a brace as he sighted the shotrifle in the direction of the oncoming attackers. Lanners, a laser rifle in his hands, took up a position on the opposite side of the car.

"No!" Ollwelen suddenly shouted as he jumped away from the car. "Look! The fuel cell has ruptured! Get away from here!"

"Into the corn! Run!" Lavager shouted and the three crashed through the rows of stalks, putting as much distance between them and the damaged land car as they could. It exploded in a huge ball of flame. The concussion knocked all three men headlong to the ground. Now fires were starting everywhere around where the trio lay, gasping and panting in the hot, still air.

"What's on the other side of this field?" Lavager wheezed.

"I think it's another road, sir," Lanners answered. "It's about a kilometer over that way," he pointed behind them, "I think. Damn, where are they?" he asked, meaning the ambushers.

"They've got those fires to contend with," Lavager grunted. As if confirming this statement someone began screaming from somewhere behind them. "Burn, you bastard, burn!" Lavager growled. "Let's get out of here. Come on." He tapped Ollwelen on the shoulder and the three resumed their dash across the corn rows. It was very difficult running because they stumbled over piping at intervals between the rows, the farmer's irrigation system. Obviously, the farmer wasn't aware yet that his corn was on fire—or that the irrigation system had been sabotaged.

They had gone only about two hundred meters farther when they stumbled out into a grassy pathway about twenty meters wide running the entire length of the field parallel to the rows of corn. "We'll make our stand on the other side," Lavager said. He sprinted across and took up a prone firing position behind a corn row on the other side. Ollwelen and Lanners flopped down beside him. The three lay there panting, their bodies running with perspiration and the air was now so full of smoke from the fires that breathing was becoming difficult. From back the way they had come they heard many voices. "We may not stop them all, but we'll slow them down," Lavager said. "They're between the fires and us. We'll really screw them over when they step out into that cleared space." He grinned at the other two, then his grin vanished.

"Where the hell's your weapon, Locker?"

"I-I didn't have a chance to get one," Ollwelen gasped.

Lavager shook his head. "Get ready," he told Lanners, then coughed when a gust of wind swept the increasing smoke into his face. "We'll be asphyxiated if we don't burn to death first," he said when his throat cleared. "When we get out of here I've got a job for you, Leelanu Lanners. So shoot like you voted for me in the last election—straight and often."

The voices of the pursuing assassins drew nearer and nearer. Many men were crashing through the corn.

"They've got to be crazy, coming after us like this," Lanners whispered.

"Not crazy, Lee, desperate. They are going to kill us or die in the attempt. Let them all get out into the open so we've got clear shots. Shoot when I do. Damnit, Locker, why didn't you pick up—?"

The first ambusher stepped out from between two stalks of corn about twenty meters from where the trio had crossed the cleared space. He carried a shotrifle in the low-ready position, the weapon angled at about 45 degrees to his body, finger off the firing lever. He stepped cautiously onto the grassy area and held up a hand for the men behind him to stay there. Slowly, he advanced to the middle of the pathway, glancing from side to side, looking for a sign to tell him where the three had crossed.

The wind began to blow. It blew toward them, from the direction of the road where the ambush had taken place. The corn was dry. A *whoosh*ing roar began to make itself heard. Lavager's heart quickened. The ambushers were between two fires now!

"Coom," the man said. Eight or ten more men—Lavager didn't bother to count them—all heavily armed, stepped out into the cleared area.

The first shot Lavager fired was a fléchette round. It hit the first man squarely in the middle of his chest, shredding his torso and knocking him over backward. Now Lavager and Lanners pumped rounds into the men as quickly as they could work their weapons' actions. The ambushers began firing back, their first shots high, cutting off the tops of the cornstalks, but as they got control of the situation their shots began to hit all around the two, who rolled into new firing positions—but in the few seconds it took them to reacquire targets, at least five more men emerged from the other side of the path and began sending accurate fire into their old positions. The remaining men began advancing, firing every step of the way.

Lavager's shotrifle was empty. He drew his sidearm and, using both hands to steady the weapon, pumped shots into the oncoming men, but they were wearing protective armor or were hopped up because none went down!

Suddenly, from about a hundred meters to the right of where the two lay, rifle fire began lancing into the advancing line of assassins and they began to falter. Lavager glanced over his shoulder. It was al-Rashid! He was walking calmly toward them, firing from the hip. The surviving attackers, about five of them, had enough. They turned and ran back into the corn, but moments later they began screaming as the fire got to them. One managed to stumble back out into the pathway, his body engulfed in flames. He whirled in agony, every inch of him aflame. Lavager shot him in the head.

"Franklin!" Lavager embraced his chief of security. "Ugly as you are, I've never seen a more beautiful sight!"

Lanners came up and started thumping al-Rashid on the back.

"They got our car," al-Rashid gasped, "rocket-propelled grenade, I think. I was thrown out by the initial blast. They got all my men, all of them," he sobbed. He'd been wounded. The bleeding from cuts on his face and neck had stopped and his left arm, although he could still use it, was peppered with shell fragments. He sat down heavily. The fire raged in the corn just a few meters away. "When the hell is the farmer going to turn on the water?"

Lavager helped al-Rashid to his feet. "Come on, let's get out of here. Lee says there's a road on the other side of this field. Uh, where's Ollwelen?" He looked around. He couldn't remember when he'd last seen the general.

"I saw him running southwest, toward the city," Lanners answered with a shrug.

Lavager swore. "Let's find that road, it's getting too hot in here."

They had made their way only a few hundred yards farther when the irrigation system suddenly sprang to life. "Allah!" al-Rashid shouted, extending his arms toward heaven. "You exist after all!" They threw themselves into the streams that spurted up from the pipes and drank in the cool liquid. "Is this water drinkable?" al-Rashid asked between gulps.

"Who cares, Chief?" Lanners answered. "We have medical insurance!"

"Lee," Lavager said, "I was going to give you Franklin's job, until he upset my plans by miraculously reappearing from the dead, but don't worry, I've got plans for anybody who's got guts like you," and he filled al-Rashid in on what had happened to them.

"Where do you think Ollwelen got off to, sir?" al-Rashid asked.

Lavager didn't answer immediately. "Maybe he went

for help?" his voice dripped with sarcasm. Al-Rashid didn't reply. He knew how close the two old soldiers were, but could see something had come between them. He didn't want to get involved, but he sensed that he would.

They reached the road at noon. It stretched away in both directions. Nothing stirred on it. "How far are we from the Cabbage Patch?" Lavager asked.

"I'm not sure, sir. Twenty kilometers, maybe less. I think we were more than halfway there when the ambush hit." He shook his head and staggered a step or two. "I-I'm not sure whether this road runs parallel to our route or at an angle to it or even if it joins up with the main highway. I-I think it does but my memory's a little fuzzy just now—"

Lavager sat down along the shoulder and the other two joined him there. "How long will it take for us to walk there?"

Lanners shrugged. "In our condition? I don't know. Hours anyway."

"I can make it," al-Rashid protested, but he knew that Lanners hedged his estimate because it was obvious that his wounds would slow them down.

"We'll make it," Lavager assured them. "That guy back there, that scout, the first one to come out of the corn? Lee, did you recognize his accent?"

"Yessir. South Solanum. That's the way they talk down there. 'Coom' for 'come.' Unmistakable. He was from South Solanum."

"Yes." Lavager nodded. "Those rotten bastards. You know what they were, don't you?"

"Yessir. They were there to ambush any relief column that might have come down the highway. Someone's attacking the Cabbage Patch, sir." He thought for a moment and then: "Or, it was prearranged to get you. Someone must have known you'd be coming."

Lavager didn't reply at once because that dark thought

had already occurred to him. "Right. Maybe. And here we are. No communications, no transportation. Franklin? Franklin?" he turned to al-Rashid but his security chief had passed out.

On the New Granum Road, Midway Between New Granum and Spondu

By the time General Locksley Ollwelen reached the road he was exhausted. He collapsed on the shoulder, gasping for breath. It had all gone wrong, terribly wrong! That bastard, Germanian, had double-crossed him! Worse, Lavager was still alive, or had been when Ollwelen had disappeared among the corn rows. Now, behind him, the fire raged.

He got unsteadily to his feet and staggered along the road back in the direction of the city. Eventually he would run into someone on the road, or reach one of the farms where he could find transportation. He could not show up at the home of the farmer who owned the cornfield. Too close to the scene of the crime and if Lavager had survived, he'd head there himself. The next nearest farmstead was some kilometers from where the ambush had taken place. If no vehicles came along he would just have to walk there. Then, once back in the city, he'd gather his loyal generals and start the coup he knew he'd have to undertake to survive after what had just happened. He'd find that Germanian person too, and talk about the trials of Job! He'd "Job" that sonofabitch!

From far down the road a tiny speck was approaching. Ollwelen's heart leaped. He stepped into the center of the road and waved his arms. Gradually the speck resolved itself into a vehicle. As it neared he saw it was a passenger car, not a farm vehicle. Excellent! He'd get the driver to turn around and take him back to New Granum. He waved his arms furiously and the vehicle came slowly to a stop.

A woman was driving. She appeared to be alone. Her hair was blond and cut very short in a masculine style.

"This is an emergency!" Ollwelen shouted, running to the driver's side.

The young woman looked out at him. He was disheveled, covered in dust and his face streaked with perspiration. "Sure looks like it," she said. Her voice was sweetly melodious.

"I need to get back to the city as quickly as possible, er, Miss," Ollwelen gasped. He did not see a wedding ring on the woman's delicate fingers. "If you will turn around and take me back there I'll make it worth your while, I really will." He leaned against the frame of the vehicle. Perspiration poured off him.

"Get in," she said. Gratefully, Ollwelen crossed to the passenger's side and climbed in. "I can't thank you enough," he said, turning to face the driver. She reached across and deftly slit his throat with the tiny surgical blade concealed in the palm of her hand. He gasped and spasmed violently. The big woman leaned across Ollwelen's spasming body, placed one muscled arm firmly around his head and pulled it back to further expose his throat while with her right hand she worked the blood-slick blade expertly across his throat, making sure both carotids were completely severed. Ollwelen gurgled and thrashed helplessly, his hot blood spurting over the woman's clothing as air whistled eerily through his severed windpipe. In moments it was all over. The woman's forearms and the front of her dress were covered in gore. She put one hand to her mouth and licked the blood, then she opened the passenger door and shoved the body out into a ditch. A few kilometers down the road she pulled off onto an access road. She cleaned herself up, with a double handful of moist towelettes, changed clothes, and transferred to her own car after setting the time fuse on an incendiary device she placed in the stolen vehicle.

Driving back to New Granum, the windows down, the warm air rushing through the vehicle, elation washed over her. She loved hands-on work. She'd drawn the town-side security team and thought it'd be boring. She wondered how the action team had let that one slip through. Oh well, her gain! Whistling a happy tune, she drove on down the deserted highway.

CHAPTER
TWENTY-ONE

**Command Bunker, the Cabbage Patch, Near Spondu,
Union of Margelan, Atlas**

Major Principale, commander of the defense garrison,
gripped the comm to headquarters in his hand though it
had become useless once the tower went down. He gaped
at the one-sided fight on his monitors. *Where are they?* he
demanded of himself. *How did they get in without being
detected?* But he had no answers. He couldn't see anything on his monitors that hadn't been visible to the
slaughtered troops involved in the brief firefight—except
for a few smudges in infrared.

But he could tell where all those bits of star-stuff had
come from, and they came from where the faint smudges
were.

"Towers three, five, seven, nine, eleven," he ordered
into the local comm. "Saturate the ground between Lab
Three and the power plant. *Now!*" Those were the only
guard towers that had a view of the area between Lab
Three and the power plant where the smudges were concentrated—the defensive layout had been designed to de-
feat a force attacking from outside, not from a force
already inside the fence.

Five assault guns began to send plunging projectile fire
into the ground between the two buildings and immediately beyond them.

Major Principale looked at his layout again and snapped

orders to the four bunkers that also had an unimpeded view of the target area. The crews in the bunkers manhandled their guns to the bunker entrances and began firing. One of the four put out grazing fire, no more than a meter above the ground, the others fired high enough that the Marines were easily able to stay low enough to avoid their projectiles.

Defenders, the Cabbage Patch

The Margelan officers and sergeants yelled confused orders to the confused troops of the reaction force from Barracks Two as they spread out to seek cover from the plasma bolts that were burning holes through their ragged ranks.

"First squad, fire toward the Lab One door!" a sergeant bellowed, then collapsed when an instantly cauterized hole appeared in his chest. Three of his six soldiers were hit, two fatally, before they could turn their weapons on the lab door.

A lieutenant stood, jerking his head about in near panic, straining to spot who was firing the bolts of blazing fire that were slaughtering his troops, but he couldn't see anyone where the bolts seemed to come from! All he could see in the floodlit night-turned-day was the eye-searing afterimages of the plasma bolts—and his own men dropping with holes burned through their bodies or thighs, or with arms or lower legs burned off.

In a rage, the lieutenant screamed out for his men to follow him in a charge into the fire to find the enemy. He led the charge but only half a dozen of his men followed. They lasted long enough to see him fall with half his neck burned away by one blaster bolt, and two others punch bloodless holes through his torso—then they fell as well, killed by the withering fire from seventh and eighth squads.

The initial ferocious firefight lasted less than two minutes. Only three of the soldiers from the reaction platoon remained alive and uninjured, and they weren't killed only because they threw their weapons away and found cover from the Marines' blasters. Most of their companions were dead; the rest were severely injured, even missing limbs.

"Section leaders report," Lieutenant Tevedes ordered on the open platoon circuit. The section leaders called for squad leaders' reports.

The only reports that meant anything were first, seventh, and eighth squads, the only squads that were involved in the firefight.

The lone casualty was Lance Corporal Thalia, who was bleeding where his nose hit the front of his helmet when he collided with the first soldier of the reaction force.

The Marines didn't have time to feel any relief, though; neither did they have time to begin planting the rest of their charges as every tower and bunker that could see it began firing into the area between and around the power plant and Lab Three.

Marines

"Move!" Tevedes shouted into the platoon circuit. "Get out of the killing zone!" The section leaders echoed him, the squad leaders also snapped commands to move, *move-move-*MOVE!

"First squad, with me!" Tevedes ordered. He and first squad raced doubled-over due south, straight at a bunker that was firing directly between the power plant and lab. Tevedes wasn't concerned with the fire coming from the bunker, it was one that was firing too high. First squad sprinted with him.

When they reached the side of the barracks the reaction force had come from, Tevedes ordered, "Take that gun out."

First squad opened fire on the assault gun visible in the

bunker's entrance. The gun let out a long burst as its barrel swiveled skyward, then it fell silent with its crew dead.

"We have to take out the towers that are shooting," Tevedes gasped into first squad's circuit.

"Which one do you want first?" Daly asked. He understood that the plunging fire from the towers was more dangerous than the grazing fire from the bunkers. He was already at the corner of the barracks, looking around it to see which was the nearest tower firing into the kill zone.

"Go to the right," Tevedes ordered. Then he raised Gunny Lytle on the command circuit. Lytle had gone north. Tevedes told him to take a squad and knock out the firing tower farthest to the west, then work his way clockwise.

"Already on it," Lytle replied.

The *crack-sizzle* of blaster fire broke out to Tevedes's right as first squad opened up on a firing tower. The tower fell silent.

But Tevedes wasn't satisfied, he wanted to be positive the tower was out of the fight.

"Let's knock it down," he ordered first squad. He fired his blaster at one of the tower's legs a man's height above the grounds. The four Marines of first squad concentrated their fire on the same spot. The five blasters fired bolt after bolt into the plasteel leg until it overheated and sagged.

"Next tower," Tevedes said, and began sprinting toward the now-leaning tower. It crashed to the ground seconds after they passed it.

The next tower firing was two hundred meters away when Tevedes stopped first squad. They quickly put it out of action, but didn't bother toppling it. By then the fire pouring into the killing zone between the power plant and the lab was almost stilled; Gunny Lytle and fifth squad had also knocked out two of the towers firing into it.

But more fire plunged into the complex and arced above the ground as the rest of the towers and bunkers joined in, their crews firing at every shadow and imagined movement.

"Take out that gun," Tevedes ordered when he and first squad took cover behind a bunker after taking out a third tower. The crew in the bunker had turned their assault gun around and was spraying grazing fire across the compound to the left of the power plant, in an area where some of the Marines were. Then, "Section leaders, report!"

Before Daly could give orders to his men, Lance Corporal Wazzen scooted around the front of the bunker to approach its entrance from the other side—which exposed him to fire from that direction. As soon as he got to the opposite side of the bunker, a randomly fired burst from an assault gun on the east side of the compound pounded into the side of the bunker, shredding him.

Daly swore, then crawled around the corner of the bunker and jammed the muzzle of his blaster past the firing assault gun and began firing blindly. Screams followed his first three blasts; he fired a few more, moving the barrel each time, before withdrawing his blaster. Nobody tried shooting through the aperture in the bunker's front, where it would normally fire from—they knew the bunker's entrance had to be a staggered tunnel and they wouldn't be able to hit anybody in it from the front.

Command Bunker

Major Principale compared the locations of the faint infrared smudges with the positions it appeared fire was coming from—they seemed to match one-for-one. He ordered his gun crews to use their infras to locate and fire on the faint smudges. He began directing fire from the guns that couldn't see the smudges onto those he could see.

Marines

"First squad, one KIA," Daly reported to Staff Sergeant Suptra, after taking out the bunker.

But Suptra didn't acknowledge.

Neither did Staff Sergeant Bos, the second section leader, respond to Tevedes's call for the section leaders to report.

"Squad leaders, report!" Tevedes ordered on the squad leaders circuit when neither of the section leaders called in.

"First squad, one KIA," Daly replied on the same circuit.

"Sergeant Bingh's down!" a shaky voice said. "The rest of second squad's pinned down."

Sergeant Kare reported, "Third squad's all right."

Fourth squad didn't reply.

Gunny Lytle reported for fifth squad, "Fifth squad's got one KIA, one wounded. We can't move."

Sixth, seventh, and eighth squads also had casualties; only eighth squad was pinned down, the other two were able to move.

Tevedes resisted the urge to swear; he didn't have the time to waste. He needed to turn the fight around.

"Third squad, have you placed your charges?" he asked.

"Not yet. We can't get to the admin building, but we're only a few meters from Lab Two," Kare answered.

"Can you get into Lab Two?"

"I believe so."

"Get in there and set your charges."

"Aye aye."

"Second squad, who's in charge there?"

"Wehrli, sir. I think." The squad's most junior man.

Tevedes forced himself to speak calmly. "Lance Corporal, can you see any of the towers without getting shot?"

"I-I think so."

"Is anybody else in your squad able to fire?"

"I'm n-not sure."

"Well, find out. If there are at least two of you, I want you to put enough fire on one of the towers to take out its gun crew. Can you do that?"

"Yessir, I can." Wehrli sounded more confident now that somebody was giving him clear orders.

"Then do it, Marine."

"Aye aye, sir."

"Fourth squad, can anybody in fourth squad hear me?" Tevedes asked on the all-hands circuit. No response.

Back to the squad leaders' circuit. "Fifth, sixth, and seventh squads. By squads, concentrated fire on towers, take those guns out." Gunny Lytle and the squad leaders replied, "Will do."

"Eighth squad, can you see a tower without exposing yourselves too much?"

"Negative," Sergeant Pudharee said. "We can't move, at least two guns are concentrating on us."

"Stand fast, Eight."

"One more down," Daly said. While Tevedes was giving orders to the rest of the platoon, he and his remaining men had concentrated their fire on the next tower down the line and silenced it.

Tevedes cautiously looked around the corner of the bunker and saw two bodies and the assault gun dangling from it.

"Got one!" Wehrli shouted into the all-hands circuit.

"Got ours," Sergeant Bajing reported. "Moving to another." Fifth squad had killed a tower and was moving into position to take out another.

"That makes five for fifth squad," Gunny Lytle said.

The near-deafening racket of assault guns firing into the compound continued, but seemed less than it had been.

"Where's the gun that hit Wazzen?" Tevedes asked Daly.

"Right . . . there," Daly said, sending a plasma bolt downrange. The bit of star-stuff plunged into a distant bunker's entrance, and the gun momentarily stopped firing. When it resumed, its fire was wild. Daly rapid-fired several more bolts, joined by Kindy and Nomonon. Several bolts hit around the bunker entrance, but more went true, and in a moment the gun fell silent.

Sergeant Kare suddenly broke in. "Third squad's charges are set and the squad is clear of the building."

"All squads, stand clear of Labs One and Two," Tevedes ordered on the all-hands circuit. He made a silent ten-count, then said, "Fire in the hole!" and set off the charges.

The roars of the explosions were muffled by the walls of the buildings, which had been constructed to contain explosions. Still, the walls were old enough that they'd weakened over the years; small clouds of dirt and pulverized plascrete puffed up from them, and cracks raced along the walls. A wall of Lab One bulged out and a corner of Lab Two's roof collapsed.

When the roar of the explosions passed, there was a brief silence in the compound as the shocked defenders stopped shooting. Tevedes snapped an order, and the Marines took advantage of the brief respite to move to new positions.

Command Bunker

"Resume fire!" Major Principale shrieked into his comm when he saw his soldiers had stopped shooting to watch the explosion of the labs. He could tell by the reduced amount of fire from the attackers that they were being hurt by the massive firepower put out by his troops, but whoever those invisible attackers were, they were very good—they were hurting his defenders even worse than they were being hurt, methodically knocking out the towers and bunkers. *Any* reduction in defensive fire could turn the battle in favor of the attackers.

"Watch for their fire!" he shouted. "That will tell you where they are. Kill them! *Kill them!*"

He examined the monitor images carefully; yes, those faint infrared smudges were definitely the attackers; the fire had slackened when he directed his men's fire, and the dots moved during the lull in the fighting. The movement put a small group along the northern perimeter in a position where a squad from the reaction platoon could come up behind them.

He began issuing orders. Later, he could wonder about who these invisible men were.

Marines

Lieutenant Tevedes analyzed the situation. The initial fire had been totally wild, until the tower guns began firing into the area between the labs. They had to be firing at the source of the blaster bolts; he doubted the defenders had any ultraviolet capability that would allow them to see the Marines' locator lights. There had to be a command bunker someplace, from which the defense was being directed. He needed to find and destroy that command bunker. The building tentatively identified as the military headquarters building was to his left—that was the most likely place to have the command bunker. First, though:

"Turn off your here-I-am's," he ordered on the all-hands circuit. Just in case the enemy could see them.

He holstered his hand-blaster and picked up Wazzen's blaster and switched to first squad's circuit. "First squad, we're going to the headquarters building and find the command bunker."

"Wait one," Daly said. He sighted his blaster and put a bolt through the entrance of the bunker to the left of the one that had killed Wazzen. Kindy and Nomonon saw where he fired and added their bolts to his. That bunker went silent. "That one could have taken us out before we got there," Daly explained.

"Good thinking," Tevedes said. "Anyone else shooting at us?"

˙ Daly snorted. *Every*body was shooting at them. But no fire was coming close to them now.

When Daly didn't say anything, Tevedes said, "Let's do it!" He sprinted to the next bunker. The others went with him.

They pounded the forty meters to the suspected headquarters and lined up left and right of the door.

"We go in hot," Tevedes ordered. "Right, left, right, left. Ready? *Go!*"

Daly was next to the door on the right. He reached for the handle and twisted, the door swung open. He crashed his shoulder into it, slamming it against the wall as he charged through and wheeled to his right, pointing his blaster where his eyes pointed. Tevedes came next and wheeled to his left, followed by Nomonon and Kindy.

They were in what was obviously a military office. No one was in it, but three doors led out of the room.

"Daly, right door, Kindy, left door, Nomonon, center door," Tevedes ordered.

Daly was at the door on the right before Tevedes finished giving the orders, kicked it open, and dove through it. There was a single room beyond the door, living quarters with a hastily vacated bed. Another door off it was open, showing a lavatory.

"Clear," Daly reported, followed almost immediately by Kindy's "clear." The door on the left was a multiunit lavatory.

"Guard quarters," Nomonon reported from beyond the center door. "There's a blast-hatch on the far wall."

Tevedes briskly strode through the middle door into a long room. Double-deck bunks, most showing signs of recent use, lined the walls; evidently the duty watch rested there rather than returning to their barracks. To the right, against the far wall, was the solid-looking metal door that Nomonon had identified as a blast-hatch. The lieutenant reached the door in a few long steps and examined it both visually and manually. His cheeks pulled his mouth wide in a feral grin, the door had been designed to withstand explosions from outside without being knocked in. The door had a handle, but there was no visible locking mechanism. So if it wasn't barred on the inside, it should simply swing open into the guard quarters. He turned about and signaled first squad to gather close. They touched helmets for secure communications.

"Turn your here-I-am's back on," Tevedes ordered. "That hatch looks like it can just swing open. I'm going to give it a try. If it opens, we go in fast and take out everybody who doesn't surrender immediately. I go left, Daly right, Nomonon left, Kindy right. Any questions?" No questions. "Let's do it."

Tevedes reached the door in a long step and grasped the handle. The door didn't budge when he pulled, but there was lateral give in the handle. He twisted it right and left, but it didn't move far in either direction, neither did the hatch move when he pulled while twisting. He pushed on the handle, and smiled when it moved forward. With the handle in as far as it would go, he gave it a clockwise turn and the thirty-centimeter-thick door swung toward him. He pulled on it hard and squeezed through as soon as it was open far enough. Sergeant Daly followed so closely he almost tripped over Tevedes's heels, and Corporal Nomonon and Sergeant Kindy briefly got jammed together going through the narrow opening.

The blast-hatch didn't open into the command bunker, but onto a landing at the head of a steep, narrow stairwell. Tevedes didn't hesitate when he got through the door, but went down the stairs three at a time. A landing at the foot of the stairs connected to another, shorter flight of stairs that went left to another landing. More stairs went down left from that landing. There was another blast-hatch at the bottom of those stairs.

Tevedes bounded down. The lower hatch had the same handle mechanism. He bent low, gripped the handle, pushed, turned, and pulled. This lower hatch was neither as thick nor as heavy as the one at the top of the stairs and swung open faster. Tevedes dove through to his left, pointing his blaster where he looked.

Command Bunker

Private Second Class Handquok turned his attention to a blinking alarm light and his blood ran cold. "Sir!" he croaked. He gasped and tried again. "Major Principale, someone's in the stairwell!"

Major Principale swore, and scanned the bank of controls in front of him, searching for the switches that would toggle the cameras in the guard quarters and stairwell. Sergeant Oble reached over and unerringly hit the right switches. Three of the monitors in front of Principale flickered as their displays changed from the battle raging outside to the interior of the headquarters. The one showing the guard quarters showed the room was empty—and the blast-hatch at its end open. The view of the upper flight of stairs was likewise empty, but the view of the bottom flight showed a faint smudge of infrared midway down and another at the hatch. On the monitor, the blast-hatch began to open.

In one motion, Principale stood, turned to face the blast-hatch, and drew his sidearm. At his side, Oble did the same. They fired through the opening blast-hatch.

Sergeant Daly almost pushed Lieutenant Tevedes out of his way rushing through the hatch into the command center. At the *zing-zing* of fléchettes flying over his back, he dove for the floor and pointed his blaster at the source of the fire. He squeezed off three quick bolts before his eyes focused on the shooters. Both of them fell with holes in their chests.

"Don't shoot, I surrender!" someone called out from behind a console.

"Show your hands!" Tevedes ordered through his helmet speaker. A pair of hands timidly poked up from behind the console where the voice was. A second pair came up from behind another console.

"I see two pair of hands," Tevedes said. "Is anybody else in here?"

"J-Just M-Major Principale and S-Sergeant Oble," the first voice said. "I-I think you killed them."

While the platoon commander checked the two bodies, Daly checked his men over the squad circuit. Corporal Nomonon was all right, but not Kindy.

"I got hit in the leg," Sergeant Kindy reported. "The bleeding's under control, but the leg won't hold weight."

"Are the painkillers working?" Daly asked.

"I'm not using them, except for a local. I want to keep my mind clear." Kindy paused, then added, "My leg's numb from mid-thigh down."

"Daly," Tevedes broke into the squad circuit, "you and Nomonon check for hidden people, just in case our prisoners are lying about how many people are here." He looked around the command center; it had eight stations. Where were the other four soldiers who should be on duty here? He switched to his external speaker and asked the prisoners, who were now standing with their hands clasped on top of their heads.

"It's night," Handquok said, "only Sergeant Oble and I were on duty. Major Principale and Private Braser were upstairs. Nobody else was able to get here from the barracks."

"Looks like he's telling the truth, sir," Daly reported on the squad circuit. The stations were close to each other, there wasn't much to the room and it had taken little more than a minute for him and Nomonon to search it.

"Secure the prisoner on the right," Tevedes ordered through his speaker. "You," he said, stepping up to Handquok and grabbing his shoulder, "show me how to communicate with the towers and bunkers."

Handquok flinched from Tevedes's grip, but stammered, "Y-Yessir. O-Over here, s-sir. H-Here, sir," he said, holding out a comm he lifted from Major Principale's console. "P-Press the button on the side to talk. L-Listen here." He pointed out the earpiece. "It's hard wired."

The other soldier yelped in fear when invisible hands grabbed him and pulled him from the console he'd hidden behind and dragged him to the small open area in front of the open blast-hatch, where he was flung to the floor and his hands secured behind his back.

"Just lie there and keep quiet, and you'll be all right," the invisible man told him.

Private Third Class Braser nodded numbly.

Tevedes studied the monitors and displays. "Which ones show the towers and bunkers?" he asked.

"Th-These, sir." Handquok pointed to a pair of schematics studded with dots. Many of the dots were blinking, about a third of them were dark.

"What do the lights mean?"

"Th-Those are stations we h-have c-communications with, sir. W-We've lost the dark ones."

"Why are the lights blinking?"

"Those stations are f-firing, sir."

"If they're steady, then they aren't firing?"

"Y-Yessir."

Tevedes nodded. He raised the comm to his helmet speaker, and pressed the button on its side without bothering with the earpiece.

"Attention all stations," he said. "This is the command bunker. Your commander is dead and the command bunker has been taken. About a third of you have been killed or severely wounded—" he glanced at the time "—in the past ten minutes. Surrender now, or you will all be killed. To show good faith on our part, we will cease fire in one minute.

"Live or die, the decision is yours." He put the comm

down and switched to the squad circuit. "Daly, you heard how to read the boards?"

"Yessir."

"Good. Take charge here, I'm going topside to call a cease-fire for us."

"Aye aye, sir." Then through his external speaker, "You, come here."

"M-Me?" Handquok squeaked.

"Yes, you. What's your name?"

"Handquok, sir," he said as he stumbled toward the commanding voice of the invisible man. "P-Private Second Class Handquok."

"Turn around and put your hands behind your back," Daly ordered when the soldier reached him. He quickly secured the soldier's hands with ties and told him to sit on the floor. "You too," he told Braser, and lifted him by the collar of his shirt. "Just be calm and you'll be all right," he told them, then walked to where he could more easily see the schematics.

Upstairs, in the front office, Tevedes toggled on the all-hands circuit. "Now hear this. We have taken the command bunker. I have communicated with the defenders and told them to surrender. Let's see if they're going to cooperate. Cease fire. Acknowledge by squads."

The Marines stopped firing and the squads acknowledged the order, beginning with Daly's terse, "One-one, acknowledged." This time, fourth squad reported as well. Outside, the rattle of the defenders' guns diminished sharply.

"One-one," Tevedes said, "what do the boards say?"

"The light for one bunker is still blinking," Daly reported. "Wait one." Daly told Nomonon to bring Handquok over. "Where is that bunker?" Daly asked on his external speaker.

"Th-That's the f-first one north of the main gate."

"Thanks," Daly said, then over the radio, "Six, the first bunker north of the main gate is the only one still firing."

Tevedes tried to imagine where his squads were. "Two-five and two-six, are you in positions to engage the bunker just north of the main gate?" When they reported they could quickly maneuver into position, he said, "Kill it."

In a moment he heard the multiple *crack-sizzle* of half a dozen blasters, then silence.

"I'm going to order the defenders to leave their weapons and posts and assemble on the drill field," Tevedes said into the all-hands, then hurried back to the command bunker to give the order.

The Battle of the Cabbage Patch was over.

CHAPTER
TWENTY-TWO

On the New Granum Road, Union of Margelan, Atlas

Toward dusk two small, bedraggled figures, obviously a young woman accompanied by a large dog, stepped out of the corn onto the shoulder of the road in front of the three men. Lanners challenged her sharply. "Halt! Identify yourself!"

Lavager laid a restraining hand on Lanners's arm. "We won't hurt you," he told the figure. "We're glad to see you. We've been in a bad fight. We need help. My friend is hurt. Can you help us? What's your dog's name?"

"Roland," the girl answered in a tiny voice. She came close enough to see them clearly and her eyes searched Lavager's face. "I know who you are!" she said, "You're—"

"Yes, the same," Lavager sighed. "We must get to Spondu. Will this road take us there?"

"Yes," she answered as she sat heavily on the ground and began to cry. "They killed everyone!" She wept.

The three men sat wearily beside the girl. "What's your name?" Lanners asked.

"Gina—Regina Medina. My father owns . . ." she gestured at the fields on either side of the road, "owned this farm," she corrected herself, "but they killed him." Briefly she told them what had happened.

"Bastards!" Lanners cursed. "They murdered the

farmer and his help so nobody would spot the ambush or interfere once it was sprung. Sir, this really is beginning to look like a well-planned setup. Gina, was it you who turned on the water?"

"Yes."

"Is there a farm nearby where we can go for help?" Lavager asked. He felt a sharp hurt in his chest, looking at the orphaned girl who was about the same age as his own daughter.

Gina shook her head. "You're closer to Spondu than to the Yatzaina place. Sir," she looked up at Lavager, "may I come with you? I-I don't want to go back to . . . I can be your guide and Roland will warn us if—if they come back."

Lavager scratched Roland between his ears. He was a big dog, at least fifty kilos, a mixed breed of retriever and something else. "Those men are never going to hurt anyone again, Gina. We'd love to have you come with us, and we can use your help. Once I've taken care of some business at Spondu, we'll send people back to your farm to—" He left the rest of the thought unfinished.

It was dark when an overloaded vehicle passed them. It came out of the night without lights of any kind, traveling at very high speed. It was upon them and past before they could react and, had they been in the middle of the road where they'd been just moments before, all four would have been hit. But carrying al-Rashid forced them to take frequent breaks and they were sprawled on the shoulder when it roared by.

"Did you see those fools?" Lavager shouted. "God-damned idiots! Probably going back to the cornfield to assess the damage. They took their own sweet time! Did you see all those men hanging on?"

"They weren't from the Yatzaina farm," Gina volunteered.

It was well after dark before they reached the Cabbage

Patch. The last kilometer of their way was illuminated by the burning buildings.

The Cabbage Patch, Union of Margelan, Atlas

Second platoon had five Marines killed and eight too badly wounded to walk; thirteen casualties out of thirty-six Marines who entered the Cabbage Patch. That was a horrendous rate—and it didn't even count minor wounds.

Lieutenant Tevedes put the remnants of second and fourth squads to work setting their charges and second section to gathering their casualties in a collection point for Doc Natron to tend to, while first and third squads oversaw the assembling of the surviving defenders on the drill field. Tevedes checked on the dead and wounded Marines as they were brought in. Most of them were hit during the first minute or two, when the towers and bunkers began firing into the area between the power plant and Lab Three. They were twenty kilometers from their puddle jumpers, there was no way twenty-three of them could carry the severely wounded and the dead that far, not with any speed, and they weren't going to leave anybody behind. They'd need transportation. He toggled on first squad's circuit.

"How are the prisoners doing?" he asked when Sergeant Daly answered.

"They're thoroughly cowed," Daly answered. "They see the destruction of towers and bunkers, and hear commands from people they can't see. They're scared."

"Are they frightened enough to try anything?"

Daly looked at the gathered prisoners before replying. "I don't think so. They don't look like they think we're about to start killing them. If they did, I'd be concerned. Anyway, we're securing them as they arrive."

"Good. Take Nomonon and go to that vehicle building, see if there's anything we can use to ferry our dead and wounded."

"On the way," Daly said.

He and Nomonon trotted to the barnlike vehicle building. He used his HUD to review the maps of the area that he'd stored en route to Atlas, checking on the roads between the Cabbage Patch and where they'd left their puddle jumpers. There weren't many, they'd need an off-road vehicle to cover the distance. He hoped they wouldn't need a driver as well.

There were five vehicles in the building. One was a standard landcar, probably the facility administrator's personal vehicle—*Speaking of which*, Daly wondered, *Where are the administrator and the rest of the civilian staff? Probably hiding out of the line of fire, which is the best place for them to be*—and one was a passenger bus that didn't look capable of driving cross-country. Of the three lorries, only one looked fit for all-terrain movement. Daly wished it rode on an air cushion instead of wheels, but it looked like it would do. Corporal Nomonon climbed into the driver's compartment and tried the motor. When it whined to life he checked the dashboard instruments and declared it ready to go. He also determined that he could drive it easily enough. Daly climbed into the cargo compartment to see what it held. Benches lined the sides of the compartment, and there were shelves above. The benches and the shelves together were big enough to hold the casualties and most of the able-bodied. There was enough floor space for the dead and the able who couldn't fit on the benches. Daly climbed out of the lorry and went to the door of the vehicle barn to report in.

"There's a lorry in here that will carry all of us," Daly said when he raised Tevedes. "We also got a present—there are two assault guns mounted in the cargo compartment, one fore and one aft."

"Let's hope we don't need them," Tevedes replied.

"Me too. But I'm glad to have them."

"Bring the lorry to the casualty collection point and let's get them aboard."

"Roger that." Daly went back in and climbed into the lorry's cab. "Find rough spots to drive on," he told Nomonon, who simply said, "Aye aye," and started the vehicle.

Doc Natron looked up as the lorry trundled to a stop a few meters away. He had the three most seriously wounded in stasis bags.

"We found an ambulance for you, Doc," Daly said through his speaker, swinging down from the cab.

Natron had his chameleon gloves off to work on the wounded, he turned a palm up in a skeptical gesture. "How are that thing's cushions?" he asked. "Some of these Marines can't take being bounced around."

"I figured, that's why we didn't come here on the road. It's a smooth ride."

Natron looked across the compound toward the vehicle building and shook his head. "That ground's a lot smoother than anything we're liable to be on after we leave here," he said.

"Sorry, Doc, but it's the only vehicle we found that *can* go cross-country."

"Then it'll have to do." He stood. "Let me take a look at what you've got, then give me a hand loading. And take off your gloves so I can see what you're doing."

While the corpsman inspected the interior of the lorry, Daly reported to the platoon commander.

"Will it hold our goodies?" Tevedes asked. He'd had a couple Marines collect artifacts from the labs, his hard evidence that the Cabbage Patch was a weapons research center.

"That's affirmative."

"How soon will we be ready to go?"

"You'll have to ask Doc, he's checking the lorry now."

"I heard that," Natron broke in. "Give me two more Marines and I can have the casualties aboard the lorry in ten minutes."

"You've got them," Tevedes said. He checked with

Sergeant Kare, who believed they could leave the prisoners alone without the soldiers realizing they weren't being guarded and trying to break loose to cause trouble. The lieutenant ordered second squad to help load the casualties.

Doc Natron was good to his word and the casualties, including the dead, were loaded within the promised ten minutes.

"Listen up," Tevedes said on the all-hands circuit, "Mount up on the lorry at the casualty collection point, we're riding out of here."

While the platoon was gathering and Sergeant Daly, as the senior uninjured NCO remaining, supervised their boarding the lorry, Tevedes went to the prisoners.

"Listen up," he said when he reached the assembled prisoners. "Some of us are leaving on that lorry over there in a few minutes. The rest of us will walk out when the lorry's far enough away. Don't bother talking to us, we don't want to hear anything you have to say.

"Sooner or later, some of your people will show up and free you. When that happens, send someone up the hillside to the east, one of your civilians is up there alone. He's trussed up more securely than you are, he'll need help getting free.

"I'm sorry for your casualties, we would have preferred to get in, do what we had to do, and get out without a fight, but it didn't work out that way.

"Don't worry about the explosions you'll hear in a minute or so, that'll be the last of what we came here to do, there won't be any more." With that, he turned and walked away.

"Report," Tevedes said on the command circuit as he headed for the lorry.

"All hands present and ready to go," Daly replied immediately.

"Stand by for the final boom." Tevedes waited until he was at the lorry before transmitting the signal that set off the explosions laid by second and fourth squads.

Mission accomplished, but at a high price.

Tevedes pulled himself into the cab and settled next to Daly, who moved to the center of the bench seat. "Take the road a few klicks southwest, then turn east," he told Nomonon, who was still driving.

"Aye aye, sir," Nomonon replied with a question in his inflection.

"The prisoners will hear the direction we're going," Tevedes explained. "This is misdirection, I don't want anybody to start searching for us to the east right away. Besides, I told the prisoners only some of us were leaving now, and the rest would guard them for a while longer before heading out on foot."

Daly snorted a laugh. "The funny part is, they probably believed you."

"I hope they did." The lieutenant then twisted around to look into the cargo compartment. "Doc, how're they doing?"

"As well as can be expected under the circumstances," Natron answered. "They'll all live until we get them back to the *Admiral Nelson*."

The five dead lay under the benches, only two of them were in bodybags, he could see the other three by the bloodstains that wandered across their chameleons. The three stasis bags were on the shelves above the benches; the corpsman thought it would be too morbid to lay the most severely wounded next to the dead. Tevedes saw the other wounded the same way he saw the unbagged dead, by the blood on their chameleons. Two of them, one laying on a bench and the other on a shelf, showed enough blood that Tevedes suspected they should be in stasis bags. But they'd been too optimistic and had only brought three. He remembered ruefully that he had thought the two bodybags they'd brought was a pessimistic number.

He turned back to watch where they were going.

They barely noticed the four people sitting on the side of the road as they sped past in the dark before dawn.

Cross-country, a Few Kilometers East-Northeast of the Cabbage Patch

Lieutenant Tevedes kept an eye on the time as the lorry trundled cross-country after leaving the highway. He hoped the rain that had started a short time earlier would wash away the lorry's tracks. He wanted to stop and send his reports to the *Admiral Nelson* as soon as they were a safe distance from traffic and the navy starship was visible above the horizon. Ten kilometers east of the highway and a few north of the Cabbage Patch, he saw a modestly tall tree on top of a moderately high hill and directed Nomonon to draw close to it and stop. The lorry would be exposed to any possible overflights for a few minutes, but no aircraft were visible in the sky in visual or infrared, so the danger was slight. He got out and recorded two messages.

One message reported mission success, casualties, and how they were returning to where they'd left their puddle jumpers.

The other was the go code to be forwarded to the sniper team in New Granum.

When the messages were ready, he coded them to a burst transmission and climbed the tree. He saw Kraken Interstellar as a bright dot halfway up the western sky. He aimed his point-transceiver at the proper distance behind the station and activated it to zero in and lock on to the *Admiral Nelson*. When it beeped to say it had a lock, he pressed the transmit button.

CHAPTER
TWENTY-THREE

The Cabbage Patch Agricultural Research Center, Union of Margelan, Atlas

It began to rain just as the four foot-weary travelers topped the slight ridge that overlooked the Cabbage Patch. What they saw made them pause. The main gate was unguarded, towers were down, parts of the perimeter fence were destroyed, and the flames of the fires they had seen from afar were everywhere. Men ran about silhouetted against the burning buildings and nobody seemed in charge.

The drenching rain revived al-Rashid and he made to shake Lavager and Lanners off. "I'm all right, I can make it!" he muttered.

Roland, who'd been enjoying the walk immensely, sat on his haunches by Gina's legs and barked down at the ruined compound.

"Man-oh-man, they did a job on the place," Lavager whispered. It was evident even from where they stood that Labs One and Two had been heavily damaged. That was bad but not disastrous. From where he was standing, the Cabbage Patch illuminated by the fires now being doused by the rain, Lavager could not make out the unprepossessing building that housed the heart of what they were doing here. Well, they'd know soon enough. He struck a fist into his palm and said, "Friends, let's get on down there, organize these people, and get after the bastards who did this!" Al-Rashid staggered after him. Gina, with Roland at her side, and Lanners followed.

"Good God," Lavager muttered after they walked through the open gate, "Hieronymous Bosch couldn't have painted anything as horrible as this!" Everywhere was chaos. Men and women staggered about with no evident understanding of where they were while others, in uniform, officers and noncoms, shouted orders nobody bothered to obey.

"We were attacked by ghosts!" a soldier shouted as he rushed by. His face was covered in blood from a head wound.

Lanners stopped the man. "Where is your commander?" he demanded.

"Dead! All dead!" the man screamed, pulling himself away and running into one of the burning buildings.

Lanners made to go after him but Lavager shook his head. "Over there." He pointed to a figure smoking a cigarette. "Who's your officer?" Lavager asked, walking up to the man.

"Major Principale, but he's dead," the soldier answered. By the insignia on his collar the man held the rank of sergeant.

"Can you tell me what happened here?"

"We were attacked. I never saw them. It was dark, they were camouflaged, they moved too quickly, I don't know who they were, but they kicked our asses good. Then they piled into a lorry and drove off to the southwest. I saw the lorry go."

Lavager turned to his companions. "Dammit," he slapped his forehead, "that wasn't farmers we saw in that truck! And I'll bet they didn't head southwest for long. Damn! Well, who's in charge here, then?"

The man looked disdainfully at the bedraggled figure in front of him and answered sharply, "Nobody is. And just who the hell are you?" He took a drag on his cigarette and blew the smoke in Lavager's face.

"He's President Lavager!" Lanners said in an ominous tone.

"Awww—" The sergeant smirked and shook his head, but he leaned forward and looked closely at Lavager in the dim light. Suddenly it seemed an electric shock went through him. He tossed his cigarette away and came to attention. "Sergeant Drew Corfram, sir! Sorry 'bout that! It's been, um, a rather difficult day."

"You don't need to explain anything to me, Sergeant. Now, let's get organized here. Get some men," he turned to Lanners, "you help him with that, Lee. Franklin, Gina, I want you two to go inside the portico of that building over there and sit tight until I come back for you. Sergeant, you are now—you said your name is Corram?"

"Corfram, sir."

"Sergeant Corfram, excuse me, you are now the ranking officer in this compound, until I can find someone to replace you. You're operating under my personal orders. Lee here will back you up. Get as many unwounded men together as you can find. You had to have medics with the security battalion. Find them, and if they haven't started one, have them get a triage going for the wounded. See what you can do to establish communications with army headquarters back in New Granum. Don't worry about security. The people who did this are long gone. Set up your command post at that bunker over there. Now, have you seen any of the civilian staff? Dr. Jullundur in particular? You know who he is, don't you?"

"Yessir. Short brown guy, little sprouts of hair on his head, thick glasses, talks with an accent. Nossir, haven't seen him. The civilians all must have gone into hiding when the attack began."

"Very good, then. I'll be with you in a minute." With that he walked rapidly off.

Corfram looked at Lanners and shrugged. "You heard the man." In only the few seconds he had been in

Lavager's presence the sergeant had gone from being a defeated and demoralized non-ranker to a sergeant again.

Lavager approached the nondescript building in the compound's southwest corner cautiously. It appeared undamaged and that made his breathing a bit easier. He punched in the access code and the door swung open. Inside, the emergency lighting system cast a dim red glow over everything. The equipment resembled nothing more menacing than a large distillery. That's what it was, but not for whiskey. Lavager breathed a sigh of relief. If the raiders had examined the contents of Labs One and Two they might have gathered some idea of what was really going on at the Patch, but it was this building, the "refinery," that held the true secret of what Lavager's scientists were doing at the Cabbage Patch. The sweet earthy smell of fertilizer permeated the building.

"Ambala?" Lavager shouted. His voice echoed metallically off the walls. He walked carefully down the rows of gleaming retorts, his pistol drawn. "Ambala! Come out, goddamnit, if you're here!" He grinned wryly and thought to himself, What a stupid thing to say, if he's not here why am I shouting?

At the near end of the buildings was a suite of offices and changing rooms. Lavager was headed toward them when one of the doors banged open and a short figure in a white lab coat appeared.

"Ambala?" Lavager raised the pistol.

"Is that you, Mr. President? I thought I recognized that distinctive voice of yours!" The red light reflected off the figure's glasses as he smiled broadly in relief.

"Ambala, are you all right?" Lavager holstered the pistol and gripped the man's outstretched hand.

"Fine, sir, we're all fine. We took refuge in here at the first sign of alarm." Ambala—Dr. Ambala Jullundur, the scientist in charge of the secret research project at the Cabbage Patch—wiped perspiration from his forehead.

"There was terrible shooting and many explosions—" Several other scientists and technicians emerged from the office rooms and all began talking at once.

"Quiet! Quiet! Now listen. We've been attacked. The raiders nearly killed me in an ambush kilometers away, and they've caused a lot of damage and casualties here. But you are all right and everything is fine in here." He turned to Dr. Jullundur. "So that means, Ambala, we're still in business, right?"

"Yes, Mr. President, we are. The damage to the other buildings may cause some delay, but there has been no harm to us or to our equipment. Mr. President, who did this to us?"

"I have a pretty good idea, Doctor, and I'm going to do to them as they have done to us. Now, you people stay put in here. As soon as I've gotten things stabilized and organized outside, I'll send someone for you." Lavager took Dr. Jullundur's hand again and shook it. "Stay calm, I'll be seeing you soon."

Sergeant Corfram had done a good job getting things organized. "They took one of our lorries, sir, a Brimmer cross-country LX6. Ident number CHO1939." He gave Lavager a handheld communicator. "I have General Ollius at army HQ, sir."

"Good work! You are now Lieutenant Corfram. General?"

"Yessir," Ollius replied. "What is going on out there? I've heard—"

"Never mind what you've heard. Now, I want you to do some things and do them quickly. You know that strategic intelligence platoon that works for your G2? I think a Lieutenant Svetlanacek commands it? Get them out here at once. Next, I want Gyrfalcons in the air to the southwest of the Cabbage Patch, I repeat, southwest of here. They are to look for a Brimmer cross-country LX6, license CHO1939. It's carrying a lot of men, how many, I don't know, but they are to take it out. Got that? Take it out. If there's more than one lorry out there that fits the description, and the pilots are not sure if it's the one, take it out too, take them all out. I don't care if one of them is full of missionaries going to a prayer meeting, get every damned lorry the pilots can spot. Next, send me a motorized infantry battalion, General, men who can move and shoot. What's left of the security battalion here is not up to pursuing anyone. Copy so far?"

"Yessir."

"Wake up your war plans people. Have them waiting for me. Call my cabinet into session at once. They can wait for me too. You are now Army Chief of Staff with the rank of full general effective from this very minute. Cut the necessary orders. I'll sign them when I get back."

"But General Ollwel—?"

"He's *hors de combat*. Forget him. Finally, get a hopper out here ten minutes ago. Have all that stuff cooking by the time I get back to the city. Out." He handed the communicator back to Corfram. "Lieutenant, you heard what I told the General. I lost some good men here today and I need replacements. You're one of them. Come with me." They spent the next few minutes rallying the survivors, organizing damage-assessment teams, and teams to search for dead and wounded. "Give me a full report on the situation out here before the end of the day. When the infantry and recon units get here, work with them to organize a pursuit of the raiders. The infantry battalion commander will have tactical control of the operation, but you, Lieutenant, represent me personally and will report to me on everything. One final thing I have to do. You carry on."

Lavager returned to the portico where he found Gina and Roland sitting. Al-Rashid had already been taken to the makeshift aid station. "His wounds are not life-threatening," Gina informed Lavager.

Lavager sat down next to her and petted Roland. The sun was just coming up. "What are you going to do now, Gina?"

Gina shrugged. "Go home, sir. Take care of my—" She bit her lip and hung her head, but did not cry.

Lavager put his arm around the girl. "No. You're coming to the city with me, Gina. I'll have people take care of your family. I'll arrange everything. Do you have any other relatives or close friends you'd like to have with you now?" Gina named several people and Lavager nodded. "I'll see they're notified and brought to New Granum. I'm going to have you put up in town for a few days, Gina. Ever hear of the DeLuxe Inn? It's a five-star hotel—" He paused as a thought struck him. No, this young lady should not be left alone in a luxury hotel after what had just happened to her. "Do you know my daughter, Candace? She's just about your age."

"Yessir." Gina's face brightened. "I've seen her in the trid news, with you. She's really feck!" "Feck" was a term the Margelan teens used among themselves to describe something wonderful and "in." Lavager had often heard Candace use it. Lavager had often thought if something were feck it'd naturally be the opposite of "feckless," so the word made some sense to him, but as with most teenage slang, nobody was sure just where it had come from.

"Well, if you agree, I'll take you back to my house and you and Roland here can stay with Candace for a while, until we get everything straightened out. Candace will like you—and Roland. What do you say?"

"Oh, yessir, I would like that! Thank you, thank you!" She put her arms around Lavager's neck.

"Look, Gina, the sun's coming up." As he spoke, the rim of the sun poked above the trees just beyond the ruined perimeter fence, casting its rays through the haze of smoke upon the ruins of the Cabbage Patch. The sight was not the most inspiring Lavager had ever seen. He shrugged. "I've always liked the dawn, even here. It's another day we're above ground." He searched inside his vest and fished out an Anniversario, which he lighted.

"That smells good," Gina whispered, her head against Lavager's shoulder.

How much she reminds me of Candace, Lavager thought. He smoked in silence for a while. They didn't need him just then; he could rest for a spell. How nice it would be to just rest, not worry about politics, war, government, anything. He thought of Ollwelen and his heart raced in anger. After all their years together Ollwelen turned traitor on him. Well, time enough to deal with that. "When this is over," he said softly to himself, "and I've got everybody on my side and everything is straightened out, Candace and I will take a long, long vacation, maybe just not come back to New Granum at all."

From far away came the sound of approaching aircraft. Good. General Ollius was on the ball. Gina had gone to sleep beside Lavager. He smiled. "Come on, Roland, old fella, let's get your mistress back to town. And then I'm going to deal with some people like they've never been dealt with before."

In the Air, East of the Cabbage Patch

"Hometown, this is Gamma Lead. Over."

Gamma Lead's radio crackled, then a voice said, "Gamma Lead, Hometown. Go."

"Hometown, does Racer have a unit at—" Gamma Lead rattled off map coordinates.

"Wait one, Gamma," Hometown said and went off the air, but not for long. "Gamma Lead, that's a negative. What do you have?"

"Stand by to receive visual, Hometown." Gamma Lead pressed a series of buttons that transmitted images of the scene he was orbiting at six thousand meters.

"Received, Gamma. Stand by." Soft static again filled Gamma Lead's earphones. After a longer wait than the previous one, Hometown came back. "Gamma Lead, Racer requests you take a closer look. Can do?"

"Right up the exhaust pipe, if that's what you want," Gamma Lead replied, then on the flight circuit, "Wing, let's take a closer look."

The flight of two Gyrfalcons of the Margelan air defense corps banked sharply and pointed their noses groundward. They were at Mach 1.25, so the object on the ground had no warning of their approach before they flashed above it at less than fifty meters.

A Hilltop Ten Kilometers East of the Cabbage Patch

The rain stopped while Lieutenant Tevedes was in the tree, but the trunk was still slick with dripping water. He had just started to climb down the tree when the sonic boom from the two Gyrfalcons slammed into him. The blast knocked him from the tree and rocked the lorry violently, throwing around the Marines inside it. Tevedes landed hard on one shoulder and flipped over with an audible cracking of bone.

"Doc!" Sergeant Daly shouted, and jumped out of the cab to rush to Tevedes's aid. He could barely make out the platoon commander in infra, but it looked like the lieutenant lay with his shoulders and head at impossible angles. Daly opened Tevedes's face shields and saw the officer's eyes were open wide and his mouth gaped like a beached fish gulping for water.

Natron reached him seconds after Daly and swore as soon as he saw Tevedes's face. "Don't touch him," he ordered. For the first time since they left the hidden AstroGhost, the corpsman raised his face screens. He bent low over Tevedes's head and turned his own head so his ear was above the man's mouth. He felt a puff of air and softly breathed a sigh of relief as he straightened back up.

He removed his gloves, then as gently as he could, felt around Tevedes's shoulders and upper body. He reached down and sharply pinched the inside of his patient's thigh, but Tevedes didn't react.

"Can you feel this?" he asked as he lifted Tevedes's hand and bent it back.

Tevedes croaked a noise. From the shape of his mouth, Natron was confident he'd said, "No," though it might have been, "Ow!"

The corpsman did a couple more quick tests, then rocked back. "All right," he briskly said to Tevedes, "here's my off-the-cuff diagnosis. I think your neck is broken, and your spinal cord might be damaged. If I had another stasis bag, I'd put you in it and let the surgeons aboard the *Admiral Nelson* worry about you. But I don't—and I can't take any of the other Marines out of their stasis bags, because they're liable to die if I do.

"So what I'm going to do is brace your neck and put you on a backboard to hold you steady. It'll be enough to keep you stable until we get you back aboard the ship. Do you understand?"

Tevedes tried to say something, but all that came out was an almost inaudible, "p-p-p."

"Planes, is that what you're saying."

"Y-Yeh."

Natron looked up. "Daly, where are you?" he called out.

"Up here," Daly called back. "Halfway up the tree. I'm looking for those aircraft." He looked all around in both visual and infra, but didn't see any sign of the two Gyrfalcons.

Directly Above Second Platoon

If Daly had looked straight up, he might have seen the two fighters turning in a very high, very slow, very tight orbit.

Gamma Lead transmitted the visuals he'd taken during his low pass over the lorry that had been identified as the same type as the one missing from the Cabbage Patch and was waiting for further orders.

They came. "Gamma, Hometown. We've got a positive ID from the registration number on that vehicle. It is the one taken from the Cabbage Patch. The intruders can't have gotten very far, so run a search pattern north and east of the lorry. Transmit your infras to me, Racer says they are impossible to spot in visual and have very good infra damping."

"Roger, Hometown. Gamma initiating search pattern north and east of the lorry." Gamma Lead switched to local and asked, "You heard, Wing?"

"That's an affirmative, Lead."

"Drop to two thousand meters, one thousand meters spread."

"Two thousand altitude, one thousand spread. Got it, Lead."

"On my mark. One, two, three, mark."

The Gyrfalcons turned on their wing tips and dove for their search pattern altitude, north and east of the lorry.

Doc Natron had Lieutenant Tevedes's neck braced and his body strapped to a metal panel he found inside the lorry in fifteen minutes. Once the injured platoon commander was loaded, he turned to Daly. Both section leaders were dead, Gunny Lytle was in a stasis bag, and Lieutenant Tevedes was strapped to a backboard—and heavily sedated.

"Well, now, Sergeant Daly," he said slowly, "it looks like you're in command. What do we do now?"

"It looked to me like those aircraft are looking for us northeast of here," he said. "We're going southeast as far as we can, then turn straight for the puddle jumpers. Mount up."

Natron didn't move. "We've got six dead, and four more so badly hurt there's no way they can travel via puddle jumper. So what are we going to do when we get there?"

"We're Force Recon. We leave nothing behind, not even footprints. We're going to pick the puddle jumpers up and take them with us. It wouldn't do to leave them behind for somebody to find later on."

"I like your thinking, Sergeant. All aboard this Ship of Fools." He climbed into the cargo compartment to tend to his patients during the journey to where they'd left the puddle jumpers.

Daly climbed back into the cab and told Nomonon to head southeast. As soon as he was sure they were far enough away from the search area, he'd stop and send an update to the *Admiral Nelson*. Maybe he'd request that the AstroGhost meet them where the puddle jumpers were hidden. That would make getting away from the searchers easier and might save the lives of some of the wounded.

CHAPTER
TWENTY-FOUR

Room 1007, New Granum DeLuxe Inn

"That's it," Sergeant Ivo Gossner said when he'd decoded the burst transmission from the *Admiral Nelson*. "It's a go." *They were going to assassinate a sovereign head of state!* He put some effort into controlling his trembling. Sure, Jorge Liberec Lavager wasn't President of a world, merely the head of a nation-state, one of several on Atlas—but he *was* a head of state nonetheless.

Gossner didn't know of another instance where Marines had carried out a political assassination. He'd never even heard rumors of Marines conducting a political assassination, and there were rumors about *everything* Marines did, and a lot of things they *didn't* do.

Lance Corporal Bella Dwan was lying on the bed in their room. She had taken off her blouse and skirt before she lay down on top of the covers wearing just the undergarments she'd bought on the shopping trip the previous day. The undergarments in question were sexier than any Gossner knew her to own back at Camp Howard, and sexier than any he'd glimpsed on her since they'd checked into the hotel. He didn't know if she was confident he wouldn't try anything or if she was deliberately teasing him. Or he had to admit that it was possible she had no interest whatsoever in sex and assumed that he didn't either.

He had to control his trembling again, but this time it was because of the sight of her scantily clad body. When

Ivo Gossner couldn't see into her eyes, he found Bella
Dwan to really be a very attractive woman. He forced
himself to focus on her closed eyes and ignore the rest of
her.

"Bella, did you hear me?"

She didn't open her eyes, but she did say, "I heard you."
She grinned. Dwan's grin was that of a big cat about to
pounce on a grazing antelope. Gossner looked away so he
didn't see the look she gave him as she curled up into a sitting position with her legs crossed camp-style in front of
her.

"Damn, it's a go," she said softly. Her eyes glittered
with anticipation.

"So we need to get out there and see if we can do it from
that empty building. Get dressed and let's make like
tourists." He rose from the chair he'd been sitting in and
went into the water closet without looking at her.

She watched him go with an expression on her face that,
had he seen it, he wouldn't have known what to make of.

Center Boulevard, New Granum

They walked past Ramuncho's Restaurant on the other
side of the street. Even though it was midafternoon on a
business day, the street was nearly as crowded as it had
been the previous evening. This time most of the people
about were dressed in business garb, and walked purpose-
fully as though they were rushing from meeting to meeting. Still, a large minority were obvious tourists out
shopping, dining, or looking for parties. There were
enough people shopping that Dwan's oversized handbag
didn't look out of place on the street.

Gossner saw immediately that they'd been right when
they decided they couldn't pull off the assassination from
the access alleys between the buildings; both foot and
landcar traffic was far too dense for the maser to get off a
full shot at the target.

They circled the block to Ranstead Street and passed the front of the vacant building they'd entered the previous night. They knew neither the name nor the address of the building, but they both had a good enough sense of spatial relations to know where it was. Even if they hadn't, they couldn't have missed it—it was the only building on the block that had a "to let" sign on it.

A dearth of shops and restaurants meant there were far fewer tourists on Ranstead Street, but there were nearly as many people in business garb as there had been on Center Boulevard.

They wouldn't be able to enter the building during the day, at least not through the front. They'd have to go in at night and simply wait until the target showed up at Ramuncho's. The maître d' had told them Lavager dined there often enough to justify holding a table for him, but how often was that, how long might they have to wait? And how might the raid on the Cabbage Patch affect his dining out? Would he stop going to Ramuncho's until the crisis caused by the raid was over?

Gossner looked down the side street toward Center Boulevard and saw a tourist couple duck into the service alley that ran behind the vacant building. None of the other people on the street paid them any attention.

"Come on," he said, and took Dwan's hand.

She skipped along with him. Her jauntiness jarred Gossner, but he didn't display any discomfort.

He glanced into the service alley as they passed it. He could barely make them out, but he saw the tourist couple, thinking themselves fully hidden, in a tight embrace.

"Is that how we're going to get in the building during the day, Ivo?" Dwan asked. "Playing the young lovers making out in an alley?"

Gossner blinked; he hadn't thought she'd even seen the tourist couple. "Do you have a better idea?" he asked in return.

"Let's try it from the other end of the alley."

"Whatever you say, dear."

"You're so sweet, Ivo." She squeezed his hand and briefly lay her head on his shoulder.

Smart move, Gossner thought. If anybody followed them around and saw them duck into the service alley, they'd think the obvious—that they wanted privacy without having to waste time going back to their hotel—or was Dwan doing something . . . Nah, not the Queen of Killers.

When they approached the alley from the other end Dwan pulled Gossner's hand around her waist and snuggled close. She looked up at him with an adoring expression and whispered something he didn't catch. At least, he was pretty sure he heard her wrong; something about "jump" and "bones" and "after the kill."

Nobody paid them any attention when they entered the alley, and in just a moment they were slipping through the shadows on their way to the rear of the vacant building. In the distance they could make out the tourist couple, who seemed to be in an even more intimate embrace than before. When Gossner looked back, he saw people passing the alley's entrance; none of them even glanced down it.

In daylight, he saw that all the detritus in the service alley was incidental rubbish, none of it organic. There was also a good deal less in the service alley than there was in the access alleys he'd looked down. Nothing was spilling from bins now, the sanitation department must have made a pickup since last night. He wondered what the schedule was.

It wasn't long before they reached their destination. They both looked carefully, but neither saw any sign that anyone had investigated the open ground-level window. In a moment, they were back in the basement.

Dim light filtered into the basement through the two windows on the alley side. It was enough to show them that the basement ran the length and width of the building and was indeed empty. They saw the stairway to the ground floor and headed for it.

They stopped halfway up at the sound of voices from above.

"—my needs exactly," a male voice said.

"And how soon would you want to move in?" a female voice asked.

Footsteps that sounded like they were headed for the front of the building accompanied the voices.

"As soon as possible, actually. There are those few items you need to fix. What's your timeline on the work?"

There was the sound of the front door opening.

"We can have it finished within a fortnight. Provided I can get a crew in to get started in—"

The voices were cut off by the closing door.

Gossner, in the lead, turned around and sat heavily on the stairs. Dwan, a couple of steps lower, put her hands on his knees and leaned in so her face was close to his.

"Let's take a look at that second floor room anyway," she said. "We might still have enough time for the shot."

"Yeah," he said, though he thought they'd have to do it from the rear of Ramuncho's or even from someplace else. He rose and led the way.

The view from the second floor rear room was a sniper's dream. The room was filled with shadows, the sniper could stand back from the window and be effectively invisible from Center Boulevard, even from the first several meters of the access alley leading to it. The view into Ramuncho's window was at an angle, and not all of the interior was visible from the Ranstead Street building, but the part that was visible included the table reserved for President Lavager.

"I like it," Dwan said. She stepped up to the window and examined the molding. "It'd be a snap to remove the glass," she said. Shooting through an open window would be more accurate and effective than shooting through the glass, and if the glass was removed they wouldn't have to risk attracting attention by opening and closing the window.

"The workers will notice if the glass is missing when they come in," Gossner said.

"They're just as likely to think it's something the bosses forgot to put on the punch list," Dwan said.

He grunted noncommittally. As a boss himself, he knew that bosses didn't always think of everything—but he wasn't about to admit it. Then he had to stop thinking about it and help her remove the glass.

"Let's go check out the Presidential Residence, just in case," she said when they were finished.

"That's a very good idea."

But there were too many tourists and soldiers around the Presidential Residence for them to find a sniper spot.

Room 1007, New Granum DeLuxe Inn

They ordered a room service dinner so they could discuss their options while they ate. Gossner also wanted to check on what the local news media had to say about the raid on the Cabbage Patch.

This wasn't the time to get exotic; they went for roast beef, scalloped potatoes, and broccoli with hollandaise sauce. They skipped dessert, but did indulge in a pot of real coffee.

Gossner activated the trid and picked a news channel. A perfectly coiffed and overly sincere-looking man in an immaculate suit was talking in front of a scene of devastation familiar to anybody who'd ever been on a battlefield after the shooting stopped.

Gossner hit the "repeat segment" button on the trid's control and the view changed slightly. It was the same location, just a few minutes earlier. This time, the view wasn't static, rather it panned from left to right. What had obviously been guard towers were tumbled to the ground. Bunkers were blackened with the scorch marks of blaster fire. Several buildings were shattered, the obvious victims of internal explosions. People stood or walked about in the middle distance; most of them looked dazed, and some staggered.

This time the reporter wasn't in the scene, though he was there as a voice-over. "You can see for yourself," he said with earnest sincerity, "the destruction wrought by unknown raiders on the Union of Margelan's agricultural research center called the Cabbage Patch. The destruction is horrendous to look at, absolutely horrendous. Words fail me."

The images panning the field reached him and stopped, as did his voice. He wasn't looking out at the viewer, but to the side, the area the image field had just covered.

It didn't take more than a few seconds for the reporter to find words again. He turned his earnest face to the front and said, "I've never seen such destruction, and I've seen more destruction than most people have in my function as a reporter for UXN Instant News. Nowhere in my lengthy service of bringing the news to you have I seen anything to match this, not even in the aftermath of the most violent storms, or the crash of the TGA orbital shuttle three years ago."

"He should see some of the things I've seen," Gossner muttered. "I've been in places that make that look like a group of toddlers were left unsupervised for five minutes."

"I guess he's never been in the military," Dwan murmured.

"Sure as shit not in the Marines," Gossner said.

They stopped talking and listened again.

". . . was here just a short while ago," the reporter was saying. "I was able to speak with him for a few moments."

The trid image wavered for a second, then steadied with the reporter standing next to a dirty and obviously angry Jorge Liberec Lavager.

"Mr. President," the reporter said in a tone of surprised awe, "who could have done this? Do you know yet? Has anybody been arrested?"

"Just give me one question at a time, Bil," Lavager said, his voice strained. "We are certain of who the perpetrators of this atrocity are, and are taking steps to gather information to confirm it. Also, even as we speak, our army and air defense corps are conducting a pursuit of the felons who destroyed this important agricultural research facility. Don't worry, Bil," Lavager turned to face the cam, "and you at home, don't you worry either. We're going to catch the people responsible for this, and when we do, they are going to pay the maximum penalty."

The image wavered again and reporter Bil was once more alone in the image. "President Lavager got rescue and clean-up operations begun here, and headed back into New Granum shortly after my interview with him."

Then "Bil" took a few seconds to rearrange his face into an expression of earnestly sincere gravity, and said, "It hasn't been confirmed yet, but normally reliable sources have informed UXN Instant News that President Lavager was on his way to the Cabbage Patch for a routine visit when his convoy was attacked, and several members of his party were killed. Again, this hasn't been confirmed, but Army Chief of Staff General Locksley 'Locker' Ollwelen is said to be among the dead."

"It wasn't us," Gossner said, surprised at hearing about the ambush.

"We're on this mission because of the Central Intelligence Organization," Dwan said, teeth clamped and eyes slitted. "Do you think maybe they've got a backup operation going here?"

Gossner considered the question for a moment, then shook his head. "No. They could screw up an ambush that badly, but I think they want to keep their DNA out of this. Remember, the target has enemies in other nation-states here, so it could have been one of them."

Dwan looked at him for a long moment, before turning

back to the trid. Gossner thought his answer mollified her, but he wouldn't be willing to bet his life on it.

Soon after, they headed out to find the target's current location. But it soon became clear that he wasn't in his usual haunts. They'd try again the next day.

CHAPTER
TWENTY-FIVE

Fifteen Kilometers Northeast of the Cabbage Patch, Union of Margelan, Atlas

The going was slower now that someone was looking for them. Daly told Nomonon to keep the lorry to low ground and under trees as much as possible. That meant Nomonon had to take a meandering route that went around hills and zigged and zagged along the irregular borders of clumps of trees.

Fearing another strike from the sky, Daly put Sergeant Kare and his third squad on air duty, scanning the sky in all directions for aircraft. Whenever they spotted one, Nomonon pulled the lorry into the deepest shadows he could find until the plane disappeared over the horizon.

"There's more than just the pair that buzzed us, you know," Kare said to Daly after the third time they'd had to hide from aircraft they'd seen heading in a generally northerly direction.

"I expect they've got a full-fledged search on," Daly acknowledged. "Once they found what we'd done to the Cabbage Patch, they probably started feeding everything they could into searching for us."

Daly checked his inertial map and silently swore; in the two hours since dawn, they hadn't covered much more than half the distance to where they'd hidden the puddle jumpers. And the search was getting larger, covering and re-covering more ground. If escape using the puddle jumpers hadn't already been impossible because of their dead and severely wounded, now it was totally out of the question because of the air search. As it was, escape would be easier if they didn't go back for the puddle jumpers. But Daly didn't think they could leave that equipment behind; if it was discovered, the equipment would point to the Confederation Marines as the raiders.

At least they had the lorry. Now if the search didn't spread too wide too quickly . . .

A Hilltop, Ten Kilometers East of the Cabbage Patch

"Hometown, Hometown, this is Walking Man. Over," said Lieutenant Rak Svetlanacek, commander of the Fifth Independent Armored Cavalry Platoon, which had been sent to take out the lorry.

"Walking Man, this is Hometown. Go."

"Hometown, we are at the coordinates where Gamma Flight saw the lorry. The lorry's not here. Over."

"Walking Man, Hometown. Are you sure you're in the right place?"

"Positive, Hometown. I'm standing in the wheel tracks where the lorry sat, but it's not here."

"What are your coordinates, Walking Man?"

Svetlanacek looked at his map display and read off the coordinates.

"Confirmed," Hometown said when he compared Svetlanacek's coordinates with those given by the Gyrfalcon flight when they reported seeing the lorry. "Tell me about the tracks, Walking Man."

"They come from the southwest. I can see where the lorry stopped. There is evidence on the ground of several men moving about and one man lying down, but there are no tracks of anybody walking away. The lorry's tracks go southeast from here."

"Follow the tracks, Walking Man, I will direct an air search to your southeast. Hometown out."

Lieutenant Svetlanacek took a deep breath and let it out slowly. "Mount up!" he shouted to his soldiers. The thirty cavalrymen broke off their search of the area and reboarded their three armored cars.

"Echelon formation," Svetlanacek ordered when his men were all back on their vehicles. Corporal Mirko, the command vehicle's driver, started his vehicle and headed out at the commander's signal. The three armored cars headed southeast at speed, with Svetlanacek's car in the tracks left by the lorry, one car fifty meters ahead of it and a hundred to its right, the other an equal distance to its left and rear.

A hundred kilometers to the west, a flight of Gyrfalcons veered from the flight path to its previously assigned search area and headed due east to take up a search pattern in support of the Fifth Independent Armored Cavalry Platoon. Fifty kilometers to the north, two more Gyrfalcon flights broke off their searches, gained altitude, and headed south to newly assigned search areas.

At the same time, a mounted infantry company on the New Granum Road turned off and headed east cross-country on an interception vector. Seventy-five kilometers to the south, an airborne battalion boarded Vertical/Short-Take-Off-and-Landing aircraft and launched. The VSTOLs began orbiting several kilometers south of the lorry's one known position. Once the raiders were located, the VSTOLs would land their battalion to trap and crush the raiders.

In the Air, Southeast of the Hilltop

"Hometown, this is Mad Max. Over," the leader of another flight of searching Gyrfalcons said.

"Mad Max, Hometown. Go."

"Hometown, I think I have something on the ground, we're heading for the deck to check it out." Mad Max Lead transmitted his location.

"I logged your location, Mad Max. You are cleared for the deck."

Mad Max Lead turned onto his right wing and dropped toward the ground, followed by his wingman five hundred meters to his left rear.

On the Ground, Southeast of the Hilltop

"Bogies, eight o'clock!" Corporal Pitzel shouted.

"Hide us," Sergeant Daly ordered.

Corporal Nomonon looked for a heavier patch of trees, someplace that would offer more screening than the thin layer of branches under which the lorry was moving. He spotted one to his left and the lorry trundled under the denser cover provided by the branches of three huge trees.

A moment later, the two Gyrfalcons shot by barely a hundred meters overhead; subsonic, the force of their passing shook the leaves and branches, but barely rocked the lorry.

Daly couldn't see the aircraft, so he listened intently to the scream of their passage. He swore when he heard them turn about for another pass rather than climb back to their search altitude.

"Stand by," Daly ordered over the command circuit, "they may have spotted us."

The lead Gyrfalcon shot past fifty meters to their left, then a change in the second Gyrfalcon's doppler told Daly it was shifting to come directly at them. A line of explosive cannon shells erupted in the treetops, raining shattered branches and mangled leaves down onto the lorry.

"They missed!" Nomonon squawked excitedly.

"No they didn't," Daly snapped back. "That burst was to make a hole in the canopy so they can see through it." Then into the command circuit, "Everybody who can, dismount. Third and sixth squads, take the assault guns! We need to try to take them out on their next pass!"

The twenty-two Marines who were still mobile scrambled off the lorry, bringing as many of their severely wounded with them as they could. Doc Natron stayed aboard with Lieutenant Tevedes, who he said couldn't be moved. Third and sixth squads set up the heavy fléchette guns.

"Here they come!" Daly said more calmly than he felt. "First section, right aircraft. Second section, get the one on the left. Wait for my command. Shoot in front of the sound."

The overhead foliage was too thick for them to see through until the aircraft were almost directly above them, they'd have to aim by sound rather than sight because when they saw the aircraft, it would be too late to hit them.

Daly listened closely. This time the aircraft on the left came first. When he thought it was close enough, he ordered, "Second Section, *fire*!" He barely had time to finish before he had to order, "First Section, *fire*!"

Southeast of the Hilltop

Mad Max Lead staggered as two plasma bolts and a spray of fléchettes struck the aircraft. The pilot flipped off the damage alarm that screamed in his ears and ran his eyes over his control panel. He had no idea what had hit him, but the control electronics in his left wing were out and his engine was overheating. He began sweating; he had little control over the Gyrfalcon now—and he had to stop the increasing heating of the engine. He eased the throttle back and tipped his nose up, which put him in danger of stalling, but he was too low to bail out and couldn't survive ditching in this terrain.

"Wing, status report," Mad Max Lead shouted into his comm.

An explosion to his rear was the only answer. The other assault gun had ripped through the second Gyrfalcon, permitting one of the two plasma bolts that struck the fighter to reach a fuel bladder.

There wasn't much left of the blast wave from the exploding Gyrfalcon by the time it reached Mad Max Lead, but it was enough to further fatigue the wing root damaged by the fléchette burst and rip it off. Mad Max Lead barely had time to see treetops rushing up before he crashed into them.

"Mount up, now!" Sergeant Daly ordered. "We've got to get out of here!"

"What way?" Corporal Nomonon asked as he hauled himself behind the lorry's controls.

"In a direction they don't expect us to go," Daly answered. "North. Go fast, let's get some space between us and anybody else who shows up here." Both the Gyrfalcon flight that attacked them and the flight they saw a few minutes before it had come from the north. If the search was shifting from the north to the south, they should go where it had been rather than where it was.

The crashed aircraft started a forest fire behind them.

Lieutenant Svetlanacek and the Fifth Independent Armored Cavalry Platoon were the first ground unit to reach the site of the brief air-ground battle. Several acres of trees and undergrowth were still burning, but because of the previous night's rain, the undergrowth and canopy ignited slowly and the fire didn't spread rapidly.

"Two and three, search for survivors from the aircraft. And watch out for the raiders! If they could take out two fighter planes, they might have set an ambush or some other surprise for us." He didn't think that was likely, though. According to what he'd heard over the command net, the raiders hadn't initiated the fight; instead they tried to hide, and didn't fire until they'd been fired on. Most likely, they simply fled after knocking out the two Gyrfalcons. He set his own armored car to make a circuit of the burn to try to pick up the tracks of the lorry.

Sevtlanacek had Corporal Mirko drive counterclockwise around the burned and burning area, checking the south and east first because that's the direction the lorry had been headed in since he began following its tracks. It wasn't until the second circuit, a hundred meters farther out from the burn than the first circuit, that he found tracks—*two* sets of tracks. One set went due north, the other west of north. Which was which? Had the raiders met up with another group?

Svetlanacek pursed his lips in grudging respect for the raider commander. Heading into what that commander had to know was the center of the search area was an audacious move. But then, that commander, whoever he was, must have guessed that the search was shifting south and east, leaving the search area uncovered. Except, which set of tracks belonged to the raiders? He couldn't tell, they'd both been made by the same kind of tires.

He ordered Mirko to make another circuit and he found the second set of tracks leading into the burn. He plotted both sets on his map, but neither exit matched the entrance of the tracks he knew weren't made by the raiders.

By the time Svetlanacek found the northbound tire tracks, his other cars had retrieved the mangled and charred bodies of the Mad Max pilots.

Svetlanacek radioed in his report and told Hometown he wanted to follow the tracks that went due north. Hometown approved his decision, but vehicles and people had been seen on the ground south and west of the Cabbage Patch, and the search and pursuit were concentrating there. Svetlanacek ordered his platoon to follow the lorry's tracks. Hometown sent one flight of Gyrfalcons to search the area west of north of the burn.

Seven Kilometers Due West of the Puddle Jumper Cache

When Sergeant Daly's map showed they were due west of where they'd left the puddle jumpers, he told

Nomonon to turn right and go as fast as he could. Nomonon went faster than Doc Natron would have wanted, but while the extra jouncing was uncomfortable for his patients, it didn't cause them any additional injury so he didn't raise an objection.

Twenty Kilometers Due East of the Cabbage Patch

"Only two hundred and seventy kilometers to go," Daly said ironically when they reached the puddle jumpers. He ordered second section to load the puddle jumpers, then changed the scale on his map so he could examine a larger area. He knew the lorry was leaving tracks on the ground, tracks that could be followed by any ground forces following them. They needed a paved road.

The map showed a road twenty kilometers northwest of them; he shrank the scale again and saw it was the same southwest-northeast road that ran past the Cabbage Patch, the road they'd first followed in the opposite direction after the raid. The road continued northeast for twenty-five kilometers beyond its closest point to their current position before turning to wend its way east through the foothills of a mountain range. It passed fifty kilometers north of where the AstroGhost waited for them.

Daly thought for a moment. Maybe he could get the AstroGhost to meet them somewhere along that fifty kilometers, closer to the road—maybe even somewhere along the road itself.

If he could find a place and time to contact the *Admiral Nelson*, that was.

It was worth trying.

He showed Nomonon the map and asked, "How long do you think it'll take to get there?"

Nomonon looked at the map and shrugged. "Half an hour?"

"Do it."

Thirty Kilometers Northeast of the Cabbage Patch

They reached the New Granum Road without incident. Sergeant Daly looked to the right, no traffic was in sight. He did see a vehicle in the distance to the left, but it seemed to be going away rather than toward them.

"Turn left," he ordered.

Corporal Nomonon looked at him. "Don't you mean right? Left takes us back where we started."

"Anybody following us on the ground will see where we turned onto the road. Let's go far enough for the dirt on the tires to beat off, then turn around without leaving the road and head the way we want to go. Nobody following the way we turn onto the road will catch up to us."

Nomonon grinned. "You're pretty smart, boss." He turned left.

A kilometer and a half after they turned onto the New Granum road, Corporal Pitzel reported they were no longer leaving dirty tire tracks in their wake. Nomonon stopped slowly enough to not leave marks on the pavement, then backed and filled without leaving the roadway until they were pointed northeast. He moved out at speed.

A couple of kilometers beyond where they'd turned onto the road, Daly saw a vehicle approaching from ahead of them.

"Take off your helmet and gloves," he told Nomonon.

"What?"

"That driver up ahead might not realize that he doesn't see your body, but he'll certainly notice if he doesn't see a driver at all in this lorry."

"Good idea."

Daly reached across and controlled the steering so Nomonon could use both hands to remove his helmet and gloves.

The driver of the other lorry waved as they passed. Nomonon raised a hand in reply, but low enough it wasn't obvious his hand wasn't visibly attached to an arm. The other driver didn't seem to notice anything amiss.

When the Fifth Independent Armored Cavalry Platoon reached the New Granum Road, Lieutenant Svetlanacek stopped his driver from turning left onto the road.

"But, sir, that's where the lorry we're following went," Corporal Mirko objected.

"I know," Svetlanacek replied as he looked up and down the road. One lorry was in sight in each direction. The one to the right was farther away, he thought both of them were too close to be the lorry they'd been following. Could their quarry already be out of sight to the left? Moreover, as slick as the raider commander was, would he still head directly back to the scene of his raid? That didn't make sense. But if the enemy commander had gone left as a misdirection and then turned back . . .

Yes, that's what Svetlanacek thought he would have done.

Svetlanacek decided to err on the side of caution. He got on the radio and requested a fly-by up the New Granum Road to check the registration number on the lorry headed toward the Cabbage Patch, and to see if the road held any other vehicles between his position and the Cabbage Patch. It took almost fifteen minutes for a flight to break off from its search pattern and fly up the road from the Cabbage Patch. The lorry Svetlanacek saw was the only one on the road. It took a couple more minutes for the flight to drop low and buzz the vehicle to record its registration number before an urgent command sent it heading back southwest.

The lorry's registration number didn't match that of the one they were following.

"That's it!" Svetlanacek exclaimed, thumping the dashboard. "He's slick, but he's not as smart as we are, eh, Mirko?"

"Not nearly as smart, sir," Corporal Mirko said, returning the grin. He turned right, to follow the other lorry, which had now vanished beyond a turn to the northeast. The other two armored cars fell in behind.

"How long do you think it'll take to catch him?" the lieutenant asked.

Mirko thought it over, then said, "The M-40 armored car has a higher top road-speed than the C-18 cargo lorry does, sir. We can do better than a hundred kph, he can't."

"What is his top road-speed?"

Mirko shook his head. "Empty, about ninety or so. I don't know how much weight he's carrying, but anything more than a driver and navigator will slow him down."

"Then let's hope he's carrying a lot of troops—and casualties," Svetlanacek said grimly.

"Don't worry, sir. We'll catch him."

Corporal Mirko speeded up. So did the platoon's other two armored cars.

The New Granum Road, Forty-Five Kilometers Northeast of the Cabbage Patch

"He's gaining on us," Corporal Nomonon said, looking at the rearview screen.

"I see it," Sergeant Daly said, also looking at the rearview. He looked at his map, calculating how much longer it would be before they pulled off to head south to the waiting AstroGhost. He also calculated when the *Admiral Nelson* would be above the horizon so he could transmit a request for the AstroGhost to meet them along the way.

He didn't like the results of his calculations—the chasing vehicles would catch up with them too soon after they left the road.

"Brigo," he said into the command circuit, "are there any aircraft in sight?"

"Negative, Jak," Sergeant Kare answered. "We haven't seen any flyers since the flight that buzzed that southbound lorry."

"Thanks," Daly said absently, and went back to his map. There, seven kilometers ahead, the New Granum cut through a low hill instead of going over it. The topo lines showed the sides of the hill were steep, which was probably why the road cut through instead of climbing over it . . . They could pull off the road on the other side of the cut and lay an ambush on its top. If the vehicles had open bodies, the Marines could lay plunging fire into them and wipe out the infantry they had to be carrying before they could react to the ambush. If not they might not be able to kill them.

"Listen up," Daly said into the all-hands circuit, and told the platoon what they were going to do. He made another time check and saw he'd be able to contact the *Admiral Nelson* while they were in their ambush position.

Lieutenant Rak Svetlanacek tensed as his armored car approached the cut hill. It was exactly the kind of place he'd set an ambush himself if he was being followed. The hill to the sides of the cut were steep—almost, but not quite too steep for his armored cars to climb. But the raiders had never stopped to fight. He didn't know why they'd stopped the first time and abandoned their lorry only to return to it, but the only other time he knew they stopped was when they killed the Mad Max fighter. He was pretty sure they'd stopped then to hide from the Gyrfalcons. They might have stopped right before they turned toward the New Granum Road, but that could have been to communicate with their headquarters or to decide what to do next.

So it was unlikely the raiders stopped to set an ambush at the cut. Nonetheless:

"Mirko, top speed. I want to get through that cut as fast as possible."

"Me too, sir. Me too." Mirko accelerated as fast as the armored car would go. The trailing armored cars also maxed their speed.

Daly nodded to himself when he saw the approaching armored cars speed up; he'd probably do the same thing himself if their positions were reversed. He swore softly when he saw the cars were covered instead of open; he didn't know if the fléchettes of the two assault guns could penetrate the armor. He waited until the lead car was almost through the cut, then gave the order over the all-hands circuit, *"Fire!"*

On the ambush's right flank, third squad let loose with its fléchette gun. Sergeant Kare, on the gun, fired in front of the vehicle, and let it run into the stream of armor-piercing darts. The darts dug divots out of the road's surface, then chewed gouges in the hood and top of the armored car—but not deeply enough to penetrate the car's top. Next to him, feeding the gun, Lance Corporal Ilon suddenly cheered when he saw the fléchettes grind a hole through the thinly armored rear of the car and shred its rear wheels. The armored car fishtailed wildly, out of control.

Kare turned his attention to the second vehicle, which was already heavily damaged by the other fléchette gun. His fléchettes joined a mass of blaster bolts slamming into and through a growing hole in the rear of the armored car. It swerved violently and slowed, and the third armored car slammed into its rear, sending it spinning and bouncing off the walls of the cut before it screeched to a stop. After hitting the second armored car, the third flipped and rolled over several times until it settled, rocking, on its top.

After a moment, hatches slammed open on the two cars and a few soldiers began scrambling out. The Marines poured blaster and fléchette fire into them. The cavalrymen were all killed or severely wounded before any of them had a chance to return fire.

* * *

Corporal Mirko worked the controls of his car, but the road was too narrow for him to regain control of the damaged vehicle in time. It slewed off the road to the right, then crashed into a tree.

Lieutenant Svetlanacek's head slammed forward and hit the navigator's control panel. He was knocked out by the blow, but regained consciousness quickly.

Mirko was dazed. At Svetlanacek's command, he fumbled with the car's controls, but couldn't restart its motor.

Realizing the armored car wouldn't start, Svetlanacek wrestled with his door and wrenched it open with difficulty. "Get out," he snarled at Mirko. The corporal's door opened more easily, but he was groggy enough that he fell to his knees when he stepped out.

The lieutenant stumbled around to the back of the vehicle. He was so surprised to find the rear door still closed he didn't immediately see the hole knocked through it by the fléchette gun and blasters. He gasped in near despair when he did. But he didn't give in; he grabbed the handle and yanked the door open.

A horrendous sight greeted him—blood-and-gore-spattered bodies were piled at the front of the troop compartment! Were all the soldiers dead?

No! Someone moaned. Someone else twitched a foot.

Svetlanacek didn't notice Mirko scramble into the troop compartment with him until the corporal began helping him sort the bodies out. Three of the ten soldiers were dead and another was dying. Two were wounded, but would be ambulatory once their wounds were bandaged. The others were only dazed from the shock of the crash.

The platoon commander of the Fifth Independent Armored Cavalry Platoon now had a command of only eight men, including the wounded, his driver, and himself. He didn't know how large the raiding party was, but he knew there had to be more of them than he had. The raiders were also far better armed than his men—he hadn't known they had guns powerful enough to break through an armored car's skin.

He grabbed Mirko and ran back to the cab. Inside, he tried the radio, but it didn't work—he couldn't report the ambush! After a moment's thought, he climbed to the commander's cupola and detached the fléchette gun mounted in it. He handed the gun down to Mirko, then hoisted the ammunition tank. The gun was awkward to carry, and the tank was heavy enough that it required two men to carry it, but they were going to need the firepower if any of them were to survive the encounter.

"This way," Svetlanacek ordered when he dismounted. He gave the ammunition tank to two of the least injured men. He led the way into the trees—and stopped abruptly. Directly in front of him was the lorry the raiders had escaped in.

CHAPTER
TWENTY-SIX

The President's Conference Room, Administrative Center, New Granum, Union of Margelan, Atlas

"This is a war council," Jorge Lavager began. "Yesterday morning, as many of you know, troops from South Solanum, possibly with assistance from other nations, attempted to assassinate me while simultaneously launching an attack on the agricultural research facility at Spondu, commonly known as the Cabbage Patch."

Lavager stood before his cabinet and other top advisors in the same clothes he had worn when he left the government buildings twenty-four hours before. Since then he had fought for his life, walked nearly twenty kilometers to safety, organized the demoralized troops at the Cabbage Patch, initiated a pursuit of the raiders, and not slept a wink. Now he was before his cabinet, looking a sorry sight in his rumpled, torn, sweat-stained clothing. But as he spoke it was as if he'd just gotten out of bed after a good night's rest.

"General Ollius," he gestured at the new Chief of Staff, "has dusted off and revised a battle plan the army staff prepared some time ago as a response to just this sort of overt aggressive act. A complete report of the events is in front of you. Mr. Goumeray." He nodded at the Minister of Information.

"Gentlemen," Goumeray, a short, balding, bespectacled man in his early sixties, began in his high-pitched voice, "when we are done here this report will be released to the citizens of the Union of Margelan. At the same time it will be released to the other nation-states of Atlas, as well as to the Confederation of Human Worlds at its headquarters on Earth. It is as factual and complete as we have been able to make it up to now. Please take a few moments to read through it, and then General Ollius will brief you on our response plan."

"Where is General Ollwelen?" the Minister of Health asked.

"He is," Lavager hesitated for just an instant but that hesitation spoke volumes to the cabinet ministers sitting around the table, "no longer with us. General Ollius has replaced him."

"That's truly shocking!" someone remarked. "I mean that General Ollwelen is—is—" The minister nodded apologetically at General Ollius.

"Yes, but no surprise," Lavager responded quickly. "As you can see from the report Mr. Goumeray has given you, General Ollwelen was with me during the ambush. I have every reason to believe he knew of the attacks. He fled while we were defending ourselves in a cornfield. For all any of us know, he perished there in the fire though we haven't found a body today. Now, General Ollius, give us the details of the war plan."

Ollius stood. "This is called Operation Sea Lion. It will be a combined air, land, and sea attack against the major cities and agricultural facilities of South Solanum. H Hour is oh-four hundred our time tomorrow, oh-seven hundred when the first targets, the enemy's military installations, will be struck by satellite weapons. Our forces are maneuvering into position even as I speak." The room had gone completely silent. "This will be followed up with coordinated attacks by combined forces, which will complete the destruction of South Solanum's defensive capabilities, and culminate with the occupation of their capital and the seizure and arrest of their government officials." As he spoke, graphic images of maps and troop movements flashed across the large screen at one end of the room.

"Is there no chance for a negotiated settlement?" Minister of Education Uhura Lunguna asked. He was fairly new in his job. He looked plaintively around the table. Some of the ministers shrugged, others refused to look at him. When Jorge Lavager said something was to be done, it was a decree, not up for a vote.

"No, Mr. Lunguna," the Foreign Minister answered at once, casting a sideward glance at Lavager. "They launched a vicious and unprovoked attack against us, against the person of our leading citizen, and we shall deal with them in the same manner."

"Sir," Education Minister Lunguna addressed himself directly to Lavager, "we are going to war, just like that?"

"You weren't with me this morning," Lavager responded drily.

"But, sir, this report," he held up the Information Minister's press release, "doesn't even present any strong evidence that the South Solanians were responsible for the attacks! How do we know it was them? We are going to be asked that by everyone."

"Tell them we have the confession of someone who was in on the attack, Mr. Lunguna. The identity of that source is confidential, that's why his name is not mentioned."

Lunguna looked again for support from the other officials at the table. None was forthcoming, so he stood. "Sir," he bowed slightly toward Lavager, "I am an educator. I explain, I enlighten, I direct attention toward facts, and when I cannot do that, I am honest about it and let people form their own opinions. On the basis of the very slim facts you have presented, I have formed my own opinion about what you are proposing."

"And that is?"

"This is an unjustified war of aggression that will lead only to tragedy for all concerned." He paused and took a breath. "I hereby resign my post in your government—a government I cannot support under the present circumstances." He turned to leave, but stopped when Lavager held up a hand and pointed at the minister's chair. Lunguna sat down heavily.

Lavager didn't reply for a long moment. "Your resignation is accepted without prejudice, Mr. Lunguna," he said at last. "I deeply regret your decision to resign. You are an excellent educator and the children of Atlas could benefit from your talents. No, I did not misspeak. What we are doing out at Spondu will have far-reaching effects on our world, and in due course I will unite all the governments of Atlas under one, and you will have a place in that government, Mr. Lunguna, if you should change your mind."

Lunguna stared at Lavager in disbelief. He felt sick at the thought that what Lavager had just said announced his megalomania. The devastating thought flashed through his mind that perhaps the attacks on the President and the Cabbage Patch that morning had been conducted by patriots, not enemies. Worse, nobody else in the room seemed aware of that possibility.

"I appreciate your honesty and moral courage," Lavager continued. "If anyone else in this cabinet wishes to withdraw from my government, now is the time to do it." He looked at the other ministers, but none said anything. "General Ollius, the attack shall begin on my command and only on my command. Marshall the forces and have them ready.

"Gentlemen, thank you very much for your support in this time of crisis. I have one more announcement to make and we are done here." Lavager paused and produced an Anniversario. He clipped it expertly and lit the cigar. When the tip glowed red he smiled affably at his cabinet ministers. "All of you except General Ollius are confined to this room, without communications with the outside world, until the attack is underway."

At first there was disbelieving silence and then all the

ministers began shouting at once. Lavager held up his arms for silence and eventually it was restored. "Just a precaution, gentlemen, just a precaution. No one here is under suspicion. You will be accommodated very comfortably while you're here. At oh-seven hundred tomorrow you will be allowed to leave, none the worse for a night spent at the office, I assure you."

"Jorge!" It was the Minister of the Interior. "I want a bottle of bourbon and a deck of cards! If you're going to confine us here until tomorrow morning, I want to get old Henri there into a game of poker and steal some of that money he's been lifting out of the treasury!" Henri Parrot was Lavager's minister of finance and no more honest official ever lived, but he was a notorious poker player.

Lavager just nodded and made his way to the door. Lunguna caught up to him.

"Jorge, please, just one more word?" Lavager paused and nodded. "Do *not* do this! If unification of the nation-states of Atlas is your goal, you do not have to do it by war! Please, aggressive wars always end tragically. Do not inflict this on our people!" He looked imploringly into Lavager's face. "I'm begging you to listen to me!"

Lavager sighed. "What we're going to do to South Solanum tomorrow is not aggressive war. I am punishing those people for what they did *here, this* morning, pure and simple. I will unite the nations of this world, but not by force. This morning's attack was designed to thwart the unification plan. What we're doing out at Spondu will definitely change the balance of power in this world and some people don't want that to happen. But it will, and soon."

Lunguna's shoulders drooped. "A super weapon," he sighed.

"'Super'? Yes; a weapon? Yes, a 'weapon' of sorts." Lavager laid a hand on Lunguna's shoulder. "Let people think what they may, you'll see the results of my plan soon enough. Now, have something to eat, get some rest.

It's a long time until tomorrow, and for me, I need refreshment and rest as well." Lavager smiled and, accompanied by his security detail, left the room.

Annie Hall, the Presidential Retreat, Outside New Granum

Lavager arrived at Annie Hall, the Presidential Retreat in the mountains outside New Granum, before noon. He introduced Gina to Candace, excused himself, and went to bed. The two young women became friends at once. Candace possessed a sophisticated outlook on politics and government that was complemented by Gina's experience of life on a farm among working people. Gina also had an intimate knowledge of the forests, plants, and animals native to Margelan that Candace found fascinating. They sat in Candace's room, listening to music and talking.

"Is that Barrabas Monk and the Abbots?" Gina asked, "I just adore them!"

"Yes!" Candace turned up the volume and the music filled the room. "Father just detests them." She laughed and added, "He just likes the old stuff." The two rocked to the rhythm as the music blared from Candace's sound system.

For a few minutes, Candace watched Gina, who seemed happy and unconcerned, then asked, "How can you be so—so—?" she began, then faltered. "I mean, after what happened at your farm, you just seem—"

"To be taking it so well?" Gina finished the sentence. "I put it in the back of my mind, Candie. I'm good at doing that, you know? My parents used to get on me all the time about my wandering in the woods, so when Mother or Father—," now she faltered, but quickly pulled herself together and continued, "—when Mother or Father would get on me about wandering off from my chores I'd just concentrate on the chores, and when I was alone in the forest I'd concentrate on the trees." She laughed. "So now I concentrate on you and what we're doing right now, and that way I can almost forget about what ... what happened. Besides, your father promised me he'd make the bastards who did that pay, and I trust your father. Everyone does. Your own mother was assassinated. You must know what I'm talking about."

"I was very young, Gina." Candace didn't speak for a moment. Then, to get away from such depressing talk, asked, "So what will you do now?"

Gina shrugged. "Run the farm. I know all about the machines my father and his hands worked. I know the planting cycles, all about fertilizer and how to breed farm animals. I turned on the water that saved your father and his friends," she added proudly. "I'll hire people to help me and eventually I'll get married." She laughed again. Gina had a pleasant laugh that made Candace feel good to hear. "And how about you, Candie, what will you do with the rest of your life?"

"Oh, I'm going to university somewhere. Somewhere offworld, father says. Have you ever been off-world, Gina?"

"No, but I'd like to go! I'd love to see Earth. My father was there once when he was young, and he told us all about the place."

"Wouldn't that be nice—I mean if we could go to university together? I'd love to have someone I like along, to be my friend and help me study. Don't you want a university education? Father could arrange it, I'm sure," Candace's cheeks flushed with excitement at the thought of her and Gina going off to college on another world.

"I don't know, Candie, I guess I was born to be a farmer." She shrugged. "I never thought much about it. My parents wanted to send me to agriculture college here on Atlas. But you know, I might like to be a forest ranger. Can your dad arrange that for me?"

There was a knock at the door and when they turned, Lavagar stood there. "I sure can," he said. His voice boomed through the music, which Candace quickly turned down. Her father frowned theatrically and then grinned. "But right now, how about something to eat?" He stood there, rested, changed, looking fresh and eager. "We'll have dinner at Ramuncho's. How about it, ladies? My treat. I hear he's got fresh dalmans."

Candace blanched at the suggestion and struggled to find words. "Father, do you think you should go out? After what's happened, I mean." Gina caught the note of anxiety in Candace's voice. She'd stood up out of respect for Lavager, but he motioned her to be seated.

"Sure. Lightning never strikes in the same place twice. Come on, ladies, be my dates for the evening!"

"Daddy!" Candace sounded desperate to Gina, who was embarrassed to witness what seemed to be developing into a family feud, but she certainly understood how Candace felt. A small knot of fear began forming in the pit of Gina's stomach. "We can have the cook prepare a nice meal right here at home!" Candace said. "Father, please, let's stay home tonight."

Lavager came into the room, took some of his daughter's discarded clothing off a chair, and sat down carefully. "You never could keep a neat room." He smiled wryly at Gina. "Ladies," he began, "I want to tell you something, so listen carefully. As the head of state, I have an obligation to our people to always be before them, to set an example, the example I wish everyone to follow. That duty always trumps personal convenience. The people expect me to lead them and you don't lead from inside a bunker! So I am not going to hide here on this mountaintop. This is my country and I will not let fear make a prisoner of me in my own land. What kind of a man would I be to do that?"

The two young women were silent; what could they say in response? Candace was desperately afraid that sooner or later she'd lose her father and she was ashamed because she knew that fear was based on selfishness. Still, Lavager was her father, how else could she feel? Gina knew nothing about politics or military affairs, but she had been brought up to believe that when work had to be done, it simply had to be done. Lavager was just telling her what her own father had said using similar words when the weather was bad and there was work to be done on the farm. She put her arm around Candace.

"So what do you say, ladies? A night out on the town with me?"

Candace nodded reluctantly. If something were to happen to her father, she wanted to be there. She'd remain alert too. Maybe she couldn't prevent something from happening but she would be there, at his side.

"I'd be happy to go with you, sir," Gina said.

Lavager smiled and got to his feet. "Tell you what, Candie, I'll even take security with me. While Franklin's recovering, my new chief of security is a man you can call Lee. You'll like him." He held out his hand and helped both girls to their feet. "Bring Roland too," he said to Gina, putting an arm around her waist and guiding her to the door. "Ramuncho can put him up in the kitchen."

Outside, two security guards made to enter Lavager's landcar. "No," he told them, "you ride with Lanners, I'm driving this crate myself. Get in, ladies!" They started off at great speed down the twisting one-lane road that was the only way up to Annie Hall. Two-way traffic was not permitted and guards stationed along the way saw to it that no intruders were allowed up the mountain. Lavager, who knew the road by heart, took the curves at eighty kilometers per hour.

"Daddy, slow down!" Candace shouted.

"I'll slow down when I'm dead!" he shouted back over the wind rushing through the open windows and laughed. Behind them the security men were having a tough time keeping up with him. He laughed again and, steering with one hand, jammed a Davidoff into his mouth. But he did slow down when he realized his driving really was frightening his young companions. "It's really fun taking this road after you've had a few liters of beer," he said, lighting the cigar.

"Father," Candace leaned toward Lavager to be heard over the roar of the wind, "the news is full of what happened yesterday. They're saying there's going to be another war."

"Ah, there are always rumors of war. Don't listen to what you hear about that. See, Gina, what a worrywart my Candace is?"

"But Father—!"

Lavager pulled the vehicle into a turnaround and slammed on the brakes. Dust billowed up around the vehicle, filtering the afternoon sun flooding the interior of the vehicle with warm, golden light. The view of the valley below was breathtaking at this altitude.

"Father, we're sitting targets from below! What if—?"

"I'm always in someone's sights," Lavager grunted. He turned to face both girls and jabbed his cigar at them. "There's not going to be a war. But I *am* going to punish the people who killed Gina's family and attacked the Cabbage Patch." His voice had grown hard and Gina could see clearly the deadly expression that had come over Lavager's face and into his eyes. "I'm going to punish them so badly they will never think of doing anything like that again. And once I'm through with those people, I'm going to kick every goddamned politician's ass on Atlas. And I don't need a war to do that. You'll see."

But before they reached Ramuncho's, Lavager gave in to Leelanu Lanners's entreaties and made a stop at the formal Presidential Residence in the city to join up with a strong security detail.

The Presidential Residence, New Granum

They saw immediately that President Lavager was in. A limousine with the presidential seal on its door and a small presidential flag on its bumper was parked in front of the main entrance.

And a full company of soldiers in battle gear was arrayed in front of the house.

Gossner and Dwan couldn't tell from where they stood in the midst of a gaggle of tourists gawking at the building, but they suspected at least two hundred soldiers were tightly surrounding the building. They were casual about looking around in imitation of the rubbernecking tourists, and spotted almost a dozen firing positions on top of and inside nearby buildings. Some of the firing positions had sniper teams, but at least two had assault guns.

Activity at the entrance of the residence drew their attention. A hard-looking man with a bandaged arm held in a sling came out and softly shut the door behind him. An officer, probably the commander of the troops surrounding the residence, marched up to him. The two conferred briefly, then the hard-looking man went back inside. He moved stiffly, as if he was in some pain.

"That was him," someone whispered excitedly near Gossner and Dwan, "Franklin al-Rashid!"

"The head of the President's security?" someone else asked. "Wasn't he injured in the ambush?"

"Yes," a frightened whisper.

"But he seems better now!" an excited squeal.

The officer called the troops in front of the residence into formation and marched them around the side of the building. After a moment there was the sound of landcar motors starting up. Soon, several small troop carriers drove out from behind the residence and took positions in the streets around it.

Gossner took Dwan's hand and drew her away.

When they reached a safe enough distance that he couldn't be overheard, he said, "I think the target is about to go somewhere."

That was confirmed a moment later when President

Lavager came out of the front door. Two teenage girls were with him. So was Franklin al-Rashid. The security chief looked distinctly unhappy about something.

Lavager was clean and looked far more refreshed and in control than he had on the trid. He stopped in the portico to smile and wave at the crowd across the street.

"I don't know about you folks," he said in a loud enough voice to carry to the crowd, "but my stomach is telling me it's time to eat; I'm taking my daughter and her friend out to dinner."

Al-Rashid's grimace was visible all the way to where Gossner and Dwan stood.

Dwan nudged Gossner. "Let's go," she said.

They hurried to a parallel street and caught a taxi back to their hotel to get what they needed.

Ramuncho's Restaurant, New Granum

Ramuncho greeted them effusively. "Your dining room is ready, sir." He bowed politely.

"You know my daughter, Candace, I'd like you to meet her friend, Gina Medina. No, Ramuncho, tonight I want the window table in the main dining room. I want everyone to see these fine young ladies who have agreed to dine with me this afternoon." Diners in the main hall paused at their meals and stared at Lavager and his party. Several stood and applauded. Lavager bowed toward them.

Candace almost shrieked when she saw the size of the window, but controlled herself and hissed, "Daddy, it's safer in the back." She tugged his arm as hard as she could.

Ramuncho, who was also nervous about his head of state sitting in front of the windows onto Center Boulevard, reluctantly gestured at a table in a far corner of the room.

"No, my usual table, in front of the windows! I want the citizens of the Union of Margelan to see me, to see me alive and enjoying a meal like anyone else. I want them to see there is no cause for fear! Dalmans for everyone, Ramuncho! Beer for me, whatever the boys here want for them," he gestured at his security detail, "and wine for the ladies, your finest, say a Katzenwasser white, a bottle of that excellent Feinherb would do for their discriminating palates! Eat, drink, and be merry!" And with that he guided the two young women toward the table by the window. "Whatever Fate has in store for us, we'll face it with full stomachs." His joyous laughter filled the room.

CHAPTER
TWENTY-SEVEN

A Cut, Twenty-Five Kilometers Northeast of the Cabbage Patch, Union of Margelan, Atlas

A silence, disturbed only by a faint whimper, descended over the gap after the soldiers who tried to get out of the second and third armored cars were shot.

Sergeant Daly watched and listened for a moment, then asked over the all-hands circuit, "Where'd that first car go?"

"It crashed into the trees," Sergeant Kare answered. "I haven't seen any movement near where it disappeared."

"Take second squad and check it out," Daly ordered. "Everybody else, keep alert; we don't know who else might be around." *Or if they got a signal out*, he mentally added. After a few seconds' consideration, he continued, "First squad, get a position with air cover and watch the road to the northeast. Eighth squad, do the same southeast. Sergeant Bajing, get the rest of the platoon ready to return to the lorry and mount up."

He got out his map and examined it. They still had thirty kilometers to go before heading cross-country to the AstroGhost. But if the convoy had gotten off a message, they didn't have time to go thirty klicks before the search came down hard on this part of the road, they had to get away from it fast. He plotted a route that kept to covered waterways and the fringes of deep woods, where they might find concealment from searching aircraft.

"Nomonon, turn on your lights so I can find you." Nomonon did, and Daly started toward him. He'd only taken a few steps before the sound of gunfire erupted from the direction of the lorry.

"Report!" he snapped into the all-hands circuit.

"We caught a squad of locals trying to board the lorry," Sergeant Kare panted as he reported—he sounded like he was running. "We took out half of them, and are in pursuit of the others."

"Let them go," Daly ordered. "We don't have time to run them down. Get your people back to the lorry." He switched to the all-hands circuit and ordered, "Sergeant Bajing, get the platoon to the lorry, double-time, let's get out of here now."

He reached Nomonon in a few more steps and handed him the map. "Study this along the way. I'll guide you." He took Nomonon's arm to lead him to the lorry. They'd just started when a long burst from a fléchette assault gun, followed by the *crack-sizzle* of blaster fire made them stop.

"Report!" Daly called on the all-hands circuit.

"They circled back and tore up the lorry!" Kare reported.

"Kill them!"

"Already did, boss."

"Let's go," Daly snapped at Nomonon. "You can read the map later."

They ran.

Daly found second and third squads forty meters east of the lorry. Sergeant Kare stood over eight dead soldiers. His men were arrayed in a defensive position facing deeper into the trees.

"I believe that's the last of the soldiers from the armored cars," Kare said when Daly joined him. "Want us to search them?"

"No," Daly said; they were leaving so they didn't have intelligence need for any documents the soldiers might be carrying. He shook his head. Why had they come back? The dumb fucks would still be alive if they'd kept going. But they hadn't known who they were going up against, had they? That kind of ignorance, not knowing who one's opponents were, had killed countless soldiers since the beginning of warfare. He turned to go back to the lorry, where he saw Nomonon opening the hood and removing his helmet and gloves to examine the vehicle's engine.

"Here, at least take this," Kare said. He bent down and took a sidearm from one of the soldiers. Between that and the shiny tabs on his collars, he must have been an officer, even though he died with a fléchette rifle in his hands.

Daly looked at the handgun. "No, you keep it. This was your kill, it's your souvenir."

"Jak," Kare said solemnly, "it's an officer's weapon. You're our acting lieutenant, you should have an officer's weapon."

Reluctantly, Daly accepted the handgun. "Thanks, Brigo."

"Can't do it." Daly could see the helmetless Nomonon shake his head as he looked under the hood at the ruined motor. "We can't fix it even if we had replacement boards; the block is cracked and the motor mount is fractured." He looked at Daly, who had his chameleon screen up so his face could be seen. "We're on foot, boss."

Daly turned away so none of his Marines could see the dismayed expression on his face. They couldn't get very far without transportation, and there was simply no way they could leave their wounded and dead. So what could he do? The *Admiral Nelson* had to send the AstroGhost to pick them up.

Daly climbed a tree and locked his point-transmitter onto the *Admiral Nelson*. He got a reply to the message he'd sent before the armored cars reached the ambush. As he expected, the reply to his request for the AstroGhost to pick them up was a terse, "No." He prepared a fresh message, telling the starship that the platoon no longer had transportation, then sent it. He settled down to wait for a reply, hoping no reinforcements or enemy aircraft were on their way.

It took twenty minutes for the *Admiral Nelson* to get back to him with a response to his request.

"Mudman," the burst transmission said when he decoded it, "bad news. There's too much traffic coming your way, and too many aircraft south and west of your position. We can't risk exposing the Ghost to discovery. You're on your own to rendezvous."

"What's wrong with you?" he demanded. "Don't you understand we *can't* travel fifty kilometers cross-country with our casualties?" But he said it to himself and didn't record it for a burst transmission. The captain of the *Admiral Nelson* was right that he couldn't expose the AstroGhost to discovery—Confederation involvement in the raid on the Cabbage Patch had to be kept secret.

But that did nothing for the Marines stranded planetside. It wasn't the first time, he knew, that the navy had abandoned Marines in a precarious position. But he couldn't think of an instance where the Marines hadn't been able to salvage an untenable situation.

Wait a minute! What did that message say? Daly read it again.

"There's too much traffic coming your way . . ."

Did that mean on the road? What direction was it coming from? Daly turned up his helmet's ears and heard the distant rumble of a lorry—to the east, not the west. He looked at the road, which was effectively blocked by the two armored cars that had crashed into each other. Thinking as he spoke, he issued orders to set an ambush and take the approaching lorry.

* * *

Ronson Gampan had been driving for thirty-three of his fifty-five years, most of that for Margelan Universal Trucking. He liked driving, and he liked his employer. He was twice married and twice divorced. All three of his children approved of Bountie Quadril, whom he intended to make the third Mrs. Gampan. One of the things Ronson liked about Bountie, and there were a great many things he liked about her, was she was young enough to make one or two more little Gampans with him. When he reached New Granum at the end of this run, he was scheduled for a week's holiday. He planned to ask for Bountie's hand during that week.

Yes, life was good.

But wait, what's this? A wreck! Someone had an accident and the road was blocked.

All thoughts of Bountie vanished from Gampan's mind as he braked his lorry and jumped out of the cab to give aid to anybody injured. As soon as he determined the casualties, he'd radio in a call for assistance. His eyes widened as he ran toward the two vehicles and saw they were mili—

Something hit him in the side—hard—and knocked him to the ground. Unseen hands grabbed his arms and jerked him back to his feet; they didn't let go, but held him tightly and yanked his hands behind his back. Something went around his wrists and held his hands securely together.

Then a voice in front of him said, "Sorry about that, pal, but we need your lorry." But there was nobody standing where the voice came from! Gampan gaped, his breath came in shallow pants, he felt faint.

The hands holding him hustled him to the side of the road and sat him against a tree trunk. Something went around his chest and under his arms, binding him to the tree.

"Don't worry," another voice said, "somebody'll be along shortly and set you free."

Gampan looked around manically for the source of the voice, but nobody was there!

He heard his lorry's engine grind and saw it buck as some unseen person tried to turn the wheels. Then he heard a raised voice curse, and another voice—was it the first voice he'd heard?—talking, followed by a soft curse.

The footsteps of someone he couldn't see approached him from the lorry, then a voice asked, "Anti-hijacking device?"

"Y-Yes." There wasn't much hijacking in the Union of Margelan, but Margelan Universal Trucking thought any hijacking was too much, and Ronson Gampan agreed; all of MUT's trucks could only be driven by their assigned drivers.

"Can you unlock it?"

"Nossir. The dispatcher is the only person who has the locking codes."

"Damn. All right, you're going with us." The voice turned to speak to someone else. "Untie him, he's going to have to drive."

Unseen hands quickly stripped off the binding that held Gampan to the tree trunk and hauled him to his feet. They left his hands bound behind his back until they got him to the lorry and he was boosted into the cab.

Someone was already in the cab. He didn't see anyone but he did see the handgun that was pointed at him from midair.

"You're going to drive where I tell you to. Do you understand?"

Gampan might not have understood invisible men, but he understood the handgun pointed at him.

"Yessir," he said.

"Fine. When I tell you to, back up until you see a break in the trees on the left, then turn into it."

Gampan nodded rapidly.

The voice told him to stop near a damaged lorry. Now

he knew why they wanted his. He heard noises and felt the
lorry shift on its springs as invisible men unloaded his
cargo and loaded something into it he couldn't see. He
thought he heard the groans of men in pain.

Metsa Forest, Three Hundred Kilometers East of New Granum

Fifty kilometers with a driver he wasn't sure he could rely
on. Farther than that, actually—Daly hadn't factored in
the additional distance caused by their early departure
from the road. He didn't even want to think about how
much farther they'd have to go sticking to whatever air
cover they could find.

But Ronson Gampan wanted to live, and he followed
Daly's instructions to the letter, even suggesting better
lines to follow once he realized what the invisible man
wanted.

The trip was ninety kilometers all told, but Second
Force Recon Platoon finally reached the AstroGhost's
hiding place without further incident. Gampan's jaw
dropped when the strange-looking shuttle levitated and
slipped out from under its cover.

Sergeant Bajing was the senior unwounded squad
leader in second section, which made him the acting section commander, just as Sergeant Bingh filled that role in
first section since Sergeant Daly had assumed command
of the platoon. He approached Daly while Bingh and
Kare saw to loading the wounded and dead on the
AstroGhost.

"You know what we have to do, don't you?" he asked
the acting platoon commander.

Daly didn't answer, he'd been grappling with that question for the past half hour. He was still holding the handgun Kare had given him, the one he had held on the
civilian teamster during the cross-country drive. He

couldn't see Bajing's face, but he knew where his senior sergeant had to be looking.

Bajing sighed. "I'll do it if you don't want to."

Daly also sighed. "No," he said. "I'm in command here. I won't order anybody to do something I won't do myself."

"You're not ordering me, I'm volunteering."

"I can't let you do it for me. If everybody else is mounted up, you get aboard the AstroGhost, too. I'll join you in a couple of minutes."

"Okay, boss." Bajing reached out to one of the UV lights in front of him and patted Daly on the shoulder, then turned to the shuttle.

Daly stood where he was for a moment, then turned and walked to Ronson Gampan, who was again secured to a tree. He removed his helmet and went to one knee in front of the lorry driver.

"Listen, man," he said after searching the other's eyes. "I'm really sorry about this, but if we just leave you, you'll be able to tell who we are, and that will cause more trouble than anybody wants."

"But, but—I don't *know* who you are! I can't tell anybody anything!"

Daly turned his head to look at the AstroGhost, then back at Gampan—the one thing anybody knew about that would identify them as off-worlders. "You can tell them more than you realize. I'm sorry, I really am." Hardly anybody in Human Space other than Confederation troops, mostly Confederation Marines, wore chameleons. And the AstroGhost was so secret, almost nobody who wasn't involved in its design, manufacture, or use, even knew it existed. The little bit Gampan could tell anybody would tell his interrogators that the raid was conducted by the Confederation, and there would be hell to pay.

Invisible men: Some armies used chameleon field uniforms, but mostly chameleons were worn by Confederation Marines, and nobody was supposed to know the raid on the Cabbage Patch was conducted by Marines.

A stealthed and highly maneuverable shuttle that didn't look all that dissimilar to an Essay: Once word of that got out, potential opponents would begin trying to find ways of defeating it, which would unnecessarily cost Marine lives.

Bottom line: When it comes to a choice between my life, or the lives of my people, and your life—you die.

Nothing personal, that's just the way the world works.

"Mr. Gampan, please believe me when I say I'm really sorry I have to do this. But I really have to do it."

"Bu—" Gampan's objection was cut off when Daly raised the handgun he still held and shot him in the heart.

Ronson Gampan jerked against his bonds, then slumped and died.

"I am so damn sorry I had to do that to you," Daly murmured. "Rest in peace." He placed a hand on the driver's shoulder for a moment, then stood and walked slowly to the AstroGhost.

Nobody said anything about the blood and bone that speckled Daly's shirt and face.

Launch from Atlas

The chief petty officer who coxswained the AstroGhost took off south, in the direction of the nation-state of South Solanum. Ground sensors detected the AstroGhost, but no aircraft could intercept it before it flew beyond the horizon and out of range. Once past the horizon from their launch point, the coxswain dropped altitude and flew at treetop level until he reached the equator, then turned on every masking device in the AstroGhost's arsenal and shot east at a high angle. Fifteen minutes later, the shuttle was in the same orbit as the *Admiral Nelson*, which blocked view of it from the Kraken Interstellar Starport in front of her. An hour later, the AstroGhost docked, undetected by anybody in space or planetside, and the wounded Marines were being sped to the starship's hospital, where surgical teams were standing by.

Mission Objective One of Second Force Recon Platoon's extraordinarily sensitive mission to Atlas was accomplished.

CHAPTER
TWENTY-EIGHT

En Route to Ramuncho's Restaurant, New Granum, Atlas

They spent hardly any time in the hotel. Lance Corporal Dwan rechecked the contents of the oversize bag in which she was going to carry the maser and visited the water closet while Sergeant Gossner checked for new messages from the *Admiral Nelson*. There were no messages.

When they left the hotel, they were dressed in the same festively muted garments they wore the second time they entered the vacant building. Gossner didn't pay any attention to the bag Dwan carried slung over her shoulder; she'd frequently carried it since the shopping trip on which he'd been her pack animal. The bag was bigger than she needed to carry the disassembled maser in, but he took her word when she told him, "A lady needs to carry many things in her handbag"—though he thought calling that thing a "handbag" was stretching matters pretty far—"and the bigger the bag, the more things she's expected to carry. So if I go out with my handbag mostly empty, people will notice and wonder. Do you want people wondering why I'm carrying an almost-empty handbag?"

Of course, he didn't, so he stopped concerning himself about the "handbag's" size and contents. Hey, at least she wasn't using him as her gun-bearer, which was a big improvement over when she dragged him out on the shopping expedition as her pack animal and he'd had to lug all of her purchases back to the hotel.

As they had twice daily, they sauntered along Center Boulevard, ostensibly window shopping and on occasion briefly stepping into stores.

They saw the military staff cars parked in front of Ramuncho's Restaurant while they were still two blocks away—and the many soldiers posted along the street.

"I knew he'd come here when he said he was going out to eat," Dwan said excitedly.

"So did I," Gossner said, controlling his excitement a little better. "Let's make sure. But let's be cool, and not go too fast."

"I'll try."

They continued to stop frequently to look in shop windows, but didn't enter any until they were almost at the intersection before the restaurant.

There was a checkpoint on the corner. Nobody was allowed past until ID was checked and parcels searched.

Gossner and Dwan entered a convenient shop before the checkpoint.

Gossner blushed and tried to back out when he saw what the shop was; it was an emporium of erotica.

Dwan laughed at his discomfort, she'd seen what the store was before she entered it. "Come on, big man," she said, patting the shoulder of the arm she had hers linked through, "there's nothing in here neither of us has never seen before."

"Yeah, but not together," he muttered. Normally, he wouldn't have had any problem with entering, even in the company of women. But he'd been having sexual thoughts about Bella Dwan and that just wouldn't do—he was her immediate superior, after all. And Dwan *was* the Queen of Killers.

Dwan laughed again, looking around with bright and curious eyes. "As much as I'd like to dally and maybe even sample, we have a job to do. *There's* what I'm looking for." She pointed at an exit sign toward the shop's rear and gave his arm a tug.

Gossner eagerly headed for the exit.

Unlike most of the other shops along Center Boulevard, the emporium had a customer entrance at the rear for the convenience of customers who might not want to be seen entering from the front.

"I was sure there would be prudes in this town," Dwan murmured when they reached the service alley behind the shop. They turned back in the direction of their hotel, then took the first side street to Ranstead Street and back toward the vacant building they'd scouted twice before.

"Got a problem," Gossner said when they reached the street before the vacant building.

Dwan looked. Two soldiers were at the entrance to the service alley between the buildings on Center Boulevard and those on Ranstead Street.

"Let's check the other end," Gossner said.

"It's probably guarded, too."

"Maybe security's a little bit slack," he said. "Not everybody's sharp enough to cover all approaches."

Dwan sniffed. "After yesterday, they're pretty sharp."

Gossner grunted. He didn't hold out any real hope that the other end of the alley wouldn't likewise be guarded. "If the security detail isn't smart enough to have the army cover the other entrance to the alley," he said, "the target and the security chief both deserve to die."

They reached the other end of the block. Nobody was standing at that end of the service alley. The buildings cast deep shadows in the alley, but it didn't look like anybody was in it.

"Someone point out the security chief," Dwan purred. "He's slacking off on the job. I'll do two for the price of one."

They'd only gotten halfway from the service alley to the back of the vacant building when they saw a patrol walking toward them from the guarded end. The patrol carried electric torches, which they shone into the refuse barrels, as well as the shadowy spaces between them.

"This is where we find out how good these clothes really are as camouflage," Gossner whispered as he hoisted Dwan into a high-sided refuse bin. He followed her into it.

Fortunately, the bin was filled with discarded packaging materials, all dry goods. As quietly as they could, they burrowed into it. Just about the time Gossner was convinced they were completely covered, Dwan grabbed him and pulled herself close.

"What are you doing?" he whispered when her hands began jerking at his clothing.

"Just in case they spot us," she said. "Now shut up and put your arms around me."

Then they had to stop making noise, the footsteps and voices of the patrol were nearly on them.

Gossner tried to ignore what he felt; Dwan's blouse was pulled out in the back and his hand was on her skin. She'd pulled his shirt open and he felt her bra and belly pressed against his bare front. Somehow, she'd managed to undo the closures on his pants. It felt like she'd also undone the closures on her own. *This is the Queen of Killers here*, he forceably reminded himself. I'm her *team* leader, we can't be doing this! Still, he had to bite his lip to keep from groaning. *Damn, but who would have thought the Queen of Killers would feel so good?*

The footsteps stopped next to their bin. A growly voice ordered two soldiers to shine their lights behind the bins and for two others to boost another high enough to see into the one the two snipers were hiding in. There was scrabbling on the side of the bin, then a light swept through it, paused, and swept back over them.

"Boost me higher," a female voice said. There were grunts from outside, then the light seemed brighter.

Dwan mashed her mouth against Gossner's just before a hand reached in and moved some plastic wrapping aside. The light shone directly in their faces; Gossner squinted so his eyes wouldn't reflect the light as he peered at the silhouetted head above them.

The light moved on. "Nothing in here but packing and other trash," the woman soldier said. The hand and light moved away. "Let me down."

There was more scrabbling, then the growly voice ordered the patrol to move on. In a few more minutes the footsteps and voices left the alley. Gossner cautiously raised himself up and looked toward the open end. Two soldiers were now stationed there. Neither was a woman, neither was looking into the alley.

"Let's go," he whispered. He could have sworn Dwan was smiling when he helped her out of the trash bin. They straightened their clothing as they went. There were no more incidents as they made their way to the rear of the vacant building and climbed through the basement window.

The building was unoccupied, though they saw signs that workers had been there. They went to the second-floor room overlooking Ramuncho's and found the window pane they'd removed on their previous visit was undisturbed.

"See? I told you nobody would notice," Dwan murmured. She took a position and peered out. "Got him," she said. Lavager was sitting with two young women at the table just inside Ramuncho's front window, the one they'd sat in.

Then she surprised Gossner by stripping down to her undergarments. He tried not to look, but couldn't help himself, especially after the trash bin, so it took him a moment to realize what she was wearing under her outer clothes; then he was surprised again when he realized she was wearing her Marine-issue skivvies.

He abruptly came to his senses and softly demanded, "Bella, what are you doing?"

She didn't look at him as she squatted to open her over-sized bag and pulled out—air? No—she pulled out a set of chameleons!

"The CIO is behind this," she said, "but we got tapped for the job because I'm the best sniper in the Corps. That means I'm making this kill for the Marines. And if I'm making a kill for Mother Corps, I'm doing it as a Marine, not as a common murderer."

She dressed with Gossner gaping at her. How had she managed to sneak a set of chameleons past the security checks they'd gone through on their way to Atlas? How had she managed to keep them hidden from him in their hotel room? They were effectively invisible, sure, but just as surely, a customs inspector could have stuck his or her hands into her luggage and noticed they felt something they couldn't see. Of course, chameleons weren't really invisible, they picked up the color and pattern of whatever they were closest to. Depending on how she packed them, her chameleons might have looked like other clothing in her luggage, and felt the same as well.

He shook his head sharply. Bella Dwan had shown him aspects of herself he'd never guessed at, that she was smarter and more resourceful than anybody gave her credit for. He decided simply to accept there were things she could do and let it go at that.

Dwan's chameleons didn't include a helmet. "I couldn't figure out how to sneak a helmet through customs," she said when she was dressed again and saw Gossner staring at her. "But this will do."

Her head bobbed down. Had she been in normal clothing, he would have seen her bending over her bag. He watched as the components of her maser rose and assembled themselves. Then, except for its sights, the weapon vanished from his view.

Dwan turned her floating face to him and smiled. "I draped chameleon cloth over it." She stepped to where she would have a clear line of sight to the target and her head shifted to a position that told Gossner she was sighting it.

"Damn!" she swore. "Where'd he go?"

Gossner held out a hand to locate her body and looked over her shoulder. He saw the table with the two girls, but the target was no longer there.

"He'll be back," he murmured into Dwan's ear, "just relax." The muscles of her shoulders shifted under his hand and he knew she was lowering the maser.

"I hate firing from the offhand position," she muttered.

Gossner didn't reply. The standing position was the least stable, and the hardest in which to hold a lock on the target. But given the angle of the shot from the second-floor room, the only alternative to standing back and firing offhand was for her to rest her maser on the window ledge and fire kneeling behind it. But doing that presented the danger that someone below might look up and see the weapon, or its chameleoned form against the sky.

Ramuncho's Restaurant, in Front of the Windows

"The dalmans were magnificent as always," Jorge Liberec Lavager said to Ramuncho when he and his two dates had finished their entrées, "and your chef outdid himself with the bokspring á la maize."

"Thank you, Mr. President," Ramuncho said, bowing magnificently. "Might I interest you in real Colombian coffee from Earth with your dessert? Complimentary, of course."

"You certainly may, my good sir. But first there is something I must do, someone I must see for a moment." Lavager stood and bowed to Candace and Gina. "With your leave, ladies?"

Sixteen-year-old Gina glanced wide-eyed at Candace—the *President* was asking her permission to leave the table! Candace saw the look from the corner of her eye and nodded solemnly at her father, who looked to Gina for her permission to leave. Still wide-eyed, she mimicked Candace's nod, and Lavager strode from the table toward the rear of the restaurant. The girls looked at each other, leaned close together, and burst into a fit of giggles. Several people at nearby tables looked at them, saw Ramuncho beaming at them avuncularly, and returned their attention to their own companions.

Lavager was gone for the length of time it normally takes a man to visit the facilities and was almost back to the table when he noticed Franklin al-Rashid standing by the maître d's lectern, looking at him. Lavager stopped with his back to the table where his daughter and her new friend awaited his return and looked a question at al-Rashid, who gave a barely perceptable shake of his head, but came toward him anyway.

"How's your arm, Franklin?" Lavager asked with a pointed look at al-Rashid's sling when his security chief was close enough. "I know you won't obey the doctors when they say you need to be in the hospital. But should you be standing?"

"I'm fine, sir. I've been hurt worse than this and stayed on the job."

Lavager shook his head. Some people just wouldn't relax their vigilance—or else they let their loyalty overrule their common sense.

"Anything to report?" he asked.

Al-Rashid shook his head. "It's just another business day out there," he said just as softly as Lavager had spoken. "I've had army patrols and my own people everywhere within a three-block radius. Nobody has detected anything out of the ordinary."

"See, Franklin? I told you there was nothing to be concerned about. Now, since you won't stop working long enough to let your arm and other wounds heal, I want you at least to find someplace comfortable to sit and rest while you mother hen me. I promise not to go running off and make you stress yourself by chasing me. Really," he added when he saw al-Rashid's skeptical look, "I promise. My daughter's worried, and I don't want to upset her any more than she already . . ."

Rear of a Vacant Building on Ranstead Street

"There he is," Sergeant Gossner said. "Must have gone to the men's room."

Lance Corporal Dwan raised her maser to her shoulder and took aim. Lavager conveniently stopped to talk to someone, and his back presented as good a target as she'd ever seen.

"What's he doing?" Gossner asked when he saw Lavager stop instead of returning to his table.

Dwan didn't answer immediately; she was pressing the maser's firing lever. When she saw her target drop and released the firing lever, she said, "Going the way of all flesh," then stripped out of her chameleons and pulled her clothes back on. Gossner broke the maser down and stuffed it back inside the bag while she changed.

"Come on, let's get out of here," Dwan said breathlessly when she finished dressing. Gossner was surprised to see the normally sharp-looking Dwan's clothing was sloppily adjusted, as though she'd pulled it on in a hurry. Which she had, but still he would have expected her to have managed to be neater about her dress. Dwan slung her bag over one shoulder and grabbed Gossner's hand, pulling him out of the rear room and down the stairs.

They exited the building via the front door and Dwan hustled them straight to their hotel. Gossner almost had to trot to keep up with her.

We must look like we started something and are in a hurry to get to a bedroom, Gossner thought, glancing at her slightly disheveled clothes.

They heard excited shouts coming from the direction of the restaurant and the wailing of sirens drawing near. But no soldiers or police were running about establishing a cordon or stopping people. Nobody had any reason to think Lavager had just been shot.

Ramuncho's Restaurant

A strange, faraway expression suddenly came over Jorge Lavager's face and sweat beaded his brow and cheeks. He swayed.

"Are you all right, sir?" Franklin al-Rashid asked, and reached for Lavager's elbow. Before his hand got there, Lavager collapsed.

Gina Medina, still in awe of having been taken in by President Lavager, watched him returning from the rear of the restaurant. Her eyes sparkled as she watched him stop to talk with Franklin al-Rashid. She gasped when Lavager collapsed. Candace Lavager looked at her, saw where she was looking, looked herself, and screamed.

Al-Rashid managed to catch Lavager enough to ease him to the floor. He knelt over the fallen President and quickly examined him for wounds while he called out, "Call emergency medical. Tell them the President has collapsed." There were no obvious wounds so al-Rashid checked for vital signs. Lavager wasn't breathing and had no detectable pulse. Al-Rashid began cardiopulmonary resuscitation.

By then, Candace and Gina had reached him.

"Get them out of here," al-Rashid said.

Sobbing, Gina let herself be led away, but a security agent had to pick Candace up and carry her. Candace Lavager kicked and screamed, fighting to break free to rush to her father's side.

Room 1007, New Granum DeLuxe Inn

Dwan dragged Gossner into the room, tossed her bag into a corner, then twisted around and shoved past him to turn on the "Do Not Disturb" sign and make sure the door was secure. Then she threw herself on him and kissed him hard enough to bruise his lips.

"What—?" Gossner leaned back and reached for Dwan's wrists to pull her arms from around his neck.

Dwan let go before his hands reached hers and shoved him in the chest, hard, staggering him back. She stepped forward as he moved backward and shoved again.

"D-Dwan—" Gossner was baffled by her behavior and was beginning to wonder if he should be defending himself from an attack.

She shoved a third time and the backs of his knees hit the bed. He fell on it hard enough to bounce. Before he could roll aside, she leaped full on him and kissed him again.

"Shut up!" she rasped and began tearing at his clothes with one hand and her own with the other. "Kiss me!" She thrust her tongue between his lips. Tears flowed from her eyes onto his cheeks.

Gossner finally began to respond. Uncertainly and cautiously, but he responded. It wasn't until they were naked, her body pressed against his and her hips grinding against him, that he realized her body was wracked by her sobs and his face was running with her tears. It was one of those moments when a man doesn't know what to do. So he hugged her and gently stroked her, while making gentling noises.

"Don't hug me, take me!" she gasped, and rolled over onto her back, pulling him with her. "Take me hard!" She kissed him violently again.

Gossner's mind ran riot with thoughts of violated regulations; a senior having sex with a subordinate, them going counter to the note in their orders that their cover of a newlywed couple was not to extend to when they were in private, conduct unbecoming, and whatever other regulation they—and more particularly he—might be violating. And he was breaking the regulations with the Queen of Killers, a woman who was known to severely injure men who touched her; and he was doing more than merely touching her.

Her hips bucked against him. "Take me, dammit!"

So he pushed away other thoughts and did what she told him.

Later, after the roughest sex Gossner had ever had, he rolled off Dwan. She sighed contentedly and curled herself into his side. He couldn't see her face clearly, but he thought she was smiling. He lightly brushed his fingertips along her arm, her side, and her flank. He blinked, he could have sworn the Queen of Killers purred in response.

CHAPTER
TWENTY-NINE

Fast Frigate CNSS *Admiral Nelson*

Within hours after the AstroGhost bearing second platoon, Fourth Force Recon Company, docked with the CNSS *Admiral Nelson*, the starship broke orbit and headed system-north to a jump point. Two days later, the *Admiral Nelson* made her first jump into Beamspace, headed back to Halfway, again via New Genesee.

The wounded Marines who were brought aboard in stasis bags were left in them; the ship's medical department had enough work tending to the other wounded Marines in addition to their normal run of underway injuries.

"Attention Marines," the carefully modulated female voice said over the ship's PA system shortly after the ship secured from the jump. "Sergeant Daly to the Captain's quarters."

Sergeants Bingh and Bajing, who were sharing a cabin with Daly, looked at him. He shrugged.

"I guess it's routine for the ship's captain to entertain the Marine commander as soon as possible after a mission," Daly said. He took a moment to make sure his garrison utilities were shipshape, then headed for the captain's quarters.

Daly identified himself to the petty officer third class standing guard outside the open hatch of Captain Emmert's stateroom. The petty officer rapped his knuckles on a shiny brass plate set into the cowling of the watertight hatch and announced loudly, "Marine Sergeant Daly reporting, sir!"

"Enter."

Daly had to stoop slightly as he stepped through the hatch. Inside, he drew himself to attention and faced the captain, who was examining something on a screen at a small desk set against the bulkhead.

"Sergeant Daly reporting as ordered, sir."

Captain Emmert swiveled to look at Daly. "At ease, Sergeant," he said after a second's scrutiny.

Daly relaxed to an easy parade rest and kept his eyes straight ahead.

Emmert turned his screen so Daly could easily read it if he shifted his eyes. Daly did. The screen showed the medical department's report on the Marine casualties.

"You had a pretty rough time down there, didn't you?"

"Yessir." He knew that Emmert wasn't probing for details of the mission; Emmert didn't have the need to know.

"I had a chance to talk with Lieutenant Tevedes before the ship's surgeon put him in a stasis bag."

"Yessir." Tevedes had gone into the stasis bag before the *Admiral Nelson* broke orbit and Daly hadn't had a chance to speak with him.

"He told me you performed extremely well after he was injured. 'Outstanding' was the word he used."

Daly didn't respond; there wasn't really anything he could say.

"Are you aware that the ship's captain on a Force Recon mission also files an afteraction report on the mission?"

"Nossir, I wasn't aware of that."

"Now you know. I think you should also know something of what is going into my report. I'm going to include Lieutenant Tevedes's remarks on your conduct after everyone above you in the chain of command was killed or incapacitated. From everything I know about it, I want to add my own hearty 'well done,' Mr. Daly."

Daly blinked. "Mister" was a proper address to use with

company grade officers, not sergeants. "Thank you, sir."

Emmett smiled briefly at Daly's blink. "You did an officer's job, and you did it well. If I need anything else from you, I'll let you know. Now rest and recuperate. Did you take care of that other matter?"

"Yessir. I gave them to the ship's quartermaster as per orders." The "other matter" was orders he was given as soon as he reported aboard: to collect the chameleons the Marines had worn on the mission and bag them without laundering, so they could be examined for traces of chemicals picked up during the mission.

Emmett nodded and turned back to his desk.

Daly snapped to attention. "Aye aye, sir. Thank you." He executed a parade-ground about-face and stepped out of the captain's quarters. His step was light on his way back to his own stateroom.

When the *Admiral Nelson* ported at New Genesee, the ship's quartermaster handed over the sealed bag with the worn chameleons, along with all the image-crystals and physical evidence the platoon had collected at the Cabbage Patch, to another navy ship headed for Earth.

Onboard the SpaceFun Lines Tour Ship *Blue Ocean*, En Route from Atlas to New Genesee

The stateroom Sergeant Ivo Gossner and Lance Corporal Bella Dwan shared on the *Blue Ocean* was much smaller than the hotel room they'd shared with little problem in New Granum. Actually, it was within cubic centimeters of the size of the stateroom they'd shared on the *Crimson Seas* on their way to Atlas.

But it felt much, *much* smaller.

On the way out, they'd been team leader and sniper. Generally, they both had done their best to ignore the fact that they were a man and a woman sharing tight quarters, just as they'd ignored the fact that they were a man and a woman sharing a bed in the hotel room after they made planetfall on Atlas. At least, Gossner knew he'd done *his* best to ignore the fact that Bella Dwan was a very attractive woman. Now he wasn't so sure she'd been ignoring the man-woman business all that time. In retrospect, he wondered if the apparent sexual signals he'd noticed had been deliberate.

On the other hand, after the one powerful bout of sex, Bella Dwan had been prim and proper to the point of prudishness. Where they'd previously shared a bed, during their remaining three nights in New Granum, one or the other had slept on a blanket on the floor, or curled in an easy chair.

Their stateroom on the *Blue Ocean* was tourist class and had two narrow berths, one above the other. Dwan had immediately claimed the upper. She didn't invite him to join her, nor did she ever descend to his berth during the journey to New Genesee. Her nightclothes were more modest than she'd worn in New Granum, and she always changed in the stateroom's minuscule lavatory with the door tightly secured.

She did, though, rumple one or the other berth every morning in such a manner that any maid who happened to come in to clean would think they'd spent time together overnight.

Daly wasn't sure how he felt about Dwan's physical remoteness. He found her physically more attractive than he had before, and now he knew how satisfyingly wild she could be in bed. He hadn't had a serious relationship with a woman back on Halfway, just an intermittent series of casual relationships, mostly with civilian women. The most recent was with a charming petty officer in the navy supply depot. The women he connected with usually broke the relationship off after he'd gone on a couple of missions; they had too many difficulties with the frequency of his deployments, or the idea that he could come back from a mission maimed or crippled—or not come back at all—to stay with him.

But Dwan was a woman who could understand and accept the fact that he was a Force Recon Marine and there were risks that had to be accepted. And, as she was a Force Recon Marine herself, he could understand her better than he could the safe-and-secure women as well.

Of course, if they had an ongoing relationship, one of them would have to transfer, it simply wouldn't do for them to remain in their current supervisor-subordinate positions. Not to mention that such a relationship was a violation of Marine Corps regulations. It wouldn't be a major disruption of the company if one of them transferred into one of the other platoons. If a vacancy came up in one of the other sniper squads, no disruption at all. They'd have frequent separations being in different platoons, one would be deployed on a mission this time, another the other time. But they were Force Recon Marines, and accustomed to being away from their friends, so neither should that create any problem.

All of which ideas he could entertain so long as he didn't look into her eyes. He did once, and the soul that looked back at him was that of the Queen of Killers, the woman who frightened men. When the Queen of Killers looked at him, he didn't even want to be in the same stateroom, much less have a personal and sexual partnership with her.

He backed off on all thoughts of resuming what they had done together after the kill.

It wasn't until they were supercargo on the Wayfaring Freight Lines ore carrier the *High Tide* that Dwan finally said something on the subject.

Onboard the *High Tide*, En Route from New Genesee to Halfway

Their cabin on the *High Tide* was even smaller than the stateroom they shared on the *Blue Ocean*. There was only one bunk, just wide enough for two people to lie spooned together, so they took turns sleeping sitting on a folded blanket on the small square of deck that was all there was between the bunk, the waterproof door, and the clothing locker. The cabin didn't have its own lavatory, they shared a head with the occupants of the other seven so-called supercargo cabins. The head could only accommodate four people at a time, so it was fortunate that only two of the other supercargo cabins were occupied on that trip.

Dwan broke the awkward silence that had fallen over them since Atlas. "It was the kill, you know," she said flatly. "Nothing personal, just the kill." She didn't look at Gossner when she spoke.

He looked at her, then away. "I know," he said just as unemotionally. "I know that happens. But you'd never given any indication before. So you caught me by surprise."

"This was my first solo team mission," Dwan continued with no more inflection than before. "Other times I had other outlets. It won't happen again." She looked at him during the last sentence.

Gossner met her eyes. The Queen of Killers stared back. He also saw something else he couldn't identify, and didn't think he wanted to.

"I don't imagine it will," he said.

Gossner looked away first.

After that, the silence between them was less awkward, and by the time they made planetfall on Halfway, they were back to normal. Or at least as normal as they'd been before they walked into Commander Obannion's office and were given the mission orders.

Fourth Force Recon Company, Fourth Fleet Marines, Camp Howard, MCB Camp Basilone, Halfway

Commander Obannion looked over his company at morning formation. Not many of his one hundred and eighty-six Marines and sailors were present. First platoon was still on a training mission to Carhart's World. Most of the squads from third platoon that had been on deployment when second platoon left for Atlas were still out and those that hadn't been gone then were now, along with three of fourth platoon's squads. Second platoon itself, with six dead and as many more too badly injured in its most recent mission to be available for duty, was truncated.

Obannion's gaze paused when it reached Sergeant Jak Daly, standing in the platoon commander's position at the head of second platoon. He'd need to do some reorganizing before replacements came in. And he had other ideas for what to do with Daly.

Other company business completed, Obannion finished with, "When I dismiss the company from formation, there will be platoon-level inspections in the squad bays. Everyone who passes inspection will be given a ninety-six hour shore liberty."

The only visible reaction to the news within the platoon was an almost imperceptible shifting as the Marines stood a little bit taller and straighter.

Obannion looked over the company one more time, then filled his lungs and shouted out, "COMP-ney, dis-*missed*!" He turned about and headed toward his office. Sergeant Major Periz walked with him, one pace to his left and rear.

"Sergeant Major," Obannion said out of the side of his mouth, "tell Sergeant Daly that I inspected second platoon and they all passed, they're free to take off. And tell him to stand by, I'm going to want to see him in my office."

"Aye aye, sir," Periz said and broke formation to head Daly off. On his way he eyeballed Sergeant Gossner and Lance Corporal Dwan. He hadn't been able to find out what that mission of theirs was, but now that they were back, he'd find a chance to corner them one at a time and find out.

Inside the barracks, Obannion signaled Captains Qindall and Wainwright to join him in his office. When Periz returned from passing the word to Daly, Obannion signaled him to come in as well and close the door. He indicated that the others should sit, and they did as soon as he took his place behind his desk.

"I've had my eye on Daly for some time now," Obannion said as soon as everybody was seated. "But you know that. Well, he just had quite a baptism of fire as acting platoon commander. According to all reports, he acquitted himself well." He looked at the others; they'd all had time to study the debriefing of the members of second platoon, including that of Doc Natron. They had also seen the deposition of Lieutenant Tevedes, taken onboard the *Admiral Nelson* before he was put in the stasis bag, and read the afteraction report filed by Captain Emmert of the *Admiral Nelson*.

"Can any of you think of a reason I shouldn't ask him to put in for commissioning?"

There was a moment of silence before Captain Qindall, the Executive Officer, said, "I'm not so sure, sometimes he gets pretty arrogant. That's not a particularly good quality in an officer."

Periz barked out a sharp laugh. "Arrogance, not desirable in a Marine? Captain, arrogance is a quality that *distinguishes* Marines!" He leaned forward, and put his elbows on his thighs. "With all due respect, sir, Daly's not arrogant, he's a Marine. A lot of people, mostly the army, think Marines are arrogant. But we aren't arrogant, it's just that we know we're the best at what we do—and we don't see any reason to hide that fact." He snorted, then continued, "Most Marines think Force Recon is arrogant. We aren't, though. It's just that we can do things nobody else can do, and we're proud of it. If Daly seems arrogant to us, it's just because he's one of the best of us—and doesn't see any reason to hide it."

There was a moment of uncomfortable silence, which Obannion finally broke.

"He's got you there, XO. From where most people stand, Marines *are* arrogant. Us more than most."

Captain Wainwright, the operations officer, chuckled.

"Skipper, I can just imagine writing an operation order for a platoon-size mission for Daly. The afteraction report wouldn't much resemble the original mission order." He shook his head. "Not that afteraction reports are all that close to operation orders to begin with, especially for us."

" 'No plan, no matter how well designed, ever survives the first shot,' " Obannion quoted the ancient military aphorism. "But for us, they should."

Qindall looked reflective for a moment, then said, "An officer does need to be flexible. Daly's proven that he's capable of flexibility in stressful circumstances."

"If nobody has any further objection," Obannion said after giving the others a moment more to speak up, "Sergeant Major, would you get Sergeant Daly, please."

Periz pulled out his personal comm and punched one button. "Skipper wants to see you. Now," he growled into it when Daly answered. Without being told to, he got up and opened the office door.

Daly appeared quickly. Evidently he'd been waiting outside the company office for the call.

"What took you so long?" Periz growled.

"At ease, Sergeant," Obannion said.

Daly assumed a relaxed parade rest.

"You did quite a good job," the company commander said. "Lieutenant Tevedes said you were outstanding after he was injured. So did everyone else in the platoon. And we all know how hard Force Recon Marines are to impress." He gave Daly an expectant look.

Daly didn't know what to say, so he merely said, "Yessir."

"You've had a taste of being a platoon commander," Obannion went on. "How would you like to have platoon commander be your usual job?"

"Sir?" The question caught Daly by surprise.

"If you would like to apply for Officer Training College, I will give my endorsement to your request. I'm sure

Captains Qindall and Wainwright, and Sergeant Major Periz would add theirs as well."

"Sir, I—I hadn't given applying for commissioning any thought," Daly said, slightly flustered by the question.

"Well, I have. And so have these gentlemen. We believe you would make an outstanding officer. Of course, we'd like for you to come right back to Force Recon after your commissioning." He turned and looked out the window for a moment, then turned back. "I believe that when Lieutenant General Indrus reads the afteraction report of the mission, he'll be happy to add his endorsement as well. So what do you say, Sergeant, would you like to be an officer?"

"Sir, if I go for a commission, I'd become an ensign. Force Recon platoon commanders are lieutenants. I'd have to go somewhere else first. I like being in Force Recon."

"Force Recon has staff positions open to ensigns with prior Force Recon experience. And a promotion can come fast for a sharp ensign."

"Sir." Daly was visibly dazed; he really had never given any serious thought to applying for a commission.

"You don't have to make a decision right now," Obannion said. "Sleep on it. Go out with some other squad leaders and discuss it over a drunken night. Whatever you need to do. When you report back for duty four days from now, I'll have an application filled out and waiting for your signature." He stood, so did the others. "That's all, Sergeant. Enjoy your liberty. That was a good job you did on Atlas."

"Aye aye, sir. Thank you, sir." Daly snapped to attention, about-faced, and marched from the company office.

When Sergeant Daly reported back for duty four days later, the application for commissioning was waiting for him. Endorsements from Commander Obannion, Captain Qindall, Captain Wainwright, and Sergeant Major

Periz were already attached to it. So was an endorsement from Lieutenant General Indrus. Daly signed the application.

That afternoon, orders arrived for him to report to Officer Training College on Arsenault. He left the next day.

CHAPTER
THIRTY

The lab was busy. Anya was intrigued by what she saw going on in the main area of the laboratory, particularly a device a technician was testing, a laser gun disguised as an eyebrow highlighter. "You've miniaturized these things since I was in the field," she remarked to Dr. Blogetta O'Bygne. "We thought the laser pen was the hottest new thing in defensive weapons."

Several technicians waved in a friendly way to Anya as she and Dr. O'Bygne made their way to the rear of the laboratory. "Come in here, Anya." O'Bygne swiped her access card through the security device set into a massive door that slowly swung open to let the women into a small lab area crowded with instruments. Pieces of equipment Anya could not identify lay scattered on tables. On one of the tables were two huge flowerpots each containing a plant. Both pots contained what looked like rich, dark soil. Each plant had extended runners down to the floor and all the way to the opposite wall, a distance of perhaps six meters. One was obviously dead, its thick tendrils shriveled and brittle looking. At intervals along the tendrils were shriveled green things that looked like tiny pepper plants. But the other plant was thriving and it was obviously a cucumber plant. But—the cucumbers! They were huge!

"You should water your cukes more often," Anya remarked wryly, nodding at the dead plant. It seemed odd to Anya that O'Bygne or someone was growing vegetables in the lab, but she and her staff were known to be a bit oddball. "Are these artifacts the Marines brought back from Atlas?"

"Yes they are, and no, lack of water had nothing to do with that cucumber plant's untimely and lamented demise. I have the answer in here to what Lavager was up to in those labs of his." She paused and looked frankly at Anya, who nodded and waited patiently for the scientist to announce what she'd discovered.

"Well?" Anya asked at last.

"Let me show you something," O'Bygne flicked on a 2-D viewer. "These are images the Marines took during their raid on the Cabbage Patch. These are shots one of them took inside a building they concluded was not being used to develop weapons components, so they left it alone. Look."

All Anya could see were huge vats. "Yes. Well? What's in those vats?"

"Those are fertilizer vats, Annie. Everything the Marines brought back from Atlas, even the uniforms they wore on the reconnaissance and raid, were shipped here for analysis. Often in weapons labs chemicals get into the environment and by subjecting impregnated clothing to microscopic examination we can tell what kind of explosives are being manufactured in them. We even collected the soil and dirt on their boots and analyzed that. You will be surprised at what we found." She nodded at the cucumber plants. "Come over here."

O'Bygne guided Anya to the table where the two plants, one drooping, the other flourshing, sat in their pots. O'Bygne lifted a petri dish and shook it. Inside was dirt. "This is soil that came from the building with all the vats in it. We've analyzed it carefully. Would you like to guess what it contains?" Anya shook her head. "It contains refined plant nutrients like boron, calcium, magnesium, phosphorus, a whole array of nutrients and," here she paused, "a catalyst we haven't yet been able to identify, probably because it's an artificial agent developed in Lavager's Cabbage Patch. Ah, what an appropriate name!" She opened another dish and took out a seed. "This is an ordinary cucumber seed, *Cucumis sativus*. This particular seed is of the gherkin variety. They usually grow to only two to seven centimeters in length. Remember that. Those two plants came from seeds like this one. One is dead, the other thriving. Do you know how long it took us to grow those plants, Annie?"

Anya shook her head. "I'd guess weeks, but I know you haven't had the seeds here but what, only a few days?"

"Now you're catching on! They were both planted forty-eight hours ago."

"What!"

O'Bygne nodded. "Forty-eight hours ago, dearie. We took only a pinch of this soil from the boots, put it in the big pots, added a little water, and voilà! Take a look at the live one. Go on, examine the leaves, pick up one of the cucumbers."

Cautiously Anya bent and took hold of a cucumber and, with some effort, she detached it from its runner. It was hard and solid to the touch but blotched, as were the leaves and the stems. But it was about sixty centimeters in length! "My God, it weighs at least a kilo!" she exclaimed. "What is happening here, Bloggie?"

"Coffee?" O'Bygne asked, offering her a cup and pouring hot kaff out of a beaker. "Sip some of this coffee. That plant is already dying. See the wilt? By the end of the day it'll be as shriveled up as number one over there." O'Bgyne grinned. "Dearie, your old buddy, Lavager, he's not building a weapon, he's developing a miracle fertilizer. Either he hasn't yet figured out how to stabilize the growth process, or we just haven't found out what it is but, Anya, if he has found out, that fertilizer will totally revolutionize agriculture on every world in the Confederation. If those plants were regular cucumbers, not gherkins, the cukes would be two meters long."

"My God," Anya whispered, setting her coffee cup down gently. "Cucumbers sixty centimeters long? Why—"

"The fertilizer in that petri dish could grow tomatoes as big as a house." She finished her coffee and poured more into Anya's cup.

"Food for everyone in Human Space! Instant crops! Lavager is—"

"An agricultural genius, Annie. The old man just wants to be a farmer. But there's a downside." O'Bygne held up a forefinger. She changed the images on the viewscreen. "Do you know what that little sucker is?"

Anya stared at the image on the screen. "Some kind of microscopic germ?"

"*Bacillus postii*, Annie. It's been around for ages. It's a form of bacterial wilt. At least that's what it was. We're not sure if this is a mutated variety or not. We sent a sample to Dakota University's agronomy lab and should have a report in a few days. But this bacterium is deadly when it comes to cucumbers. No, no, it's been safely isolated so it had nothing to do with what you just saw. Those plants died of 'old age,' I guess. But do you know where this little devil on the screen here came from?"

Anya shook her head.

"Off the Marines' uniforms. *Bacillus postii* is not native to Atlas. The Marines went in clandestinely. Get the picture?"

"Oh, Allah's pointed teeth!" Anya wailed. "They couldn't have been sanitized! Atlas has a strict decontamination procedure. They brought this bacterium in with them."

"Yes. Have you seen the Board of Trade reports lately? There was a sudden dip in Atlas's crop exports yesterday. It'll get worse, much worse before they figure out what hit them."

"Does the Director know any of this?" Anya's voice had gone tight and slightly high-pitched.

"Sure. We filed a full report. He has all the data."

"Can you do me a really big favor? Can you download this data onto a crystal for me? I have the necessary need-to-know."

O'Bygne waved a hand. "Don't pull that crap with me, dearie. We've been friends too long. You bet your sweet ass you can have the data."

R-76 Quadrant Desk, CIO Headquarters

Back in her cubicle Anya Smiler rested her head in her hands. She felt like crying. She had just checked the outgoing messages, and so far Adams had not reported O'Bygne's findings to anyone. Would he? Well, that was the question. What advantage would there be to withhold something like this? Anya thought she knew.

It was then she was summoned to the Director's office.

Office of the Director, Central Intelligence Organization

Anya Smiler stood hesitantly in the middle of the Director's inner sanctum, a nervous smile on her face, and after the briefest hesitation, gave his proffered hand a perfunctory squeeze. J. Murchison Adams beamed beatifically at the young woman. "Please, have a seat, Anya. My, my, my, we haven't had a chat in a long time," he said as he guided her to the coffee table arrangement where he entertained visitors in a relaxed atmosphere.

They took seats in ortho-sofa armchairs opposite each

other. Anya had never sat in one of the things before. They were too expensive for her. Besides, she'd heard too many stories of them malfunctioning, particularly the one about the senator who'd been assassinated when someone rigged her chair to crush her to death. Almost as if he read her mind, Adams grinned and said, "Wonderful things, aren't they?" He adjusted his position and moved his chair closer to Anya, to where their knees almost touched. "Perfectly safe, these conveniences," he smiled. "Anya, excuse me, but some caviar?" He gestured at a sideboard containing crackers and cloacaian caviar. Anya shook her head. "When was the last time we had a talk, my dear?"

"Uh, we never really have, sir." Anya felt faintly uneasy, being this close to Adams, whom she'd never really liked but had grown to hate. The director was too thin for one thing and his face too narrow; to Anya, he always looked as if he were hunting for something to eat. When he grinned at her, as he was doing now continuously, showing his long, yellow teeth, she had the uncomfortable impression he was regarding her as—prey. She longed for that highlighter she'd just seen being tested in the lab. She imagined what it would be like to direct a laser beam into Adams's Adam's apple, watching him die screaming, blood spurting from his ruptured aortas. Oh, it would be so nice!

"Well, more's the pity, my dear. Valued employees such as yourself, Anya, deserve more attention." He waved a finger, as if to forestall contradiction. "Yes, 'valued employee,' Anya, that's you! I know a lot about you, my dear! You are a top-notch analyst! That is why I personally— personally, Anya—selected you to replace old Whatsisname in R-76. You're on your way up now, my girl!" He beamed.

"Thank you, sir—"

Adams held up a hand. "You are disappointed at the

transfer, I know. What professional wouldn't be? You know your sector, you've spent time on one of the worlds there, you are experienced in field work, wonderful combination of talent and practical knowledge, Anya. But I am thinking of bigger things, Anya."

"Sir—?"

"I am thinking of the future of the Confederation Intelligence Organization, Anya. Oh," he shrugged, "Atlases come and they go; political and military crises boil up all the time everywhere in Human Space. Dealing with such things is the price we pay as professional servants of the Confederation, Anya! But the crisis of the moment passes and we move on. My job is to see that we all remain sharp and engaged and that I have the best possible people in the right positions to deal with things." He leaned close and placed a hand on her knee. The hand was cold.

"Sir, I appreciate that you took the time out of your busy schedule to see me. But—"

"Never too busy for one of my best analysts, Anya!" His hand remained on her knee.

"—but I would like to ask to be sent back to the Atlas desk, sir—"

Adams leaned back in his chair. As soon as he removed his hand from her knee, Anya let out her breath. He tilted his head to one side and regarded her with one eye half closed, as if he were a huge bird eyeing a potential meal. "Um," he said, steepling his fingers, "impossible."

"But, sir, now you need me on that desk more than ever! I-I know that sector better than anybody. I see a trend in the reports coming from Atlas that is very disturbing, sir, and—"

"Yes, very disturbing, Anya, so disturbing that I have personally taken over monitoring the events on Atlas. As you know, I've already had two conferences with Madam Chang-Sturdevant about events there. But Atlas is in good hands, and so is R-76. The former because I am closely watching things there and the latter because you are now on the job. And I might add, Anya, that my job is made all the easier because of the fine work you did down there. You really know what's up, and your profile of this Lavager fellow has been most helpful."

So far, no mention of O'Bygne's report. Anya felt a flush of anger. And was he saying to her now that her profiles on Lavager were being used to portray the man as a threat to the Confederation? How monstrous! Her face reddened and thinking it was modesty on her part, Adams hurried on. "But Anya, that was then, this is now. Must I point out to you, my dear, the substantial increase in pay that your new job carries with it? Your base pay rises by three thousand credits per annum and your locality allowance by an equal amount. Now, my dear, you can afford one of these." He thumped the ortho-sofa he was sitting on and grinned. The grin bore no warmth and Anya detected a hint of impatience in the way Adams inflected the words. Clearly, the interview was near an end.

"Yessir, thank you. Uh, sir, has the lab reported yet on the materials brought back from Atlas?"

"No, no, net yet, my dear. Maybe in a couple of days." Adams smiled again, this time more relaxed. "I think we should have these talks more often, Anya."

"Yessir. May I ask one question, sir?"

"Certainly."

Anya hesitated. "Well, what are we going to do about Atlas, sir?"

Adams did not let his expression show what he was thinking: This goddamned meddlesome little bitch! Another one of these dedicated fools who refused to see the Big Picture. It's a good thing I got her in here and felt her out like this. She's trouble. Time to send her little ass far, far away. "Well, Anya, of course we need to know more about what Lavager is really up to out there. We've sent our own team, undercover, of course, to investigate. One can never really trust these military folks completely, you know." He moved his chair back to its original position and stood.

Anya felt sick. A "team"? Did that mean someone like Wellers Henrico? Among Anya Smiler's many fine qualities, stupidity was not one. "Well, I understand, sir, but I only thought I could be of more immediate service if I volunteered to return to my old job. Thank you very much for explaining things to me, and thank you very much for taking the time to talk to me."

Adams guided Anya to the door, one hand resting gently on her shoulder. "Come and see me anytime you like, Anya, always a pleasure to talk to a professional of your caliber," the director said. As he spoke his hand slid gently down to the lower part of Anya's back. "Do come back, Anya." The hand slid down even farther.

Twenty years of training, experience, dedicated service, concern about the security of the Confederation, her career prospects, all that vanished in a flash of red-hot anger. Anya whirled suddenly, her eyes flashing with indignation and disgust. "I don't think so!" She gritted in a voice so loud that Adams, a sudden expression of alarm, almost fear on his face, started and stepped back from her.

Back in her cubicle Anya sat at her station and tried to calm herself. Her hands were shaking and she was nearly in tears. She took several deep breaths. All right, all right, she told herself, Take it easy! With effort she managed to control her breathing. Cautiously she fingered the crystal in her pocket. The information on that crystal had to get to President Chang-Sturdevant. After a few moments her hands stopped shaking. What to do? Well, first priority was get herself out of the CIO! It was clear to Anya Smiler that she would be persona non grata at Hunter, and the sooner she got out the better it would be for her. Besides, she couldn't continue working for swine like Adams. Anya had a friend at the Ministry of War. That ministry hated the CIO.

She knew what she had to do.

CHAPTER
THIRTY-ONE

Office of the Deputy Minister for Intelligence, Ministry of War, Fargo, Earth

Anya waited three days before asking for an interview with Adams's counterpart at the Confederation's Ministry of War, Jeremy Boast, Marcus Berentus's Deputy Minister for Intelligence. Anya had known Boast ("J. B." to everyone in the intelligence community) for some years and he had frequently tried to entice her away from the CIO. She had politely declined those offers, but the seed had been planted. When she asked for an appointment it had been granted immediately.

"Come to spy on us, Anya?" Boast asked, laughing, as she was ushered into his office. She could not help contrasting J. B.'s office with Adams's. The furniture consisted of old-fashioned straight-backed padded chairs and plain tables. On one wall hung an artist's rendition of the Battle of New Reading that had taken place in 2253, where an understrength Marine infantry division had succeeded in holding off an entire army trying to force a strategic pass in the Gondular Mountains. The action was known as "New Thermopylae," only with a happy ending. On the opposite wall hung a very old painting depicting Custer's Last Stand at the Little Big Horn. "The Alpha and Omega of military tactics," Boast was fond of remarking. On the wall directly behind his desk—a massive affair made of real wood with a polished top covered by a huge piece of glass—hung his military award certificates engraved on vellum and trid images of Boast's career as a Marine intelligence officer. "I'm a double-dipper," he'd tell visitors, meaning he was drawing both his military pension and a civil service salary.

Boast himself was in his early nineties, spare, energetic, a man who never minced words. The office décor matched his personality perfectly. As soon as Anya entered the place she knew she would be taken seriously there.

"Sassi?" Boast asked. Sassi was a popular soft drink. Anya, who for the past several days had spent too much time communing with a bottle of bourbon, accepted gratefully. Boast served her himself from a cooler that sat in one corner of the office.

"Are you still on the Atlas desk?"

"Until a few weeks ago, sir."

"Promoted?"

"Yes, kicked upstairs, so I quit that fucking disaster, sir," she said bitterly.

"Umm. I see. What you been up to these past weeks, then?"

"Spending too much of it getting drunk, sir, washing my cares away," she said lightly.

"That's an honorable enough pastime, Anya, I used to do a bit of that myself." Anya could not possibly imagine J. Murchison Adams drunk.

"You don't by any chance have an ortho-sofa, do you, sir?"

"What?" Boast laughed, imagining one of the monstrous devices in his Spartan surroundings. "No, I don't trust the hedonistic things, Annie. We had a senator squashed to death in one of them a while back. Maybe you heard about it? I don't trust anything I can't install and fix myself. All those outrageous technicians, they're becoming the new priesthood, know what I mean?" He handed her the Sassi, which he expected her to drink right out of the bottle. "Besides," he continued, sitting behind his desk and putting his feet up, "those damned conveniences make a man—or a woman—soft, too comfortable, takes the edge off." He drank from his bottle of Sassi. "I have a job opening, if that's why you're here, Anya."

"Nossir, that is not why I'm here." She took the crystal out of her pocket and held it up. "I have this, and I'd like you to read it and tell me what I should do with it. Uh," she looked around, "you do have a reader, don't you?"

"Yes," he laughed, "some of this razzle-dazzle technology really is worthwhile." He pressed a button and a tiny reader emerged on a platform from somewhere under his desk.

Anya laughed as she handed over the small plastic container; most people at his level had desks that could morph consoles out of their tops.

"What's in here?" Boast asked, holding up the container.

"A lab report on the analyses of the material brought back from Atlas, sir, and other information about what the CIO is up to on Atlas."

Boast regarded the crystal in its little box. "You know you could get fired if anybody over there at Hunter knew you were sharing this stuff with me? Hell, girl, you could even face criminal prosecution for giving this to me!"

Anya sighed and her shoulders slumped. "Frankly, sir, I just don't give a damn. Besides, they can't fire me, I already resigned."

"Um. Well, if this is of any use to us, we'll give you a medal. I've got a whole box of them over there." Boast inserted the crystal and pressed a button. What popped up on his screen kept him engrossed for about twenty minutes. Finally he closed his eyes as if getting control of himself. "Anya, come here, around behind me, so you can see this screen." A questioning look on her face, Anya complied. "I want you to read this. It's an Ultra Secret backchannel message from J. Murchison Adams to President Chang-Sturdevant. She in turn shared it with Minister Berentus and he with me. Read what it says." He exited the crystal report and entered a password. Anya took in her breath as a short message popped up on the screen. She read:

```
                    ULTRA SECRET
    FLASH
    EYES ONLY, CHANG-STURDEVANT
    LAB ANALYSES REVEAL LAVAGER BUILDING A
    "PLANET-BUSTING" NUCLEAR DEVICE. PRECISE
    TRIGGERING AND DELIVERY SYSTEM UNKNOWN
    AT THIS TIME BUT UNDER STUDY. ESTIMATED
    YIELD BASED ON ANALYSIS OF SAMPLES RECOV-
    ERED FROM LABS ON ATLAS @ 1,000 (ONE THOU-
    SAND) MEGATONS PLUS. URGENTLY RECOMMEND
    SPECIAL TEAM IN PLACE @ NEW GRANUM BE
    GIVEN CLEARANCE TO PROCEED IMMEDIATELY.
    ADAMS.
    EXCLUDED FROM AUTOMATIC DOWNGRADING
    PER ADAMS
    ULTRA SECRET
```

"This is all lies!" Anya shouted. "This is not what Dr. O'Bygne's team discovered! We have to stop this!"

Boast sighed. "Look in the header, Anya. It was dated last week."

"Last week!" Anya exclaimed.

"Please sit down, Anya." He got up and guided her back to her chair. "We can't stop this, Anya. It's too late. Lavager is dead."

Anya's body went rigid. The word "No" formed on her lips but when she tried to say it only air came out. "My—" she gasped, "my fault," she whispered. She mumbled something ending in "sooner."

"I don't think it would've done any good, Anya," Boast whispered, laying a hand on her shoulder.

Anya's grief turned instantly to white-hot anger. "Goddamn you! Goddamn all you meddling, power-hungry motherfucking bastards! Goddamn you!" she shouted, half rising out of her chair and banging her fists on its arms as she screamed curses at Boast and through him at the entire Confederation government.

Boast bowed his head silently and let Anya rage on.

"Sir? Sir? Is everything all right?" Boast's secretary asked over the intercom. She had heard Anya cursing and screaming through the wall.

"Yes, Judie, everything's all right. Would you get Marcus for me? Tell him I've got to see him at once?"

"He's in a conference with the Chief of Staff, sir. He's told us to hold all calls until he says otherwise."

"Judie, you get his goddamned secretary right now and tell him to tell Marcus that I'm on my way to his office, and I'm bringing someone with me who has something he's got to know about right away." He turned back to Anya. "Anya, you're right, we are a bunch of meddling, power-hungry idiots and worse, much worse. But by God, somebody's going pay for this mess, I swear, Annie, I swear it."

Anya Smiler's anger turned as suddenly to grief and she began to weep in long, wracking sobs, like a person whose heart has been broken. Hers had.

"Annie, will you come with me to see Marcus Berentus, and then the President? Can you do that? Are you up to it?" He took her gently by the shoulders to steady her shaking.

Anya caught her breath and wiped her eyes. They were bright blue, Boast noted. "Yessir, I will. Goddamned right I will!"

Office of the Minister of War

"What have we done, what have we done?" Marcus Berentus muttered after viewing the crystal Jeremy Boast had given him. As he read his face had gone white and then turned red with anger. "This is nothing but catastrophic!"

Berentus's office, like Boast's, was Spartan, if slightly larger than his intelligence chief's. He often hosted private conferences there, so along one wall was a long table equipped with individual viewers for participants. But Berentus had invited Boast and Anya to sit at a small coffee table arrangement where they could talk more intimately. "I ought to kill that bastard," Berentus said of J. Murchison Adams. "Anya, I guarantee you, nothing shall happen to you for blowing the whistle on the people at Hunter."

"I know that, sir. Mr. Boast promised me the same and I know I can trust you."

"You're absolutely right that you can. And the reason I can say that is because when the President sees what I've just read, J. Murchison Adams and that whole crew he's installed over there will be out on their pinstriped asses! You can work here for us from now on. I'll match the grade they gave you at CIO."

"Thank you, sir, but I'd like to think about it for a while, if you don't mind. Right now I'm just—well, I need some time off. And—and if the President is going to clean things up over at CIO, well, maybe I can go back to my old job?"

"I understand, Anya. Think about my offer." He sighed and shook his head. "What was this man, Lavager, really like, Anya?"

Anya felt tears coming to her eyes again. She struggled to get a grip on herself. "He was a fine man, sir. Anybody could sit down and talk with him. He treated everyone the same. He was direct, open, and honest with everyone. And he enjoyed life, more than anyone I've ever known." In her imagination she could smell the rich aroma of Lavager's Anniversarios again. For the rest of her life the smell of cigar smoke would remind her of the man. She struggled again to control her emotions. She focused for a moment on a holograph image on one wall of Marcus

Berentus standing beside what looked like a fighter aircraft, a huge grin on his youthful face. He was pointing to several large holes in the fuselage of the fighter. Anya thought, Lavager would have liked these men. "He was no dictator, sir," she concluded.

"We played God and came up short," Jeremy Boast said.

"Sir, what happened to his daughter, Candace?" Anya asked suddenly.

"She's fine. She'll be going to an off-world university, Anya. I'll see to it that she'll be looked out for from now on. She's got a future." He paused and drummed his fingers on the arm of his chair. "I don't need an appointment to see the President." He got to his feet. "Anya, will you come with me to see Madam President?" He held out his hand to help her up.

"Yessir, I will."

Anya smiled on her way home after meeting the President—such a gracious woman. Maybe Anya would call Tim tonight, try to patch things up . . .

EPILOGUE

"I'm drunk," Madam Chang-Sturdevant said with drunken gravity. "And I don't give a damn." She lay stretched out on the old-fashioned leather couch in her private office, a glass of bourbon in one hand and a smoldering Davidoff Ambassadrice Senorita in the other. She drew on the cigar and slowly exhaled the aromatic smoke.

"Oh, I wouldn't say you're 'drunk,' Suelee," Marcus Berentus said. He sat enfolded in an overstuffed armchair, his own drink in one hand and an Anniversario in the other. Nobody in government had ever called Madam President Suelee except, recently, for Marcus, and then only in private, intimate situations, such as the one they were in now.

"Oh, yeah?"

"Just a little lit, Suelee. You deserve it, after what we've just been through."

Suelee drew again on the cigarillo, sucked the smoke deep into her lungs and expelled it slowly through her nose. She sipped at the bourbon. "After what we've been through, Marcus?" she asked bitterly. "Don't you mean after what we've put the people on Atlas through, not to mention that poor man, Lavager? We made his daughter an orphan, Marcus. No, correction! I did all that, me, the fucking President of the fucking Confederation of Human-fucking-Worlds. I did all that." She finished her drink in one gulp. "Marcus, would you be a perfect dear and plour, pour me another?" She held out her glass.

"Suelee, you've been in politics all your life," Berentus said over his shoulder as he refilled Chang-Sturdevant's glass, "and you know that even the best leaders are only as good as the advice they're given. You got bad advice that you thought was reliable and you acted on it." He handed her the glass. Yes, there were some new lines in that still-handsome face, and maybe another strand or two of gray hair on her head, but Cynthia Chang-Sturdevant still turned heads when she walked into a room.

"Oh, bullshit, Marcus! Pure bullshit! Don't try to soften the blow! I made the decision, I gave the orders, the disaster on Atlas is all on my shoulders, nobody else's."

"We've sent people to Atlas to help out with this crop disaster. Lavager's scientists never did discover that stabilizing element, but we have our best people working on it. And I've personally seen to it that Lavager's daughter is taken care of. The Smiler woman is now on my staff, Suelee. Nothing will happen to her now."

"I find myself wishing she'd never come to us, Marcus. Ignorance is such bliss."

"Suelee, this is all the fault of Adams and that crowd—"

"Screw them! I can't put what happened off on them! I should have known, I shouldn't have trusted him! I knew he had his own agenda. I should have replaced him months ago, ordered a reorganization of the CIO top to bottom. By Christ, that's what's going to happen now—he's going to resign and the whole mess'll be swept under the rug." She smiled bitterly and sipped her drink. "We can't have my administration embarrassed by any of this, can we? And while all this was shaping up all I did was sit here on my ass and do nothing." She made a gesture of frustration with her cigar. "Marcus, those Marines who went to Atlas and did the dirty deed on my direction. They are never to be told the truth about the mission, about how they committed murder and half destroyed an entire world's economy because of some-one's lying personal agenda, and because of my rank stupidity."

"To the best of my ability, they will never know. Though, Suelee, if they learn on their own about the crop damage, they're smart enough to figure out at least part of it for themselves."

She sighed deeply. "I know," she said in a small voice.

They were silent for several moments, then she sat up-right, put her glass on a sideboard and her cigar into an ashtray.

"Marcus, I've come to a decision. I am not running for reelection."

"What? Suelee, you can't be serious!" Marcus leaned forward in his armchair. The leather squeaked pleasantly as he shifted his weight.

"Yes I am. I'm tired of other people's problems, Mar-cus. I'm tired of running other people's lives, too. I'm tired of being polite to other politicians, of begging the Senate to do what any decent person would do. And most of all, I am tired, I am sick, of sending other peo-ple to their deaths." She held up a hand. "Do not argue with me, Marcus." She was not drunk now and her voice carried steely determination as she spoke. "I've made up my mind." She sat back on the couch and sighed. "It's the price I have to pay." She sat silently for a long moment, then, "Marcus, I think I shall have a cry."

Berentus moved quickly to her side and put his arm around her. She lay her head against his. He ran a hand through her hair. It smelled of aromatic cigar smoke and lotus blossoms. People referred to Chang-Sturdevant as "The Iron Lady," "The Dragon Lady," and so on, the so-briquets normally applied to a woman of power, but to Marcus Berentus she was a soft and warmly human per-son and when he was close to her, like now, he imagined warm summer nights in a fragrant Chinese garden.

"Marcus, when I'm no longer President, when I'm retired and a lonely old maid again, will you still love me?"

"You bet, more than ever! If you go, I go, and wherever you go, that's where I'll be." He kissed her forehead and smiled. He didn't know if she had heard him. She was fast asleep.

There was something Marcus Berentus would never tell the handsome woman sleeping on the couch. He'd already told the whole sorry tale to Hugyens Long. If he knew the Attorney General, one day, not too far in the future, when J. Murchison Adams was out of the public eye, he would quietly vanish, along with his deputy Palmer Quincy Lowell, and never be seen again—except by the other denizens of Darkside.

Annie Hall, the former Presidential Residence, outside New Granum, Atlas

"Ladies, hurry with your packing," Franklin al-Rashid said from the doorway, "your flight leaves in an hour. It's a wonderful morning, just right for a drive into town. I'll be outside when you're ready."

The heavy luggage had already been sent ahead, but neither girl had much to take with her. Candace was leaving Annie Hall forever. Soon the next president and his family would move in—the government of the Union of Margelan had leased it from the Lavager estate. All of the Lavager possessions, the accumulations of lifetimes, had been put in storage and Candace would take with her only the things she'd need on the long journey to university. She planned to major in political science as an undergraduate and then law. She would return to Atlas. Her father's name would carry her far in Margelan politics, and she would achieve the unification of Atlas her father had only dreamed of. That was her plan, anyway.

"We're both orphans now, adrift in the cold, cruel world," Gina Medina remarked and smiled. She hefted the little bag of toiletries she was taking with her. She would major in agronomy and someday return to Atlas and her family's farm. It had no mortgage and her parents' insurance was enough to pay the taxes until she could finish her education and get the place running again.

"Actually, I'm excited, Gina. We're going far, far away from here, and we'll be friends now for the rest of our lives! Just think, we can get a room together at the university." An endowment had been established for the two young women, neither knew by whom, to pay for their education and get them started in their lives. Candace assumed the money came from friends of her father. The lawyer who managed the funds would not tell either girl how the trust was financed.

"Well, I'm going down now, Candace," Gina announced, "I want to get a good seat in the car. And say good-bye to Roland for me."

Candace Lavager picked up her bag and walked slowly out onto the landing at the head of the staircase. For as long as she could remember, she had lived in Annie Hall. The smell of her father's cigars was still prevalent everywhere and even though she'd pretended not to like them, she loved their aroma; all the rest of her life cigar smoke would remind her of him. She loved this old house, the floorboards beneath her feet; every inch of the place was somehow a part of her. She looked down the stairs and remembered the time as a little girl she'd slid down the banister and cracked her head on the floor at the bottom. The house was quiet now. She stood there listening intently. In her own mind she could hear the voices of her parents, her mother's, soft and tender, her father's rich tenor. She would never hear them again. "Mommy, Daddy," she whispered, "I'll always love you." She walked down the stairs, out into the sunshine and the rest of her life.